THE
LOST COLOURS
OF THE
CHAMELEON

THE
LOST COLOURS
OF THE
CHAMELEON

MANDLA LANGA

To Fergus

With best wishes.

PICADOR AFRICA

First published 2008 by Picador Africa,
an imprint of Pan Macmillan South Africa
Private Bag x19, Northlands
Johannesburg 2116

Reprinted 2009

www.panmacmillan.co.za
www.picadorafrica.co.za

ISBN 978-1-77010-0848

© Mandla Langa 2008

Editing by Michael Titlestad and Andrea Nattrass
Proofreading by Alison Lockhart
Cover design: Donald Hill, Blue Apple
Design and typesetting by Triple M Design, Johannesburg

Printed and bound by Ultra Litho (Pty) Limited

To my wife, June Josephs, with love

ACKNOWLEDGEMENTS

I would like to thank my brother Pius Nkonzo Langa, whose anecdote about the consequences of the abuse of power became a creative crucible for this narrative. I would also like to thank a few people for their contribution to the book: Jyoti Mistry for an impossible role as editor and agent; Andrea Nattrass for her fine work of editing and giving coherence to chaos; and Andries Oliphant, Michael Titlestad, Gillian Slovo and Andy Metcalf for suggestions that gave the narrative its shape. Any mistakes, however, are all mine.

Count your colours, oh chameleon,
Aborigine of wood and wind,
Count your colours in the rainbow of the fern,
In the thick, ashen hide of the sapling tree.
Niyi Osundare

'We'll walk you through every step of the way.'
A soldier accompanying a condemned man to a firing squad

PROLOGUE

I

AUGUST THIS YEAR has become a very important month for the people of Bangula. There is expectation that President Abioseh Gondo, who was actually born in August, will not survive the inquiry. Rumour has it that Zebulon, in league with the Provisional Authority for Progress, has already tasked the carpenters to construct a gallows. Not waiting for the rumour to be confirmed, people are fleeing the island in droves.

Mr Hieronymus Jerome remembers the day of his own flight.

IT WAS IN August, almost a lifetime ago, when he was just ten years old. In the sugarcane field that day, he felt the rise of the wind and the snap of the tall grass against his shins. His anger came in waves of nausea and then subsided.

He ran.

Confused by the runner's frantic footfalls, a multi-coloured snake wiggled crazily like a hula dancer and retreated into the dead blades of

3

grass and crunchy sugarcane leaves. The boy knew that the snake reigned here but, even though too scared to worship it, he could still pray. He prayed to the god of the Irish priest, Father Mitch Mitchum, remembering what he had heard in the shelter where the derelicts congregated, the songs from throats scarred by alcohol and despair. And Father Mitchum telling them to speak what was on their minds. Bangula was, after all, a democratic state.

There were no borders on this island. There was no occasion to trespass into another country. The only boundaries were man-made and they differentiated people into the haves and the have-nots. There were others in the middle who from time to time experienced great hunger. When starving, they cursed the gods and the rulers who had condemned them to that condition. But every now and then they ate their fill, and thanked the government for the bounty.

The land itself was indifferent to the drama being played out by the have-nots who wanted to escape their condition and by the haves who didn't wish to be dislodged from their lofty perch. Those caught halfway between the two conditions kept their heads down and their guards up, eyes peeled for the slightest rustle of the foliage.

Hieronymus couldn't tell where he belonged in the scheme of things, except that he was always hungry and his teeth were forever set on edge, mostly when his father was home and his mother was terrified.

Earlier that day, the boy had been in a group that crawled under the fence into the plantation. Their plan had been to cut the cane quickly and then, in the parlance of his beloved cowboy films, skedaddle. His more agile friends had skedaddled when their illegal harvest was interrupted by one of the workers, a terrifying hulk of a man wielding a machete. The boy was left cowering behind a thicket of cane.

His friends had been like the new cars that picked up speed like cheetahs. He had waited, listening to their thrashing through the cane. He heard the worker swearing in the thick accent of the mountains, the hundred-and-one things he would do to the boys once he laid his hands on them.

Following the heavy summer rains, the cane breaks had become gullies full of stagnant water, where mosquitoes bred. His heart thumping, the boy saw the droppings and imprints of wild animals on the loamy ground. He climbed up a sacred rubber tree but, as he crouched within its rough folds, he grew less concerned with wild animals than with a drumming and a slow march from the easterly direction of the shanty town that neighboured the wide acreage of the cane fields.

The boy saw, in the gathering dark, a glow that resembled a savage sunset shimmering above the bushes. Night fell swiftly. A drum sounded a tattoo that was echoed by a general thumping of feet that reached all the way up to the branches of the boy's tree, in counterpoint to the chanting voices. Above the rhythmic pounding, women ululated intermittently, their cries lending an eerie effect to the evening.

The marchers carried aloft their flaming torches whose brightness penetrated the corners and drove out field mice and various tenants of the night. The boy saw a white goat attached by a length of rope to a group of young men whose bare upper bodies glistened from exertion under the violent mixture of lights. The orange and white chalk smeared across their foreheads together with the black and crimson paint under their eyes gave them an alien appearance.

One of the men picked up the goat and carried it in the crook of his arm to the base of the sacred tree. Kneeling, he looped the rope around the trunk and, in a single movement, tied the bleating goat to the trunk.

The people gathered around the boy's tree, creating a brightened clearing that seemed holier than a shrine. Their singing gave way to an atonal incantation delivered by an old man. Standing shirtless and barefooted in unremarkable bleached denim overalls, he was the undisputed spiritual leader of the crowd. Beside him crouched another man, his head covered with a blanket.

Transfixed, the boy stared down at something he couldn't understand even as it felt familiar to his bones. At once repelled and fascinated by the ritual of light and blood, he remembered a cousin's initiation ceremony that Father Mitchum had once severely condemned.

But this was no initiation, at least not in the sense of a boy reaching manhood, although something transcendental seemed to be taking place. The boy understood that it was the transfer of spiritual power onto an earthbound person.

When the blanket was whisked off the head of the crouched man, the boy saw the Colonel, the champion of Reform, before the healer in denim overalls. Although kneeling barefooted, the Colonel still managed to look stately. Making incisions on the Colonel's brow with a sharp blade, the healer then rubbed a dark, sticky ointment into the fresh cuts. The boy saw the Colonel wince, this reaction triggering off rapid-fire pounding on the drums.

A woman strode into the light, lunging forward and lurching back, her legs moving spasmodically, her feet raising up the yellow dust. She went on dancing for what seemed a long time before another woman gathered her by the waist and pulled her back into the shadows.

The healer raised his arms, invoking the gods that dwelled beneath the surface of the earth and their counterparts in the skies, saying that the gods had vast stores of energy above and below. That energy was needed here. 'We walk upon the ancestors,' he prayed, 'because they give us the right to do so. We do not have a book of instructions on how we should communicate with you. Everything we do is instinctive, like the spontaneity that brought us here under this tree.'

One of the young men grabbed the goat and, with teeth gritted, twist-ed its neck so that the animal could be slaughtered. The boy watched the goat. Its chest seemed to rise and fall, its legs thrashing as it took great lungfuls of air. Another young man handed a long-bladed knife to the healer before sinking to his haunches to help his colleague subdue the goat that was already intuiting its own death. The goat's eyes increased in size, gathering its last image of light.

'We implore you,' the healer said, 'to strengthen our son who's assuming the mantle of leadership in these troubled hours of the blood plague ...'

When the healer raised the knife into the sky, the boy thought he had never seen such a weapon before. He tried to close his eyes, but couldn't.

'... so bring us a sign, you who voyage in the shadows ...'

The blade sliced the goat's neck. A geyser of blood spouted into the air. Fearing that the blood would spray him, the boy on the tree ducked. Since he wasn't an expert tree climber, he lost his balance. Crying out with fright, he came tumbling down, partly landing in the blood newly sprayed on the ground.

Winded, he peered up at the faces that now looked at him from above, the roles reversed. He could see some of the men reaching into their waistbands and producing guns that seemed like tools with which to commit sacrilege. But when the Colonel murmured something, the weapons were returned to their holsters. Everything was still until the Colonel said, 'Who are you, boy?'

Nauseated by the sight and smell of the bloodied goat, the boy tried to get up. The Colonel extended his arm and helped him to a sitting position. 'Who are you?'

The boy studied the face he had seen countless times on the 7.00 PM news on television. It was a narrow face with eyes that were clouded, perhaps from engagement with something outside of the ceremony, a more urgent matter. There was kindliness in the face, the chiselled nose and the full lips; it was a face that contained the knowledge of its own power.

'I'm Mr Jerome's son,' the boy answered. 'Hiero. And who are *you*?'

The Colonel gave him a long look and smiled. 'That,' he said, 'is a good question, Hiero, and I'm here to find the answer.' Then he turned to the young men. 'Make sure he didn't break anything in the fall,' he said. 'Take him to the Mariposa clinic. They should look at him.'

Then he looked at Mr Jerome's son again, shaking his head. 'You broke through my security. You could have easily taken a pot-shot from that tree.'

'No sir.' Hiero shook his head. 'I was hiding from the sugarcane man.'

7

'You were stealing the sugarcane.'

'Yes, to sell it. A sheaf of a dozen stalks fetches twenty Bangdos.'

'Bangdos?' The puzzlement on the Colonel's face made Hiero smile.

'That's Bangula dollars, Colonel,' one of the security men translated.

'Oh,' said the Colonel. Turning to the boy, he went on. 'When you're done with the doctors, come and see me. I think it's time I also learnt how to fly.'

'Yes, sir.' Hiero didn't know what the Colonel was talking about. He debated with himself whether he should report the man who had chased them with a cane knife, but thought better of it. He was happy to get out of there in one piece. And he had made friends with the Colonel. 'I *will* come and see you.'

'Yes.' The Colonel was no longer addressing himself to the boy. 'Please do.'

2

ON HIS BIRTHDAY on the 22nd of August, on the twentieth floor of the Commodore Hotel, His Excellency the President of the Republic of Bangula, Mr Abioseh Gondo, looks down from the window at the spread of Jambora, the capital city, and closes his eyes. Briefly overcoming a rush of emotions, he studies his room, especially the elaborate bed that has allowed him no rest.

It is a strange, custom-made affair, adjustable in all respects, like one of those reclining seats in First Class that provide insomniacs with a hammock-like sensation of being in flight while flying.

Everything in the hotel room conspires against comfort. The air-conditioning unit has become ever more capricious, sending out a daily blast of hot air redolent of raw sewage. Two days ago a handyman with insolent eyes was assigned to the job. Things are bad, thought Abioseh, when the hired help can hold you in contempt. As the repairman was explaining the complex mechanism of expansion valves and cold coils, there was a sudden blast of a reggae song from the radio along the passageway. The workman interrupted his recital to do a stylised shuffle and sing along with a tune decrying the government's 'betrayal' in the face of the blood plague. Abioseh threw him out, but the song lingered on:

> *Dem got dollars and pounds for fight disease*
> *Dem blow millions on bushwa with so much ease . . .*

TODAY, THE GRILLE fronting the unit growls and then the bedroom reeks of wild gardens. Mr President suspects a plot. *Bring it on*, he thinks, *bring on the whole malodorous blitzkrieg. I have a stomach for these things.*

From this height and distance, the houses and office blocks all sport a khaki uniform, the film of dust that covers everything. Out of this graininess that blows into people's every orifice and sets their teeth on edge, scorpions, spiders and rats emerge into the blinding sun and declare that they, too, are alive.

But the real rulers are the dust mites and sand fleas that hatch their eggs under the skin, causing victims to break out in pustules that are less sore than scary. At the back of Abioseh's mind lingers a trivial detail from the story of creation, that man was moulded from dust to rule over other life forms. *Since man has eternally failed to control his own instincts,* he thinks, *how is he expected to extend his dominion over others?* Apropos of nothing, the slogan insinuates itself into his head: *There is only one Reform and the Colonel is its Architect.*

Mr President gazes at the morning people and Jambora's restless traffic below, the people foreshortened into ants and the vehicles into toys. The silence created by the conspiracy of height above sea level, distance and double-glazing is eerie but comforting. He wonders about the destiny of the unknown walkers, barefooted or shod, or of the unknown drivers in sleek sedans or rickety minibus taxis held together by wire, tape and prayer. Here and there walks a child who will either be shadowed by ill fate or showered with blessings. The schools these young ones are perhaps headed for or playing truant from will determine whether the graduates will be armed for the future or are to be scarred forever.

Regarding them, the blessed and the damned, the drowned and the saved, he wonders whether he, Mr President, features in any of their thoughts, dreams or nightmares. Remembering his late father's warning about people, he laughs grimly to himself. 'No matter how gentle and decent you might be,' the Colonel had said one day, 'people will blind you with their smiles while they hood their sabre eyes. Trust them at your peril.'

Then again, Mr President agrees with what Jacqui Morgan once said: 'The people pounding the pavements or driving their cars are almost singularly incurious about you.' She went on to say that, since Mr President was everywhere and nowhere at the same time, people found it easier to consign him to the realm of myth. In the hotel room, he knows that he looms large on billboards and posters and on the frayed texture of paper money. He can be seen on television, heard on the radio and his words are made immortal by newspapers that regularly show pictures of him at conferences, reviewing troops in some location abroad or embracing his embattled or exalted counterparts elsewhere. It amuses him that the only thing that seems stubbornly alive on the billboards is the presidential gaze, which seems to follow you everywhere you go.

This morning, he is alert to the special character of the country and its people, in the same way a sleeper wakes up to the sharpness of sound and colour following narcotised slumber. He appreciates that while he was asleep, the world moved on without him. The machines rumbled on in the all-night factories. He can see the wide river snaking all the way to the mist where it becomes one with the mountains that form part of the horizon.

In that moment, he wishes for the sea-facing part of the hotel, from which point he would see almost the entire southern side of Jambora, the city that pulses in time to his heartbeat. He yearns for the lush vegetation on the other side, the wide splashes of green that relax his eyes.

He feels the onset of a headache, which comes from the knowledge that he is just another vulnerable man. He is just another man, not special. The events of the past fortnight, the handyman's rudeness, have alerted him to his ordinariness. The pain is one of the few indulgences he allows himself.

There is a timid knock at the door. 'Come in,' says Mr President.

The uniformed Chief of Protocol tiptoes into the room carrying a tray with the president's breakfast, black coffee and toast. Under his arm, he has newspapers and the diary. 'Morning, Sir,' he says as he places the tray on the writing desk. Taking two steps back, he stands, waiting. Tall and angular, the Chief of Protocol somehow manages to give off an effect of smallness. He has served Abioseh for many years but the latter doesn't quite know him. For two weeks now, they have been engaging in this pantomime. Enacting the rituals of power, the Chief of Protocol pretends that all is normal.

In character, Abioseh asks, 'What do we have today, James?' He sits down, takes a sip of the coffee and starts buttering his toast.

James takes his boss through the diary. 'At 6.50 AM,' he reads, 'the president has breakfast.'

'Ah, that's right,' Abioseh says, biting into the toast. '*I'm* having breakfast.'

Impervious to irony, James nods. 'Fair enough,' he says. 'At 7.30, you're on your way to your office.' He looks around. 'I suppose that's not possible today.'

'Yes,' Abioseh agrees. 'That's not going to happen.'

'Hiero, the Chief of Security Affairs, is next at 8.00 to 8.35.'

'I'll see Hiero,' Abioseh says, dismissively. 'Give the rest of the diary to Wonderman. He'll know what to do.'

As he heads to the door, the Chief of Protocol pauses. 'Is the president still in good health?'

'I'm fine, James,' Abioseh says. 'In fact, never better.'

'I'm pleased to hear that.' James smiles, a grim flutter of facial muscles.

'And you still keep time, I see.'

'Time,' Abioseh says almost to himself, 'is all I have.'

Hearing the door click shut, Abioseh reflects on his diary, which was always full from morning to late in the evening, the meetings normally taking no more than half an hour. The punctuality is in line with his sense of himself. He wakes up at 5.00 AM as regular as clockwork. From the time he was a schoolboy, through the long days and nights of love and war, Mr President (even though he wasn't president then) would wake up at this hour. This hour operated and continues to operate somewhere inside his mind. It galvanises his body into wakefulness – an alarm, it appears, that is ready to go off any time his body has rested for five hours.

He is therefore a nightmare on foreign missions because ambassadors have to ensure that they are the first people he sees in the morning and the last before he retires. The five-hour man, these diplomats call him behind his back.

He thinks of the meetings he has missed, the addresses he hasn't made to various august bodies, including the Chamber of Commerce, and the withdrawal of the privilege to play host. Weary that the presidency has become inseparable from his own personality, he determines to free himself from concerns about a way of life that has rejected him. It won't be easy.

There is another knock on the door. This time, the Chief of Protocol enters without waiting for permission. 'My profuse apologies,' he says. 'Your mother wished to come up and have breakfast with you.'

'I hope you turned her down, James,' Abioseh says.

'Yes, Sir,' James replies, the corners of his mouth twitching. 'Politely.'

'Thanks, James.' Abioseh Gondo looks at the door swinging shut, cutting off the snarl of a vacuum cleaner elsewhere on the floor. He imagines his mother trying to bully the hotel staff, encountering firmness beneath their outward complaisance. *She will hit back at them in her own way,* he thinks, *binding them to her through random acts of kindness.*

AT THE AGE of eleven, a year after his friend Hiero's encounter with the Colonel in the Panza sugarcane field, Abioseh was moved from the Panza junior primary school to a more modern and well-equipped institute in Jambora, which catered for the children of the country's elite.

When he objected to his parents, he was told that it all had to do with security. 'It's for your own good,' MaZembe, said. She was an accomplished carrier of bad news. He would miss his mates, especially Hiero. But he had to accept the dictates of his position in society.

The fact that it was his mother who'd tried to sweeten the pill brought about a spasm of resentment towards his father. Abioseh was proud of his mother's beauty and her great dress sense and didn't want her to have to do anyone's dirty work. He sometimes wondered if she wouldn't have been better off without the Colonel.

During the Colonel's occupation of high office, from the modest four-bedroom house in Panza to the official presidential residence of Mariposa in Jambora, it was MaZembe who kept everything orderly. The servants — and there were times when these constituted a platoon — were perfectly useless without her guidance, even though there was some major-domo forever on call. She was gracious even when she was hosting people who she privately loathed, even known enemies of the Colonel. In time, however, Abioseh started hearing of his father's indiscretions with women, some of them married, who brazenly accepted invitations to Mariposa in the company of their cuckolds. It was then that MaZembe became the very incarnation of kindliness. 'Never,' she once told Abioseh, 'let people in to what stirs in your heart.' It was after hearing these words that he started suspecting that his mother despised his father.

It was not in anything she said or did. When the Colonel came back from days of meet-and-greet gatherings in the outlying areas of Bangula, his clothes still holding the musty smell of outdoor fires and stolen moments of passion, she supervised the laundry herself, ensuring that the servants never caught sight of telltale white blotches that had congealed in the Colonel's underwear or collars soiled by rouge. Even though her face sometimes revealed that she suspected that the servants knew — *how couldn't they?* — the set of her jaw simultaneously conveyed to any watcher that anyone found peddling this knowledge would be crushed.

It was only last night that Abioseh had overheard his parents squabbling. Even when they thought he was asleep in the big house, they still spoke in code. The Colonel sounded angry over something. 'How long,' he asked, 'will you keep on with those know-nothing bookclub, marketplace gossipers?'

'It's not gossip,' MaZembe said. 'The way *they* look at me tells me why *you* no longer look at me.'

'Of course,' the Colonel snapped, 'I look at you!'

'You know what I mean.'

'I don't know what you mean. I've got a country to run, and you want me to look at you.'

'Ever since Abi was born,' MaZembe started, and then seemed to change her mind. 'Don't you think that he might have wanted a brother or sister?'

'How the hell would I know what he would have wanted? I'm not a mind reader or a wizard. That's more your department.'

'What do you mean by that?' There was a sudden chill in MaZembe's tone. 'Are you implying that I'm dabbling in juju?'

'Hell,' the Colonel said carelessly, though caution had crept into his voice, 'I just mean I don't have a bloody crystal ball. I don't know what the boy wants. Maybe he needs a brother, maybe he needs to get out a lot more and mingle with people instead of moping like a lovesick cow.'

'Maybe,' MaZembe said, 'he craves his father's love.' Then, in a voice that was accompanied by a sob so soft that Abioseh thought he might have imagined it, she added, 'Like I need your love.'

Abioseh had hardly attended his new school for three months when Emma-May, Hiero's mother, arrived unannounced one late Sunday afternoon and requested an audience with the Colonel. Still carrying

her overnight bag and dressed in last night's clothes, which were rumpled by the train journey from Panza, Emma-May looked harried and
overwrought, the bushy wig on her head adding to the impression of
dishevelment. When Emma-May was escorted into the lounge, Abioseh saw his mother's face stiffen. She took her time inspecting her son's
craftwork, a series of woven grass strainers for the brewing of sorghum
beer. When Emma-May coughed politely, MaZembe turned to greet her
guest with a dazzling smile.

'Emma-May!' she cried, spreading her arms. Embracing the woman,
MaZembe asked, murmuring into Emma-May's wig, 'Why do you ambush me like this? Dropping in without giving a woman time to prepare?'

'Ah,' Emma-May said, settling into the settee, taking in the decor.
'The matter that brings me here didn't allow me to give you a warning,
Mama.'

'Who gives warnings in times of urgency?' MaZembe asked no one
in particular. Looking around, she snapped her fingers. 'Something to
drink, then?' Without waiting for an answer, she rattled off a series of
orders to a young woman in uniform. 'And bring something for Abi.'

The attendant retreated, mumbling, 'Yes, Mama.' Abioseh wondered
if this was his mother's ploy to shorten the meeting by ensuring that he
stayed on in the lounge, since it was uncommon for children to be around
while adults talked about weighty matters. Was this her way of lowering
the importance of the session and making it awkward for Emma-May to
request something of value?

However, Emma-May's request was neither ambitious nor hard to
achieve; the Jerome family was moving to Jambora and they wanted little
Hiero to get a place in 'Abi's school'.

Having expected to be asked for something that would have meant
her calling on favours, MaZembe was visibly relieved. She smiled.

'Do you think you can do that, Mama?' Emma-May asked.

'Do it?' MaZembe repeated the question eagerly. 'Of course, I'll *do* it,'
she said. 'I'm the patroness of the school's governing body, and little Abi

here has been asking after his friend, haven't you, Abi?'

Abioseh couldn't remember asking after Hiero, but since he couldn't contradict his mother, he ducked his head slightly instead of telling a lie. He wondered if Hiero would cope in the new school, which was strict. He was somewhat pleased because they had so much unfinished business together. Looking out the window at the lawn, the gazebo and the swimming pool, he experienced a moment of acute loss. Had MaZembe agreed so promptly to intervene on Emma-May's behalf so that he, Abioseh, would have a friend? For, he realised as he sipped the chilled ginger beer, he had not really made friends at the new school. The attitude of privileged children rubbed him up the wrong way. They were spoilt, insolent, used to taking the world for granted.

The students at other schools were unreachable, but for different reasons. They evinced their own brand of superiority. They knew that the world wouldn't do them any favours. Fiercely competitive in sports, they played as if losing to the rich kids were punishable by death. They wore their uniforms in style, the shoes unlaced and the shirt-tails hanging out, the grey flannels slung so low that the crack between their buttocks would show whenever they were crouched on the floor in a game of cards or dice.

'You're a kind woman, Mama,' Emma-May said, accepting the cup of tea the servant had brought. 'May the good times befall you.'

'Thank you,' MaZembe said, 'for letting me be of service to my sisters.'

'Ah,' Emma-May sighed as she contemplated the piece of cake before her, 'the future looks bright.'

'The future *is* bright,' MaZembe said.

ABIOSEH IS BROUGHT back to the present by strains of the irreverent refrain of the reggae tune. Ebbing and flowing, pleading and teasing, the lyrics remind him of the charges he still has to face. He wonders if he actually has a future.

3

Dem amass weapons to boost the treasury
Dem leave the poor on slabs in the mortuary . . .

SUPINE ON A LUMPY pallet covered in crinoline, Zebulon hears the thump of the bass guitar, insistent and arrogant. He is grateful to the person with the radio, who has been keeping him company in his isolation. Today, his visitor hums along with the melody; Zebulon feels so thirsty he debates with himself whether to ask the visitor to get him an ice-cold Coke. But that would be sabotage.

He can feel his thoughts pouring out of his head like perspiration oozing out of his pores. *I am the emptying gourd of my soul.* He wonders if this is an original thought or something that has lain dormant in his brain, a long-forgotten line from one of his mother's poems, one of those things that comes out in times of stress. *Yes,* he thinks, *the words are a poem of sorts,* only he can't remember the poet. Zebulon comforts himself that even at school, the few years he attended, he wasn't big on poetry. He wasn't big on anything. He merely liked the words to sing like a waterfall. Although soothing, the words were far from trustworthy for they earned him a beating from the teachers when he forgot their sequence.

He thinks he can see the words, which have now merged with his thoughts seeping out of him. They are elongated lucent tubes streaked with green, like tendrils of discoloured kelp. They will nourish some aquatic creature that feeds on viridian dreams. This thought causes him to smile as he is amazed at the flow of words, but he quickly rearranges his facial muscles, the only part of him capable of mobility. He must shut down his brain and shut his trap. He has seen what happens to people who have been drained of everything.

Zebulon starts to cry to himself, the tears trailing down his cheekbones into his ears, irritating him. Everything that has happened to him has given him no option but to seize any opening to fight what his halfbrother – and the government he heads – stands for. On one occasion, a psychologist with a fondness for Shakespeare, wrote that even if Abioseh Gondo were to spend his entire tenure giving alms to the poor, Zebulon would have found some missile to hurl at him. 'Was it,' the psychologist asked, 'a classic case of sibling rivalry, where one of the half-brothers had been born to advantage while the other had not had such a lucky break? Was one "doomed for a certain term to walk the night" and the other to be encased in the luxury of the leather and chrome of limousines the size of battleships?'

ZEBULON WAS DRAWN to Jambora's smart cars from a very early age. He was no different from any other boy. When he was eleven years old, he watched the vehicles and their occupants and sensed the onset of an anxiety that he couldn't quite describe. He always stood and gazed as the cars whizzed past, leaving clouds of dust behind. Although he couldn't explain all the details, he knew at that age that they were poor and that his mother was battling. He understood, moreover, that her poverty was somehow connected to the fact that he had no father. He was aware of other single women who, like Madu, his mother, also went to church on Sundays. But they were at ease with their lot and their clothes didn't scream poverty. They weren't hobbled by needy children, as Madu was with him.

He went to bed each night praying that she wouldn't abandon him at midnight. In the morning, it cheered him to hear her singing to herself, perhaps something bluesy or a spiritual number borrowed from the church choir practice:

> *I want to be ready,*
> *To go to Jerusalem just like John ...*

Knowing that she had other chores, he scrubbed and dressed himself unaided and got ready for the day. Then he watched her preparing breakfast: a mug of tea, a slice of bread and porridge. One of the boys had organised him a newspaper route that started at the crack of dawn, which earned him ten pence a round. At night he memorised – and, alone, rehearsed – her every move when cooking, all the time telling himself: *Mother's got to be free of me.*

But Zebulon's well-laid plans towards a unilateral declaration of independence from maternal supervision suffered a setback on the morning of Madu's birthday, which was on the 15th of March. He had marked the day with the aim of waking his mother up with a cup of tea (coffee was banned in the small household) and toast that would have been made on the Welcome Dover coal-burning stove, which took up most of the kitchen space. As a bonus, in recognition of the important and unusual day, he would have boiled her an egg.

The first indication of trouble was a tingling at the back of his throat, followed by a lively to-and-fro sensation inside his cranium, as if the brain tissue were struggling for direction. And then the pain started from somewhere inside his ear and detoured behind the eyes to hit him at the base of his skull. Engulfed by nausea, he jumped out of bed and had just emptied the contents of his stomach into the washbasin when his mother entered the little cubicle to do her toilet.

Madu took one look at him and placed her cool palm across his brow. She removed it as if it were red-hot. 'You're running a fever,' she said, 'and you'll soon be raining sweat if we don't do something quickly.'

'But I'm fine,' said Zebulon, cursing the weakness in his joints, '*really*.'

'Really was a Silly Billy,' Madu sang – something picked up in the schoolyards of her own childhood, which didn't make a lot of sense, but its lilt made Zebulon realise how much he loved her. 'Come here.'

She rummaged in the cupboards, upended suitcases and various tin boxes and came out with handfuls of dry herbs and phials containing dark violet liquid or magic crystals that came out entangled in twine and sewing bits and bobs. Lighting the wick and then pumping a Primus stove, she threw the mixture into a saucepan to boil, steam rising and filling the kitchen with a pungent smell.

Awash with shame, he let her strip him naked, then sit him down on a low stool and place a steaming vessel on the floor between his legs, with an injunction to watch it didn't burn his pretty pink privates. Madu covered him from head to toe with a heavy blanket. Zebulon was sure his penis was neither pink nor pretty but, weak as he was, he couldn't argue with his mom.

The steam swirled around his genitals before enveloping his face, stinging and causing his closed eyes to water, heating the back of his head, which had been, he felt, the starting point of the fever. And just when the heat inside the blanket was nearly unbearable and her son was almost suffocating, Madu whipped the cover off and handed him the saucepan. 'Go,' she said, 'and douse yourself with this stuff in the pot. Some of it will stick to you; don't worry. Just go to bed and you'll wash properly once you've recovered.'

Later, as shadows danced arabesques across the curtains, somewhere in the realm of dreams and feverish wakefulness, he was lifted up, lighter than a feather and brought to the sound of his own voice. He knew that he had been talking in his sleep. At the same time, however, he could feel her placing on his forehead a compress that had earlier been dipped into a blend of herbs.

Although he couldn't tell what time it was, he knew that she couldn't have gone to work, not with him ill, and this filled him with sadness as if he had failed her. He surrendered to sleep when he felt her body warmth against him and he turned – although it could have been a sequence in a dream, a hallucination – and held her in a grip that even death would have failed to unclasp.

He wouldn't know, until much, much later, how dearly Madu had paid for that day's absence from the cleaning job she held at Charlie Bonheur Dry Cleaners, a facility run by a consortium of Francophone Africans and Creoles.

Every time he came to see his mother at work, especially on Saturdays when he would help her to run the weekend errands, Claude, from Gabon, would ruffle Zebulon's hair and ask: '*Comment ça va?*' and offer to teach him French. Zebulon, as he had been taught, would respond, '*Ça va bien, merci*,' hating the man for mussing his hair. He even asked his mother, 'Ma, what's with all this *komosava* and *bee-yen messy*? Why can't he just speak English?'

But it was much more than a concern over grooming that made it hard for Zebulon to warm to his mother's employer. It was the way Claude addressed her, as he did other young women, with a certain careless and disrespectful edge.

What further mystified him was Madu's reaction. Her laughter became louder and her eyes smiled as they'd never smiled for him, even though there was something watchful in the smile.

And at school, the other children would say that he and his mother were fools, for it was known that he, Zebulon, was the Colonel's son. So, some of the school bullies would ask, why were they living in a poky little shack like lowlifes, with his mother fucking married men for extra cash?

This, of course, became a source of countless fights, in which Zebulon would wrestle anyone to the ground for suggesting his mother was less than perfect.

One evening, she came back, a whiff of alcohol in her breath that she had tried to mask by popping breath mints, singing to herself, something not entirely right with her eyes. It was on that day that he asked, 'Ma, are you a whore?'

Madu looked at her son as if seeing him for the first time and from an overwhelming distance. She had been seated on the bed watching the news on the television whose screen was so small that Zebulon feared she would ruin her eyes. At first she recoiled as if he'd punched her under the heart, and then slowly, slowly, as if she'd never finish the act of straightening up, she rose and, seemingly without effort, leaned forward and struck him with her open palm across the mouth, drawing blood. 'Don't *you* ever,' she said, breathing hard, poised to slap him again with her other hand, 'don't you ever call someone's mother's child a whore, *ever!*' She paused, her chest heaving. 'Do you *hear* me, Zebulon?'

'But,' he persisted, his face aflame, 'that's the word on the *street.*'

'Since when,' she asked, lowering her hand but keeping her fingers clenched, 'do you go along with the talk on the street?' She made to stroke his head and, as he flinched, she softened. 'I'm not going to hit you,' she murmured, 'but one other lesson you need to learn, boy, is that you must *trust* me. I'm your mother, for Christ's sake … If there's something being said behind my back, which makes you unhappy, ask *me* first, don't just come out and call a woman a whore.'

She gathered him to her and wiped the blood and snot off his face with a handkerchief that smelled of lavender and dry-cleaning chemicals. 'Okay?'

'Okay.'

Then she told him why she had chosen their way of life for them. While her account made sense, it filled him with a great sense of inadequacy, like a soldier fated to fight against a superior enemy. He felt himself a feather in a whirlwind.

HERE HE IS, condemned to immobility and nearly suffocating in the cloying August heat. Even as he suspects that his mind is wavering and trickling out in droplets onto the pallet, he accepts the notion that his flesh is capable of betrayals. That shouldn't come as a surprise because he is an older man now. He has had a long life. It feels like a miracle that he was once a young man.

PART ONE

FLESH

I

YEARS ELAPSED WITHOUT Hiero honouring his promise to visit the Colonel. The move to Jambora's Alfredo Romero High School, which had once catered solely for white and Creole students before Ramala's takeover, had been less than smooth. His dada, Mr Jethro Jerome, had found it difficult to accept his wife's engineering of such a huge change in their lives. When drunk, his abusiveness reached untapped levels. He accused Emma-May of lusting after anything that was remotely white. 'They rejoice at common people like you fighting over their leavings,' he roared.

'It's to secure Hiero's future,' Emma-May said with lethal patience. 'It's to take care of *me* in my old age.'

Hiero wondered if Abioseh's parents ever fought, although he suspected that his dada's rages came from a sad and fearful place inside him. The Colonel was as sure-footed as MaZembe was dignified. It would be in bad taste to ask Abioseh, even though they were in the same class. They were both fourteen years old and had known each other from when they were toddlers in Panza. Much as Hiero would have liked to share the details of his life, there was something about Emma-May's stubborn pride — and sorrow — that had to be kept away from prying eyes. With his life suddenly full, even if its fullness was a type of emptiness, seeing the president had become secondary. It had found a place among misty memories.

Practically, he also couldn't just stroll over to Mariposa and tell the guard at the gate that he had come to see the Colonel. *And who might you be?* Hiero imagined the guard asking him, feigning politeness the way people do when disarming a madman. He had no desire to end up in a straitjacket.

THE WEATHER WAS beautiful. Although September was normally prey to strong winds that blew from the mountains down to the sea, this Friday afternoon was calm. The sun, normally harsh, felt warm against Hiero's back as he and Abioseh stepped out of the school gates to wait for David. The eldest son of Chief Justice Gwandon Kone, David was a storehouse of information about women. To Hiero, women — girls — were an enigma, a species that elicited fear and revulsion in equal measure. Although he knew that Abioseh was the son of the most important man in the land, he took his hat off to David. Anyone who could crack the arcane code of femaleness was zibby zabba.

Six Creole girls were next out of the gate, serene, their hair in scarves or flowing freely, their eyes scanning the road for their lifts home or to the mall. There, Hiero knew, they would sip coloured cocktails and blow illegal tobacco smoke through sculpted nostrils. These young women's self-importance made him feel sorry for his dada, whose impotent dislike for white people had latterly found a target in the Creoles. He would even hum a little-known ditty about the Creoles whose bodies were in Bangula while their spirits were ensconced in Europe. Looking at the young women strutting to the cars, Hiero was struck by the fact that there was nothing European about them. Their skin tones ranged from chocolate-brown to olive; the eyes and hair could have belonged to many a native of Bangula. It was a matter of attitude.

David Kone, tall, handsome and smiling as he scoped the Creole girls, was in the company of five members of the basketball team. Three of the girls got into a four-wheel-drive, and the boys watched the dust billowing into the air.

'One day,' David said, 'I'm going to own a car like that.'

'How do you know?' Hiero felt he had to be the first one to engage David in a discussion. 'You're what? Fourteen? You still have years of school before you earn real money. You'll be an old man before you can buy a spare tyre of a car like that.'

'Not me. I'll go work for the Colonel.' David had it all figured out. 'There's work to be done in government that brings quick rewards.'

'Like what?' This was Abioseh. He found it intolerable that people could ignore him while they discussed his father.

'Oh,' David said airily, 'stuff. Secret stuff.'

Hiero looked at David with a mixture of disbelief and annoyance. 'People,' he said, 'don't just choose to do secret stuff for the president. They are appointed.'

'Yes?' David put in evilly. 'Like you were appointed when you fell out of a tree? Come on, Hiero.'

'That was a brilliant bit of gate-crashing,' one of the basketball players said.

'If it really happened,' David said.

'What was he wearing?' Abioseh asked, ignoring the doubters. At this, three of the boys ran off from the main group and started playing chicken with a few cars, mainly military vehicles, as they played catch along the road.

'Who?' Hiero asked, although he knew.

'The Colonel.'

'I can't remember,' Hiero replied in a tone that said that he could still be persuaded to dig deep into his memory if this were truly important.

He recalled staring with fascination as the open-necked white cotton shirt became speckled with blood when the healer made the cuts on the Colonel's brow. At fourteen, he already appreciated the currency of information.

Abioseh was silent beside Hiero, irritated by Hiero's reluctance to tell the story. David Kone repeated his refutation. 'Nothing happened in the cane field,' he said. 'Hiero's just selling us a pile of crap.'

'Yes,' Hiero said huffily, 'David's right. I made it all up.'

Abioseh shot David a warning look. 'David,' he said, 'this is my old man we're talking about here, so please shut up.'

'Why don't *you* just ask the Colonel what happened?' David teased. 'He's your father, after all.' Catching Abioseh glaring at him, David put up his hands in a gesture of surrender. 'Okay, okay.'

Back in the limelight, Hiero told the story of meeting the Colonel, his account fluent. 'The Colonel,' he said, 'wore a checked shirt.'

'Strange,' Abioseh said, 'because I don't remember the Colonel owning such a shirt. And you've just said you couldn't remember what he was wearing.'

'It's just come back to me now,' Hiero said. He gave Abioseh a side-long glance. 'Do you want me to go on with my story, or what?'

'Tell the story, tell the story,' one of the boys, nicknamed Baluba, urged. Tall and chubby for his age, he evinced an aggressiveness that made other boys give him a wide berth. 'Is it true that the Colonel was naked?'

'And that he has a big one?' another sly adolescent asked.

'I don't know about that,' Hiero said truthfully. 'I just know what I saw – and it gave me a thrill.'

'We must never,' Abioseh said cryptically, 'lose ourselves inside the stories of others.' He waved at someone inside a black sedan that stood with its engine running on the side of the road.

'Trust me,' Hiero said, 'I'll never get lost in someone else's story.'

The group suspected that Hiero could sometimes live in a fantasy world. But, like all boys, they loved a good yarn and didn't worry about the inconvenience of facts. As the rest revelled in the story, breaking into gales of laughter at Hiero's impressions of the fateful evening's droller moments, Abioseh whispered something into Hiero's ear before striding off to the official-looking car. 'See you fellows Monday,' he called.

'What did he say to you?' David asked indicating the disappearing sedan.

'He said: *Help me find the Colonel's son,*' Hiero replied.

'Find the Colonel's son,' David repeated. 'What do you think he meant?'

'God knows.' Suddenly sensing a divine plan to elevate him to the ranks of the exalted of the island, Hiero shivered. 'Throw me the ball,' he yelled to the frolickers on the road, needing some form of distraction. 'Throw that ball here!'

THE LITTLE SUBURB of Cinnamon Hill lay between Alfredo Romero High School and the bus rank, whose human traffic had spawned one of Jambora's busiest markets. The residents of the suburb sometimes experienced a surge of pride when they saw the students from Alfredo Romero: the boys in grey flannels, white shirts, green-and-gold ties and green blazers sporting the motto *Mens Sana in Corpore Sano*, a sound mind in a sound body, the girls wearing similar blazers over green tunics. These examples of ripening manhood or womanhood were destined to be a credit to the race. Second only to the University of Bangula in prestige, Alfredo Romero was a sure-fire crucible for future leaders, the way a reputable bakery guaranteed good bread.

The inhabitants of Cinnamon Hill would, of course, be chastened by the sight of some of the schoolboys behaving badly. These would sway, under the influence of the brew peddled in some of the illegal taverns in the market. Or they'd be walking arm-in-arm with known women of ill repute, who plied their trade from airtime kiosks. On Mondays, their dreams deferred, the residents would hose the pavements of vomit and caked blood.

Occasionally, people would gather and sign petitions for the reloca-
tion of the market and the bus rank. Being middle class and owning their
own means of transport, they wouldn't be inconvenienced by the move.
They also didn't really care where the buses and the septic tank, as the
market was also called, moved to, preferably into the Indian Ocean. But,
of course, officialdom being notoriously hard of hearing, nothing was
done. Alcohol, drugs and disease – especially the blood plague – would
be the ruin of many a student, the people predicted.

ON THIS FRIDAY, three elderly women, Cinnamon Hill's oldest residents,
watched the boys they called 'David's chums' passing by as avidly as they
had watched Bangula's journey from childhood to adulthood. The whole
of Bangula, from Jambora to Panza – and even the smaller towns and
villages – spoke of Jutaita, Jumaima and Josephine in tones reserved for
royalty.

No one had lived long enough to know how these women, daunt-
ing presences who gazed on the world with clear eyes, had come to be
in Cinnamon Hill. Their faces were gaunt as if the elements had done
their worst – and failed. They incarnated a thumbing of the nose at the
grave.

They went against tradition, appearing in public wearing clothing
made of skins of animals both wild and domestic, challenging the protocol of the totem of the Jirovuma royal house by using leopard skin.
Sometimes all three would appear in men's dark jackets and top hats or,
more bizarrely, in colourful short fringe aprons of fibre cords strung
with beads covering gingham skirts. Their progress around the suburb
would be accompanied by the clang of iron and wire bangles, some of
which were shot with precious stones of indeterminate origin. Sometimes all three walked to the municipal offices with long-stemmed clay
pipes whose ornate bowls were filled with exotic tobacco.

Unaware of their effect on others, the trio was engaged in mundane
chores this early afternoon. There were the four or five eight- to ten-

year-old girls who had been dropped off by their mothers in the morning, who would be picked up in an hour or so. They had to be fed so that they wouldn't spread negative stories about having been starved, especially since their mothers paid for this service. Running a playschool had been Jumaima's initiative. She believed that no matter how old a person was, money mattered, and she had popularised the phrase that had so scandalised the local pastor. 'Nothing,' she said, 'can take the place of God except money.'

But the house of the three old women was also a sanctuary, an informal shelter for women, young or old, fleeing marital unhappiness or the inconvenience of parental arrangements that rode roughshod over the wishes and aspirations of marriageable women. Inside the house, the other two Js were baking and cooking and brewing ginger beer. Now and then they'd emerge to check if they might be missing out on any action in the neighbourhood.

'Ah,' said Jumaima, 'you'll burn the pots if you can't curb your curiosity, you two.' She was the self-appointed director of the drama provided by the unwitting cast of actors on the potholed road.

'How are the babies?' Josephine asked, not about to be intimidated. 'Are they enjoying themselves?'

'You can see for yourself that they're all right, homegirl,' Jutaita said. She was impatient with people who tended to state the obvious. 'Maybe,' she suggested evilly, 'you should join them in their play, seeing as your brains have gone on vacation.' The three women always addressed one another as 'homegirl'.

Josephine looked at the girls dancing, carefree. 'Hope their folks don't turn into monsters,' she growled wistfully. 'Fill their heads with nonsense.'

'They will become monsters,' Jumaima said. 'Especially if they meet monsters.'

A few minutes later, the children fed, the old women approached two workmen from a gang building the road and bullied them into carting their old couch from inside the lounge and placing it outside. Accompanied by tumblers of still-warm ginger beer and golden scones on the tray covered with doilies against the flies, the women sank into the settee and readied themselves to survey and intimidate the passers-by. The schoolboys appeared, their loud yells nearly drowning the scream of the siren at the sugarcane mill as it heralded the 4.00 PM shift.

This afternoon as they watched the boys, hearing adolescence creep into the timbre of their voices, the old women welcomed the first two mothers who had arrived to fetch their children. The mothers were about to leave when the boys suddenly stopped their frolicking and stood on the side of the road, as still as statues. The women got to their feet and watched as a funeral procession went past. Leading it were seven little girls, each holding a bouquet of white flowers. Their bare feet unsettled the dust, browned their cream dresses and stained the petals. Behind them the priest in black strode decorously as if giving the beat to fourteen pallbearers carrying seven small coffins on their shoulders. The whitewashed caskets were daubed on two sides with green crosses denoting the ages of the deceased. Taking up the rear were the mourners, hundreds of them, their gait suggesting that they had been on this march since morning and would accompany their dead children until hell froze over. Unsmiling and silent, they filed past the house of the three old women, who stood to attention.

'Where do they come from?' Jumaima asked.

'Possibly Vitoux,' Josephine said. 'I hear people are dying in droves there.' Vitoux was a village half a day's march from Jambora.

'I didn't know,' Jutaita said, 'that the fingers of the blood plague were already touching people there.' Her face betrayed a certain pride that she and her homegirls were still alive and not being carried inside those wooden boxes.

'It's touching everywhere,' Josephine said. As the mourners disappeared around the corner, Josephine glanced at the little girls on the veranda as they clung to their mothers, uncomprehending, awed by the afternoon that had become so serious. The mothers themselves seemed troubled, especially Mrs Badawi, who was pregnant and whose daughter with doll-like eyes gazed at the old women as if seeking an answer.

'This is terrible,' Mrs Badawi said, shaking her head. 'It has to end somewhere.'

'It's the end of paradise,' another mother said. 'It wasn't always like this.'

BUT THE THREE old women were thinking about the schoolboys from Alfredo Romero High. That David Kone, they knew, was going to the tavern. He was sure to drag someone down with him.

2

IN THE MIDDLE of August, the Colonel paid an unusual visit to Abioseh. Hiero, who had advance knowledge about everything, broke the news. In the locker room where the rest of the soccer players were changing into their kit, Hiero looked odd in his grey flannels and green blazer.

'Why are you always in that blazer even when it's so hot?' Abioseh asked. 'People will think you're hiding a pregnancy.'

'Yes,' Hiero answered, adjusting his tie. 'I'm five months gone, already.' He sniffed the air, which smelled of disinfectant, dirty socks, sweat and adolescent lust. 'Smells like a billy goat just farted in here.' And then, 'The old geezer's here for you, Abi boy,' Hiero said. 'Want me to come along?'

'It's okay,' Abioseh said. 'Don't worry about it.'

'You sure?' Although jocular, Hiero's tone belied seriousness. 'Our old man can be intimidating ...'

Abioseh wondered where the possessive pronoun came from. 'I'll be fine.' Hiero's attention to him was beyond friendliness.

'If you wind up needing some backup,' Hiero said, sauntering to the exit, 'just give us a shout.'

Even as he strode from the tiered benches for spectators to the gravelled path, just in time to see the state car entering the gates of the sports grounds, Abioseh was marvelling at his father's sense of timing. Although he was the captain of the squad of fourteen-year-old soccer players, due to a sprained ankle, Abioseh was not playing today. The kit was for the rallying of the troops.

The weather was superb; the unseasonal July rains that had lashed Jambora had stopped. Abioseh hoped that the good weather would hold.

But his elation soon waned when he climbed into his father's official car. 'Don't bang the door,' the Colonel said gruffly. Abioseh felt something like goose pimples rising at the nape of his neck; he respected and loved the Colonel, but today *he*, too, deserved to be loved and respected. Throughout his life, his father had made him feel like an outcast; this had to end.

'If you don't want me here,' he said, 'please allow me to get back to my friends.'

'I admire your spirit,' the Colonel said, giving his son a long look, a small smile on his face. 'But please spare me the theatrics.' He paused. 'And if I teach you just one thing in life: never, never show people that you're angry.'

'I'm sorry, Father.' Something up-tempo was playing inside the car.

'What I tell you today is something you might choose to ignore,' the Colonel said, 'but I'll say it, in any case, for you're my son. If we had our way in everything, we'd be guilty of skewing nature's design. Those we love would live forever and fill our homesteads with joy, but we'd probably end up hungrier with the state forced to provide for geriatrics. That would mean no ancestors. There'd be no crime, no need for the prison population. Did you know that with every new political dispensation comes a refinement of criminal methods?'

'No.' Abioseh didn't know.

The Colonel looked at the teams tussling for the ball, the late afternoon sun beginning to set and the shadows lengthening. 'Anyway,' he said, 'if we'd had our way, there'd be no divorces, and no need for men to cheat on their women, no men to force their wives into a perpetuity of rage or the sanctuary of adultery.' A trumpet solo preceded the rasping voice of Dodo Madelia, Bangula's celebrated singer; it wove into the fabric of the conversation:

What happens when we all see the hidden lion
Don't we wish for the colours of the chameleon?

It suddenly grew cold in the car. The Colonel signalled to the driver, who was also the bodyguard and thus privy to unwholesome secrets, to close all the windows. The Colonel cleared his throat. 'When I was young,' he began, 'before I met your mother, straight out of the military academy, I fell in love.'

The simplicity of the words – *I fell in love* – struck Abioseh. 'I'd seen this woman before and made enquiries. She was beautiful in that strange way of women who aren't classical beauties but who, when they look at you, personify everything you've ever dreamt of: large, liquid eyes, the whites like milk, the eyes themselves darker than rivers. She literally took my breath away.'

The Colonel paused. 'Madu,' he said, 'Madu.' He seemed to ponder. 'We had one of those whirlwind …' the Colonel groped for a word, and then he snapped his fingers, '… romances. I wanted to marry her then and there. Every time we made love, it was perfect. But she would say that she wanted to tell me something. *There's something I've got to tell you.* Sometimes I would say, *What?* and she would fall silent.'

Uncomfortable with what amounted to a confession by his father, Abioseh squirmed at the notion of his father making love to someone. He rolled the expression off the tongue of his mind, *making love*, and it didn't make sense. At fourteen years of age, he knew that men and women 'did' it; he had heard that sometimes men and men and even women and women 'did' it. But these were people outside his immediate grasp of the implications of the stirrings of flesh and blood. And soul. Although he had already heard of his father's indiscretions, he was still uncomfortable with their corroboration.

'Sometimes, in sleep, in the middle of the night,' the Colonel went on, 'I'd feel her thrashing like someone in the throes of a nightmare. I'd wake her up and she'd look at me wildly, eyes unfocused, like I was an animal she had encountered in the middle of a forest. In those moments I'd feel an alien, disconnected from her, and I would ask myself: *What brings strangers together?*'

He glanced at his watch, more from force of habit than from a need to find out how late it was. He couldn't have read the dials in the gloom. 'I didn't probe. I believed that whatever was eating her would go away.' He shook his head. Then he sighed and it was the loneliest and, ironically, the most human, sound Abioseh had ever heard his father make. 'We listen but we do not hear.'

'So what happened?'

'Do you remember the Blood of the Ancestors?'

Abioseh remembered.

Who hadn't heard of the terror that gripped the country at the beginning – and carried the seeds of the end – of General Gabriel Ramala's administration? Recently graduated from the local military academy, the Colonel – who was a mere captain then – was part of the task team sent to investigate a spate of seemingly random family murders across the land. The killings were intriguing because robbery was clearly not the motive. It had to be something else. Revenge? What?

The breakthrough came with the murder of two families. 'When we checked the identities of family members,' the Colonel said, 'one thing stood out. These were great-great-grandchildren of leaders and warlords who had collaborated with the slave-owners. This piece of information was given to analysts at HQ who confirmed that their ancestry pointed towards some benefit from the past.'

'As you know, when Ramala took over,' the Colonel explained, 'he granted pardons to warlords. Angry people sought to nullify these pardons. People died. Their crime was that they were descendants of some previous beneficiary of an obscene system.' All the victims had been beheaded.

It was perhaps this chilling method of killing, at once intimate and detached, which struck fear into the population. In the violence that had tapered off towards the end of Ramala's rule, people had used guns and the country was awash with firearms. Killing with a knife had become rare; there was no glamour in it. The closeness of the victim to the stabber made its use one of the messiest methods of murder. The knife struck fear based on people's terror of ancient weapons, since these linked humanity to a primeval past.

'A knife,' the Colonel said, 'is used in all rituals involving blood; the wizards and witches and healers are all familiar with the strange power of the blade. The planning of these murders showed skill and precision. The killers had access to secret files, which had not been released even under the Freedom of Information Act. They coordinated a series of attacks in areas hundreds of kilometres apart.'

> ... *in this thrashing hour under the boot of iron*
> *We'll be safe in the skin of the chameleon* ...

Night fell slowly, softly, deepening the edge of the russet sky. Although it was somewhat warmer, the strength of the wind could still be felt inside the car. Abioseh sensed the shadows swallowing the remnants of the sun.

Giving his father a sidelong glance, he felt that the Colonel was leaving out a lot. Perhaps the Colonel thought he'd protect him from the nastier aspects of life. But the grim expression on the Colonel's face showed that he suspected that the son had already seen his fair share of horror.

'And Madu?' Abioseh asked. 'Where was she in all this?'

'She followed the case without at first showing any real interest,' the Colonel said. 'When we discussed it, she said that the murders only confirmed that the world wasn't really safe in men's hands. Sometimes I was irritated by her casual approach to my work. As time passed, she took more notice, and would ask me for some kind of progress report.'

On some hot nights when mosquitoes whined and dive-bombed them until they covered up with a sheet, the Colonel and Madu would argue about the morality of the manhunt. Intelligence reports had come up with the ringleader's *nom de guerre* – Vezi. When Madu was told of this development, she forbade the Colonel from further discussion of the campaign to capture Vezi.

People followed Vezi's bloody adventures in newspaper reports. The country was split into different camps. One faction felt that the long route towards nationhood had skipped a crucial phase, namely, the shedding of blood, and had for the moment averted the inescapable through appeasement. Others urged the government to track down the killers. Murderers were murderers, no matter how skilfully they covered themselves with the cloak of revolutionary respectability.

The Colonel belonged to a third camp that believed in the law of causality and the occasional brutality of karma. Although obliged by the security code to pursue and prosecute, he felt a grudging sympathy for Vezi. Beneficiaries from the spoils of the past had got off lightly. The violence unleashed to lay the foundation for their privilege called for blood. This was perhaps the reason Vezi and his people operated under the name of the Blood of the Ancestors.

As was known by any African, no matter how brainwashed he or she might have been, ancestors were all round – and their restlessness could cause chaos lasting generations. 'What's going on today,' the Colonel had told Madu, 'is destiny in action: what goes around comes around.'

He believed it unjust for the world to pretend that the benefits from the slave trade hadn't given the rich of the land a head start. 'Today, in commerce and industry,' he had lamented, 'in the education gained by evil means – all this gave these people the upper hand. If we'd have a tally of the casualties of struggles, they got off very lightly. It's about time they bled.'

'But,' Madu had asked, 'doesn't that pave the way for anarchy?'

'Anarchy will always come from anger,' the Colonel had put in cruelly. 'The unequal distribution of land has always been the root cause of fire. Then there was poverty and general carelessness about how people should be treated. The landed didn't care when farmers' dogs savaged old black men and women and vulnerable young children. And what was their reaction, these bedbugs fattened by slavery? Their radio talk shows received calls sympathising with the traumatised dogs that must have been provoked by the victims. People drew up petitions and launched campaigns to save the dogs from being put down!'

'Yes,' Madu had argued, 'that might have been the case. But dogs still kill people under Ramala's term.'

'That's right,' the Colonel had answered, 'but Ramala has tried to gain some internal cohesion. I understand his position as I also understand that of the Blood of the Ancestors.'

NOW, DRAGGED TO the present, he looked at his son. 'Vezi was captured in September.'

'How did that happen?' Abioseh asked. Throughout, Abioseh had listened politely, but this development promised excitement. He was, after all, fourteen years old and weaned on a regular diet of adventure stories. This one involved a real-life hero, his father.

'Events developed their own logic,' the Colonel said. 'One night, Madu and I had ...' he paused.

'Made love?' Abioseh prompted, smiling. 'You'd been doing that a lot.'

'Yes ... *that*.' The Colonel chuckled. Madu had been unwell, so, this particular session had been characterised by sorrow and rapture. Yielding while resisting, Madu had clawed at him as she drew him into herself. Then she had murmured that she was pregnant.

Later, watching his cigarette smoke spiralling into the air and merging with the flames of the scented candles, he had asked her how far gone she was. 'Far enough,' Madu had answered. He had thought of probing more. But she would only reveal what she wished to be revealed. 'I knew it would be a boy.'

He had expected to sleep in the following day, a Sunday. But there was no rest. A loud banging on the door shattered the morning. The unit of five soldiers, already sweating in slept-in uniforms, told him that one of Vezi's men had been captured and was due to be interrogated at the police station.

'Who is it?' Madu had asked nervously, a warning in her tone. The Colonel had stood framed against the doorway, his hand on the brass knob.

'It's the men,' the Colonel had answered, his mind already erasing the texture of the night and its passion. 'Seems like *they've* hit on something,' he had added, hoping that this detail that distanced him from the expedition would somehow take the edge off her irritation. 'I'll be back soon.' Bidding the men to wait a while, he had stepped into the room where Madu, the sheet pulled up to her neck, watched with fretful eyes.

'Be back soon,' he had repeated, and had stooped in an attempt to kiss her. She had averted her mouth and his lips had brushed against her cheek, now slippery with tears. Madu had wiped the point of contact with the back of her hand. Stung, he had still forced her face to look up at him. 'We'll be all right.'

Madu had ceased counting on him for anything. 'Don't worry,' she had said in a voice so low that, years later, the Colonel still couldn't be sure that she had actually made the bitter pledge. 'I'll have your bastard baby – *alone!*'

All he could remember of the journey up the hill was the grainy texture of the atmosphere – the charged ions – of their room of love. Emptied of all emotion, he watched the scuffed boots of his colleagues as they marched past the burst of lean-tos and ramshackle houses, broken-down cars, bicycle skeletons, rusting farm equipment, incurious dogs, a wakening settlement and pot-bellied toddlers in rags.

The men stepped over and sometimes splashed through pools of stagnant water, disturbing swarms of mosquitoes. Through peripheral vision, he saw a brace of goats nibbling at the leaves of guava trees that rubbed shoulders with thorn trees amidst knee-high grass that was yellowing furiously under the spring sun.

As they marched towards the hill, the men could look down on the stone quarry with its boulders and yellow rock, the scar on the earth as clinical as if something precious had been gouged out of the earth with a giant plough. From this vantage point, the village below spread like a patterned quilt, the smoke from the first cooking fires snaking and rising and adding to the low clouds. Women lined up at a communal tap. The Colonel wondered what had happened to the promises of free and abundant running water.

'Someone once told me this story about Algeria,' the Colonel told his son, 'where the Front for National Liberation was debating whether violence could be justified in extreme circumstances. The question was whether the fighters could suspend their own humanity for the sake of a greater good, in this instance, the total liberation of Algerians from the French. The discussion ended with a debate on whether they could set their favourite dog on fire and let it loose in a wheat field owned by French farmers or sell-outs.'

'Did they agree,' Abioseh asked, disgusted, 'to set the dog on fire?'

'I don't know how that story ends,' the Colonel said, 'in any event that's not the point ...'

'What's the point, Father?'

'The point is ... are we capable of extreme cruelty in order to make sure we don't lose what we've gained in our own liberation struggle?'

'Well,' Abioseh said, wanting to say more, 'I don't know.'

'No one does,' the Colonel said. 'People grapple with situations where informers undermine the very possibility of that liberation. Or traitors sell out millions of people. Should they be treated with kid gloves and given bound copies of the Geneva Convention? Most regimes wouldn't know the Geneva Convention if it were served up with their breakfast cereal. In war, there's no percentage in playing by the rules.'

'You have to set the dog on fire?' Abioseh asked, hating his father.

'Yes,' the Colonel said, remembering something that caused him to stare into the air. 'It didn't take long for Vezi's man to break down,' he said. He recalled the man walking ahead of the squad, connected to the lead rider by a length of long rope with the noose around his neck. Even from where the Colonel rode behind he could see the green swarm of flies that had been drawn to the feast of the man's open wounds. And, as the day's temperature rose, with the sun seeming to hang above their heads, he had wondered if the prisoner would make it.

'Have mercy,' the man had cried, and the Colonel had fought with the notion of snapping off a quick shot and putting him out of his misery. That, of course, would have been gross insubordination, and would also have alerted Vezi.

The caves would have been impossible to access without a guide. To reach them meant dismounting because the horses would have needed the agility of mountain goats to negotiate an almost sheer cliff that was the same colour as the quarry: yellow, friable sandstone out of which trickled dislodged pebbly stones that would be transformed, in time, into gravel for some construction project.

As they inched up the face of the rock, a gust of wind blew, carrying in it an astonishing odour. It was a concoction of the prisoner's stale blood, sweat, urine and fear. Like something alive, it entered the Colonel's mouth and nostrils, tasting of death. At that moment, he struggled with the implications of oblivion, of the world continuing without him and experienced a moment of displacement: *What am I doing here?* He felt an intimacy with the man struggling for his life ahead, the contact

45

with his fluids an omen, and wished he were God, because he certainly would have banned the creation of days like these.

The answer to an unasked question lay in the inventiveness of the zealots. Makeshift olive-green camouflage netting covered the entrance to the cave. The young commanding officer feared that the opening into the cave – whose narrowness only allowed one person to slide and crawl in at a time – was probably booby-trapped. The wiry and stern career soldier indicated with his pistol, whose muzzle was extended by a silencer, for the prisoner to slide in and keep his mouth shut. 'Or your bum develops a second hole.'

As the Colonel thought that the captive would die of fright, he also found the group leader very funny. He envisaged a man trying to move bowels that were confused by the existence of an extra rectum. The prisoner looked a sight. His one unseeing eye dangled from its socket and seemed about to drop and shatter into bloody fragments. The men followed him, the rank odour of his terror proving a reliable olfactory guide, into the dark womb of the earth. Inching forward on their bellies, they halted intermittently, their ears primed for an ambush. Finally they emerged into a wider chamber that was lit with paraffin lamps and torches made from straw and rags. The smell of fuel increased the Colonel's anxiety. No one – neither the tenant nor the intruder – would survive an underground explosion.

His eyes adjusting to the dim chamber, the Colonel could make out forms that became, slowly, distinct shapes, much like an image emerging out of a negative in the darkroom. Gradually he heard the monotonous drone of machinery, probably a generator, sounding as if it came from somewhere inside his own head. This explained the smell of diesel.

Further ahead, the cave opened into several sizeable halls each sectioned off by sturdy timber panelling that, although seemingly scavenged from building sites, still gave the area an air of expert construction. Daubed on the plywood screens were a series of representations of the journey the country had taken.

The panels showed coarsely executed pictures and posters harvested from art galleries or billboards. Here was a collage of black-and-white prints and colour cut-outs from magazines depicting the first Portuguese explorers, fresh from the vessels that had carried them across the oceans on to the shores of the island. There was a group who was led by Pedro Alvares Cabral, which had split into factions, with Cabral landing in Brazil and Fernando Cassamo on the coast of Bangula. Once-glossy illustrations torn out of coffee-table books featured explorers in feathered hats and uniforms, all reminiscent of hotel porters, their rouged lips stressing depthless arrogance.

Moving along the panels, like visitors in a gallery, the armed men inspected assorted symbols of plunder dating back to ancient times. With love and terror, instruments of torture and restraint, chains, pillories and gallows were all laid out for exhibition. On the stone floor were littered, in uncharacteristic sloppiness, sleeping bags and blankets that spoke of interrupted sleep.

'Vezi had been expecting us,' the Colonel told his son, 'all along.'

Above the drone of the solitary generator, the Colonel could hear drumming and the voices of women singing. On a lower register, he heard footfalls. The squad tensed. Vezi came out of the gloom and walked the gauntlet purposefully to his injured comrade.

Forming a semicircle behind Vezi, a dozen muscular drummers, whose bare torsos gleamed in the diffuse light, stood alongside eight women dressed in black robes. He was tall, with a full head of uncombed hair that was peppered with grey, giving him a patrician look. He was the natural centre of attraction.

'I'd never witnessed such tenderness in a man before,' the Colonel said. 'Vezi helped the captured man up and stroked his face, his eyes lingering on each pore. He soon looked up and said, *So now you'll try me in court. Your courts are a travesty of justice. You'll try me in court,* he repeated, slowly articulating as if addressing himself to the hard of hearing, *and my capture will give succour to all those who have plundered and been unjustly rewarded. As a moral human being* ... he laughed at the word as if taken aback by its very texture, its brittleness in the cave, ... *I hold the view that that which doesn't belong to you must be returned to the treasury of the people. But if the law is itself lawless and protects sons and daughters of lawbreakers, what are we, the people, to do?'*

'He wasn't expecting an answer,' the Colonel said, 'and it was time to finish this nasty business. Then Vezi asked for a short moment to pray. I asked if *he* had given his victims time to pray. It was exactly at the moment of the half-light dancing across Vezi's face and highlighting his cheekbones, bringing out a burred jaw line that I saw his eyes – and everything fell into place.'

'*Yes*, Vezi said, with fierce pride, *she is* my *daughter.*'

'Somewhere in the distance,' the Colonel confided in his son, 'a prayer meeting was in session, which I heard as a dull buzzing in my head. The congregants spoke in tongues, their voices raised to praise an unseen power. Amidst the prayer and the singing, which sometimes rose to the strength of a lament, I imagined I could make out Madu's contralto. The voice of my own lover, who carried my seed in her womb, would mingle with Vezi's rich tenor, contributing to a melody at once as melancholy as it was triumphant.'

The Colonel blocked out of his mind the details of the trial as efficiently as Madu had excommunicated him from her life. He operated as if in a narcotic daze. He would scan the newspapers, somehow knowing that his baby in Madu was growing with each edition. The days became weeks, and weeks, months until, in a quirk of fate, Vezi and six of his followers were sentenced to death by firing squad on the same day a sympathetic nurse phoned him from the hospital to tell him that Madu had given birth to a baby boy. Her tone was subdued, as if she suspected that this birth would be another addition to the troubles already heaped upon her world.

'YOUR BROTHER,' THE Colonel told Abioseh, 'is called Zebulon. And he's out there, somewhere.' The Colonel gestured into the omniscient night.

3

'THEIR LEARNING,' MADU told Zebulon, 'will not match what I will teach you.'

They were seated inside the shack, on the first Sunday of October, listening to the rain bucketing down on the zinc roof. The wallpaper consisting of pictures cut out of magazines, which had the effect of re-ducing the size of the room, together with the sound of the driving rain, increased Zebulon's sense of being under siege. At sixteen, something was bursting from inside him. His difficulty in concentrating on his geo-graphy homework had more to do with the restlessness of his blood than the distraction posed by the rain. He looked up at his mother, ignoring momentarily the library books and notes scattered on the floor.

'What's the matter?' Madu asked from the bed where she was read-ing a book of poetry, the new glasses perched on her nose giving her an owlish look.

'This ...' Zebulon indicated a section on rock formations. '*The transformation of rocks under tons and tons of pressure . . .*' His face was a study in hopelessness. 'I can't get the hang of this.'

'Well,' Madu said, striving to be heard above the torrent, 'you'd better get the hang of *something*, Zebulon, because the world out there is exceedingly unkind to ignorance.'

'But rocks,' Zebulon remonstrated, 'how will that help me in the future?'

'Perhaps it won't,' Madu said, 'that is, if you read things literally; if you look for deeper meanings, then you're getting somewhere. Let me see the book.'

He handed her the book, still open on the perplexing chapter. She leafed through, pursing her lips, mouthing some of the technical words, whistling in awe at the schematic representation of the formation of igneous, sedimentary or metamorphic rocks.

'This is serious stuff,' Madu conceded, 'and it might take a lot of studying to understand it. I won't pretend to know what it means, except that you need to apply pressure if you want things to be different. And pressure fosters the build-up of heat – and heat causes change.'

Madu told him that she was certain their future would be strewn with thorns and glass shards. 'You can see it in the way this country is shaped. The government will never lift a finger to support the poor. The poor have to apply the pressure – and the heat – or the rich will tighten their hold on the spoils. Right now,' she went on, 'Abioseh, another addition to the Colonel's menagerie, is at the school for future leaders, where they'll teach him how to be an effective thief.'

By now, Zebulon understood the source of his mother's indignation.

This rainy Sunday afternoon, Madu quoted lines from poems and miscellaneous writings by known or obscure scribes. The afternoon session stretched into the evening, where her words flickered as if in accord with the unsteady yellow flame from the paraffin lamp. She loved Ezekiel Manolo, the blind poet who had renounced his position in the royal house of the Buzaki, whose epic poem, *Coming out of the storm*, seemed to infuse her slight frame with light and strength.

'Listen to this,' Madu began, and, having caught his attention, started to read, occasionally looking up to see if he was still attentive, lowering her bespectacled face into the book. She read:

> There is no beauty in this wasteland
> Just a collection of wooden crosses
> And small children that lie at the bottom of our bellies.
> We people the colour of fingerprint ink.

That was the first of many such evenings, when he would listen to her, mesmerised by the rise and fall of her voice, watching her neck muscles expanding and contracting with each breath drawn, each syllable expelled, wondering what had happened in her life that had so effectively banished for her the possibility of dreams. How could she ever imagine that he would be inattentive? Or doubt that his universe didn't revolve around her? What was it about him that elicited uneasiness in others? Perhaps sensing the hesitancy of his soul on its own solitary journey towards the future, she would turn her eyes to him, smile and continue reading, not so much educating him now as paying homage to something unseen, which pulsated to the rhythm of her own heart. She would go on:

> The children of vengeance will ensure
> The future of our own creation.

Sometimes she would mumble verses from the Old Testament, especially the tribulations of Job or Ezekiel, punctuating these spells by observing that she trusted the Old Testament because it contained lessons for human beings. 'If any harm follows,' she would say, her eyes bright, 'then you shall give life for life, eye for eye, tooth for tooth, hand for hand, foot for foot, burn for burn, wound for wound, stripe for stripe.' Madu would pause, her mind envisioning the enactment of retributive justice.

Zebulon couldn't really grasp the full meaning of his mother's teachings, but he knew that her words held a key to his own survival. When he sometimes caught her alert eyes fixed on him, her frame rigid as if she were straining to hear the heartbeat of a concealed assassin, he somehow knew that her troubles were linked to some man or men, and that they wielded power. Although he knew about the Colonel, that he was related to him by blood, it all seemed so abstract, so remote; for all he knew, there were a thousand other Zebulons who had been fathered by so many Colonels of this world.

Swearing softly under her breath, Madu sat him down one evening after supper. It was towards the end of October, which had become a month of revelations. She told him that her rejection of the Colonel and his world was an expression of her love and pride in herself and of her faith in him.

'I'd be a crazy mother,' she said, more to herself than to Zebulon, 'to bring up my son in this sinkhole where the walls are so thin you can hear people fighting, fucking, shitting, dying, giving birth and killing each other. I would be crazy to pass up the possibility of you having all the nice things that the Colonel – may his bowels turn into maggots – can offer, but I cannot do that because I'd be going against my word. I promised that I would have *nothing* to do with him and all the people who murdered my father. So, Zebulon,' she said, her chest heaving as she looked at him with tenderness and love and rage that had the power to kill, 'no matter how *much* a man owns, and never mind even *whom* he owns, and how much power he can unleash, if that man has no honour, then, God strike me down, he's *not* a man.'

Shaking him now, fervent in that quiet and scary manner of hers, she hissed: 'Promise me that you'll stand by your word – always.'

'Always, Ma.'

Madu confirmed what he had already suspected, that there could be hundreds of women in the same boat and thousands of little boys like Zebulon, running around all over the republic, all without fathers who could help them grow into manhood. Some of those, she maintained, received maintenance money from the Colonel. But they, Madu and her boy, were all right the way they were. They would survive.

THEY DID FOR a while. Madu continued with her work at the dry cleaners, seeming more and more beaten with each passing day. He volunteered and, mercifully, she agreed that he do more of the household work, even cooking, seeking to astound her palate by studying recipes in women's magazines he found at school or in the malls and applying his newfound knowledge to the pots.

He managed to elicit genuine praise from her one Sunday when he made her favourite meal of samp and beans. He had soaked the crushed corn and black-eyed beans and had allowed it to simmer for hours. Then he had thrown sliced red onions into the mix, some coriander, parsley and neck bones with some meat on them. Although Madu had eaten with no visible appetite, she'd applauded his effort, her 'little man' who'd make a great cook one day.

At around that time, MaZembe paid them a visit. Zebulon knew that someone of great importance had arrived when he saw the great, black limousine parked on the street outside the house, as he returned from some errand.

Peeking into the car, a difficult enough enterprise since all the windows were tinted, he saw the driver busy filling in a lottery slip. Sensing the young man's eyes, the bald, bullet-headed driver with an enormous chest, a shade darker than the car, pressed a button and the passenger-side window rolled down with a sibilant hiss. Zebulon's eyes popped wide at the splendour inside.

The seats looked soft; the dark leather whispered untold dreams. The phone on its cradle was silent, poised for instant connection with the mightiest seat in the land. The dials and clocks and enchanting instruments were much more elaborate than the pilot's cockpit Zebulon had seen in the same magazines where he got his recipes. Ah, he imagined the speed of this four-wheeled animal, the distances it could cover at the touch of a button.

'Cool, huh?' said the driver, reading the great joy on the youngster's face, glad that he was even obliquely associated with its cause.

'Not just cool,' Zebulon answered in the language of the streets, proving that even though he cooked for his ma he wasn't a sissy, 'it's zibby zabba.'

The driver, whose face showed the scars of the streets, grinned. 'Come in here, kid,' he said, but Zebulon was his mother's son and had learnt not to accept invitations. Seeing his face becoming instantly guarded, the driver flashed him a thumbs-up. 'You're the Colonel's sharp kid, you'll be okay.' He rolled up the window and went back to his dreams of hitting the jackpot.

IT WAS BY reading the concern in MaZembe's eyes that Zebulon discovered how ill his mother was. When he entered the house, Zebulon sensed something deep and hidden passing between the two women, something to do with him.

'So,' MaZembe said in a voice made unnaturally loud by anxiety, 'this is my other son?' She was older and more matronly than Madu, her clothes evincing taste and originality. She wore a simply cut, two-piece charcoal grey suit and a matching headscarf, with spangles and silver in her ears conveying innate elegance. Although years younger, Madu looked far older than MaZembe.

'Say hello to Auntie MaZembe,' she said, getting up from the bed.

MaZembe laid a hand on Madu's shoulder, not unlike a preacher laying hands on the ailing, cautioning her not to strain herself. 'He's such a big boy; soon he'll have to meet my Abioseh.'

'How old is Abioseh now?' Madu asked, trying to inject some enthusiasm into her tone. But Zebulon could tell she didn't give a damn, really.

'He's fifteen in August next year. Maybe Zebulon can come to Abioseh's birthday party.' Bending from the waist, she nuzzled Zebulon's cheeks. Raising her eyes to Madu, and obviously continuing a conversation they had been holding, MaZembe said, 'You'll tell him what I said.' It sounded like a warning.

'Of course.' Madu's tone indicated that she would do nothing of the sort.

'You're a stubborn child,' MaZembe chided. 'Not that I blame you. But I also want you to think about what's best for the boy.'

'Think about what?' Zebulon asked and earned himself a *watch-it* look from his mother, who believed that children's voices were best for singing and had no place in big people's conversations. She was no different from MaZembe, who had carried on chatting about Zebulon as if he weren't there.

'Your ma will tell you,' MaZembe promised, 'when she's good and ready.'

MADU NEVER TOLD him anything because she withered away quickly following MaZembe's visit and died and was given a pauper's burial. Then people with papers arrived with a truck at the shack and alleged that Madu owed them money. Claude was among them, and this time he wasn't offering any free French lessons. They seized the property, turned the boy out and drove off. He lived on the streets, roughing it with the roughest the city of Jambora could offer, until, after being stabbed in the stomach with a broken bottle and spending two weeks in a trauma ward, he realised that he needed food and shelter, but not at any cost.

Death became Zebulon's major provider. Knowing that people died every day, and that somewhere in Jambora there would be a vigil where guests would be fed, he did the research. He went to the charismatic churches where believers sang and spoke in tongues as they baptised the newly converted or gave a holy name to the newborn. Here Zebulon met people who weren't swift to judge others and who shared their successes as well as their setbacks. It was from them that he learnt of deaths and imminent burials. Since Zebulon was tall and could pass for someone much older, he was trusted by the members of the congregation. He accompanied bereaved people to the mortuary. His natural eloquence, inflected with Madu's mordant dictums and the authority of prophets, made him an appropriate companion for mourners. People took him in and gave him a place to sleep. Since he had no problem with cooking, he could always tell himself that he was contributing to his board and lodging.

On these days and nights of activity, he would sometimes think of how Madu had died. In December, he had visited her at the hospice, when it was clear that she was going. He had found her lying alone in the ward, tubes entering and passing fluid into or out of her nose, mouth and arms. Madu was scabby, reeking of the grave, emaciated, voiding herself, the light gone out of her eyes. She gave off a stench, her tissues beginning that long walk away from one another, like long-time friends who had to bid each other farewell.

On New Year's Eve, as he kept vigil – now and then dropping off – he woke up to a hazy figure of a big man whose face was in the shadows. In profile, he recognised the Colonel, who stood staring at the sleeping wo-man, his hands clasped behind his back as if about to inspect the troops.

As if sensing his presence in the ward, Madu released a low, harsh sob that must have put too much pressure on her lungs, until the volume of the laboured breathing increased enough to alert the night nurse. She ap-proached the Colonel on soft footfalls and whispered something to him. The Colonel summoned his bodyguards and they left, without so much as a glance in the boy's direction.

Zebulon asked the nurse what his mother had said to the Colonel. '*Getoutofhere*,' the nurse said without taking a breath, '*Getthehelloutofhere!*'

FROM THE MIDDLE of January, a week after his mother's simple burial, Zebulon could still wangle his way into the ICU ward, bypassing med-ical staff, often pretending to be a close relative of a patient. He had a favourite hiding place where he would listen to the soft hiss of the ma-chines and watch the metronomic regularity of the indicators and dials of life-support equipment, somehow knowing, even before the doctor on duty could ascertain, if the sufferer would live or die.

On certain occasions, he would bring in his schoolbooks and study in the half-light while listening to the progress or otherwise of the sick. As night dragged on, Zebulon would do the rounds of the ward, imitating the medical staff. In the geriatric ward, he would see old people embarked on the irreversible journey to the grave, wondering if he, too, would one day shrivel like that. Sometimes he would stop and stare at a patient who looked like the Colonel. He was as distressed as he was fascinated one evening when he entered the neonatal nursery ward with its complex ventilators, monitors and incubator cots in which small, premature babies lay struggling to breathe. The babies were pink and almost translucent in their fragility; their navels covered with strips of plaster rose and fell with every breath drawn. He went back to his den wondering why people made babies. *What is the point?* he asked himself. He heard the noises of the night, the trundling traffic below, determining the nature of the emergency from the sound of the sirens.

Sometimes he would imagine he could hear the chatter before lights-out in the children's wards, which would occasionally be punctuated by a sharp scream, someone receiving an injection, he was sure. And then on weekends, there would be more urgent activity around the wards as they brought in people injured in fights, most of their voices thickened by alcohol and rage. And on two or three occasions, unexpectedly, the brawling would carry over from the streets into the hospital lobby, mostly men but sometimes with women also getting into the fray, squaring up, kicking, spitting, punching and clawing at one another, skirts pulled up and bunched into the elastic securing the sides of their panties, cursing in language so coarse that it must have speeded up the progress of a few of the malingerers from sickness to health.

Seen from the balcony or the winding staircase, these transitions, which would be marked by great turmoil, would seem surreal, like a slow-motion sequence of a film, to the soundtrack of shrieks, catcalls and wolf-whistles. Churchwomen, some still carrying the flowers to comfort a sick friend or en route to adorn a neglected tombstone, would stop in mid-stride and regard the unfolding tableau with that ageless acceptance of human folly in their eyes, shaking their heads: *What's this world coming to?*

ZEBULON CAME OF age, at seventeen, by, well, coming.

It was difficult to know exactly how old Melinda was. On the one hand, she evinced a grasp of issues that would put many a grown-up to shame. On the other hand, she had an innocently vulnerable side that recalled the helplessness of the premature tots gulping for air in hospital incubators. Melinda was wise to the ways of the world, which she claimed to know and which were mapped in the blood that coursed through her veins.

Her father, she said, had been a gift, and when Zebulon asked her what kind of gift, she said, 'G-I-F-T, stupid – Greek-Italian-French-Tanzanian.' That's where, she said, she got these exotic looks. Then, pirouetting, whirling like a dervish and stopping, leg extended and foot curved in a balletic pose, she smiled and pouted. The dancing was from her mother, a Hungarian-Namibian-Jew.

To demonstrate the dark swirling in her soul, Melinda would dance anywhere the spirit moved her and leave watchers spellbound. She guided Zebulon, whom she once accused of having two left feet, on how to move, as she put it, 'like a prince across the dance floor, and not shuffle like some common numbskull'.

Taking him under her wing, she showed him how to survive. 'It's okay to be a cook, but you don't make it in this city by making nice,' she said to him as they fled from a supermarket, their shoes clattering above the clanging of store alarms. 'Forget that little old lie about the best way to a man's heart and all that bullshit ... it's not through his stomach.'

'What's the route, then?' Sounding like he was asking for the best way to Cinnamon Hill.

58

'Through his balls. Squeezing them or stroking them, either way you get his attention.'

'You're such a small ...' he struggled for a word.

'Piccaninny?' Her own suggestion made her laugh. 'That doesn't work for a girl. The best I've been called is gamine ...'

'What does it mean?'

'A girl with boyish or mischievous charm,' she replied quickly; it was something that must have been repeated back to her numerous times.

'You're a *gamine*, or what*ever*,' Zebulon said, 'with these small hands; when have you ever squeezed men's balls?'

'Or stroked ...'

'Or stroked, yes.'

'You'd be surprised,' Melinda said, her tone already changing the subject, 'what small girl hands can achieve.'

THEY RAN ALONG the outskirts of Jambora, marvelling at its changeableness in the mornings, the smoke rising, blue and white edged with a saffron hue, like the plumage of some rare and malevolent bird. They crawled through the hole in the wire fence to the train depot to witness the magic of the orange-and-black engines pulling out. These were en route to picking up workers and dreamers, the rail lines crisscrossing and snaking like something alive and full of nameless energy. They watched the people waking up in the shacks, heard a baby wailing out of some discomfort dissociable from hunger and smiled at a toddler gurgling with mysterious and grateful pleasure — as if her mother had earlier burped her successfully — at the silvery plane streaking overhead. Together they listened to the distant sound of a bell ringing and summoning schoolchildren to early morning classes. Soon other urchins got up; they rubbed sleep out of their eyes, rolled up their cardboard homes and drab hospital- or Salvation Army-issue blankets. Melinda and Zebulon and the orphans and the discarded with runny noses and eyes that needed attention, ran.

They ran and scattered to regroup later in the evening to escape the police or agents of property developers who were embarrassed by undesirables whose presence affected the Stock Exchange. They ran because bigger and tougher children, whose state of grace had long been mortgaged to crack cocaine, via glue and alcohol, were on the way and needed this piece of prime real estate, which was close to shops with faulty alarms and fruit and vegetable stalls owned by old Asians and Creoles who'd long given up chasing fleet-footed adolescents. There was no percentage in that; these kids carried 'homemake' knives and some even packed guns that could blow a hole bigger than a saucer in a man's head.

It was in the days and nights of running and, sometimes, dancing with Melinda that Zebulon started having wet dreams and would wake up in the morning with his shorts glued to his crotch. When he reported this to her – omitting the detail that all the dreams involved her – she grinned and said, 'Come, let me show you something.' She led him by the hand to the crest of the hill, where the shack dwellers didn't dare go for fear of murderers and rapists who roamed there, to a cold-water tap, and stripped him naked.

He shivered as the spring evening air washed over him, before she wet his T-shirt under the tap and washed him, from head to toe, he, gasping at the coldness of the water and feeling on fire from her touch. Here, bent on one knee, she touched him with her tongue and he moaned, the fire, the ice, and she grasped him, once cruelly, as if she also needed something that was just for her, for the void created by so many thousands of miles her ancestors, her gift, had travelled for a place they could call their own. He, tumescent, felt her pulling him down on top of her, funnelling him with her hands, opening up, yielding, and he felt a warmth that was different from any warmth he had ever felt before, and he was lost, thrashing in a jungle.

He heard her saying something, giving a low, throaty cry that was almost like a chuckle in a foreign language, seeing her face transformed in the moonlight, and he felt it, starting at the base of his neck, coursing down his spine, washing over his buttocks to become a pain of incredible pleasure along his stiffened muscle – no longer the little pink penis – and he cried out, feeling her nails digging into his back, she, gazing at him with eyes full of sadness that were already consigning him to the past. And he knew, now, that nothing would return him to where he had been, *never*, there was no going back.

Melinda got up earlier than usual in the morning and smartened herself up, applying skin-tone lipstick and slapping circulation into her cheeks. Picking up her tote bag full of all her life, she gave Zebulon a valedictory peck on the lips. She let her fingers linger along his jaw, committing to memory and yet purging herself of all impulses of intimacy. She left, kicking a can on her way down towards the railway terminus.

Zebulon levered himself up on his elbows as he watched her figure receding. He meant to call out her name but was restrained by something he felt powerless to oppose, and then got to his feet and waved goodbye to her memory. That was the last time he saw Melinda; as had happened with his mother, it was as if the earth had swallowed her up.

He had not grieved for Madu. Even though her death had rocked him, he had long anticipated it. His unstated fears had been realised – and Zebulon struggled with the guilt of one who might have inadvertently cast a malevolent spell. Melinda had been different. Zebulon had come to take her presence – that vitality – for granted. It was as if a landmark had disappeared overnight. With her gone, Zebulon was left with nothing, and he was young, at an age when it was difficult to remain unselfish about memories. To forget her, he had to do everything to remember her.

Leaving the other children who were no longer children, he went back to the funeral circuit, attending vigils and commemoration services, willing himself to look – when the time came to view the bodies – at each representation of death, no matter how grotesque, and superimpose Melinda's face over it. This way, he could accept that she was dead and gone. He mourned her passing by recalling some of their moments together, for instance, the day they had borrowed wheelies to skid across the smooth tiled floors of the mall when a photographer took a picture of them with one of those cameras whose giant lenses are used to capture unforgettable moments in sport.

'Don't you wish,' Melinda had asked, 'that you could see yourself the way others, like that cameraman, see you? Wouldn't it be freaky to freeze all those instances people have looked at you and use them like a mirror to see yourself, from the minute of your first cry at birth to the picture in the family album of your own funeral?'

ZEBULON WOULD REMEMBER his mother's funeral, the unspeaking sky, the gravediggers embarrassed for the boy because there was no one there to hold him or sing a song that would accompany the body in the pale box on its journey to eternity. The priest conscripted to conduct the service was sullen to the point of rudeness, his face grim as if he, too, were thinking about the certainty of departure. To brace himself against crying and hurling his own body onto the coffin, Zebulon recalled the words that Madu had committed to memory, which had been sculpted somewhere in the heart of a Buzaki prince:

> We will traverse these paths in search of the beauty
> That makes us who we are in this wilderness
> Others will retreat into the cocoons woven by their masters.
> We will move.

PART TWO

BLOOD

I

A BORN STORYTELLER, Hiero couldn't, however, find the language to express what was happening right in his own back yard. His dada was succumbing to something that was eating him up from the inside. Already there was a rumour doing the rounds that an epidemic of the blood plague had again broken out. Despite their strained relationship, Emma-May brought about a suspension of hostilities between husband and wife. She ensured that her man received the necessary treatment in their Cinnamon Hill house, even though others were advising her to commit him to a hospice if not an incinerator.

These advisers called Emma-May a fool for taking care of a wastrel whose chickens had come home to roost. 'We were all brought into this world,' she said, 'so that we can improve on our humanity. I'm not a saint; I have in my own way wronged this man as much as he has wronged me. But I could never live with myself if I left him for vultures to feast on his flesh. Being right doesn't mean you're correct.' The other women hissed and banged the door, leaving Emma-May to her martyrdom, wondering if she hadn't actually called them vultures.

It was at this time that Alfredo Romero High School was invited to the inter-school games in the Panza district. Worried that he would be leaving his mother alone to deal with his sick father, Hiero suggested that he withdraw from the school commitment, but Emma-May would have none of it. 'Go,' she said, 'you have my blessings.'

Guiltily elated, Hiero got on the bus with the other students. As he had a window seat, he watched Jambora, the outskirts dominated by brown fields readied for development, past despairing shanties and the higgledy-piggledy brick and mortar structures, shops and homes of the middle strata that fought a desperate war with unappeasable poverty.

The scenery changed dramatically as the bus rolled further away from the city and its tall buildings to the flattening countryside, the rolling sugarcane plantations a swathe of green that merged with the blue of the ocean. He slept fitfully through the journey and woke up when they were entering Panza.

The tournament took a week. Hiero had no recollection of the games except that they involved much cheering and flexing of muscles. As part of the school debating team, and as no such cerebral activity was on the programme, he cruised along, taking in the sights and looking up old school friends, who still found his store of fantastic tales interesting. Whatever joy he felt, though, was slightly marred by the anxiety over what could be happening with his dada.

On his return, Hiero had to go to the Jambora Civic Hall for an afternoon meeting where the youth of Bangula were being inducted into Civilian Service. This was a more elevated version of the Boy Scouts or Girl Guides, which stressed the virtues of service, volunteerism (a word that caused Hiero to giggle and earn himself a dirty look from the man on the lectern) and vigilance. This was all part of strengthening the Fabric of the Reform (another phrase that brought about much clearing of phlegm from the assembly of adolescent throats). Hiero was all for the youth being initiated into the cult of wholesomeness; it was common sense, really, and the government didn't have to send a pompous spokesman to tell them about it.

As he returned home, he was still smiling at the memory of the moustachioed mouthpiece when he saw a car and two bicycles parked outside the house; there was also a huddle of neighbours, some wearing shawls despite the late afternoon heat and humidity. Figuring that something awful had happened, he hurried past the visibly anxious neighbours, murmuring, 'Excuse me, excuse me.' Finally he made his way inside.

The house had been taken over by strangers. He was on his way to the bedroom when he collided with his Aunt Hilda in the passage. Even before she clutched him to her ample bosom and exclaimed how much he had grown, Hiero realised that the car outside had ferried in a number of relatives, including a battery of half-brothers and -sisters mostly from the countryside, living evidence of how his father had sown his seed far and wide. One of his half-sisters, Sigone, stood watching, a tense smile on her face.

'My word,' Aunt Hilda said, 'you're taller than Wilberforce!' Aunt Hilda had not outgrown her massive girlish crush on the seven-foot-one player who had made the Harlem Globetrotters synonymous with basketball.

'It's *Wilt* Chamberlain, Aunt Hilda,' Sigone said, gently reproaching the woman. In that instant, Hiero saw how much Sigone looked like his dada. The two women led him to the bedroom, everything suddenly surreal. As though a stranger, he was being guided through the house in which he lived. His acceptance of this change as natural contributed even more to the feeling of dislocation.

The bedroom was dark, all the curtains drawn. The smell hit him and led Hiero to the conclusion that things would never be the same again. It was a veritable explosion that no laboratory could have concocted, an accumulation of odours that spoke of decaying flesh and the failure of all things.

When in secret dialogue with himself, Hiero owned up to the fact that he had never really liked or respected his dada, but it was shocking to see him laid out on the bed like a rag doll. The bones of his dada's face and skull stood out from beneath a translucent skin that hinted at the texture of parchment paper; the protruding bones called to mind the sign, DANGER: KEEP OUT, which was tacked to the fence prohibiting entry to the chemical plant.

But it was the smell to which Hiero could not accustom himself, a smell which spelt out the finality of death. His dada, he could see, was still alive, but that was just a formality, a cruel technicality imposed on the dying by a code that no one believed in. For, even though Hiero had never really seen a dead person up close, he knew that nothing could have prepared him for this ruin. 'Come in, Hiero,' he heard his mother call.

She sat on the bed, resting against the headboard rather than the plumped-up pillows that were, like all the linen, damp with perspiration and the body's fugitive fluids. Emma-May held one of her husband's claw-like hands in both of hers, periodically stroking it.

His mother looked smaller, as if the tragedy perching on the windowsill had shrivelled all her tissues. Only her face remained the one feature that Hiero recognised, the eyes, especially; they alternated between scanning her husband's face, a smudge against the pillow, and her son's. Emma-May's eyes were bright, with pinpointed pupils as if she had sniffed some narcotic.

While it was clear to Hiero that Emma-May was looking at him, here in this fetid hole, she was actually outside the confines of the room. This was how she had outlived the loveless marriage and all the years of watching her youthful life ebb away as surely as that of the unlovable man on the bed.

At that moment of silence, when people sat and waited for the intervention that would release the spirit from the body, Hiero accepted that all he had thought he knew about human beings added up to nothing. The moment, the loaded silence of waiting for his dada to die, marked the beginning of a journey that every fatherless boy was fated to make. In some remote corner, in that space in people's hearts where selfish thoughts pulsed with the pride of Lucifer, he accepted that this imminent death was a release for both Emma-May and for his dada and an initiation for him, the son. From then on, he knew, he had to depend on himself.

Just as somewhere in the lounge someone started to sing, Hiero heard a faint rustle, like the rattling of the wings of a praying mantis. Aunt Hilda and Emma-May, bonded by something they would have rather forgone, something more ancient than time, looked at each other. Then they stood up and, bent over the body, they closed his dada's sightless eyes and folded the bony hands into an attitude of prayer across the breast that no longer heaved with a beating heart.

'He's gone,' Sigone said in a voice breaking with grief. Then she started wailing, a signal for the relatives and the believers and the thrill-seekers to come into the room that held the unique smell of death and lavender.

One of the mourners was a young man who possessed authority that was beyond his years. Standing in a baggy black suit, looking uncannily like a younger copy of the deceased, his eyes shone as if ignited from somewhere inside him. 'My name is Zebulon,' he said in a voice that strangely rasped against nerve endings and soothed at the same time. 'I have come to pray for the dead.'

Shortly after his dada's demise, Hiero, who had despised his dada's weakness, left the house and stumbled into the first tavern from which he had repeatedly fetched his insensate dada, and ordered his first drink. The landlord, who specialised in various homemade brews but held a legitimate liquor licence, advertised himself as a distiller as opposed to a bootlegger. He knew what had just happened, death being its own publicist, and understood that he would burn in hell if he succumbed to the boy's request. But then, as they said in Cinnamon Hill, heaven could wait. And to hell with hell.

'What's it you want here, boy?' the distiller asked.

'I have come,' Hiero said, 'to pray for the dead.'

IN DECEMBER, SEVEN months after his dada's funeral, Hiero was thinking of how to break the news to his mother that he wanted to leave school. The subjects were proving too difficult, except maths. Many of his teen-age friends had long turned their backs on the classroom, responding to the imperious call of the hotels or the boats. The Commodore Hotel was still the most attractive prospect, but opportunities were limited; you had to be connected. Most boys knew it was either the hotel (and the attendant possibility of rubbing shoulders – and, sometimes, other choice parts of the anatomy – with celebrities from home and abroad) or a life shovelling manure in the sugarcane plantations. There was of course the military, which was widely signing up young men who had reached that age when they could kill or be killed on behalf of their country.

As if on cue, he heard the trucks rolling out again, the second fleet in as many days. Hiero peered through the window and saw the trucks that were covered with dirty-white tarpaulins, their sides marked with giant red crosses to denote vehicles commandeered to transport sufferers of the blood plague to quarantine. Some of the uniformed men propped on the tailgate and holding rifles with the muzzles pointed skywards directed low wolf-whistles at the group of women in the nearby outdoor market. Since the women were mostly widows and well past their prime, this tomfoolery was without longing.

Above the indifferent roar of the engines, as the last of the hulking vehicles pulled out, leaving behind a cloud of dust and smoke, Hiero thought he could hear the stifled groans of the ailing occupants when the suspension bounced off the humps and crunched into potholes. This corrugated stretch of purgatory had consigned many a once-treasured motorcar into the scrapheap. He derived grim satisfaction from the fact that his dada had been spared the indignity of being ferried halfway across the countryside to die anonymously.

It was happening everywhere, people dropping from the blood plague as if from great exhaustion, but the Colonel was quiet despite the nationwide clamour for him to say something. *To give direction*: this was what people said they wanted the Colonel to do. Hiero's dada had been swept away by the tide that had engulfed hundreds in just a few weeks.

But today, whatever the complaints of the rest of the populace, Hiero and Emma-May were focused on the invitation to visit Mariposa, the official residence of the president. This was part of the year-end festivities launched separately – though not in rivalry – by government and the private sector, with the invitation to the president's banquet being the year's most desirable social event.

Turning away from the window that opened on the mood of uncertainty that had taken hold of the people, Hiero took in the dining room with its huge sideboard that supported certificates and official-looking photographs showing his dada seeming scrubbed and happy. In most of the photographs Jethro Jerome was in his role as interpreter, posing beside formidable men in gowns and wigs of the judiciary. There were a few photos of his dada in the company of his half-brothers and -sisters, whom the son remembered from the funeral. None of the judges or magistrates had shown up. The only lawyer who put in an appearance had come to solicit business, as he put it, 'to ease the pain of surviving members of the family'. He was quickly booted out.

The other pieces of furniture had been covered with sheets throughout the mourning period and uncovered three months later. In that period, as was the custom, he and his mother had slept on grass mats with their heads resting on carved wooden pillows. On the nights when he was sober, Hiero would hear his mother weeping silently. He wasn't certain whether it was due to her despair over his own drunken excesses – which must have rekindled memories of a punishing past – or a sudden grasp of what lay ahead for them.

From the minute Hiero was hit by the full impact of his father's death, to the awkward leave-taking by the relatives and assorted mourners, he had found it hard to cry. Perhaps the fourteen-year-old boy had been insulated from the impact of death by liquor, something for which he had developed a sudden and great fondness. There was a strange and savage irony about his lifelong abhorrence for alcohol and how it had ruined his father. And now, at the ripe old age of fourteen, he was already a full-blown alcoholic. Even as he tried to clear his head, he knew he was in the grip of something powerful.

He had been dry-eyed as he watched his mother saying goodbye to everyone, and had been unmoved even as Emma-May turned to give full vent to her grief. It wasn't due to the loss of a husband since, for her, he had been dead a long time ago. It was something else that was perhaps born of a history she couldn't articulate, a loss of something in her that she had once cherished.

Through the years, Hiero had watched as his mother effectively cancelled her tormentor out of her life. When the frustrated ex-interpreter railed against her, she merely looked at him and through him as if he weren't there. Indifference, she must have learnt in a school for women fated to unhappiness, was a most devastating weapon. Hiero prayed that he'd never meet someone who'd give him the silent treatment. Suddenly the fury of the Spanish Inquisitors made sense.

But today, his mother was a lot more amiable. 'Which dress,' she called from the bedroom, 'do you think I should put on tonight?'

He stood at the doorway to the bedroom watching his mother arrange five or six dresses on the bed that was covered by an aubergine bedspread embroidered with ochre and gold stripes. The dresses were mostly of a sombre fabric with straps; they all looked the same to Hiero. Moreover, he knew that his mother had already made up her mind which dress she would wear.

'Why don't you wear the one you have on already?' Hiero teased.

'This?' Emma-May asked, looking down and picking at her loose gingham dress with mottled yellow designs on a light-blue field. She was amused at the idea. 'The president knows we're poor market women, but if people saw me in this at the banquet, they'd probably laugh me out of town.'

'But,' Hiero pressed on, 'wouldn't that be just grand? Coming into the party in your own original design?'

'With everyone looking splendid,' Emma-May exclaimed. 'Do you want people to say you have a lunatic for a mother?'

'That wouldn't surprise anybody,' Hiero answered, 'since I had a real madman for a father.'

It was mid-morning on a pleasant day, with birds singing outside and cattle moving purposefully to graze in the pasture, their bells tinkling in sharps and flats. Hiero was reminded of the book they used at school, an English primer, which supplied jawbreakers in lieu of simpler language, where he read *tintinnabulation*, a highbrow word for the ringing of the bell. It was when his lips formed the word *madman* that his mother motioned him to sit down on the bed. Careful not to crush the dresses, he complied, feeling the spring mattress creaking beneath his weight. He looked out the window. There was a momentary softening to the light as a cloud floated across the face of the sun. Somewhere beneath the chatter of women traders and customers, a radio station broadcast a school programme featuring children with high-pitched voices torturing the unemployed. Hiero felt the humidity rising, like steam.

'Your father,' Emma-May said, '*wasn't* a lunatic. You have no right to say what you're saying.'

'Sorry, Ma,' Hiero apologised. 'I didn't mean it the way it came out.'

'Whatever you meant,' Emma-May said, 'it's just downright disrespectful. Your father had a troubled life. And his trouble meant that none of us could find peace. He wrestled with demons daily because, once, he had been a man with his eyes on the stars.'

He wanted to quip that it was no surprise then that his dada had been partial to Star Lager, when he could still afford his legitimate drink of choice before the lean times overtook him and left him with an undiscriminating palate. However, he was still on parole. His mother might be in a good mood today, but, if pushed too far, all that would change.

'The day we got married,' Emma-May began, her face placid, 'I knew before the night was over that it had all been a dreadful mistake.' She looked at Hiero, her eyes asking for forgiveness. 'You mustn't think that you *were* a mistake, because I loved ... *love* you. But your father came into our marriage bed carrying a past that had scored his back as though with a whip.'

Although she was telling him the story, Hiero knew that his mother was wrapped up in a world of her own, reliving a past that would have tested the patience of Job. Soon after the funeral, when Emma-May realised that the bug of fermented grapes and juniper berries that had ruined her husband had now bitten her son, she had consulted Father Mitchum, the Catholic cleric from the local parish of St Theresa.

He had told her that there was an alarming rise in substance abuse, especially alcohol, among the youth – and Hieronymus Jerome was under enormous strain and thus particularly vulnerable. There was also the little wrinkle affecting the personality: addiction could be hereditary. The boy needed spiritual guidance.

Emma-May had taken it upon herself to frogmarch her son, drunk or otherwise, to the all-purpose Bible, catechism and anti-addiction lessons that were held in the church hall twice a week. It was here that Hiero encountered Zebulon again. Possessed of a voracious curiosity, Hiero read the King James Version of the Holy Bible from Genesis to Revelation. He was enthralled by the adventures or transformations of heroes and villains told in a language that was as apocalyptic as it was redemptive. He soon traded the bombast of the *Student's Companion* for Moses' disastrous venture with the Children of Israel: *Therefore God dealt well with the midwives: and the people multiplied, and waxed very mighty.*

This drove him to ask questions that would sometimes leave Father Mitchell stumped for words. For instance: 'How's it possible for people to spend forty years wandering in such a small stretch of desert?' Or: 'Would people have followed Christ if He had not been resurrected after three days in the tomb?'

Hiero hoped that he and his mother would wax very mighty indeed when the time came for them to step out to the president's banquet. But, first, there was the little matter of his runaway tongue, which had earned him a dressing-down or, more precisely, a forced sitting next to his mother. He determined to listen to her story, which, he suspected with the single-mindedness of youth, held a key to his own life. Although he was a great talker, Hiero had long started to value the need to listen. He tried to imagine the weals across his dada's back. 'Go on, Ma,' he prompted.

'Okay,' Emma-May said. 'For most of the time, I don't think we're actually aware of the places where our actions can take us. We treat each other so *uncaringly*, especially we who speak in the sacred name of love.'

Her late husband had been popular with the ladies, spending time and money with them. 'There was,' she went on, 'something unsatisfied, always seeking, an impatience with what *was* and a hankering for what *should* be. In that period, your dada dressed in the finest robes and was a welcome guest at every social gathering. Everybody knew him, and he counted the president as one of his friends.' She shook her head. 'It takes someone truly insane to think they're friends with the president.'

Hiero held his tongue, aware that his mother had just aired the same sentiment for which she had almost chewed off his head.

'Like all men,' Emma-May said, 'he met a woman whom he imagined to be the love of his life. A schoolgirl, really. Do you know,' she asked randomly, 'that in life there's always someone brought onto this earth who'll cause our downfall?'

Hiero shook his head. 'No, Ma.'

'Well,' Emma-May said grimly, 'you'd better know this, for your own safety. There's a man or woman who is born with your name stamped on his or her brow, the same way other people's names are inscribed on a killer's silver bullet. That person, the silver bullet, will catch up with you one day – and you will fall helplessly in love. That love will contain the seed of your own destruction.'

At fourteen, Hiero knew that between men and women, women and women or men and men, unspeakable things were done in the name of love. This knowledge was picked up from the streets, the school locker room, the toilets where boys boasted their latest fantasy conquest, or the taverns where blood and sweat – and, often, tears – added a piquant flavouring to the national brew of lust. At fourteen, Hiero had seen love or a reasonable facsimile thereof thrashing in unlit alleys; he had watched it in his own father's maddened eyes and heard it in the moan of his mother in the midnight hour.

But, he reasoned, he was still young and open to what the future would offer; those who were disenchanted with love and its bitter fruit had themselves to blame. Even with his limited experience, Hiero reasoned that love should have the power to transform and need not necessarily be destructive. Maybe the others had gone about it the wrong way. Hiero wouldn't make that mistake; he would first sample *liking* without rushing headlong into *loving*. He would touch without feeling; that way he would maintain control. Obliquely, he wondered who would be his mother's silver bullet now that Dada was being transformed into manure six feet under. Perhaps, and this thought filled him with trepidation, his dada had never, really, been Emma-May's silver bullet. It was possible, then, he thought, that some people were destined to wander the world searching for the right configuration of arms and bodies – and souls – that would embrace them and provide them with sanctuary.

'Your father fell in love with this woman,' Emma-May said, twisting her lips as if about to bite into a lemon, 'who was half his age but had clocked up experience that was as ageless as time. She turned him around and made a fool of him. Even when his friends were telling him, *Hey, this woman is turning you into an idiot; she has fucked* – excuse me – *the whole Appellate Division of Panza and is halfway through the Supreme Court*, he would turn a deaf ear to it. He figured everyone was jealous.'

Suddenly Hiero didn't want to hear the rest of the tale as drowsiness took hold of him and poured tepid water in his joints. He felt that, in telling the story of his dada, his mother had slowly sloughed off the outer casing that had held her dignity intact. In his short life, he had come across women – and men – embittered by the card life had dealt them, and there was something beaten and unattractive about people who wore their defeat on their sleeves. In that moment of languor, he half-listened and half-dreamed as his mother continued with her story. He heard how his dada became more and more dependent on the woman, who strung him along unashamedly. She used him to gain entry into the core of high society; frustrated, he started hitting the bottle heavily. The invitations to society events stopped. His dada had become an outcast and his erstwhile friends looked at him pityingly through self-righteous eyes and shook their heads as they released a long drawn-out sigh: *Isn't that Mr Interpreter?*

In this account, Hiero intuited that his mother wasn't really telling him a story about her late husband. The story was for the improvement of the son who had survived, whose feet were leading him on a path to perdition. It was this image of himself as an alcoholic indigent; it was this moment when he got a full measure of his mother as being no different from any old and bitter woman who'd been bested by the wiles of a voluptuous siren; it was this feeling that bad things actually happened to good people and then changed them forever, which brought the tears that he had held in check for many months. A dam somewhere inside him burst and he shivered and his mother held him and wiped the tears and snot with the back of her hand. It smelled of talcum powder.

'Let's get ready,' Emma-May said to her son.

'Yes, Ma.'

AND THEN IN the early evening, when the shadows were long and the light capable of investing people with beauty, mother and son stepped gingerly into the back seat of the thirty-six-seater microbus that had been sent specially by the presidency to collect those guests without transport. Inside the bus that was already three-quarters full of mothers and sons – for some reason, there seemed to be a dearth of girl-children in Bangula – the air was rank with the combined perfumes applied liberally to disguise the smell of poverty; the teenage boys, some with faces already breaking out in acne, recognised one another from schoolyards, video-game arcades at the mall, playgrounds or soccer fields, their adolescent syllables suggestive of a thin line between deference and buffoonery.

As the bus rolled on towards Mariposa, Hiero looked at the few men, the fathers who sat in stolid and slightly uncomfortable silence, like spectators forced to sit through an unenjoyable performance. Some of the boys stared back at Hiero with eyes that mutely objected to the ne-cessity of this forced outing. But it seemed that they all accepted that the Colonel had sent out an invitation, a privilege extended to a very small minority of the people of Bangula – and so they had better show some enthusiasm.

At the gate, the driver produced his ID card before proceeding along a stone driveway to an open area half the size of a soccer field, where he parked the microbus. Standing strategically at various points, armed men, uniformed or in civvies, helped with directions, ushering the large groups of invitees. The sight of weapons, especially the machine-gun emplacements and sandbag fortifications, enlivened even the most dis-gruntled boys.

Hiero was surprised at how he was so taken with everything associ-ated with the banquet and the evening. He paused at the entrance, which was arched like the doorway into a house of dreams. Porcelain-smooth orbs of lights hung above the heads of the guests moving decorously as if to honour an appointment with destiny, illuminating the ornate head-dresses of the women and highlighting the pomaded hair of some of the important men who had gone to such lengths to enter the fellowship of the great. Emma-May, next to him, usually striding purposefully but now with a provocative, slow gait, grinned at him as they both waxed mighty in fulfilment of a promise they didn't know they had made.

Here, his mother, in a dark dress that fitted her snugly and empha-sised those parts of a woman's body that, he knew, inspired thoughts of blood and heat. Here, on the carpeted floor, Emma-May suddenly becoming the focal point, eclipsing the other mothers, delicately accepting her drink in a fluted glass, the bubbles seeming to dance under her nose. Emma-May sounding sophisticated even as she warned him *sotto voce* to keep away from hard liquor. Here, the band playing something lively and full of hope, the people breaking into groups of familiarities, some fighting for exposure to or fleeing from the stills camera. Here, the television camera crew directed by a gimlet-eyed shrew, simply called Sarsaparilla, whose syndicated column, *The View from Sarsaparilla's Window*, had led to either the meteoric rise or graceless downfall of many a powerful figure. Here, the toastmaster in a flawless cream tuxedo stepping forward and waving the music to a diminuendo with a flick of a pampered hand, and then raising his long-stemmed glass and leading everyone in song. It was a song that spoke of the triumph and grandeur of the Reform:

> *Once upon a time this land was bleeding*
> *From teeth of marauders that showed no pity*
> *But now that the Reform has started leading*
> *There's joy from the countryside to the city ...*

Even though Hiero had heard the song countless times, it had never sounded this real and completely representative of the wishes and gratitude of the people. Although still a young man given to enjoyment of the fast and fashionable things of life, which included popular music from home and abroad, the anthem to the Reform had become one of the very few things that could gladden his heart. He joined in the singing, as did the other boys, even those who had been expelled from the school choir.

As the singing reached its highest point, it sounded as if the larynxes of the people in the front had opened to an even higher, seemingly impossible, register. The celebrants who had gathered to praise the power of the day separated into two camps and created a passage. A man appeared in orange-and-red livery and spangles. He seemed weighed down by golden epaulettes and military-style braiding and held a golden mace in both hands, a lead athlete holding up the country's colours at the opening of prestigious games. Behind him, flanked by equally power-ful men in dark suits, blindingly white shirts and bow ties sporting the colours of the republic, the Colonel walked barefooted to the centre of the room, a smile of humility on his face.

Abioseh stood behind the Colonel. He wore a grey suit that made him look wrapped up for a celebration. A half step behind to the left, Ma-Zembe watched with a look that simultaneously embraced both father and son and still managed to send out a guarded welcome to the assem-bly. Because — and this stunned Hiero — she must have wondered how many of the children present were Abioseh's half-brothers or -sisters, it being known that the Colonel had ensured his place as a future ancestor of legions. But it was the faces of men she seemed to watch from a chaste distance. How many of them had been betrayed?

At this, Hiero puzzled over his own origins. When the blood had gushed out of the goat's neck and he had fallen from the tree into it, into the blood that was meant to strengthen and sanctify the leader of the republic, what did *that* say about him? Was that not a sign that was more profound than mere words that he, Hiero, had been included and made part of the blood sacrifice — and was therefore the anointed one? In his mind, he went back to his solitary readings of the Bible, his debates with Father Mitchum, the Epistle of Paul the Apostle to the Hebrews, 9:22: *And almost all things are by the law purged with blood; and without shedding of blood is no remission.*

He listened attentively to the Colonel, hearing words meant to assure people that all was under control. 'We're on top of it,' the Colonel said, *it* being any activity, real or imagined that could disturb the peace. Dis-missing an impudent question about bandit activity and skirmishes in the mountains, the Colonel smiled indulgently, swatting away the query with a wave of his hand. Another question referred to the blood plague: *Are we on top of that, too, Colonel or are we bathing in blood?* At this, the Colonel laughed good-naturedly, perhaps admiring the journalist's nerve. 'There will always be blood,' he said. 'Don't the religious ones make us sing about the power of the blood of the Lamb?'

That evening Hiero grasped a few things, already displaying the acumen that became his hallmark in his later role as a gatekeeper of state security. Observing his mother in profile, he noticed that throughout the evening, not once did she raise her eyes to look at the Colonel. Even if convention required women to drop their gaze in the company of men, this was odd. There was more to this than met the eye.

Hiero became increasingly at peace with the idea that there was no such thing as reality. We see, he mused, what we are meant to see. That evening, he began to question every time anyone mentioned calm because, he knew, there was an undercurrent of turbulence. In the unfolding of all the schemes for the benefit of the masses, leaders were speaking in a subterranean language. But much more importantly – even if this was going to be a secret he would take to the grave – he, Hiero, the son of his despised dada, was not a commoner. He waxed mighty in the knowledge that he bore on his brow the mark of greatness.

2

IN THE EARLY evening of the 15th of July, Zebulon stopped on the road outside the parish of St Theresa. As he rested his hands on the wrought-iron gates, tiredness rippled through him from the crown of his head to the soles of his feet. Scattered on the grass, almost covering the paved footpath to the arched doorway into the church, were blankets and cardboard strips that would later be used for bedding. About twenty men of varying ages, mostly in denims, overalls, chinos or greatcoats stood in groups, smoking furiously.

Zebulon realised that there was something frustratingly familiar about the sight of men who seemed as though they had a lot of time on their hands. Everywhere he looked, there were people standing in a line or loitering around the grey stone and glass edifice that housed the Ministry of Labour. The unemployed, it seemed, suffered from an inability to accept failure. They refused to give in even when some of the recently retrenched ministry employees swelled the ranks of the unemployed. A memorable line also formed outside the hospital. Starting at the bustling taxi rank, the queue almost broke his heart because, nearer the glass hospital doors, it split into two ragged sections, one for patients headed for medical wards and the other for visitors to the mortuary. Some of the patients entering the wards would stare at the line to the mortuary, as if already thinking about the time when their own turn would come.

Zebulon was mulling over how such a small country like Bangula with a population of around a million could bear to lose so many people when the church door opened and let out the stocky, white-haired Father Mitchum in his customary black suit, followed by a matronly woman, Emma-May, with Hiero in a blue-and-white tracksuit and white trainers bringing up the rear.

Zebulon had last seen Emma-May on the day her husband died. He remembered that, even though she was grief-stricken, something told Zebulon that she was vaguely uncomfortable around him. He didn't know what caused this reaction but had long decided that he wouldn't take responsibility for what people thought. He'd just offer his condolences and leave. Melinda had influenced this attitude. One day Zebulon had been at pains to explain to a bunch of sceptical street children why he didn't want to discuss his relationship with the Colonel. 'Shut up, Zebulon,' she had said. 'Nobody gives a shit what you think.'

Father Mitchum greeted the men milling on the lawn. Seeing the cleric conduct a last-minute consultation with Hiero and Emma-May, Zebulon was suddenly struck by the thought that he had no parents; he had no one. Not a single person would stir if anything happened to him and he ended up on a porcelain slab in the mortuary. He remembered his mother's funeral, the ring of the spade glancing off a rock and the heavy, flat sound of earth crunching onto the pale pine box. Seized by a feeling beyond his control, Zebulon lowered his head, determined to disappear into the traffic roaring behind him. The action inadvertently alerted Hiero to his presence. The latter said something to his mother, who seemed about to protest before the priest laid a supportive hand on her shoulder. Then Hiero strode across the lawn, nodding at some of the men along the way, until he was at the gate.

'Zebulon,' he cried with genuine joy, 'what are you standing out there for?' Without waiting for an answer, he opened the gate and pulled Zebulon inside.

Hiero led Zebulon past the men to where Emma-May was still talking to Father Mitchum. Zebulon had an idea that Emma-May was going to ignore him. But she stopped talking and turned, her face sporting a cautious smile.

'Ma,' Hiero said. 'This is Zebulon. Ma, you might not remember him, but he came to help us mourn for Dada and we have been together in some of Father Mitchum's lessons.'

'Of course I remember him,' Emma-May said breathlessly, studying Zebulon's face and shaking his hand. 'How are you, Zebulon?'

'I am well,' Zebulon said. He wanted to say more. Instead he turned to the priest. 'And,' he asked, 'how is the Holy Father?'

'Whoa, hold it, hold it,' Father Mitchum said. 'That's not how you address a lowly priest like me, Zebulon.' He snorted good-naturedly. 'Holy Father,' he murmured. 'That's for the Pope.'

'How do you address a priest, then?' Emma-May asked. 'I'm also a little like Zebulon. Can't make head or tail of all these titles.'

'It's *Father*,' said Mitch Mitchum. 'Call me Father Mitch. Or even Mitch. I deal with people from different denominations and I always see them struggling. There are some who are older than me who find it difficult to call another man *Father*. I suppose it's even harder if you're dealing with a white man. In fact, Matthew 23:6–9 reads: *They love places of honour at banquets, seats of honour in synagogues, greetings in marketplaces, and the salutation Rabbi. As for you, do not be called Rabbi. You have but one teacher, and you are all brothers. Call no one on earth your father; you have but one Father in heaven.'*

'Zebulon and I,' Hiero piped up, 'have one father.'

'Don't talk nonsense here,' Emma-May said sharply. 'What father?'

'I mean in *heaven*,' Hiero said. 'Like Father Mitchum said.'

'Well, *Father*,' Emma-May said, with a small laugh, 'I must say I've learnt more than I bargained for this afternoon. But I must love and leave you.' She looked pointedly at her son. 'Don't be late coming back tonight. And you must bring Zebulon along to come and visit one day.' She gave Zebulon's arm a slight squeeze. 'Don't be a stranger now, you hear?'

'Yes, Ma'am,' Zebulon said.

'MY NAME IS Zebulon,' he had told the twenty-five or thirty people in the church hall. Clearing his throat to launch into his speech, he realised that his voice had broken and sounded strange to him. And, like most young men grown too tall too soon, he was conscious of his height. His elbows were too bony and had a life of their own, knocking into doorjambs, upsetting things.

'My name is Zebulon,' he repeated, looking down at the faces that stared up at him. Even the priest, who stood next to him with a smile of cautious piety, had to look up, as he was a head shorter. Outside the hall, the roar of traffic became a backdrop to the ebb and flow of voices of men and women returning from work. Since it was the last Friday of the month, a payday, voices wafting into the church hall sounded excited.

Zebulon's nostrils twitched to an amalgam of smells of different art materials: paper glue, cement or paint that had been used earlier in community art classes. There was also the rank odour of unwashed bodies and poverty. Spread around the hall were worktables on which skeletal figures were riveted to their bases atop a veritable forest of newsprint; the miscellany of work in progress, under the weak light of the late afternoon, seemed full of life. Zebulon could almost hear the flutter of the wings of the figures representing birds. A few of these sculptures looked more real than the emaciated beggars, drug and alcohol addicts and those who had given up hope who looked at him from heavy-lidded eyes. One of the men let off a resounding fart, sending the younger derelicts into hysterics. As Zebulon hesitated, letting the laughter die down, Father Mitchum raised his hand. 'You have to give Zebulon a chance to tell his story,' he said.

'Why?' Intrepid Farter asked from the floor.

'Because,' Father Mitchum answered, 'that's what we do here with all newcomers. When you came here for the first time, Francis, you were worse for wear, but we allowed you to say your piece.'

'Not that there's been any improvement now,' another joker put in. He was a younger man who, once upon a time, must been of noble stock but had since been dislodged from that privileged perch by the ravages of raw liquor.

'What the hell,' Francis asked, getting to his feet, 'do you know about my life, you lowlife?'

'*Lowlife?*' the one-time aristocrat shrieked. 'What would *you* know, you filthy thing that's even beneath the underdog?' Before his fall from grace, the young man had been a staunch admirer of Charlie Mingus, tending to speak in a style he imagined was characteristic of jazz musicians.

'SHUT THE FUCK UP!' The priest's roar cut through the room like an electric buzz-saw. This had an immediately sobering effect on the men. 'Many of you,' he continued, 'don't understand that we're serious here … we're dealing with issues of health and survival and spiritual growth. Most of you were at death's door when you first joined us. If you don't want to listen then you'd better get out of here!' He paused, glowering, letting it sink in. Satisfied, he turned to Zebulon. 'Go on, son,' he said gruffly.

Zebulon gave his testimony, starting on the day his mother died and how the shack and its contents were snatched away as if by a cyclone. He told them about witnessing the Colonel standing above his mother's bed in hospital – and how he had heard about the shelter. Listening to his tale, the group reacted with *oohs* and *aahs*, grinning knowingly when Zebulon came to his adventures with Melinda, accompanying him on his journey of discovery in the garden of delight and despair. A round of applause greeted the end of Zebulon's story, the hands clapping more vigorously as Zebulon dipped his head in embarrassment. Father Mitchum stepped forward.

'Now,' he asked, 'what have we learnt from Zebulon's sharing?'

A confusion of voices followed, each person striving to advance his or her theory on Zebulon's contribution. Father Mitchum banged his fist on a desk, his reddening face showing the mighty struggle he was having with himself not to utter a devastating oath. 'One person at a time,' he said, shaking his head, and then jerked it towards Hiero, who had been quietly watching the early evening lurching from order to chaos and back again. 'Yes, Hiero?'

'The kids at school were spot-on,' said Hiero. 'The lad *is* a jester.'

'That's interesting,' Father Mitchum said. 'How come?'

Hiero seemed to consider. 'When he saw all these things happening to his mother,' he said, speaking guardedly as if he feared that he might stumble over the words, 'he should have spoken to other people, because a young person is not supposed to experience all this hardship alone.'

'And you think other people would lift a finger to help?' asked an ageless grizzled man wrapped in a brown blanket that had absorbed all the smells of the night. 'Come on. People don't want to know. Stories spell trouble.'

'He could have gone to a traditional healer for help,' Hiero suggested. 'Anyone.' He sounded angry all of a sudden. 'It's bloody wrong,' he added, shaking his head.

'In truth,' Father Mitchum said, 'Zebulon's case is not unique. It's true he might have found help if he'd gone out looking for it. But I believe that what he has gone through has toughened him. What do they say about that which doesn't kill us?'

'Makes us stronger,' Hiero prompted.

'Yes,' Father Mitchum continued. 'I'm certain he could have gone to the Colonel and demanded his birthright. An easy route that would make him as soft as the spoilt brats of powerful parents.' He laughed, sensing a paradox. 'Children of the weak are strong and vice versa.'

AS THEIR FRIENDSHIP blossomed, Zebulon and Hiero started visiting different haunts of the destitute. They listened to first-hand accounts of the wickedness of the world. Zebulon told Hiero more about Melinda. But he didn't tell him of his quest to forget. Or how the exorcism of her memory had led him to a life where he comforted the bereaved as a balm for his own soul. While Hiero puzzled over Zebulon's obsession with mortality, Zebulon couldn't understand how people could be addicted to alcohol.

The two friends came across runaways who had fled neglectful parents. They encountered women fleeing loveless marriages, some ending up on the treadmill of prostitution and disease. Here, Zebulon thought of his mother. What would she have made of the characters whom they met, business executives – some bearing an uncanny resemblance to Claude – who had squandered their future on the needle or the bottle? There were many stories. The poor, though, formed the overwhelming majority of the down-and-out.

'I tried,' the grizzled man confided to Zebulon after a session with Father Mitchum. 'I tried to hold on. I had a wife and two children, two girls, but it all proved too much. She left and took the girls. Strangely, I'm happy she took the girls with her because children are uncomfortable around poverty; they can't see the fucking point.'

When Hiero and Zebulon attended to certain urgencies together, they learned that sections of the population still held Vezi's memory in high esteem. But this veneration had a price, since the Colonel had put in place an effective network of informers. It was a strange time, when speaking ill of the order of things did not go unpunished, often resulting in the withdrawal of a benefit. It was not unheard of for a malcontent with a loose tongue to be suddenly out of a job, with all avenues closed. These people then swelled the ranks of the unemployed whose inevitable end was a pauper's burial in an unmarked plot via a stint among the homeless.

It was then that Zebulon frequently visited the families of the bereaved, occasionally in Hiero's company, usually alone, offering solace with his presence. It sometimes seemed as if a funeral service was incomplete without Zebulon. It was then that they dubbed him 'Holy Boy', not so much for any singular act of piety as his appearance – a reassuring face and unruffled bearing. Some pastors invited him to address their congregations, the charismatic holy rollers going as far as allowing him to minister to their flocks, testify and even take part in the laying on of hands. Others, alarmed that this young newcomer would form his own breakaway church that would wean their members off established ministries, denounced him as an upstart.

Oblivious of the effect he was having on people, Zebulon was indiscriminate in his acceptance of invitations, until Hiero directed him to avoid those that could have put him at risk. 'The world,' Hiero would say, 'is not as innocent as you think. There are some seriously jealous people out there.'

'I'm just doing what has to be done,' Zebulon would answer.

'The famous last words,' Hiero would muse, 'of someone fast on their way to becoming a corpse.'

SEVERAL MONTHS AFTER their meeting at the church, Hiero suddenly disappeared. When Zebulon asked Father Mitchum where his friend was, the burly cleric became evasive. 'It seems,' he said glumly, 'that your Hiero wasn't entirely what he'd led us to believe he was.'

'Meaning what, Father?'

'Meaning,' the priest said quietly, 'in addition to his own issues, he was here on behalf of the government.'

'What does the government want from the church and the shelter?' Zebulon asked. He was suddenly angry, everything that he had found distasteful about his father returning, like the memory of a bad dream. As best as he could, he had expelled the Colonel from his most immediate concerns. But now it seemed that the Colonel had infiltrated a world in which he could find safety. Somehow, the Colonel's influence tended to make all the people Zebulon valued most disappear. The old man had drawn a line in the sand.

When not at the shelter, Zebulon spent night after night walking, listening to his stomach growling, feeling the thinness of the soles of his shoes and the lightness of his jacket and trousers. When he finally fell asleep under a bridge or in a classroom during school holidays, he dreamt of his mother. Sometimes Melinda's face, scornful and furiously alive, laid itself over his mother's, and he would wake up ashamed that he had an erection.

ZEBULON STARVED. FOR a long period there were few burials, to the extent that humorists suggested that undertakers and gravediggers should consider petitioning the government to give them some slack. Even columnists whose wherewithal consisted of obituaries found themselves out of a job. On the brink of starvation, they decried this strange drought. Like vultures, they watched old people who seemed destined to live forever, trailing them to see if there was perhaps a secret elixir that was the cause of this inconvenient longevity.

And then, in February, when the sun was so hot the ground seemed to dance from the heat, death arrived with a vengeance. It cut a swathe through the population. People collapsed all round – sometimes in midstride on the busy Revolution Boulevard. It was unclear at first what the cause was, with many attributing the toll to the midnight ministrations of conjurers. Confusion reigned until medical experts, led by Dr Ahmod Badawi, a little-known virologist, announced that Bangula was again in the grip of the blood plague.

The first disavowal came from the Ministry of Tourism, which prevailed upon the Ministry of Health to announce that the blood plague did not exist; those who claimed otherwise were in the grip of a communal hallucination. A curious state of affairs ensued; a posse of prominent government officials routinely paid visits to some of the sufferers and explained to them in the most pleasant tones the imprudence of disclosing to the jeering world the full nature of their condition. The logic was that it was in the national interest that the victims and their relatives stayed their collective tongue since anything disclosed would strengthen the enemy.

And who was the enemy? The enemy was unemployment; it was poverty; it was crime; it was the lack of national esteem, where the country would be pilloried in international councils and put up as an example of African lowliness. Government agents who showed exemplary solicitude transmitted these messages in the most unthreatening way. A few of the patients knew they were going to die anyway, but they worried more about the fate awaiting their surviving families if word got out that they had broken ranks with the authorities by admitting to being infected by the dread disease.

Months passed. Even though he was now busier than ever before, Zebulon did not accept the fact that people were dying like flies. Sometimes he visited Father Mitchum. The priest always prefaced his comments with a disclaimer that what he was about to say were his own personal views and not the views of the church.

'What we have here,' he said one morning, 'is a violation of human rights. Health is a human rights' issue. Bangula is not alone in this. But what makes us unique are the unending efforts to justify what cannot be justified. Unfortunately,' he went on, sipping his tea, 'I'm just another white man with a big mouth. It's up to you to put this right.'

3

ON THE DAY in December that Abioseh Gondo wrote his final matric examination paper, he made a few enemies.

He had woken up in his parents' house, which was one place in the world he felt a stranger. Nothing in him found comfort in Mariposa. He even hated the name of the residence, how could his folks allow some pretentious Spanish architect to name the presidential residence 'butterfly'? Tiresome, too – by his own assessment – was the whole palaver around meals. Breakfast was served at 7.00 AM in the dining room, a cavernous chamber in which you could fly a small plane, accommodating a table and chairs that must have denuded a forest the size of a sports arena. In addition, as the Colonel wasn't a breakfast person and MaZembe took her cue from him, especially when he was in Jambora, Abioseh dined alone. He didn't so much as crave his folks' company as find government wasteful.

It was unacceptable, especially since the Colonel's government promoted some form of austerity. People were always being advised to tighten their belts. To Abioseh, this was hypocrisy. The spaciousness of the building of the office of the president, which housed the presidential residence, was an insult to the thousands of Bangula's homeless. While he was sipping his coffee that morning, something snapped. He rang the bell, summoning the steward. On the wall, the framed portraits of eminent leaders, religious or secular, scholars or philanthropists gazed disapprovingly down at him.

'Yes, Master?' The elderly man who had appeared out of nowhere had been with the family as long as Abioseh could remember. In the past, Rupert had been pleasant, a part of the family. Then he had a run-in with MaZembe when he brought in a young woman he claimed to be his niece. Sporting a noticeable bump a few weeks later, Donyen, the niece, had told MaZembe that Rupert was the father. As he had lied to his patrons, MaZembe wanted him fired.

The Colonel intervened and said that it would take time to find someone with Rupert's experience. Furthermore, the presidential domestic staff had been handpicked and vetted by Security Affairs. They also reflected the regional and language diversity, so, firing one person on the basis of volcanic hormones could upset the sensitive process towards nation building, blah blah blah.

'He's building a nation all right,' MaZembe had snapped, 'right under our noses.' She was more alarmed than indignant that Rupert, who must have been in his late sixties, could indulge in extramural activity that could result in the production of a baby. In time, MaZembe relented and Rupert was restored to heading the kitchen detail. But the incident had soured his relationship with the presidential family. Not given to surliness, Rupert had simply decided to keep his distance. 'Something wrong with the eggs?'

'No,' Abioseh said; he hadn't touched his eggs. 'Can you get my mother?'

'She's with the Colonel,' Rupert said. His eyes pleaded against being sent.

'I know that,' Abioseh insisted. 'Could you get her? Please?'

When it dawned on him that he was sending a man who was years his senior to run a personal errand, he got up from the table, meaning to track down MaZembe himself. He did an about-turn at the entrance when he heard his father's unmistakable baritone, a rarity at this early hour. 'Let's see who's ringing the bell,' the Colonel said.

'He might be missing school,' said a soft yet forceful voice. 'Hence the bell.'

The two men laughed. 'Hence the bell, indeed,' said the Colonel. Abioseh had an impression of the Colonel resisting a lapse into irony. They entered, the Colonel first, followed by the leaner and younger Carlos Nobrega.

Before the Colonel could do the introductions, Nobrega grasped Abioseh's hand and shook it vigorously, his grip firm like someone who worked out a lot. He was very light complexioned with wavy black hair that was slicked back, the chin showing even at this early hour the exact location where the five o'clock shadow lay in wait. 'I've heard so much about you, my brother,' he said. 'And it's all good.'

My brother? 'Pleased to meet you,' Abioseh said, figuring Nobrega for a liar because the Colonel was notoriously close-mouthed about his family. Since he impacted on the lives of so many people, he couldn't afford to have the secrets of the one life crossing the border into the domain of the other. Peace came from the maintenance of absolute silence.

Nobrega was dressed in a light tropical suit, a yellow tie and tan shoes; he exuded vitality and, as he moved to lean against the wall, Abioseh got the faintest whiff of cologne. He was normally prejudiced against men who wore any form of perfume. Deodorants were okay as part of personal hygiene: the island was, after all, very hot and he found bad body odour offensive. He wasn't so much leery of covert femininity as scornful of vanity.

But, the cologne notwithstanding, Carlos Nobrega displayed no sign of femaleness. His face was lean, squarish, as if it, too, had benefited

94

from the sessions at the gym, the nose speaking of ancient European ancestry. His deep brown eyes missed nothing. It was a face whose rigidity recalled a rock sculpture, a physiognomy belonging to heroes in space adventures. But, despite the symmetry, something was lacking; perhaps it was the absence of defects that could have given a clue into the personality behind the mask.

'I was taking Carlos to see plans for the new wing to the building,' said the Colonel. 'He's just come back from a conference on youth.'

'How nice,' Abioseh said. He judged Nobrega to be in his early thirties, but someone who carried himself with supreme seriousness, the minister with a special responsibility for the youth, people with disabilities and women's affairs. It never ceased to puzzle Abioseh that women were always lumped together with children, in this instance, the youth, and the disabled. On the last day of high school, he suddenly found himself at odds with the way society articulated itself and its processes. Women were called 'the weaker sex' and old people 'senior citizens'. Depending on your family status, you were either a thief or a kleptomaniac and a 'flexible labour market' stood for the prerogative of employers to hire on slave wages and fire without adequate compensation. There were many more such words to legitimise the illegitimate. He wanted to ask his father whether he still remembered that, once upon a time, Bangula had been hailed as an island of hope, an exemplar of stability in a turbulent ocean region.

'Were the youth there?' Abioseh asked. He didn't know what had prompted him to ask that particular question.

'What kind of conference on youth would it be,' Nobrega asked, smiling, 'without youth representation, my brother?'

It was the smile that got to Abioseh. 'I mean,' he said, 'there are various youth groups. At Alfredo Romero, for instance, we do Civilian Service with the community – and we encounter so much that affects the youth.'

'Such as what, my brother?'

'You go to the market, near Cinnamon Hill,' Abioseh said, 'and look at the human waste there – the youth, some dying from diseases. The blood plague.'

'I need to chip in here,' the Colonel said, pulling rank. 'There's no plague in Bangula. You have a limited outbreak of communicable diseases. The people dying have turned their back on the principles of sanitation that the rest of the world adheres to. Some are unwilling to get into the government's health programme on religious or cultural grounds.' His chest heaving, the Colonel turned to Nobrega. 'We can't change that.'

'You could set some funds aside for public health education …'

'We're doing that already, my brother,' Carlos Nobrega said.

'That's right,' said the Colonel. There was sorrow in his eyes, as if he was accepting that he had neglected his son's education. 'The budget to combat contagions outstrips even the military allocation.'

'And so it should,' Abioseh said. 'We don't need to spend on defence.'

'Perhaps,' the Colonel said, 'but we could also be throwing good money after bad, trying to stem the tide of infections when Nature has decided to curb the population explosion.' He paused. 'Have you thought about that?'

'I haven't,' Abioseh conceded, 'for the simple reason that the thought is so monstrous as to be unimaginable …'

'But it could be the case, couldn't it?' asked the Colonel gently. 'Why is it that natural calamities tend to befall overpopulated regions of the world? Africa. Asia. Latin America. Isn't there some … *monstrous* design at work?'

'Father!' Abioseh was exasperated and horrified. 'Do you hear what *you're* saying? Are you justifying the plunder of the environment by the industrial nations? They don't, unfortunately, have their populations dying in droves, but their greed and consumption and gas emissions and reneging on treaties and environmental agreements cause so many deaths in the so-called Third World.'

'That might be the case,' the Colonel said patiently. 'But we're a poor country, with a population of around a million. We can spend so much on health. Keeping dying people alive is very expensive. We have to think about the living. And the unborn.' He sounded tired. 'And,' he added, 'we *do* have enemies.'

'The Colonel is right, my brother ...'

'Listen, you,' Abioseh had had enough. 'I'm *not* your *fucking* brother. I've got enough brothers already ...'

Abioseh realised too late when Nobrega gave a gleaming, full-toothed grin of martyrdom, that he had been cleverly unseated from his perch where he had assumed the moral high ground. Losing his temper and spitting invective in front of the Colonel and Carlos Nobrega was mortifying. Deciding that he might as well be hanged for a sheep as a lamb, he let out a long, drawn-out sigh. '*Sheee*-it.'

'Let's go, Carlos,' the Colonel said, after a long silence while the expletive settled on the floor. He hooked an arm around Nobrega's shoulders. 'Good luck with your exam,' he said. 'Later we'll discuss what you'll do after matriculating.'

'I think I'll look for work,' Abioseh said. He hadn't really come to that decision, but he felt he needed his father to understand that he meant to have a hand in designing his own future.

Eyes narrowed, the Colonel promised, 'We'll see.' It sounded like a threat.

Before exiting, Nobrega did a smart about-turn, still smiling. 'I really enjoyed our little talk,' he said. 'Perhaps we'll find time soon to continue?'

'With pleasure,' Abioseh said. *My brother.*

THE FIGHT WITH Baluba had been inevitable from day one at Alfredo Romero High School. It was one of those situations where two people had a mutual aversion for each other. In times when the young men got together as a group to, say, listen to Hiero's stories or marvel at David Kone's amorous adventures, Abioseh always preferred to keep quiet and let the others do the talking. On the day when he'd already had a fight with his father and his Cabinet minister, he sought a quiet moment to have a smoke. He also needed to think about his future. He was confident he would matriculate with a first-class pass. The prospect of finding a job that wouldn't be tied to his family, though, was remote. Except if he left the country and went overseas. But where?

Since the whole school had become one noisy camp, solitude even in the usual places was impossible. Everywhere clusters of excited adolescents stood talking, exchanging the last gossip, stocking up on stories that would tide them over the festive season. As they were all in civvies, gone was the restraint imposed directly or indirectly by the school uniforms. The men, who had been boys until recently, looked like the old men they'd soon become. The girls, who had not too long ago appeared gawky or stout – certainly characterless during the academic year – seemed to have reached a stage of sexual attractiveness. The butterflies had emerged from their chrysalises. He wondered if these young women would find Carlos Nobrega's stone face charming.

Miraculously, the canteen was still trading and there were a few unoccupied tables. Abioseh found a corner table near a group of six new butterflies who carried on a conversation about career prospects in Panza. One of them, a tall girl-woman in tight jeans and an orange tank-top shook her non-existent tresses and declared that she wanted to become an actress, to hell with getting a degree in maritime studies. 'What's more,' she said in a nasal twang, 'I just can't stand fish.' And gave a theatrical shudder.

'But your father is a fisherman,' one of the friends said.

'Exactly.'

'Well,' her friend pressed on, 'you've got to keep it real. Do what your folks want you to do.'

'At least you're not being forced into an arranged marriage,' another friend put in. 'That's scarifying.'

Something about these women, their preoccupations with private life and personal problems gave Abioseh insight into his parents' minds. The older generations, he reasoned, would see any subsequent age group as flawed. Although they never seemed to crow about it, the Colonel and MaZembe saw themselves as belonging to movements that strove to change the world. They had been in the struggle; they saw the changeover from the old dispensation to the new. They still had memories of what had been done in the name of the old flag, which was spattered with the blood and sweat of compatriots – and they had rejoiced when the banner of shame was lowered and theirs unfurled.

Abioseh was sitting in the corner by the window, looking at the sun splashing on the little plots on which struggling cabbage and beetroot grew amidst scattered clutches of weeds. He was thinking that revolutions were like these gardens: the fruits could be sweet or bitter – and there was no scarcity of weeds which, left unattended, would choke the life out of the life-giving vegetation.

'There you are,' he heard someone say and shook himself, for he realised that he must have dozed off a bit, must be the sun. He looked around and saw that the wannabe actress and her posse had left, leaving behind crumpled paper cups and dead cigarette ends swimming in tin ashtrays. He reckoned that, before they enrolled for any course in maritime studies or got married off to some unloved fisherman in Panza, they needed a crash course in home economics to learn the rudiments of hygiene. *I am getting to be as bad as my parents*, he thought.

'There you are.'

It was David Kone and Baluba Jambo.

It was about 11.00 AM but David looked already like he'd had an early start and smelled a little of alcohol. This was surprising because they were still supposed to sit for the biology paper at 1.00 PM. After that, they would be as free as birds. Baluba, who was sober, had a strange look in his eyes, perhaps as a result of having taken a few tokes of marijuana. Both had wide smiles on their faces, like people who had just hit the jackpot.

'What's up, guys?' Abioseh asked. He really wished to be alone.

'You won't believe what we've just done,' David said, his smile widening. Not waiting for Abioseh to respond, he went on, 'We've got the biology paper.'

'What?'

'Yep,' David boasted. 'We've got it. Don't ask how we did it, but we have it here.' He patted the sides of his backpack. 'Want to see?'

Abioseh was very good at drawing, which made him take to biology where drawing was an important skill. Drawings helped him to record data from specimens. Some of his schoolmates preferred working from photographs. He preferred drawings since they could show features that would take several photographs. 'No,' he said, disappointed in his friends. 'I don't want to see it.'

'Why?' This was Baluba. 'What's wrong with us sharing a paper?'

'*You* go ahead and do whatever,' Abioseh said. 'Just don't involve *me*.'

'Why?' Baluba pressed on. 'Because we're mere slugs and you're a superior being?' The ill-gotten biology paper must have featured questions on molluscs.

'Because …' Abioseh started to explain, then stopped. 'Forget it.'

'We can't forget it, Abioseh,' Baluba said. 'You already know we've got the paper. We came here because we trusted you. Now you want to betray us.' Suddenly a knowing smile appeared on Baluba's face. 'Is it because you know that my dada and David's dada said your old man's full of shit?'

David, possibly sensing that the matter was taking an ugly turn, laid a calming hand on Baluba's shoulder. 'Let's drop it,' he said.

'Listen,' Abioseh said, lifting his face to Baluba's. 'Listen, I don't know what your father's gripe is. Frankly I don't care. I just want you two to leave me alone and go and sleep off whatever it is that's addling your brains. Perhaps,' he added, 'you need to discuss this with your fathers; maybe they'll give you some pointers on how to run your lives because – at this rate – you're heading for a crash.' He paused. 'On second thought, leave your fathers out of this. Talk to your mothers.'

If Abioseh had slapped Baluba across the face, the reaction couldn't have been more dramatic. Baluba banged his fist on the table, the crash startling some of the students. He started to lunge for Abioseh but got blocked by the table, which was riveted to the floor. Abioseh kicked a chair out of the way and was squaring up. 'If it's a fight you want,' he said, 'come on, then.'

Just then Hiero came in. It took time for Abioseh to recognise him in an orange pair of overalls and white trainers. When he saw the two men circling each other, he broke into a run. 'Hey, hey, hey,' he said. 'My brothers . . .'

Oh, brother, thought Abioseh. *It's getting to be that kind of day.*

'Why don't you guys wait until after the biology paper?' asked David.

Surprisingly, Hiero, who had rushed to the scene as a peacemaker, now agreed. 'Yes,' he said. 'After the paper and after a square meal.'

'Never,' an invigorated David advised, 'fight on an empty stomach.'

ABIOSEH COULDN'T REMEMBER how he managed to collect his thoughts and apply his mind to the exam paper. In one instance, when he had to draw and label the cross section of an eyeball, he kept seeing Baluba's maddened and bloodshot eyes jumping up from the page. The morning had been temperate; after the exam, the sun was merciless, reminding all and sundry that Bangula was hot.

As Abioseh started heading to the clearing that was immediately out-side the school premises and which served as the arena for students with disagreements, he concluded that the fight was a set-up. There was noth-ing spontaneous about David's suggestion that the matter between Abi-oseh and Baluba be settled via fisticuffs. Something told him that every-one, Hiero included, was in on the game. And the expectation was that Abioseh would get the hiding of his life. Baluba was bigger and stronger – and had proven more than equal to any task that involved pummelling some unfortunate adversary into the ground. *Whatever*, Abioseh thought,

mentally shrugging, *there's no way to back out now.* He supposed he was fated
to be taught a lesson for the simple reason that he was his father's son.
Moreover, his apparent detachment from activities that the other fellows
had taken to with gusto was an affront. There was a code of conduct that
everyone had to abide by. His sin was appearing disdainful of the simple
pleasures that others took for granted. It wasn't personal.

News of a fight was a guaranteed crowd-puller; that the combatants
would be students in their final year, and one of them the president's son,
meant that the curious and bloodthirsty would reserve their 'seats' long
before the fight. And so it was that Abioseh proceeded to the designated
place, swept along by an excited throng that kept up a continuous chant:
'*Fight, fight, fight, fight!*'

As he walked down the concrete path, leaving the sanctuary of Alfredo Romano High School for the hostile world, Abioseh could hear
nothing but the chant, which reached a crescendo when Baluba emerged.
His upper body glistened as if he had worked up a sweat practising his
punches.

Other young people from neighbouring schools, residents of Cinnamon Hill (who were experiencing a power outage and so couldn't watch
their favourite soap operas) and commuters on their way to the taxi
rank, massed around the clearing, forming a circle. Abioseh had no illu-
sions that this human wall was for his protection. Some spectators were
holding hands, like members of Alcoholics Anonymous about to say the
Serenity Prayer.

Abioseh knew he might need to say a prayer himself when he glanced
at Baluba, whose body was made for wrestling, his long, ape-like arms
rippling with muscles. Although they were about the same age, Abioseh
knew that Baluba was a lot more experienced in street fighting. From
scars that crisscrossed his upper body and head, he had survived serious
knife duels. What was he to do?

The answer came from the five-fingered slap that Baluba delivered
with snake-like speed, catching Abioseh across his face, causing tears

to spring into his eyes and stars to dance before him like tiny sparklers in a field of deep blue. Somewhere in that haze, he heard a roar go up, recalling, irrationally, a scene in a film he had once seen where spectators convulsed with delight at the sight of the Roman Emperor Nero feeding Christians to the lions. Wobbly for an instant, he regained his balance and fixed his eyes on Baluba, whose grin conveyed that this would be a quick demolition job and everyone could then go home and crack a beer. *Fight back,* his mind told him, *find an opening and ...* But his mind turned into mush when his forehead collided with another punch, this time from a fist that seemed to have started its journey halfway around the world.

The shouting was a lot more frenzied now, Baluba being urged on and Abioseh hearing someone screaming with nervous disgust: *Why don't you just lie down and get it over and done with?* Abioseh realised with shock that this voice had leapt up from somewhere inside his own head. *The treachery,* he reasoned, *is everywhere* — and he became determined to stay on his feet, whatever the cost. To accomplish this, he first ducked a roundhouse punch that would have taken off his head and then held Baluba around his slippery waist. He got a whiff of Baluba's breath that was stale with tobacco and something that Abioseh interpreted as terror, pinning his one hand in the clinch.

The crowd, which craved blood, howled its displeasure at Abioseh's lack of sportsmanship. At the same time, Baluba was wriggling to free himself, bringing the free hand to Abioseh's throat, hissing, 'Get your hands off me, sissy boy!' And then, 'I'm going to *fucking* kill you!'

It was this threat, perhaps — much, much later, Abioseh still couldn't tell for sure — that convinced him that the stakes were high indeed, and if he wished to get out of this alive, he had to devise another plan. The dust, loosened from the clayey ground by the feet of the fighting young men, rose like a yellow cloud and filled their nostrils and eyes.

Momentarily free, now, Baluba snorted like a buffalo and brought his fist down like a hammer upon Abioseh's neck; the latter felt as if something had broken up inside him and was ready to heed that mocking voice which had earlier suggested that he give in. But it had now changed tune. *Stay on your feet*, the voice was urging, *stay on your feet!* On another level, he heard his father's voice, dripping with contempt, telling him he wasn't a man.

Looking up, through the mist of dust and fear, Abioseh saw a depthless arrogance reflected in Baluba's eyes. Accepting now that he was probably going to die anyway, Abioseh lashed out and caught Baluba flush on the chin, the force of the blow snapping his head back. A hush fell over the crowd. The surprise on Baluba's face soon gave way to fury; the short punch had stung him. Roaring and clawing at Abioseh's face, Baluba seemed to have lost his air of invincibility, which depended on his being in total control. The angrier he got, the easier it was for Abioseh to step in and strike, now to the midriff, which felt as if he had socked a brick wall. Baluba let out a whoosh of air. Still, he was able to kick, flail and draw blood. *I'm not going to fall*, Abioseh thought, swallowing a gob of saliva that tasted metallic, his own blood. *I'm not going to fall!*

As the fight dragged on under the harsh December sun, Abioseh and Baluba became exhausted. Their punches were a mere formality, having lost all sap. The crowd from Cinnamon Hill, which had come for some diversion, retreated to their houses to stare at their silent television sets and hope. The expected crucifixion had degenerated into a normal fight, with neither side giving in.

When they were finally separated, Abioseh decided that all his future friendships would be on his own terms because he could no longer trust people.

When he got home, bloodied and tattered, he first cleaned up in the servants' quarters, grateful that he hadn't broken anything. Scrubbed and salved, he sneaked into the house and made a beeline for his bedroom. That night, he slept until morning without once waking up. MaZembe saw him in the morning and screamed at him. He looked as if he'd been through a mangle. Was Abioseh trying to send her to an early grave? In contrast, when the Colonel heard about the fight, he was impressed.

'Must arrange self-defence classes for you.'

'Thank you, Sir,' Abioseh said dutifully, knowing that the only viable self-defence against Baluba was a gun. But he didn't tell the Colonel.

'I bet the other guy looks worse, hey?' asked the Colonel. 'Who was it, by the way?'

'Baluba.' Abioseh guessed that his father already knew.

'Oh,' the Colonel said. 'One of the Jambo brothers. You must watch them. Their father runs a mortuary, so they are familiar with death.'

Father and son didn't know how prophetic those words were. Later in the month, on Boxing Day, Abioseh took a call from Hiero.

'What's up, Hiero?' Abioseh was still upset with him.

'David's dead,' Hiero said. Then he wept.

4

THE FUNERAL WAS at 8.00 AM on New Year's Eve. Early that morning, Hiero arrived by taxi at the gates of Mariposa, dressed in a sombre black soutane-style tunic, matching trousers and black shoes. A few minutes later, the presidential limo edged out and stopped to pick him up. He joined Abioseh, also in black, at the front, it being a rigorous security measure that the president always occupied the back seat beside the bodyguard and diagonally opposite the driver. MaZembe had elected to stay behind.

As the car wove through the morning traffic, connected, as it were, by invisible thongs to the outriders on motorcycles, Abioseh was struck by the gulf, both physical and spatial, between the Colonel and the two young men. He had barely responded to Hiero's good morning, staring straight ahead. The Colonel's body language was of someone who wanted to be left alone. Abioseh wondered if Hiero's story of the encounter in the field hadn't been the product of a febrile mind.

The traffic rolled on outside, the minibus taxis adding to the noise of the city with their indiscriminate honking. The streetlamps, in defiance of the government's injunction towards saving energy, were ablaze; so, too, were Christmas decorations strung along Revolution Boulevard like the illumination guiding aircraft along a runway. The Colonel gave no sign that he was aware of what was happening outside the car; his interest only seemed to be pricked at the sight of a man in rags sitting inside the fenced-in park at the traffic circle. 'Where's the service again?' the Colonel asked.

'St Theresa's Catholic Church,' answered the bodyguard, startled; Abioseh suspected that he had begun to doze.

'Is that Father Mitchum's church?'

'Yes, Colonel.'

'What really happened?' The Colonel sounded genuinely curious – and troubled. 'To the boy.'

There was silence as if everyone wanted the Colonel's question to answer itself. Then Hiero spoke. 'It was a car accident,' he said.

Abioseh looked out of the window at the morning people. Some were dressed in their finery, others in clothes that spoke of a struggle. Here, young people, elderly people, walking, trudging the pavements, a few stopping in mid-stride to gaze at the magnificent sedan rolling past. Here, on the long boulevard to honour the heroes of a forgotten revolution, policemen controlled the traffic, their arms spread wide as if they were about to push back a deluge threatening to engulf the island. The buildings of the city that had once been the pride of the pioneers, which were now encrusted with stubborn layers of dust, stood silhouetted against the dirty sky. *Does the Colonel ever see the state of the city? Of the country? Of the people?*

He couldn't, Abioseh concluded; *it is difficult to see anything if you have lent your eyes to others.* The bodyguards had to test the Colonel's food against poison; everywhere he went, there was a presumption that someone wished him dead. In a life so full of measures to eliminate surprises,

what could one look forward to? The Colonel saw what he was supposed
to see; he met the people he was supposed to meet at the stipulated hour.
His somnolent pose in the car was occasionally animated by the sighting of an attractive woman, the eyes scanning height, weight, age – the
vital statistics – and filing data away for future application. To Abioseh,
the naturalness of this behaviour, the lack of self-consciousness simply
meant that the Colonel couldn't help himself. In a life where mysteries
were taboo, it seemed to Abioseh that the only mystery the Colonel
could get pleasure from was the probable texture of the anonymous flesh
that would enfold him in assignations far from home.

In spite of the judgements against his father, Abioseh could still appreciate that the Colonel had interrupted his busy schedule to attend
David Kone's funeral. Even though propriety called for his presence, as
the deceased was the son of his Chief Justice, he could have easily delegated the unpleasant task to one of his ministers, Carlos Nobrega for
example. *Where was the Rock of Ages?* Abioseh wondered. He also pondered
what the real reason for his dislike was. He didn't have long to think
about it, though, because the driver said, 'Here we are.'

THE CHURCH SEEMED smaller and somehow different from what Hiero
remembered. The homeless had disappeared and the pews were occupied
by a well-scrubbed congregation in raiment of mourning. He had a hard
time keeping a straight face when he saw Zebulon sitting on the last row
but one, bent forward with his ungainly arms hovering over his ankles,
staring at the altar. He was conscious that he was in the presidential
party. The group of eminent persons was aware of its power. Hoping to
minimise its impact on such a tragic occasion, it entered as silently as it
could. But heads turned at their entrance, alerted to the presence of the
Colonel by the urgent smile of the usher. While hurrying on tiptoe, he
gave off the effect of walking slowly and respecting the dead while paying obeisance to the living president. He conducted them to the front
row where the family sat, Gwandon Kone's hoary head contrasting with

the general gloom of the church. David's mother sat with her face hidden under her great black hat, her shoulders shaking as she sobbed, now and then dabbing her secret eyes with a lacy white handkerchief.

Although the coffin on the bier was a little lower than the altar in the front, it still dominated the church; a riot of flowers covered almost every inch of the mahogany box and its shiny golden handles. A formal portrait presented to the assembly a smiling and vividly alive David Kone, a slightly raised eyebrow accentuating his boyishness. The picture reminded Hiero of an exhibition he had seen in Panza, of Ga coffins in Ghana, where people could order caskets reflecting their lives and loves. One vain character was buried in a coffin replica of his favourite Mercedes-Benz, complete with registration plates. One or two others requested to be buried in wooden representations of mobile phones or bottles of their choice beer. *What vehicle would have tickled David Kone's fancy, for him to arrive in heaven in style? And,* Hiero asked himself, *what's my coffin of choice?*

Father Mitchum stood up from behind the altar and strode to the microphone, which was to the left of the coffin. Seeming weary, he started off by welcoming the Kone family and expressing his hope that the short service for David would go some distance towards assuaging their sense of loss. Then he acknowledged the president. This was the first time His Excellency had graced the humble house of God. He hoped that this would be the start of many such engagements, hopefully under more propitious circumstances. Then he sat down.

A middle-aged black priest Hiero had not seen before, who had earlier been chatting to Father Mitchum behind the altar, stepped forward and cleared his throat. 'Today,' he said in a strong voice, 'we'll depart from procedure and do exactly what the Kone family requested us *not* to do.'

He paused and smiled, the strange and pained smile of someone about to make enemies. 'For those of you who don't know who I am,' said the priest, 'my name is Father Aloysius Rodrigues. From my name you'll gather that I'm a Creole and proud of it.' He stood watching the congregation for a while. 'Many of you will wonder why it's so important to tell you that I'm a Creole. The reason is simple. We have these names, these labels, so that we may identify each other and lock each other up in the prison of our fears.'

'I'm glad that the president of the republic has graced this occasion,' Father Rodrigues continued. 'I'm also happy that all of you are here, because it is you who'll have to call by their true names all the things we've been speaking about in whispers. David is dead – and all of you wonder what happened. Some of you might have heard that he died in a motor-car accident. He *was* driving, all right. But the truth is,' Father Rodrigues said, glancing at the family, the mother's weeping rising in volume, 'the truth is, David took his own life.'

If the church had been quiet before, the silence that followed was almost complete. Then it was punctuated by muffled sobs and by two or three people who blew their noses loudly. 'David took his own life,' the priest repeated. 'We'll never know what depths of despair drove a young man to that decision. What we know – what has been disclosed to us and the family – is that he had contracted the blood plague. Yes,' Father Rodrigues said, 'the blood plague. The family had sworn me to secrecy that this would never be disclosed. But I'm a man of God; I'm a product of my conscience. And my conscience tells me that there'll be many more deaths if we don't name the horror that stalks us all.'

Hiero caught Abioseh shooting a sharp glance at the Colonel and then looking straight ahead. The Colonel had an attentive look on his face, like someone listening to a report, perhaps in a Cabinet meeting.

'Anyway,' Father Rodrigues said, 'there are people here who've offered support to the family, who were with them from day one. I'll ask Zebulon Gondo and Baluba Jambo to come forward and stand at the head and foot of the coffin. That is a request from the family. It is also the family's way of saying thank you.' He paused. 'The choir should also prepare to give us a musical item.'

Hiero wondered if Baluba Jambo and Zebulon Gondo, who were

walking up the aisle, would also be joining the choir to ease the sorrow of the bereaved. He watched them going up the short flight of stairs to the altar. Zebulon, stunned, was in his usual dark suit although he had spruced up a bit; Baluba, still sporting a black eye, which must have given Abioseh a measure of satisfaction, was visibly chuffed with the accolade, bowing to his father the undertaker, who also sat in the front row with the family. The two young men took up their respective positions in relation to the casket. The choristers, all dressed in flowing blue robes, filed past the coffin and arranged themselves behind Zebulon and Baluba, their conductor off to the side, baton in hand.

Someone hidden must have given the nod, because the conductor suddenly hunched his shoulders and slashed the air with his baton. Then voices filled the church with a song that spoke of thousands who had never reached the Promised Land. Hiero had heard the song before, including at choir practice at Alfredo Romero. They used to peep through the crack in the plywood room divider at the young women, mainly from the higher primary classes. David had had his eye on one Zoya Badawi, who, although the youngest and shortest in the choir, could render outstanding soprano solos.

Now Hiero watched her singing, her arms folded across her stillgirlish bosom, the sound mingling with the many voices, surging into the air and becoming part of the subdued weeping:

> *Thousands and thousands*
> *And thousands are marching . . .*

The singing that rang through the church was stopped by a signal from Father Rodrigues. He then proceeded with the funeral prayer. After that he bowed towards the family and the assembled dignitaries, his eyes lingering on the Colonel. Father Mitchum came forward and took the microphone. He thanked all the people present and then invited the Colonel to say a few words if he wished. The Colonel declined, waving a polite hand.

Then the pallbearers, consisting of Zebulon, Baluba, two basketball players and two members of the family lifted the casket to their shoulders and started down the steps to the aisle. The front row with the family and the dignitaries followed. Hiero walked in step with Abioseh.

'Are we going to the cemetery?' he asked.

'The Colonel's going back home,' Abioseh said. 'I guess I'll join him.' He paused, looking at the backs of the pallbearers. 'So,' he said, 'that's Zebulon.'

'Yes,' Hiero said. 'If you were coming to the cemetery, I'd introduce you.'

'We'll find the right moment for that.'

'Yes,' Hiero agreed, 'the time will come.'

IN THE CAR on the way back to Mariposa, the Colonel pressed his face against the window, looking at the crowds that had gathered outside the church. There was a crush of bodies all along Revolution Boulevard to the traffic circle, where the cops were still busy directing traffic. 'I hate funerals,' he said.

'Why didn't you accept the invitation to say a few words?' Abioseh asked.

'I'd have been forced,' the Colonel replied, 'to defend the government I head. Funerals are a good place for malcontents to vent their spleens.' He laughed grimly. 'I couldn't possibly steal their thunder.'

PART THREE

POWER

I

HIERO WAS AWARE of a different thunder that came from the mountains. Four years after David Kone's memorable funeral, people started speaking, at first in hushed tones and then with stronger voices. They said that many young men had disappeared into the mountains following David's death. As Hiero was a relative newcomer to Security Affairs, with just twelve months' experience, he still had a lot to learn. What he knew, though, was that the young men had gone for military training and he believed that he might know some of them from Alfredo Romero.

But why, he asked himself, *would anyone drum up a revolt against the Colonel? Didn't the Colonel institute the Reform, a system that has changed the lives of so many people for the better? But then — was life better, now?* For instance, in addition to the unending scourge of the blood plague, Bangula was in the grip of a maize shortage. And while people endured the hot sun as they queued for their rations of yellow kernels, they voiced their suspicion: *The Colonel is giving all the maize to the army.*

As a liaison officer between the military and Security Affairs, Hiero was privy to confidential information; he was best placed to know if there was any truth in the accusation. He knew there was nothing of the sort. In fact, and this was scary, there were rumblings in the army over the conveyance of infected patients, most of them already at death's door, to the quarantine camp. But, even there, the grumbling was mainly directed at Dr Ahmod Badawi, who was seen as the architect of the scheme. The Colonel was a past master at deflecting unwanted attention to others. But, Hiero knew, it was only a matter of time before the spotlight was put on the leader.

Hiero felt that the Colonel needed defending. In this regard, he differed from his friend, Abioseh. The latter, a member of the select committee on communications, tended to be less than complimentary about his father. Although Abioseh had found his own place away from his parents, he would still go and see them.

'Every time I visit the old folks,' he told Hiero, 'I come back depressed.'

It was midday on the 18th of February, the first day after the opening of parliament. The parliamentary canteen was still festive with streamers and buntings and the colours of the different political parties on every table. The food, too, had the flavour of leftovers from yesterday's feast as Abioseh discovered when he took a bite of a steak and kidney pie. Quickly he washed it down with a Coke. 'Tastes like cardboard,' he commented.

'Parents,' Hiero said, 'were invented by God to depress their kids.' He paused, looking at the parliamentary clerks trailing MPs. 'Point to remember, however, is that the time for this mutual aggravation is short. Before you know it, the Jambo brothers are helping you choose a coffin for one of them.'

'My folks,' Abioseh said, 'look set to live forever.'

'Don't count on it.' Hiero started laughing. When Abioseh gave him a puzzled look, he asked, 'Did you hear what happened to Father Rodrigues?'

'The priest at David's service?' Abioseh asked. 'What happened?'

'Well,' Hiero said, 'you know he's been a right royal pain in the arse, banging on about the blood plague, writing letters to the editor and giving poor old Dr Badawi a shitty time.'

'Yes?'

'Well,' Hiero said, laughing ahead of the punch line, 'seems like he's been dabbling in a little sideline involving altar boys. They caught him in flagrante delicto with two of them, drunk as a newt, in the Commodore.'

'But does it make sense to go to such a public hotel for hanky-panky?' Abioseh asked. He recalled sincerity blazing in the priest's eyes.

'Who's to know,' Hiero commented, 'what motivates men?'

'I thought that understanding our weaknesses was your department,' Abioseh said. 'That way you can lay a trap for us.'

'Are you suggesting that the priest was trapped?' Something grating had come into Hiero's tone. 'Our job is to safeguard the state. It's got nothing to do with providing temptation.'

'Perhaps,' Abioseh said, 'you're focusing on the strong part of the state and leaving the weak side unprotected.'

'Perhaps,' Hiero said, shrugging. 'Who knows?'

Who knows, indeed? Abioseh thought. The ongoing deaths from the blood plague, an epidemic that did not exist officially, were an affront to him. Every week, scores of bodies were buried in the cemetery near Cinnamon Hill. There was an unfunny joke doing the rounds that, since the mortuary was full to bursting, Mr Jambo was the only one not complaining.

He forgot about death when the two men braved a sudden downpour to rush to Hiero's car. 'I want to show you,' Hiero said, 'that, for all your protestations, you're no different from us.'

'What do you mean?' Abioseh asked, panting slightly.

'You're part of the ruling class,' Hiero said slyly. 'And what's more — you love it.' He laughed as he started the car. 'You're like those animal rights' people who have no conflict with eating chicken curry.'

I'm not a hypocrite, Abioseh thought. 'Where are we going? I didn't even lock my office ...'

'We're going to see power in action,' Hiero said. 'Your power.'

LIKE MOST PEOPLE in the maw of transition from one social system to another, Abioseh was still tentative towards the exercise of power, however essential. He had watched the Colonel slowly accepting as inevitable certain practices that he had earlier dismissed as unnecessary trumpery. Abioseh had been amused when the Colonel winced whenever guns were discharged during gun salutes on state occasions; but now, it was all par for the course. Still, Abioseh felt a twinge of shame when, despite his protestations, the parliamentary office still laid on a chauffeured sedan to ferry him to and from work, especially since his workplace was less than two kilometres from his house. There were many MPs like him who enjoyed a lifestyle unattainable for the vast majority of the population. For him, it was not so much the embarrassment of extravagance as a fear that he might acquire a taste for this lifestyle. In his reckoning, the Reform, which emphasised a kind of humanism, need not squander resources; conspicuous consumption, he knew, gave birth to greed and unrealistic expectations that could lead to illicit practices.

As a member of the select committee on communications, he tried to do his work diligently, avoiding conduct that would reflect badly on the Colonel. He knew that the self-appointed protectors of the public primed journalists to investigate him. They waited for him to slip up so that they could swat him like a fly; *the media giveth*, it had been said, *and the media taketh away*. Behind the scenes, there were all sorts of probes to determine if he was taking bribes.

Those who would benefit from his downfall were not limited to the media. There were people waiting to take over once 'the Colonel loosened his grasp on the levers of power', a euphemism favoured by editors. For instance, on Sunday, during the week of parliament's opening, the

Colonel had been particularly peeved.

'Why,' he had thundered, throwing aside the newspapers he'd been reading, 'don't they just come right out and dance on my grave? We're all going to die one day!'

'What's wrong?' MaZembe feared he might rupture himself.

'All that claptrap about levers of power. I'm not a tractor driver,' he had snapped in a momentary lapse into immodesty, 'I am the *Colonel*.'

He *was* the Colonel and Abioseh and the government lived under his shadow. For the son, the subdued chatter and murmured rumours about succession were particularly tiresome because he had no ambitions to the presidency. It was enough that his father was the head of state; this was not a dynasty, but a modern democracy. Moreover, not all of the people who *coveted* the presidential seat would step forward and throw their hats into the ring. No. These things were done better via proxies, through praise singers and political cheerleaders. In these situations, a lot of money passed hands.

Abioseh knew that he was as hungry as the next man, but he had drawn a line on active campaigning for any position and was proud to have attained his current position on merit.

After majoring in electrical engineering, Abioseh had entered the public broadcasting service responsible for both radio and television. Hardly a year later, the national telecoms giant, Bancom, which needed indigenous personnel to take over from the Americans, poached him. Even though he sometimes wondered, as he rose swiftly from Chief Technical Officer to CEO whether his family name had influenced his ascent to these heights, Abioseh could justify the appointment. He *was*, after all, one of the few qualified people in Bangula. Then he was forced to quit his job at the top, taking a pay cut, on orders from the Cabinet, when one of the MPs died in a car accident and the Cabinet invoked a little-used statute to swear in a deserving public servant. Abioseh Gondo was that candidate.

Life at the select committee was routine, with long meetings among some members given to admiring their own voices. The debates over certain provisions of legislation, in which the lobbyists from Bancom traded insults with public-sector activists, provided the only periods of excitement. Each of the two groups proclaimed its value to consumers. 'I do declare, Honourable Members,' an exasperated Dr Caramel Sebone-Prah, the chairwoman of the committee, quipped one day, 'at this rate the consumer is bound to choke on an excess of goodwill.'

In these meetings, Abioseh tried to stay unobtrusive, declining to show up the ignorance of his colleagues. Some arrived at the meetings having neglected to read the literature, ending up being bamboozled by the official opposition that came to sessions readily armed with sheaves of research findings and accomplished condescension. 'Why can't the ruling party,' Graham Hollingsworth, Leader of the Official Opposition (or LOO), would ask, 'make *proper* use of Mr Abioseh Gondo, seeing as he's the only one in the committee with the formidable qualifications of poacher-turned-gamekeeper, ha ha?' Knowing that the proceedings were being broadcast live, Abioseh would keep a straight face while he fumed. *You pompous oaf*, he thought, *it would be nice to poach your backside in a dark alley one day.*

He watched as people played their games, occasionally attempting to embroil him in them. There were some of the Cabinet ministers who couldn't have made it anywhere else, but the Colonel turned a blind eye to their incompetence. It was widely believed that he didn't want to create ructions with the ministers because he needed all hands on deck against rebel activity growing in the mountains.

Vice-President Carlos Nobrega, a scion of Creole nobles who could trace their bloodline to the royal court of Carlos I of Portugal, never passed up an opportunity to demonstrate his suitability as the Colonel's successor. A man of legendary competence, he kept himself and his achievements unobtrusively visible. He was, however, smart enough to credit the Colonel's wise leadership as the inspiration for any of his own accomplishments.

Even though their relations had been strained some years earlier,

Abioseh could still admire Nobrega, who had matured gracefully. Tall and angular, his black hair streaked with silver, he had an aristocratic air about him, which might have earned him the nickname of The Hawk. But Abioseh knew that the name came from the widespread knowledge that Nobrega's specially selected people were his eyes and ears in all the country's security structures. Even though he had nothing to hide, Abioseh was determined to watch himself around Nobrega.

HE WAS STILL in a watchful mood, wondering where Hiero was taking him, when they pulled up at the marina.

'You go in there,' Hiero said pointing at a yacht, 'and I'll see you in a minute.'

'Whose yacht is it?' Abioseh asked, hating Hiero's mysterious ways.

'Just go,' Hiero said, driving off. 'And loosen up.'

He was therefore cautiously looking forward to enjoying himself when he found himself at the launch of Nobrega's boat. It was a beautiful forty-eight-foot symphony of wood, chrome and fibreglass boasting an engine capable of doing a speed of twenty-three knots. Carlos Nobrega, informal in a loose cream cheesecloth shirt, lemon chinos and tan moccasins, appeared nothing like a no-nonsense leader a hairsbreadth away from the most powerful seat in the land. Paradoxically, his casual attire gave off an air of understated power that was sometimes voiced when the prosperous of the land dressed down. 'Welcome,' Carlos Nobrega kept saying, nodding, pointing to two young women standing with trays loaded with drinks in tall glasses, 'welcome.'

Speaking in a tone that belied his pride in owning such a vessel, Nobrega extolled the virtues of boating. 'It's more than a pleasure,' he said. 'It's a passion.' Taking them on a guided tour, he waxed lyrical about the use of aluminium, pointing out that it was optimal for structural integrity. 'Fibreglass,' he went on, 'tends to crack under stress, especially after electrical installation.'

Most of his audience, with the exception of Abioseh, didn't know what Nobrega was on about, but were willing to indulge him if it meant access to the sophisticated styling of the salon, staterooms and the huge master suite. It was like walking into a luxury apartment. Back in the sunlight, Nobrega demonstrated the fire and safety procedures required before setting sail.

The day was in agreement with the magnitude of the occasion, the guests getting a soft waft of the salty noonday breeze, the sea bluer than the sky, waves scudding gently against the hull. Other yachts and an assortment of smaller craft bobbed and danced as if in rhythm with something pleasurable pulsating from inside them. Catamarans sliced through water, tourists standing on the decks, holding onto rails, content with the government of the day, which could lay on such splendid sailing weather.

But beneath all this, the sea gave off the smell of the rotting of ancient things. It was a ubiquitous odour, speaking of the squalor behind the fences separating the waterfront from the shanty town, which spread out in waves, a galvanised iron replication of the configuration of the sea.

One by one or in twos and threes people clambered on board, onto the foredeck, helping themselves to bubbly and snacks. Abioseh exchanged pleasantries with three or four captains of industry and a few sports and entertainment personalities. There were women in slinky dresses and borrowed blonde hair extensions either braided and shot through with coloured beads or simply left flowing freely. The women's burnt-umber skin tones suggested an unclaimed lineage. There was a model known simply as Jacqui, who smoked a long cigarette held between her thumb and forefinger. It was only when the smoke wafted in his direction that he got a whiff of the sickly-sweet smell of marijuana, surprised that he was taken aback even though the weed had long been legalised. She sensed him looking at her and, without turning her head, extended her arm in the fashion of a knife thrower hefting a new dagger. 'Smoke?'

'No thanks,' Abioseh declined.

Jacqui turned to him. 'Why?' She smiled, 'Papa's spooks spooking you?'

'No,' Abioseh replied, a trifle irritated. 'I just don't smoke.' It was a lie since he took the occasional puff under controlled circumstances. But it rankled that people imagined he needed his father's permission.

'Pity,' Jacqui said, shrugging and flicking the joint into the water. For a moment he watched her profile as she stood gazing absently at the water, seeming smaller and frailer, certainly different from the magazine photos and the images on television. Barefooted, she padded to where Nobrega was holding court amidst a gaggle of eager faces, her scent of wild flowers infiltrating the trace of salt in the air. Jacqui must have said something because there was a brief pause in their conversation as they turned to gaze at Abioseh. He was aware of the croak of a seagull that preceded peals of laughter. Somehow he felt a strange calm and an absence of rancour towards Nobrega, Jacqui and the group of young men and women resplendent in garments acquired from exotic shores.

There was a sudden flurry of activity as the marina was cleared of vessels and gave way to two coastguard boats manned by armed policemen wearing flak jackets. They were escorting a group of VIPs, including some of the military top brass, Cabinet ministers and two or three Bancom executives. Dr Caramel Sebone-Prah beamed with girlish excitement as Wonderman Bhele, who had recently landed a Cabinet post, lifted her and set her delicately on the deck as Ministers Caswell Stone, Hamilton Sodoku and the eternally quiet and unruffled Marcia Baraka, looked on. In a minute, Hiero, leading the procession with the Colonel standing head and shoulders above a phalanx of bodyguards, climbed up the wooden steps and stepped into the boat.

Forgetting the well-dressed hangers-on and gently edging Jacqui aside, Carlos Nobrega turned to his illustrious guest. He opened his arms and received the Colonel in a generous embrace. Above his deputy's shoulder, his nostrils working as if prickled by something suspiciously sweet, the Colonel's eyes locked with his son's. *I wonder*, Abioseh thought, *if he smells a rat?*

Then Abioseh heard the sound of music coming from the lower berths, as if carried by a cloud, soft and full of unendurable longing; the wind suddenly stilled. Feeling out of place, Abioseh stared at the light that crowned a cake and counted seven candles – a candle for each decade – embedded in icing and coloured sweetness; the legend *Happy 70th Colonel*, in honeyed lettering, bled into a depiction of the national flag executed in minute detail, which nestled in the corner.

Held aloft by the hands of young people, the cake seemed to have a life of its own. It was no longer the sum of its sweet parts but a magical object, an enchanted incarnation of the pricelessness of the honouree. The voices that accompanied its ascent increased in volume, the melody segueing into a conventional rendition of a birthday song:

> *Happy birthday to you*
> *Happy birthday dear Colonel* ...

Nobrega's rich baritone led the guests in a song that took the edge off the cawing of birds and subdued the hooting of shipping vessels. In the distance, a speedboat trailing a water-skier cut through the waves soundlessly, like a pantomime of itself, the spray churning against a field of turquoise.

During all this, Abioseh could feel his father's eyes on him although he was sure that the old man wasn't actually seeing him but was staring at something buried deep inside him. Abioseh berated himself for forgetting the birthday, even though as a family they weren't big on anniversaries; he couldn't even remember when his mother's birthday was. Besides, the actual day and time that the Colonel had emerged covered in blood out of his mother's womb was shrouded in mystery.

The Colonel, it was widely held, had been born in the midst of a devastating cyclone; today's festivities were derived from information supplied by historians and government image-makers. *Whatever the actual date,* Abioseh thought, *it was exactly this neglect, this lapse, on which people like Nobrega capitalised*. Even if his father weren't given to pomp and circumstance, there was something satisfying about people observing your birthday. As with visiting the sick or comforting the bereaved, it was a degree to which friends showed that they cared.

He was brought back to the present, when a light flashed across from the whitewashed building at the top of the hill and rebounded on the aluminium fittings of the boat. Abioseh looked at the men and women who were still assembled on the foredeck, Jacqui belting out a bluesy coda to the birthday song:

> *For he's a jolly good fellow . . .*
> *And so say all of us . . .*

Somewhere off the top of the hill that had been gashed as if by giant chisels to construct a chalk-white quarry, from which jutted out a fort that faced the water, two cannon originally mounted to protect the enterprise of slavery shuddered and discharged bluish smoke as they announced midday.

Even as Jacqui sang, standing dwarfed between Nobrega and the Colonel, their arms laced over and around her exquisite bare shoulders, she held Abioseh's gaze steadily in hers. Smiling, Jacqui invited him to join the two men's disastrous attempts to follow a dance routine she was trying to teach them, the spur-of-the-moment lesson progressively degenerating into an inelegant shuffle punctuated by self-mocking laughter. It occurred to Abioseh that he'd never seen his father this carefree. The realisation brought forth a spasm of craving; the wine was flowing, but doctor's orders were that he couldn't have a drink. Cursing the cold that had given him the sniffles which seemed destined to last forever, Abioseh wondered if the men – singly or in concert – had ever slept with Jacqui.

Abioseh was also tired of people – women – losing faith in him. Having grown up on the island, he felt the claustrophobia of everyone knowing everyone's business. As the child of a prominent family, he sometimes wondered when women offered themselves to him, using words or the ageless language of the body, whether it was because he was his father's son. And sometimes, at the urging of his flesh, he succumbed and quenched his thirst, often waking up in the morning next to an anonymous body, overcome with self-loathing. Here, though, he watched his father and his deputy and the woman, their gestures speaking familiarly of days and nights of exploration.

Just then, Hiero approached from the head, zipping up his trousers. 'She's beautiful,' he asked, 'isn't she?'

For a moment, and since she had been on his mind, Abioseh thought that Hiero was remarking on Jacqui's visible attributes, but then realised that he meant the boat. Hiero was not alone in this; a crew member was giving a running commentary to six or seven young people, directing their attention to the bunk with a locker and hanging space in the forward starboard cabin; the lazaretto and packing space amidships and aft; the fluorescent lighting in the cabins, galley and cockpit and the intricate navigational instruments. Correcting his attitude, Abioseh agreed. 'I wonder,' he said, 'how much Nobrega paid for this little baby?'

'It must have cost a pretty penny,' Hiero answered. And then, out of the blue, he asked, 'When last did you hear from Zebulon?'

'Strange,' Abioseh said. 'I've had my mother asking the same question only last week. I must be missing something.'

MAZEMBE HAD DROPPED in on him unannounced last Friday, her timing perfect for he had just driven from parliament to the gated village where civil servants and MPs enjoyed a secluded existence. Abioseh hated the place, christened, possibly in bitter irony, Fear-the-Dog Village. It was a square mile of a passably bland, face-brick housing complex with all the modern trimmings, including maids and pools, which boasted the greatest concentration of the canine population throughout Bangula.

As civil servants made their way from their offices along the paved walkways to Fear-the-Dog, the air would be filled with the excited yelps and yowls from breeds that ran the gamut from the Affenpinscher to the Yorkshire terrier. It was Abioseh's conviction that the rise or decline of any civilisation could be determined by dog owners' attitudes towards their pets. He believed that the middle- and upper-classes of Bangula, whose fortunes had dramatically improved in inverse proportion to the impoverishment of the multitudes, regarded dog ownership as unAfrican, and therefore as close as possible to the ideal condition of whiteness. Of course, he knew, there *were* people who really loved animals, but it was the status-seekers, the social climbers, who got his goat.

Fear-the-Dog was separated by a gravel dual carriageway from the neighbourhood of Desoluso, whose most prestigious villa, Mariposa, was the official residence of the president. From where Abioseh stood, the Commodore Hotel loomed above and behind the antenna and satellite dishes on the roof of the president's place. The gardens and orchards were a riot of greens, reds and oranges, an explosion of flora common along the seaside. The thick and pampered lawns were much like the dogs and flamingos imported to the island by the French.

As the day died, servants moved quietly and purposefully to their modest neighbourhoods, some armed with plastic bags containing samples of their masters' garbage, like watermelon rinds, which they would exhibit among their peers as testimony to their own indirect prosperity.

On this late Friday afternoon, Abioseh had meant to drop his bag, shower and change and then rush to his favourite bar twelve kilometres away. The Blue Parrot was a spot that allowed Abioseh to be the young man he thought he was rather than his father's son. He regretted having turned down an offer of a lift with some of his colleagues, known party animals who would also be doing the nightclub circuit. Abioseh had already mentally prepared himself for the solitary drive, a rare opportunity for someone constantly shackled to a chauffeur, when he could wrestle with his own demons. And there were many.

He loved his mother but could have killed her then and there; he studied her with rising irritation as she bent to pat a neighbour's bulldog at the entrance to his four-roomed bachelor's residence.

Absently stroking the exact bulldog that her son couldn't stand, Ma-Zembe stared into the distance, shrugged and sighed. 'Abioseh?' she called softly, 'Is that all you're going to do? Make your mother wait instead of opening the gate?'

'The gate is not locked, Ma,' he grumbled. On the lawn were four or five plastic shopping bags. MaZembe's well-kept black sedan stood parked on the side of the road. Her bodyguard must have helped her carry the shopping, but she would be damned if she would be seen lugging bags into her son's place. This had nothing to do with a First Lady putting on airs; she was his mother and it was his duty to act like a son.

'So many people all of a sudden,' she commented, waving at the faces that had massed on lawns and in loudly congested doorways to stare at the wife of the president. 'Where do they all come from?'

'They are your subjects, Ma'am,' Abioseh said.

Before opening the gate, he had meant to give her a token kiss on her cheeks as usual, but she held him with a surprising intensity, forcing him to look at her. She was always dressed in some dark fabric. During rare pleasant exchanges, he debated whether to ask her why she was in mourning even though her husband was still alive. At the back of his head was the mischievous notion that MaZembe was in mourning exactly because the Colonel was *not* dead.

Today, though, her head was covered in a brocaded aquamarine head-scarf, which set off her regulation, shoulder-padded, cobalt-blue two-piece suit and low-heeled leather pumps. The new worry lines around her eyes alerted him to the inexorable march of time that would finally end in the grave. The thought that his mother would one day disappear quickened his pulse. There was something disloyal about even thinking about the possibility of her death.

Unaware that she could be the cause of a certain level of anxiety, Ma-Zembe chattered on about the barrenness of the ground and the unadorned lawn, swiped at the lack of flowers and, as a solution, offered to loan him her gardener to spruce things up. Convinced that the gardener would be another one of her many spies, Abioseh sidestepped the offer and chose another tack. 'How's the Colonel?' *Howz de Kolonel?* Assuming the mountain accent.

'How come you never call him your father?' MaZembe sounded genuinely cross. It could have been that she had been sincere in her offer and was unhappy that her son had chosen to judge her. 'He's your father, you know that?'

Abioseh opened the door and ushered his mother into the lounge, hoping that Abdullah's housekeeping would meet her superior standards. The room, as hot as it was stuffy, was mercifully tidy. Depositing the parcels and his bag on the floor, Abioseh quickly opened the windows, silently cursing Abdullah for turning his place into a hothouse. 'Abdullah thinks that thieves are going to pack up the house and steal everything,' he said. 'But what is there to steal here, except for official government furniture?'

MaZembe stood in the middle of the lounge, looking around as if she were the only survivor of a shipwreck. Her attentiveness directed him to examine his home. He noticed the bleak wallpaper, which was peeling off in parts, and the curtains that suddenly seemed drabber than usual, which folded to expose the lace lining flecked with the remains of gnats and flies. The vinyl covering was scuffed and cracked in the section nearest the door and the tables and chairs were bruised by constantly bumping into unyielding walls, perhaps in the process of moving. A flowerless vase rested on the crocheted table covering, the only ornament that spoke of the creative generosity of a human hand. Abioseh was suddenly very thirsty. 'Something to drink, Ma?'

'A glass of water.' MaZembe eased herself onto the settee, which, from her facial expression, must have been clumpy and uncomfortable. The large piece of furniture seemed out of place in the lounge, like an article snapped up in a street sale during an unguarded moment. As he was about to turn towards the kitchen, MaZembe called out, 'And don't bother with bottled water. Tap water will do.'

Having given up on any plans to slake a different type of thirst among workmates and women whose charms would increase with the emptying of a glass of brew, Abioseh rummaged in the fridge and was able to give his mother a glass of orange juice. He still brought her the water she had requested, but felt that he needed to redeem himself in her eyes. Even as she sat, sipping at her drinks without enthusiasm, her lips puckering at the bitterness of the stale citrus, he knew that his mother's disappointment probably had its genesis long before he was conceived. 'Are you happy, Ma?' Abioseh asked.

She looked up at him, a sad smile on her face. 'I was about to ask you that same question,' MaZembe said. 'I'm glad to see that there's another mind reader in the Gondo stock.'

'Who else reads minds?' Abioseh asked. 'The Colonel?'

'I wish,' MaZembe said, 'that were the case. Then all of us would be spared the trouble of trying to second-guess the traditionalists and their newfound allies, the Creole League. But I'm talking about Zebulon, in this instance.'

Zebulon. He had not cropped up in any real conversation Abioseh had had with members of his family in a long time. In fact, there seemed to be an unwritten law that Zebulon would not be discussed in any of the circles in which Abioseh found himself. People were reticent in Abioseh's presence, even while the media were loud in the land about Zebulon's exploits. It wasn't in anything said. There was no rule that outlawed people from broaching the subject of his half-brother. It was society's way of getting around awkward family secrets.

But what was the secret? Maybe MaZembe held the key. 'Whose mind has Zebulon read?' Abioseh asked. He wanted to add, *in the past twenty-four hours*, even though MaZembe was particularly averse to sarcasm or any nastiness. But he wished to say something that would cut to the quick; his mother had no business cluttering up his Friday evening with negative energy. 'The Colonel's?'

'No one can read the Colonel's mind, least of all the Colonel,'

MaZembe said. 'But I hear that the churches are now supporting Zebu-lon. They say he has a gift and can see into the future.'

'How nice,' Abioseh said. He wasn't interested.

'Yes. They say that the Colonel has reached an age when his back could get tired, so he needs a staff with which to prop himself up.' Ma-Zembe had flattened her voice, making everything sound matter of fact. 'A strong staff.'

'I always thought that the Colonel could use the Creole one,' Abioseh said. 'Carlos Nobrega.'

'Carlos Nobrega is temporary,' MaZembe said, 'a stop-gap.' She paused. 'They say that their first choice would be the Colonel's son. Blood they can trust.'

'And they trust Zebulon's?'

'Why not? Yours is too precious for such mundane duties.'

'Good luck to them,' Abioseh said. 'I'm glad that issue is now re-solved.'

'Your obstinacy will send me to an early grave, Abi,' MaZembe said. 'You refuse to come to terms with what is staring you in the face. Your father would like you to take over from him.'

'I'm not carved from quality wood, Ma,' Abioseh said, 'not cut out to make a strong staff.'

'Your father,' MaZembe began, 'did not start out the strong man he is today.' She paused, staring as if picturing a feebler version of the Col-onel. 'In fact,' she said, 'there's no such a thing as a man who's strong of his own accord; strength is acquired, nurtured, like you nurse something precious.' She paused. 'However, I didn't always know this. When your father took over from Ramala, he became the country's most powerful man, but inside he felt as weak as a baby. And he was lonely.'

'Lonely?' Abioseh couldn't imagine the Colonel, who drew people to him like bees to honey, being lonely.

'Yes,' MaZembe said. 'Something had happened to him ... or he must have seen something that undermined him. He would be with people, his friends and colleagues, but there was always a part of him that was elsewhere.'

'Where were you in all this?' Abioseh asked.

'I was there,' MaZembe answered, 'but I don't think that I was there for him. Do you know what I mean by that?'

'Tell me.'

'I suppose,' she began, 'I thought that I'd allow him to grow into the role, become the president of the republic, the Colonel, the man of the people, who was sought everywhere. But what I didn't know, until it was too late, was that he really wanted me to be *with* him, to *talk* to him, to make him feel that we were together ... in that sense, he could consume you, his demands sap you of energy.' She gazed into the gathering night. 'The mistake we make,' MaZembe said softly, 'is to keep at bay those who need us. And by the time we wake up to the fact that *we* also need *them*, they're long gone. Human beings are incapable of accepting rejection.'

'Is that why,' Abioseh asked tentatively, 'he's so cold ... to you?'

MaZembe looked up at him as if surprised that he could speak. 'It's not a deliberate coldness.' she said. 'He's just never been exposed to warmth.'

Or opened himself up to it, Abioseh wanted to say, but decided against it. They sat, mother and son, in the room that had been taken over by the night, listening to a medley of sounds that amplified the silence – dogs barking excitedly at their own shadows, the sighing wind, workers bidding one another goodnight and the rising tide.

'You deny your father the possibility of a peaceful death,' MaZembe said, her voice sounding as if it had been dreamt up by the dark. 'Zebulon will take your place. Is that what you want?'

'And what place might that be?' Abioseh asked, his irritation starting up again.

'You know,' MaZembe said, 'you know.'

'Seriously,' Abioseh said, 'I don't know what you're talking about, Ma.'

'People will choose him over you, Abioseh,' MaZembe answered, un-willing to be intimidated. 'They'll crown him leader while you play your little games.'

'I've heard it said,' Abioseh put in, 'that mothers are the real king-makers. But you don't have to bother because I've no desire for the high seat, Ma. After this stint …', pointing at nothing in particular, embrac-ing the whole world, '… I might go back to university and pick up an-other degree. Another career.'

'And,' MaZembe countered, 'you'll be an educated fool without any practical skill.'

'What is practical about being a president?' Abioseh asked heatedly. 'What is it that gets put on your cv?' He adopted the formal tone of someone making a presentation to a panel: 'I led this republic into ruin for four years; in year so-and-so my tenure resulted in so many deaths from the blood plague and the deflowering of one thousand virgins …'

'Go on,' MaZembe said, 'and poke fun at your father and me. The truth is that you are not able to ridicule the strivings of someone who does nothing, who plays it safe. People think that being in power is one long and endless party, but, whatever we ultimately think of them, we do need people like your father, people who risk everything to push the frontiers.'

'Nobody asks them to do it,' Abioseh said, the words sounding petu-lant and unconvincing even to his own ears.

MaZembe shuffled her bags, a signal that her work was done and she was ready to leave. 'I'm not educated like you,' she said, 'I don't have the luxury of choosing jobs, of getting another degree. I don't think your father has that option, either, things being what they are. But, with the white man gone and the Creoles readying themselves to be the new mas-ters, we, who know dispossession, could have been guilty of the crime of omission if we hadn't gone out there and written history anew. And we can only write the history that *we* make, with our own hands. Your father is in the process of making history, but he is old and his bones scream for relief. That relief will possibly come from the stable of strangers, from his other son who doesn't know that he is also inscribing his name in history, even though it's through the unseeing eyes of the dead. But he is the one who will be remembered.'

Abioseh stayed in the house, reflecting, the last words hovering in the air like a living curse. He knew that it had taken a lot of courage for his mother to goad him that he needed to be resolute about life if he meant to have any impact on his country's history. He still didn't harbour any noble notions about his role in history; he would be long dead and buried when his own name was appended to the footnotes of history.

However, fast-forwarding to the future, he saw himself dead, unable to influence anything, with Zebulon gazing down at his corpse, and a chill gripped him. He knew he was headed for one of those bouts of flu that sneaked up on him whenever he was totally run down. *Does the fear of making crucial decisions induce infections?* His mother had made a decision that had guided her life. She had shelved her own capacity to dream to dedicate herself to realising her husband's dream.

That is what makes mothers so formidable, he thought. *They dream dreams and hope hopes and inhabit the lives of others while theirs become unliveable, a cross to bear.* In that moment, he knew that he feared his mother. It was futile to go against her, suicidal almost. Trembling in the silence of his lounge, Abioseh listened to his bones urging him to chart the course they should take. Otherwise, they would be picked clean by vultures. 'What,' he asked, 'is to be done?'

BACK IN THE boat, Abioseh hadn't realised that he had actually voiced the words in his head until Hiero put in his own question. 'You mean,' he asked, 'generally in Bangula, or is there something in particular you'd like to know?'

Adjusting quickly, Abioseh decided to risk it. 'My mother literally dangled the presidency in front of me on Friday,' he said.

'And like a believer in the wickedness of power,' Hiero prompted with unexpected annoyance, 'you turned it down.'

'I abstained,' Abioseh lied. A young woman approached them with a tray loaded with drinks and snacks: cold cuts, potato wedges, shrimp curlicues pasted onto triangular pieces of unleavened bread, sausages daubed with mustard, everything skewered with toothpicks. He watched as Hiero casually dislodged something wedged between his molars with a toothpick and sucked on his teeth. Feeling his gorge rise, Abioseh substituted the lemonade with a glass of Coke, hoping the gas would pressurise the nausea back to its source.

'Knowing MaZembe,' Hiero said, 'I can't see her letting you get away with anything less than a resounding *yes*. The country's in for a serious shake-up, and all of us want to pretend otherwise.'

'What does that have to do with me?'

'Plenty,' Hiero said. He looked around them furtively. 'Carlos Nobrega will send this country back hundreds of years.'

'The Creoles?' Abioseh's mother had sounded worried about the Creoles.

'They are a factor,' said Hiero. 'They are the only ones not resting on the laurels of liberation. Except for aristocrats like Nobrega and a few select families, Creoles are without a discernible cultural continuity, legacy or heritage. And there's nothing more desperate than unanchored people. They have to reinvent themselves and they need a power base.' Hiero paused. 'With the whites gone,' he went on, 'people are in search of new enemies. And among this diffuse mass there's an increase in elements, such as healers and cultural nationalists, who are suddenly finding glory in the past. This group feels that if the native Bangula, who are now in power, do not fulfil all those election promises, then, Reform or no Reform, they'll cast in their lot with the Blood of the Ancestors.'

The promises had been the Colonel's rash lapse into magnanimity, a guarantee that all peoples would be allowed to express their distinct national character. It was an assurance to mark a break with the past where the previous political order had promoted a policy of homogenising the blacks while separating them from the other components of Bangula society.

'So,' Abioseh asked, 'a coalition of the Creoles and Vezi's children?'

'Yes,' Hiero said, mouthing *Vezi's children*. 'The Colonel has said we must watch Zebulon. We *can* keep an eye on him, but who's to tell what'll happen if there's a change?'

'What *can* happen?' Abioseh thought he detected an ominous edge to Hiero's words. 'Zebulon, from what I can gather, seems pretty well established, the darling of the left and assorted malcontents.'

'From your tone,' Hiero said, 'he might be a figure of ridicule, unschooled, unsophisticated. But that rawness has won him followers. People gravitate towards him almost instinctively. And the majority of his supporters are loyal to the Blood of the Ancestors. For them, Zebulon might represent a fulfilment of an ancient prophecy. The Colonel feels particularly distressed by this and, knowing him, this time he won't be pulling any punches when he launches an offensive against *them*.' He gazed upwards at the gloomy sky. 'The Colonel believes that if you want to get at a bird's nest, you've got to destroy its tree.'

'And one of the eggs in the nest,' Abioseh put in, 'is his own son.'

'Unfortunately,' Hiero said.

And then the rain came down. It was a downpour of wanton savagery, the huge drops let loose by the clouds in a tropical assault. Four coastguardsmen bulked up by uniforms and weapons under umbrellas and oilskin coats transferred from their boat and boarded Nobrega's yacht. Saluting first and then standing to attention, they listened to crisp orders from a now businesslike though thoroughly soaked Hiero, who had to raise his voice to be heard above the roar of the water. Nobrega ushered six or seven of the guests off the boat. 'It's one way,' he said as a form of light-hearted adieu, 'of ensuring the correct ballast.'

'It's the same thing,' Hiero asked, 'in a political movement, hey?'

'Balance is impossible,' Carlos Nobrega replied, 'in any political environment.' Then he seemed to remember that the Colonel was in the master suite. 'Excuse me,' he said politely and disappeared among the guests. He came back in a minute and rang the bell. The Colonel wished to say a few words.

It occurred to Abioseh that this was going to be one of the very few occasions when he would hear his father speak. Of course, he'd seen the Colonel address parliament or the media or launch a philanthropic initiative. Abioseh was nostalgic for the rare times when the family had dined together and the Colonel had held court. Dressed unfamiliarly in a navy-blue windbreaker, beige slacks and loafers, he seemed more kitted out to exercise his golf swing than to run a country.

To Abioseh, however, the casualness was designed to mask fatigue; it left the Colonel's body seemingly fit, but expressed itself around the eyes. Mindful that he was on display, the Colonel smiled, turning into the young man he once was.

'One of the biggest mistakes I made,' he began, 'was to become a politician and then to allow people to persuade me to do this job.' He smiled, looking at the sea, the waves growing bigger as the yacht sailed further away from the coast. The land itself looked like the hull of a giant ship engulfed by fog. 'My wife,' he went on – his eyes resting briefly on Abioseh – 'asked me, when I was sworn in, *What will people call me?* And I answered, *Why, they'll call you* Mrs *Colonel!*' He gave a short laugh. 'But MaZembe also asked me if I really wanted this responsibility. What she was actually saying was that a presidency is not so much a career-limiting move as one that severely shortens lives.'

Nobrega now led his guests in laughter, slapping the CEO of the state power company on the back, striving to catch everyone's eye as if to cue them in to a session of synchronised applause. Even as Nobrega smiled at him in apparent friendship, Abioseh resisted being taken in by his antics.

It was perhaps this smile that led to Abioseh's conversion. Not five minutes earlier, he had been utterly indifferent towards the undeclared war for the throne in Mariposa. But now, seeing the speculative smile dancing at the corners of Nobrega's lips, Abioseh felt a spasm of hatred towards Carlos Nobrega that was almost overpowering.

This feeling became more intense when he saw Nobrega encircling Jacqui's waist in a discreet though proprietary manner, all the time staring at Abioseh, the smile widening in tribute to its own power to torment. It was the woman's browned shoulders, isolated and seemingly not part of Jacqui herself, that elicited a rush of lust so sharp in Abioseh that he had to avert his eyes and grab hold of the rail to steady himself, not a second before intercepting a fleeting exchange of glances between Carlos and Jacqui, so brief it could have been in his imagination. It was this moment that decided him that, indeed, a lot was at stake. Abioseh's disinterest in the race was a blasphemy against the memory and energy that had thrust the Colonel onto the supreme seat of the land.

2

RETURNING FROM THE market, where they'd walked in between the stalls picking out merchandise, the three old women shared a bowl of roasted nuts and rough-skinned and white-fleshed yams rare in summer. Later, sitting on grass mats outside their house, their splayed legs covered in bright calico cloths, Jumaima and Josephine were fanning themselves. They grinned at the antics of grandchildren in their charge while monitoring the brewing of heady sorghum beer in outsize pots. Oblivious of two lizards copulating just above her head, Jutaita, to ease a damnable itch, was rubbing her back against the whitewashed wall of their thatched house as she carried out a meticulous search-and-destroy operation on lice in a young woman's hair. The wide-eyed young woman winced occasionally as one louse after another met its crunchy end between her granny's fingernails.

As if responding to an alarm bell located somewhere inside her spindly frame, Josephine suddenly shot to her feet, her abruptness sending the frisky pair of lizards scuttling back into the thatch. Feeding an armful of firewood into the half-hearted fire, she then removed the iron lid off the steaming pot to control the consistency of the beer with the aid of an enormous wooden scoop. Satisfied, she gave a thumbs-up. Then she saw Zebulon ambling past.

'Jutaita? Jumaima?' she cried, addressing her friends without turning round to face them. 'My age-mates: help me make sense of this ...'

'Make sense of what, Josephine?' Jutaita asked. Then she called out in triumph. 'Ah, another swine dead!'

'Isn't that Vezi's grandchild?' Josephine asked, pointing with her ladle still dripping with porridge-like beer.

'Josephine,' Jumaima asked, 'why do you call him Vezi's grandchild and not the Colonel's son?'

Josephine sucked on her teeth. 'Because,' she said, 'the Colonel's a piece of dung and Vezi was a man.' She was quiet, reliving an ancient moment, her eyes concentrating on a spot somewhere in the region of her soul. 'Vezi *is* a real man.'

The young woman, who had been watching the old women and making an effort to follow their conversation, could no longer contain herself. 'What is a real man, Grandma?' She vaguely remembered Zebulon at David Kone's funeral service.

'What do you mean by that, Zoya?' Even as she asked this question, it was clear to her friends that Jutaita was buying time while she mulled over Zoya's query. 'Sit still.' Her bony fingers were greasy with dead lice and liquid paraffin.

Exasperated by the adult world's trick of avoiding giving answers by posing another question, Zoya asked, 'I mean, what is the difference between a *man* and a *real* man?'

'That's a good question,' Josephine said. She laughed as Zoya gave her a dark look that said she was wise to *that* old ruse, too, of praising the quality of the question and then ignoring it.

'A real man, my baby,' Jutaita said, slowly, closing her eyes as if to avoid being distracted by a chance sighting of an unreal man, 'is one who holds truth above everything else, someone who, while everyone goes *this* way, will choose to go *that* way if the path he follows will lead him to the fulfilment of that truth.'

'A real man,' Josephine said airily, the young girl inside her coming out, 'is one who fulfils *me* ...'

'Stop thinking with what's left of your hormones,' Jumaima snapped. 'The child is serious.'

'All right, all right,' Josephine grunted, extending her arms, palms out as if warding off an assailant. 'You don't have to be so bloody solemn about it.'

'In short,' Zoya said, 'a real man is the one who'll do the right thing even if others think it's dumb?' She turned round to look at Jutaita. 'Is that right?'

'Dead right,' Jutaita said.

'Have the three of you come across many such men?'

Josephine laughed out loud when the two women looked at her. 'We've met men, Zoya,' she said quietly. 'Some were real; others were disappointments.'

The three women, whose accumulated age could have been a few centuries, sat in the late afternoon sun, thinking back on what they had forced their bodies to forget — encounters with men and what these had precipitated. They remembered the musky smells, the sweat and the strange texture of the hands that had touched their nerve endings with tenderness and passion; they recoiled at the remembrance of the stiffened fingers and fists that had pummelled them into the groaning earth, mainly because the men had needed female company in that lowly dust. They reminisced over men who had stood up for their ideals and paid a heavy price; and they recollected charlatans whose words were sweeter than honey and emptier than banana peels. They revived the memory of the tears that men strove to hide from them, the blood that flowed like so many rivers when the warriors, confronted with the awesome power of the armed bringers of civilisation and earthly representatives of the Holy Ghost, stood up and declared that they were men and would no longer bow before anyone, certainly not before the arrogant wielders of the cross. In remembering the men who had been reduced to mere memories and therefore as unreliable in the realm of imagination as they had always been in reality, the women sighed and celebrated whatever force resided within them that had conferred the twin gifts of the grace to bury the good and the spirit to survive the wicked.

The scuttling of the lizards on the thatch broke their communal reverie. One of the reptiles jumped out of the dry grass and landed on Zoya's lap. Screaming, the young woman jumped up, knocking the wind out of her groomer. Jutaita, hopping on one foot, let out a stream of obscenities, kicking the lizard straight into the live coals. The air was immediately filled with the smell of burning flesh. Jutaita, her hands supporting her head, started shouting and calling Jumaima and Josephine. 'Come and see,' she yelled. 'Come and see.'

'What?' asked the two old women. Zoya added, 'Yes, *what?*'

'We've burnt a lizard,' Jutaita said. 'Someone big has died.'

3

IT WAS WITH a sense of déjà vu in the second week of March that Abioseh found himself in a discussion with Carlos Nobrega. They were in the dining room in Mariposa and the table was laden with food although no one seemed to have any appetite. The windows and the portraits were screened with black damask cloth, the artificially lit room deliberately stripped of diversions, its occupants forced to look one another in the eye.

Of the twenty-odd people present, only Abioseh and Hiero and one or two others were not Cabinet ministers. MaZembe, who would be consulted every step of the way, was too overcome by grief to attend. At the moment, they were waiting for the arrival of Malachi, her brother, to constitute the committee for the funeral of the late president of the republic, the man known affectionately as the Colonel, the premier champion of the Reform.

'It's difficult,' Carlos Nobrega said, 'to think of the Colonel in the past tense. He was so alive.'

'Yes,' Dr Caramel Sebone-Prah murmured, 'such a colossus.'

'How did it happen?' asked Marcia Baraka, the latest addition to the Cabinet. She turned her eyes to Abioseh and he read genuine pain in them.

He wanted to tell them that his father had died exactly three weeks after the opening of parliament in February. 'The Colonel died in his sleep,' Abioseh said laconically. 'My mother found him dead in the morning.'

The ministers heard the words. They glanced at Abioseh and then looked at one another, for this simplicity, this unembellished account, was not in keeping with their own imaginings. The Colonel deserved a much more spectacular exit. And what did Abioseh mean by saying that MaZembe had found him dead in the morning? Were they not sharing a bed, then? Was Abioseh deliberately withholding crucial information?

When Malachi arrived, the business of setting up the committee began. Abioseh studied the ministers vying to be part of the committee. He knew from history that the death of a leader created tension. It made people ambitious. And ambition led to more funerals.

Abioseh accepted that his sardonic outlook was nothing less than a failure to face up to his loss. Although he was the Colonel's flesh and blood, the Colonel had never, really, embraced him as he would a comrade. The son had belonged to the father the same way an elbow was part of his anatomy – a fulcrum, admittedly, but something given to banging into unyielding surfaces.

'How do you feel?' Hiero asked.

'Not good,' Abioseh said. He looked at the faces in the room again, realising that he'd need Hiero's help to get through the period following his father's death. He further discovered that the Colonel, as president of the republic, belonged to everyone who could lay a claim on him. The funeral arrangements were in the hands of strangers and some people who he simply didn't like. *People like Dr Caramel Sebone-Prah*, he thought, *regard the death as a stepping-stone.* He watched as she cosied up to Nobrega, the second-in-command, now head honcho.

On day two of the arrangements, Abioseh became convinced that the Colonel was really dead and gone when Malachi handed him a poem sent to the family by Ezekiel Manolo. Abioseh prevailed on the family for it to be added to the other symbols of mourning. Somehow, for him anyway, it matched the fragrance from the mountains of bouquets, some as high as a man, which pervaded the air at the stadium where the state funeral service for the Colonel was being held:

> ... *the lizard burns*
> *In hearths fashioned in corners*
> *Of our hearts where a great tree falls*
> *And banishes cowardice from the land* ...

The line *cowardice from the land* rang repeatedly in Abioseh's head, a refrain that mocked him even as he marched. Abioseh was in lockstep with the soldiers as part of the military procession that also involved the gun carriage from the private resting chamber to the Great Hall. This was where the body had to lie in state for three days. Dazed, he observed the protocol that had greatly influenced the funeral planning. Malachi and MaZembe, the family seniors, had taken the lead and determined the exact sequence of events. Abioseh saw his mother seated on the dais with other dignitaries, all of them in black, splendid and elegant in grief. In this she was matched by most of the other female relatives, mourning being a loyal supporter of astonishing wardrobes.

It was one of those days made for funerals. The Saturday sun was high up, seeming to rise towards a never-ending blueness, the woolly clouds scudding across the sky, promising rain even though the seers had said it would be a good day for a funeral.

Looking beyond the heads of the throngs, Abioseh still couldn't take his eyes off the casket that was bedecked with national colours on the catafalque. As the service rolled on, Abioseh knew that the box would soon be placed amid more wreaths at the back of the gun carriage. Eight uniformed pallbearers picked from various units guarded each corner of the coffin. They appeared alert to their commanding officer while the chaplain recited words that produced a fresh spell of moaning among the mourners.

Abioseh couldn't quite hear the eulogies as they were distorted in the recording system and rendered useless to the dignitaries and family members. The only people they seemed to rally, those who responded with heartfelt affirmations, punching their fists into the air and chanting the Colonel's favourite slogans, were the common men and women, whom the Colonel had called *the great unwashed*.

It was then that Zebulon marched across the soccer field. There was a ripple around the tiers, with people getting to their feet, unsettling the speaker on the podium. Zebulon stepped onto the crimson strip of carpet that bisected the soccer field. The strip ran across from the gate, past the gun carriage and the catafalque into the shadow of the marquee for dignitaries and foreign guests who sat in different poses of sorrow.

Although the viewing had been done at the earlier service in the resting chamber and the Great Hall, the pallbearers gave way to Zebulon, who gazed at the face beneath the glass. For Abioseh, it was a moment when he, too, was transformed. When Zebulon was directed by the two men into the empty chair among members of the family, he took the seat as though he knew it had always been reserved for him, glancing at Ma-Zembe, nodding in acknowledgment of her grief. He was two or three rows behind Abioseh. Somehow it seemed as if the further Zebulon was from the centre of power – the table of honour which was the nearest to the casket – the more that power remained contestable. As Malachi read the obituary, Abioseh knew that he had never known his father.

THE COLONEL HAD made it known as a young man that he had no wish to become a soldier, even when, at the age of seventeen, he joined the army. He had agreed with his parents that the military was not for him. After matriculating by correspondence, he joined the Permanent Force, a model from neighbouring islands, and went to an officer's course at the Military College.

Although not academically inclined, he ended up at the university with a B.Sc. Military degree, after which he became an instructor and, much later, a staff officer at Army HQ. While evincing the attributes of a professional soldier, he kept up the song that he was a mere civilian in uniform. It was in this self-deprecatory frame that the Colonel accepted his failure to distance himself from the military when for two years he attended an army staff course at Fort Leavenworth that included an attachment with the 85th Armoured Division in Arizona.

Even though he had some particularly uncomplimentary things to say about Americans when he returned, the Colonel couldn't hide the fact that he was impressed with their degree of organisation. It was as a major-general that he was promoted to Head of the Army; from there, the politicians nominated him an MP and then on to the Cabinet as minister of safety, security and national intelligence. It was here, now as a civilian, that he saw the country racked by strikes and restlessness that didn't augur well for the government.

General Gabriel Ramala was very unpopular. He had let power go to his head instead of leading; he dismissed the popular rumblings as the figment of his detractors' imagination. Some whispered that he was senile.

After a few months, the Colonel assembled the generals and heads of all units of the armed forces and presented them with a blueprint. In two weeks, the president was relieved of his position and the Cabinet dissolved. It was a coup, but, after two years of martial law, during which the Colonel headed a junta, new elections were held. The state of emergency was lifted and a new government put in place, with the Colonel as the first president of this reformed and reconstituted country. It was here, also, that he emerged as the founder of the Reform.

Throughout, he declared that he was merely a peasant and would like to try his hand at farming. 'This is not for me,' he'd say. 'I'm just a caretaker.'

And his accompanying gesture would embrace the desk covered with important papers and files, the seal of his office. The flag was positioned a little behind him to his left. On the wall hung his official photograph and beneath it an array of Cabinet ministers. There was a pictorial odyssey of occasions with foreign luminaries in which the Colonel's face had perfected a look of interested disengagement. There were trophies, citations, framed certificates and awards from home and abroad.

WITH THE AIR blue from the smoke and thick with cordite from rifle muzzles following the twenty-one-gun salute, the family and presidential party were choreographed into their positions behind the pallbearers who marched slowly behind the gun carriage. Abioseh found himself in step with Zebulon, as if they'd been rehearsed together. Here, now, at the hour of the long shadows, on the quiet afternoon, a streak of lightning flashed across the sky followed by a muffled crash. Looking up into the dark-blue void, Abioseh thought he could see the last of the seven peace doves, each dove representing a decade of the Colonel's life, released after the ceremonial salute, barely a minute before the singing of the national anthem.

Abioseh, the reluctant heir, had to oversee his late father's transportation by train to his ancestral home for burial. It was a special train, guarded by paratroopers, the body in a huge custom-built fridge, an engineering feat signifying the ingenuity of Baluba Jambo, the undertaker.

It took two days from the departure ceremony to the burial. Although the train was a train of sorrow, local industries thrived along the way for the hawkers were able to sell their wares as the train stopped at all stations to let people show their respect. It was one of the Colonel's last wishes that consideration be given to all parts of the land, even unimportant stations whose platforms were the size of postage stamps that had been bypassed by progress.

4

ZEBULON EVENTUALLY FOUND work at the dockyard, first as a casual labourer with a squad that chipped rust and old paint off the hulls of the
giant ships and rigs. Suspended on a plank while the water swirled bluely
in the distance and dirtily a hundred feet below him, he could lose himself in the deafening noise from so many hammers banging against the
steel plates before they could be painted with industrial coating followed
by the spot-colour of the shipping line.

When the shop-floor steward, who was also known as the Flying
Monkey on account of his agility on the planks, heard of Zebulon's
reputation on his regular funeral expeditions — which had a quality of
pilgrimage about them — and of his parentage, he invited him to join
the union, which would mean Zebulon's promotion from casual labourer
to full-time worker. This was opportunism on the part of the Flying
Monkey, who reasoned that even if the Colonel was dead, the young
man was still the issue of influential testicles. Zebulon was told that the

Flying Monkey was puzzled by his activities and overheard him remarking on Zebulon's habit of spending his entire waking hours moping over corpses like some bloodsucking undertaker. 'Thank God,' he said, 'that lot isn't in *my* union!'

Zebulon stopped huddling in derelict buildings where he had warmed himself over braziers and had slept wrapped in fetid and scratchy blankets and rags. Gone, for a moment, he felt – because he still didn't quite believe that the change in his circumstances wasn't just an illusion – was the constant danger of life at the margins, where blood was sometimes spilt with voluptuous glee.

Although his circumstances changed, his previous condition remained like a healed wound whose memory lived in the scar. It conveyed itself in Zebulon's impatience with what he saw as insincerity on the part of the bosses or, even, the Flying Monkey himself, spurring him on to confrontations.

At first the Flying Monkey welcomed the young man's spunkiness, which he saw as a lever with which to prise open the sealed corporate vault of Bangula, but in time it started to present a challenge to his leadership. Using his prodigious powers of organisation, the Flying Monkey went about conferring with the workers, offering his analysis. 'The man is crazy,' he said.

In Zebulon, the workers saw someone unafraid to speak the truth and measured him against the union leadership. Stripped of artifice, his language found resonance with their own unspoken feelings. In one instance, the men delegated the Flying Monkey to negotiate with management about the need for protective gear, especially when they scoured the engine rooms of noxious grease. The Flying Monkey came back to them and said that the management had turned them down. It transpired, however, that the Flying Monkey had not raised the workers' concerns although the opportunity had been there.

'You've lied to us,' Zebulon said. 'You made us believe you could represent us. You are worse than management.'

Spluttering with rage, the Flying Monkey picked up a tappet wrench and advanced on Zebulon, vowing to knock sense into him. The other men held him back. Looking at him with eyes that had looked on so many dead faces, Zebulon said softly, 'You threaten me with that thing again and I'll make you eat it.'

The Flying Monkey left in a huff, carrying his lean frame stiffly upright. Two days later, he broke his left leg when he failed to negotiate his trademark leap from a plank scaffold to the steel ladder temporarily fastened to the hull, ending his long career as union leader. This mishap confirmed that tangling with Zebulon could prove a health hazard. Although the men didn't – or couldn't – say this, they felt that he had somehow caused, or *willed*, the accident. More out of a need to move forward and get on with the job at hand than a disregard for their erstwhile leader, they gathered into a conclave and elected Zebulon as their union representative.

And so, at a relatively young age, and seemingly moving to an inner rhythm, he walked into the offices of powerful men and negotiated, sometimes successfully, many times not, terms and conditions to change the lot of workers. Because he did not talk much, the workers trusted him and the management felt that their own confidences, and these were many, would not be compromised by loose tongues that reputedly sank ships. To compensate for his lack of formal education, on alternate days Zebulon skipped the vigils to attend night school. Eventually, though, he had to be at evening meetings that were unavoidable for shop stewards in Jambora.

These activities ate into the time and rituals with which he remembered Melinda in other deaths so that he could forget her. Slowly – and it quickened with the passage of time – there were days when he would discover that she hadn't once crossed his mind. This filled him with a strange sadness, as if he had betrayed her. Zebulon now had the chance, when not at work, to visit other regions where the union had a presence, mostly the coastal towns with their networks of ports and harbours. He found himself in high-powered meetings on the waterfront, sleeping, for the first time, in hotels, affronted and astonished in equal measure by the power of money.

ZEBULON WAS DRIVING with Cameron Jele, a shop steward from the Eastern Region. It was a little after midnight following a lengthy congress. They were headed to their hotel when Jele suggested that they go into the nearby township and see if they couldn't find a spot where they could rustle up a late-night meal. From his girth and weight, it was easy to see that Jele enjoyed his food; Zebulon was feeling a little hungry himself, although at this late hour he would have settled for his stash of dried fruit and tea in his room, but he fell in with the idea, thinking: *What the hell?* Snacking on prunes and apricots and raisins had suddenly lost its appeal.

The congress had been a somewhat bitter victory for the Eastern Region chapter of the union, which had been under pressure from the 'No Lies' campaign by dockworkers who had felt that the union wasn't applying enough heat to stop the government from enforcing pension cuts. Since the dockworkers had threatened to go on strike even without the union, it took some skilful negotiation before the workers accepted that the union would be behind them on the strike, should it take place, but was appealing for calm, because the strike was likely to be ruled illegal by the authorities. The union was not calling for a halt to industrial action; it was merely proposing that people box smart. *Discipline*, someone said, *does not mean defeat.*

Ultimately, there was agreement that a deputation would investigate the legal implications of going on strike. Zebulon had thought that there was merit in both the workers' and the union's cases, albeit for different reasons. The workers were sick and tired of inaction and scared to death that they could soon find themselves on the breadline if nothing was done. And the union felt that it would lose its relevance if unguided strike action took place, especially if it yielded results. To build a union was hard; to destroy it took a single misguided decision, especially one informed by emotions. Since the two forces were not mutually exclusive, they could explore ways to support each other. He noticed, also, that there was a certain degree of posturing, where speakers played to the gallery, imagining their names on banner headlines.

Eventually, however, the hot tempers were cooled and the stratospheric egos brought onto steady ground. The men and women who had glared at each other from across a great gulf now cheered and toasted one another and declared a great victory. Gone was the enormous anger behind the sentiment, which Zebulon had heard, of putting the 'right-wing leadership out on its fucking ear'. Although pleased that the matter had been solved amicably, Zebulon still experienced a twinge of discomfort that the union had not really taken cognisance of workers' concerns, especially their vulnerability because their benefits of unemployment and disability, health and pension were being interfered with. Unemployment was rising with thousands of people joining the ranks of the jobless every month. He asked himself: *What is our role?*

This was just one of the many issues that preoccupied him. He felt that the people of Bangula had the power to change the situation. *Why are there so many kids begging on street corners?* he thought. *Why has there been a frightening increase in the number of women with wide-eyed babies strapped to their backs, with begging bowls, some breaking into song-and-dance routines for the amusement of the bored and moneyed motorist? Why is the fruit of liberation so bitter and so unreachable for the majority of the people?*

As they left the town, the bright lights gave way slowly to the darkness. The skyscrapers and symphonies of glass and chrome yielded to brownstone and corrugated iron warehouses and squat residences that lay almost slap-bang on the dusty road, the once-whitewashed walls bearing the legacy of the unceasing traffic, the few straggling trees up front stunted and choked by the oil fumes and smoke. Zebulon hoped that the children were mercifully asleep. For, he thought, *there must be children, since the wretched of the earth religiously hearkened to that verse in the Bible that advised them to go forth and multiply.* They passed an empty lot in which the darkness snarled ominously. Further along was an eight-foot fence topped by a tangle of coiled barbed wire enclosing a red-bricked military barracks, the observation tower silhouetted against a grey sky.

They heard the music long before they reached the nightspot, a she-been set among rows and rows of similar four-roomed dwellings built in the time of black labour that would serve white interests. Parked along the scraggly lawns, two lines of elegant and average cars stretched all the way to the corner, leaving a narrow lane on the road for one car to crawl through. Young men in fluorescent jackets waved cars into or out of impossible spaces.

'Seems like a cool place,' Jele said. He was a jazz fanatic, sometimes bopping to an internal rhythm, even in meetings. He was the only man Zebulon knew who still had a collection of vinyl records, in an age when CDs had already lost out to electronic media. A trumpet wailed as if in the grip of excruciating pain, the sound billowing into the night, spilling out like liquid gold. 'Yeah,' Cameron Jele said, now walking the walk, his instincts confirmed, '*this* is the place all right!'

Although Zebulon had come across musicians and artists of every stripe, he accepted that he tended to judge them unfairly as people who should be doing something meaningful with their lives. He had therefore never taken them seriously.

Here they were, a drummer, a bassist, a trumpeter, a tenor saxophon-ist and a pianist, all squashed into a corner of the packed room. Furni-ture had been shoved into the corner closest to the entrance. The more elderly of the clientele occupied the chairs; the younger ones standing were voluble in their support.

The trumpeter was negotiating a particularly tormented solo, his face contorted and his blistered lips puckered as if about to bleed into the mouthpiece. Some of the patrons were yelling encouragement, urging him to coax out of his instrument the final note signifying the peak of his pain. Next to him, wearing a black trilby that gave him a raffish look, the bassist plucked at the strings desultorily, as though trying to find the channel that would connect him with others, his scarred face showing the mileage his short life had clocked. The pianist, who wore an olive panama that resembled an Australian bush hat, was the oldest, also lost in a cacophony of notes as he studied the ivories beneath his fingers as if they held an answer to an ancient secret.

A counterpoint to the music was the sound of glasses clinking in the kitchen, beer bottles knocking against each other and people conversing in muffled and respectful tones punctuated by occasional laughter. And then someone, a stout, balding man in a fashionable though ill-fitting cream suit, emerged from one of the rooms and stood in front of the musicians. 'The fun's just starting folks,' he said. 'I have here something that's going to warm the cockles of your hearts.'

'Isn't that Baluba Jambo?' Zebulon asked Jele. People who seemed completely at ease among strangers intrigued him.

'Yes,' replied Jele. 'He is the boss man here. In addition to the funeral parlour he runs shebeens and entertainment places.' He framed the word 'entertainment' in quotation marks.

'For some people,' Zebulon said, 'funerals and entertainment are one and the same thing. Didn't his father stand against the Colonel some time back?'

'Yes. But now his old man's no longer in politics.'

Zebulon wanted to say that no one who'd been in politics took a re-tirement package. But something stopped him, perhaps the rumbling of his stomach. He was suddenly ravenously hungry. 'Where's the food?'

'Soon,' Jele said, giving his colleague a sidelong glance as if to say: *What's up with you?* He turned to feast his eyes on what had been vaunted as likely to warm the cockles of people's hearts.

In front of them stood a young woman. She was tall, her hair cropped so short that when she stooped to check the microphone, Zebulon could see her scalp; her big gold earrings dangled and matched a copper necklace shot with an emerald pendant that rested in the hollow of her throat, complementing a sheath-like cotton dress of aubergine and black on a field of ochre. When she looked up, her eyes settled on Zebulon's and he felt as if he knew her from an earlier encounter, going back years and, yet, speaking of a future that was still unknowable and therefore mystifying.

'She,' Cameron Jele said, nudging Zebulon with his elbow, 'can warm the cockles of *my* heart any day of the week.' It was Zebulon's turn to shut him up with a look.

Then, without any introduction, she started to sing, softly and slowly as if the evening were dedicated to her own emotions, nothing else. The eyes that sometimes flickered in the direction of the customers were mainly turned inwards to her own private universe, refusing to corroborate the truth or lie of the existence of anyone else.

Although young, the woman sang of the banality of sentimental journeys, conveying a lot of experience in the lyrics about encounters and partings. She phrased her anguish in a tone at once clear and deep, about crossing oceans and rivers, forests and deserts, being lifted to the mountain-tops and sinking to the depths of valleys – all these journeys acknowledged in all the trouble that people had seen.

The musicians, who were on their own separate crossings, accompanied her, taking turns to imbue her voice with vigour. The horns were clear and distinct, melding into a melody that was textured like honey and coloured amber like a warning. The soprano, alto, tenor and bass filled the air with tonal arabesques as the piano pealed in triumph and then rumbled like a tuba. The men allowed her to lead, now and then straining to catch up with her when she hurtled too far ahead. They drew her back into the tempo and phrase of the moment, knowing that she was their little sister who spoke for all the women who were lost and the men who bore the guilt and who needed to be lifted up from the mire onto steady rock.

The set ended to scattered polite applause. Zebulon was still replaying the last note in his head as he watched some of the patrons congratulating the musicians, the woman looking over their heads, her eyes seeking like the eyes of an intolerant buyer in a crowded marketplace. He watched her collect her bag, copying the actions of the musicians who were also packing their instruments into cases.

Even when he had been a boy begging for a living with Melinda, Zebulon had always found the end of concerts a sad and lonely business. The packing of the instruments, with the musicians' backs turned to the audience, had a melancholy finality that made him wish for performances that lasted forever, where no one would have to go home. In those years he had no home to go to; much later, he would learn that home was invariably the awareness of the freedom and the surrender of shuddering in someone else's arms.

And so, shrugging off Cameron Jele's restraining hand, Zebulon walked across the floor, which now felt like the widest floor he had ever crossed, broader by far than Revolution Boulevard, to where the woman stood stuffing castanets and a marimba into a raffia bag. He stood behind her, vaguely aware that people were staring at him and that, even though she hadn't turned to look at him, she was conscious that he was there, perhaps alerted by a hush that had now descended over the room.

'Will you please get away from behind me,' the woman said softly in a voice that could be heard halfway across the room. 'Your presence is heavy on my shoulders.'

'I'm a little afraid,' Zebulon said, 'of facing you.'

'Why?'

'Because you might see the nakedness in my eyes.'

'I will turn around then,' she said, the dress and the cape she had over her shoulders rustling like the feathers of a giant flightless bird, 'because I am more frightened of people who cannot trust their nakedness.'

'Are you coming, Zoya?' asked the pianist, who wasn't burdened by his instrument, but who carried a bag slung over his shoulder. 'The car's waiting.'

'Is it time, already?' Zoya asked, her eyes on Zebulon, studying him.

'Yep,' the pianist said, regarding Zoya as coldly as he might have looked at a stranger. 'It's time.'

The rest of the band, their bags packed, crowded the doorway, their faces impassive, their bodies saying that whoever this big man was, they'd wait for Zoya till hell froze over.

'Will you come with us?' Zoya asked Zebulon. 'We've been invited to a party in Jamestown.'

'He *can't* come with us, Zoya,' said the pianist shaking his head in exaggerated amazement. 'You hardly know the guy.'

'I don't know him but I have seen him around,' Zoya said. 'Neither did I know you when we first met, Stefan, but in time we got along like a house on fire.' She paused, toying with an idea. 'We're only strangers when we meet. You remember that song, Stefan?'

Sensing the tension, Cameron Jele, who harboured the suspicion that Zoya, or any woman who accompanied musicians, must be mixed up with a bad crowd, came up from behind and tapped Zebulon on the shoulder. 'We should make tracks,' he said. His anxiety, which he fought hard to suppress, had diminished his appetite.

'We'll go in time,' Zebulon answered. He turned to Stefan. 'I can sense that there is a little history between the two of you,' he said. 'But is there anything now that gives you the power to have a say in what she does with her time?'

'Who the fuck are you?' Stefan asked, unslinging his bag and handing it to the drummer, suddenly looking leaner and wirier in his dark clothes. Although he took a step towards Zebulon, his eyes that had clouded with his growing rage were fixed on Zoya. 'Do you know me, man?'

'Stefan,' Zoya called, quietly, conversationally, 'get a grip.'

'I'm *not* going to get a fucking grip,' Stefan said. There was something deliberate about his anger, as if he had stored, fed and fattened it, and now its time had come to be released, 'certainly not for this smug fucker.'

'My name is Zebulon … Zebulon began. He stepped out from behind Zoya and stood slightly to her side as if to ensure that even though
she was in the orbit of Stefan's rage, she would be out of harm's way
should he open fire. It did seem as if Stefan's anger was building up to
the inevitable moment of a strike. His litheness in the dark suit suggested a capability, an appetite even, for violence; he looked like someone
who compensated for his smallness with a weapon.

'I don't *fucking* care what your name is!'

'*Stefan!*'

'… and I realise you're angry,' Zebulon went on as if he hadn't been
interrupted. 'I see it in your eyes and hear it in your voice. And it's very
likely that right now you're preparing to do something that will justify
the way you feel, that will make you go home and have a beer, satisfied
that you've dealt with this smug fucker, me.' He punctuated the last word
by jabbing his own breastbone with stiffened fingers as if easing the aim
Stefan would take to hit the target.

'When you stab me or shoot me,' Zebulon said, 'when you ensure that
I'm dead – and no longer the smug fucker who makes you feel small in
front of a woman – my brain will take some time to shut down and the
tissue will soften. My cadaver will probably lie dead here before police
take it to the mortuary, where it'll stay on a tray for almost a week.
Maybe there'll be an autopsy although the cause of death – a death that
you've caused – will be quite clear. In another week people will get together and probably gloat or mourn over my passing, but I'll no longer
be involved with that. They'll be dealing with a shell that was once me,
which now belongs to *you* because, when you kill someone, you take away
their spirit and for the period you, the killer, are still breathing, that
spirit will be with you. To bargain with that spirit, you'll have to enter
into negotiations with the ancestors. That's what will happen to you and
to me – or what remains of me.' He paused. Even though he had been
addressing Stefan, his stance completely disregarded him.

'As for you,' Zebulon went on, 'you'll probably have to run all your life, with my spirit on your back like white on rice. In the event that you're caught — let's say you intimidate everyone here to let you flee — you'll be shot by firing squad. I'm not sure what will happen to your cadaver; it'll probably be taken by the University of Bangula and sliced into parts and used for medical research. And your spirit will wander looking for a body that will give it purpose. Maybe it will enhance the existence of another murderer. I don't know.' He suddenly sounded very tired.

For a long moment there was again silence, punctuated by Zebulon's breathing. During Zebulon's speech, Stefan's expression had registered a series of changes, from rage to incredulity and frustration to disgust.

'Fuck this,' he muttered and stomped out. Hesitating for a moment, as if wishing to make sense of what had just happened, the rest of the musicians filed out quietly.

'Now look what you've done,' Zoya lamented, turning to Zebulon, 'you've lost me the best bunch of musicians I've ever worked with.'

'Maybe they weren't meant to work with you in the first place.'

'Do you always talk like that?'

'What do you mean?'

'I am Zebulon,' Zoya said, mimicking his deep voice. 'My corpse … no, my *cadaver* — what a word, *cadaver* — my cadaver will lie for three days and three nights in the government mortuary … yours will rot in a dark alley.' She giggled at her own hopeless impersonation. 'Weren't you scared Stefan was going to pull a gun on you?'

'I was shaking,' Zebulon admitted, 'near to pissing myself.'

'But it didn't show. I was watching you *all* the time.'

'It's when we lose our fear that we make mistakes.'

'There you go again,' Zoya said resignedly, 'putting on The Voice.'

IN THEIR DAYS together, which became weeks and months and years, Zebulon and Zoya helped each other to discover what they didn't know about themselves. In looking at her, he started understanding how others saw him. And this frightened him, a feeling to which he wasn't accustomed.

For a very long time he had existed without appreciating the need for the human touch. And now that he was with her, he wondered endlessly how he had managed all those years without it. Then there was the gradual understanding that the island was much more than sugarcane and banana plantations. The people, the sugarcane cutter together with his songs and the woman dressed in sacks at the mill daily humming a tune from her favourite soap, in whose houses he had mourned and sought food and shelter, were more than the work they did – or didn't – do. The island consisted of these people and their children, a few with grandparents, and their animals. The rulers sat in the seats of the mighty; he knew something about that, since – and everyone knew this – it pulsed in his spirit and in his blood. And the ruled bided their time.

What Zoya knew consisted of her education and what she had picked up in her life experience. She came from a relatively well-to-do family and had kicked out against tradition from when she was a little girl. The only people she held in esteem were her three grandmothers, none of whom was related to her by blood.

'Do you know,' she asked Zebulon one day, 'they got together just because all their names began with the letter "J" – Jumaima, Jutaita and Josephine. Isn't that funny?'

And she took him in her little runabout, an ancient Peugeot that ran on inspiration, to her place where he was formally introduced to the old women.

The three centenarians, who were still as sharp as tacks and knew exactly who he was, overwhelmed him. They gazed at him with their clear little girls' eyes, asking him questions, performing a three-way good cop/bad cop routine, in which the interrogators seemed to fuse into one haranguer.

'Who did you say you *are* again?'

'Zebulon.'

'Zebulon *who*?'

'Yes. What's *your* surname?'

'You didn't just fall off a tree, boy.'

'My surname is Gondo.'

'Who is *your* mother?'

'Who's *her* father?'

'Who *killed* Cock Robin?'

And so on, leaving him exhausted. He caught sight of Zoya in the kitchen fixing lemonade drinks in a huge jug that looked older than the crones; she seemed to be going about her chores happily oblivious to his discomfort. She handed him the glass and he took a grateful sip, only to splutter from the drink's unsweetened harshness to the throat.

'Why are you coughing? You don't like the drink?'

'Prepared for you with so much love …'

'No, I like the drink.'

'And what do you know about loving?'

'I love Zoya.'

'Come again, what was that?'

'Speak up boy; cat got your tongue?'

'I LOVE ZOYA!'

He didn't realise that he had raised his voice until he heard his hoarse cry reverberate in the room. In his mind's eye, he saw his voice carrying the fateful words wafting out of the house onto the street, where they got picked up by a hundred pairs of ears that would send the information to the brain and store it for transmission to other ears. And so the cycle would start again and go on and on. Somewhere, people would sit down at a table for a meal and one of them would say, 'Hey, people. Can you help me make sense of what I've just heard? Did you listen to the words of that Zebulon?' In that infinitesimally brief minute when the words hung in the air before escaping into the sunlit afternoon, he became aware that for perhaps the first time in his life he had admitted to the stirrings of his soul. He had disclosed to the world what he actually felt. And he didn't care.

PART FOUR

WITNESS

I

FOLLOWING THE DEATH of the Colonel, Carlos Nobrega served for sixty months as acting president at the head of the junta before its dissolution. During this period Abioseh was still in parliament. He sometimes missed the life of a highly paid executive. Parliamentary pay was atrocious, throwing a few of his colleagues into rhapsodies over a life outside the hallowed halls once their terms ended.

Abioseh kept his head well below the parapet of political intrigue in the period of the junta. He watched how Nobrega tried to stamp his authority as the public face of the military rule. This exposed him to criticism, since the blood plague was again on the rise and there were no strong measures to combat it. Further, the traditionalists constantly reminded Nobrega that he had the blood of the oppressors coursing through his veins and was thus unsuited to hold such a powerful position.

This raised the spectre of ethnicity, which the Colonel, with his soldierly dedication to strengthening the Reform, had almost succeeded

in stamping out. Abioseh broke ranks with the traditionalists and reminded everyone how the fabric of Bangula society was strengthened by
non-racialism. During the hearings in parliament on amendments to the
communications bill, the traditionalists made a representation towards
the exclusion of Creoles from ownership of electronic media or telecom-
munications networks. Abioseh lobbied his colleagues. Not only was
the exclusion rejected, but a fresh provision was inserted. It made it a
criminal offence to discriminate against any community on the basis of
cultural, religious, sexual or linguistic affiliation.

It was this, perhaps, which made Nobrega more accommodating towards Abioseh. It was as if, deep down, he actually did have a soft spot
for him, ensuring that he received invitations to Mariposa for state func-
tions. Knowing that the role of a regent was always tricky, Nobrega used
his closeness to Abioseh and the political aristocracy to drive a wedge
between the rest of the junta and the traditionalists, who were mainly
unelected and unelectable chiefs. Abioseh was sceptical that Nobrega
was taking him under his wing, knowing all too well that people used
people.

Then, halfway through the junta's term, Abioseh was led to appreciate
the huge price of high office. It was on his birthday. He returned home
at around 2.00 AM from his party, which had been held at the Commodore Hotel, with Jacqui Morgan, the model he had first met on Carlos
Nobrega's yacht. He opened his remote-controlled gate and drove into
the garage. He had moved from his residence at Fear-the-Dog, but was
still in the same area. As the car rolled into the driveway, something
registered at the back of his mind as amiss, but he couldn't put his finger on it. The interior of the car, smelling of leather and perfume, was
flooded in warm and ambient light as soon as he killed the ignition.

'What a beautiful house,' Jacqui said. Even though he knew she was
stating the obvious, he had to agree that he'd been lucky to get the place.
Advised by a developer, he had gone to great expense to buy into this
exclusive neighbourhood of high walls, electric fencing topped by razor

wire and regular security patrols. The lethalness of the armed security companies, consisting mainly of retired policemen, was intimated in plaques riveted to walls. Garish depictions of dogs with dripping fangs, snakes and scorpions were visual deterrents situated alongside a warning, DANGER, in large red letters, superimposed over skull and crossbones. Accompanying these representations, in less frenzied script, were translations in various languages. Bangula was a democracy where would-be felons needed to be apprised of danger in their mother tongue, if they could read, that is.

This signage always amused Abioseh, with its suggestion that criminals either had the time or the inclination to read. Even all-night convenience stores or garages displayed signs that declared no cash was kept on the premises. Was this helpful advice aimed at prompting the would-be robber to scratch his head and ask himself: *If not here, where?* Often Abioseh would recall a sign that had caught his attention in a magazine featuring photographs by Gordon Parks of the American Civil Rights' struggle. Scrawled on a board at the entrance to an Alabama railway station in the early 1960s was a sign reading: *Nigger, if you can read this, run for your life*, and then, as an afterthought: *Even if you can't read it you'd best run anyway!*

Back at his house, the only instrument associated with running was the treadmill, which both Abioseh and Jacqui could see squatting in the anteroom. Abioseh regarded the device with mounting guilt as it crouched stubbornly, as if daring someone to use it. Silently he acknowledged Jacqui's evident fascination with his place by taking her through the sliding doors that opened into a well-equipped kitchen with tiled floors. 'I like this place,' he said, 'mainly for giving me the freedom to move in and out.'

'Facilitates the playboy lifestyle?'

Abioseh could think of no appropriate response and after a pause he said, 'I'm not a player.' He continued, for he imagined he had a healthy, if cautious, attitude towards women, 'And I'm not responsible for the speculations in the newspapers.' The gossip columns had named him,

among a gallery of testosterone jockeys, as one of Bangula's most eligible
bachelors. It had irked him to be in such average company.

JACQUI HAD LONG been an enigma for him, arousing a curiosity he hadn't
known he possessed. He had pursued her with an intensity that bor-
dered on madness, a contradiction that he quickly realised since, he had
convinced himself, he really wasn't attracted to her. Of course, she was
the epitome of glamour and intelligence, but there was something about
her that kept him on his guard. He didn't know what it could be, but
suspected it had something to do with the brazenness of her approach at
the marina, during the Colonel's 70th birthday celebration.

Jacqui had been a model, which meant that her wherewithal was located in her physicality, a frighteningly changeable currency whose worth
was dictated by the subjectivity of the beholders. And since most beholders on any island were likely to suffer from fatigue, boredom or the
effects of rum in the bloodstream, a girl had to devise other means of
survival if she wasn't going to end up counting the stars as she supported
the weight of some grunting official or marvelling at the cars of the rich
and the great as she sat on a high stool in the market peddling unsale-
able fish.

Diligently, come rain or shine, Jacqui had trudged the pavements, going from door to door, trying to convince the mandarins in financial
houses that there was room in the country for more beauty salons and
boutiques. She hit pay dirt with Gwandon Kone, the retired judge, who
invested in her initiatives out of a perverse need to prove reluctant investors wrong. In time, her businesses took off, with some of the shops
getting substantial cash injections from offshore companies that found
her ideas in line with their own growth strategies.

Watching these developments, Abioseh became convinced that Jacqui
was destined for greatness if she continued using her skills acquired in
securing businesses. He told himself that any intervention from him
would stifle the momentum of her achievements. The girl was on a roll.

He marvelled at her independence and was considering asking for her hand in marriage. When he broached the subject with MaZembe, she lost her temper. It was not a sudden flare-up but a gradual glowering that started with a bulging of her neck muscles before the veins popped out at her temples, giving Abioseh the impression that his mother was going to explode.

'You want to do *what?*' Before he could answer, she silenced him with a wave of a hand. 'You will do nothing of the sort,' she added. 'What are you trying to do – turn me into a laughing stock for all of Bangula to poke fun at? Over my dead body!'

Then MaZembe confirmed what he had long suspected. 'Everyone in Bangula,' she said, 'knows that she was one of your father's concubines.'

'That might have been the case, Ma,' he said lamely, 'but what does that have to do with me?'

'Do you want to dip your stick in the same well as your father?' Ma-Zembe looked at him with eyes that declared this question was unanswerable. 'You'd be going against tradition.'

But my father is dead, Abioseh wanted to say, but thought better of it. His mother was certainly headed for a stroke and he didn't wish to be credited with it. He considered sitting her down and taking her through reasoning which she, as a woman, would have had to understand and accept. And that was the fact that no one person belonged to another, not even a child to a parent. Past liaisons, however publicised, had nothing to do with the path that a person chose to follow today. Jacqui was an adult woman who had the right to be with whomever she chose to be with, as did he.

He realised – and this insight wearied him – that aspects of the past, and the eminent personalities that inhabited it, became handy ammunition against progress. Wrapped up in this was tradition, which had been central to human development for millennia. Everywhere in Bangula, there were men who called for a return to tradition, to the nebulous beliefs and modes of thinking inherited from the past. But they needed select chunks of the past that complemented their view of the world. It was this syndrome in the thirteenth century that had led the Catholic Church to mount crusades against what it regarded as heresy. It had been behind the American South's attempt to eradicate the collective memory of African slaves.

Abioseh supported tradition only in so far as it helped people to move forward. The notions of purity and continuity that his mother espoused, which were wrapped up in her discomfort at the continued prominence of a woman who had been her husband's lover, did not have a place in modern society. He might not marry Jacqui, he told himself, but he'd be damned if he wouldn't make her a part of his life. Come what may. He didn't care that others might see this liaison as a round-about, posthumous way of supplanting and challenging the Colonel in the sexual arena.

THIS EVENING, WITH something still nagging at him, he preceded Jacqui into the lounge, which was roomy by any standards and well lit by down-lights recessed into the ceiling. The sense of space was accentuated by mirrors and framed oil landscapes that were a song of praise to the freedom of an untamed land. Abioseh quickly fixed their drinks and flicked a switch that simultaneously dimmed the lights and issued forth the strains of a strings and horn collaboration by Eumir Deodato and Ali Farka Touré. The home theatre system was wrapped around the fire-place, the speakers unobtrusive in the corners, the bass solid, resounding through the lounge. Handing her a crystal glass of scotch and water, he was quick to assure her that this was not a prelude to a seduction.

'Looks pretty much like that to me,' Jacqui said, kicking off her high-heeled shoes and lowering herself onto the cream leather settee.

'No, really, it's not,' he said. 'When I was a younger man, I thought I was a hit with women; you know … that they were dancing to my tune. But it has long since dawned on me that I've been a puppet at the end of a female string.'

'You mean women have manipulated you?'

'No,' Abioseh said, 'that's too strong a word, and I don't like the idea of being a victim. What I mean is that we, men, simply don't have the foggiest notion what women are all about.'

'*I* don't give a damn about *men* as a species,' Jacqui said, an edge to her tone. She could have been remembering something that might have happened to her a long time ago, and which had very little to do with her host. 'We're talking about you here – that's what I'm interested in. You mean, then,' she asked, fixing him with an unwavering look, 'you don't know women?'

'I mean, women are the best in the insurance of life.'

'That's interesting. What do you mean, though?'

'Whatever women do,' Abioseh said, suddenly feeling tired, 'has something to do with the following day, the future. If it had been your birthday, I'm sure you'd not be thinking about the birthday party, the decor, the music and the illustrious guest list ...'

'But?'

'You'd be thinking about the implications of the next birthday,' he said. 'You'd be planning the next milestone, the eventual big five-oh, halfway house to a century and a death knell for many. I believe that when a woman meets a man, she's already got it figured out where to place him in her hierarchy of needs.'

'I don't get it ... isn't that how all human beings are supposed to behave?'

'Yes,' he replied, 'but it's a sharpened reflex with women. When they get into, say, a social situation, they know within the first minute of entering the room who they can pair with: for stability, for looking good, for fun, which includes sex ...'

'You mean for a good fuck?'

'Probably that, too,' he said. 'And the beauty of it all is that, when questioned about this, women will probably deny it – and they'd be meaning it. Some don't know that these are their innate reflexes.'

'And when did you become an expert on women's behaviour?'

'I must admit I don't know anything about women,' he began, 'since my parents didn't think it wise to have other children after they'd had me. So I don't even have a sister to study. Must have been my mother, perhaps, who put a stop to things, because the Colonel seems to have tried to create a clan of his own outside the family. Maybe,' he went on, looking pointedly at her, 'you'd know something about that ... Another drink?'

'No,' Jacqui said, 'not just yet.' She stared back at him. 'If you think I'm going to give you titbits on the Colonel, forget it.'

'Anyway,' Abioseh went on, shrugging off her defiance, 'at university, I thought I'd do a course in Women Studies, which meant I'd be one of the few men in women's company the whole day. I'd been told that was the best way to pull women.'

'Think the sisters would have fallen for the sensitive male feminist?' Jacqui was smiling, for the first time genuinely amused. 'You might have evolved your theories about women, but let me tell you something. Women aren't dumb; they've mastered insincerity ... shit ... they can smell insincerity a mile off.'

'That's strange, coming from you.' Abioseh grappled with words that wouldn't come out as patronising. 'I thought that as a model, selling the illusion of skin ... sex ... you'd prefer guys who would want to be with you for who you are and not ...'

'A bimbo?' Jacqui laughed. 'Come off it, Abioseh. Women will tell you all sorts of stuff about being objectified by men and so on. I suppose with all the porn and abuse – especially child abuse – around, people need to be on the level on the gender question. But, and this is my personal belief, I do want men to want me, to appreciate me for what I am, for the beauty and the brains that I possess. So long as somewhere we grow into the realisation that I'm not just a bunch of fine curves, tits and a bum. I'm much more than that. I'm a businesswoman. When I meet a man, a client, we talk business. No more, no less.'

'And the clients are cool with that?'

'They're fine.' Her look impressed on him that the clients had no choice but to accept her outlook. 'Before all this, I wanted to run a publishing house.'

'That's a strange move,' Abioseh said. 'From beauty to brains.'

'My point exactly,' Jacqui countered. 'They work in tandem.' She lit a cigarette. 'If you look at what's going on in this country,' she went on, 'the education, the industry, the commerce, everything is stacked against the blacks of Bangula. They're poor; they've never written anything of note that puts them on the map. Ezekiel Manolo is the only voice. But,' she went on, 'look at all the studies that have been done about the people of Bangula. Creoles are the ones writing bestsellers about our people. We're not a people but an anthropological study, guppies in a big fish tank, to be studied and interpreted for the world. Even your *acting* president, Carlos Nobrega ... did you know that he was a university professor? An industrial psychologist who specialises in the effects of slavery on the production capacity of the natives of Bangula?'

'I thought he was *your* buddy,' Abioseh said with a touch of malice.

'I don't know what's come over you today,' Jacqui said. 'But, whatever it is, deal with it before it kills you.'

It was late and he felt curiously disengaged from Jacqui, who had finished her cigarette and now stood with her arms folded beneath her breasts.

Given their surroundings, the ambient dark, this intimate space of magnificent furnishings complemented by music and understated lighting, Abioseh felt that they could have easily wrapped themselves around each other and exercised various muscles, enlivened the skin and let the glands go haywire in the appeasement of lust, for, he knew, there could be no love-making, no, not here, simply because there was no love.

Probably attuned to men and their vagaries, Jacqui gave a dramatic shiver. 'There's a certain ugliness in how we have related to one another this evening,' she said. 'Maybe the gods are trying to tell us something.

But, right now, I'd like to hit the sack. There must be a guest room in this mansion.'

'I feel like a swim,' Abioseh said. 'Join me?'

This gave him another opportunity to show her around the house, the bathrooms with ceramic tiles and glittering fixtures, the wooden panelling that ran through the passage to the sliding doors that led to the pool. Even here, through some ingenious sound engineering, the earlier track had given way to Wynton Marsalis blowing something cool and sad and memorable. Jacqui, with a sense of claiming every new space in which she found herself, had wrapped herself in a bathrobe Abioseh couldn't quite remember as one of his possessions. She was striding purposefully to the lip of the deep end of the pool, her calves rippling in a manifestation of rude good health he found vaguely enviable.

Looking up from her legs, past her rounded rear to her now exposed shoulders, the robe slipping to the floor, the strong arms raised to the sky as if in supplication, Jacqui preparing to dive, he noticed the element that had been nagging at him, like an irksome piece to a puzzle, and he shouted, 'Jacqui, *no!*' Although the momentum of her own enthusiasm nearly tipped her into the water, the horror in his voice effectively galvanised her mind and muscles, and she stopped, spun around and faced him.

'*What?*' She followed the direction of his gaze, which had settled fleetingly on the churning chlorinated water before lingering on an object that resembled a bundle of unwanted woollens bobbing on the water. In that instant, he recalled that Showa, his housekeeper's German Shepherd, hadn't come to greet him at the entrance, as was her habit. Abdullah, her owner, frowned on his bitch's antics, feeling that she was ignorant of her station in life and would one day cost him his job. But Abioseh, who normally didn't like dogs, went to great lengths to assure his housekeeper that Showa was okay. He'd come to like the dog, which had spirit; it was agile and balanced, longer than tall, giving an impression of strength and nobility. Where was Abdullah? Realising that the water might be infected – and, in any event, Showa was certainly dead, ruling out any urgency to retrieve her – he escorted a shaken Jacqui into the lounge and phoned Hiero.

'THAT'S THE REASON,' Hiero said, after leading the police forensic team to secure the grounds as a crime scene, 'I've always advised you to get body-guards. It's crazy living alone here.' He glanced at Jacqui, who was still wrapped in the bathrobe, as if the attire she had worn earlier might have become implicated in the events of the night. The handful of policemen tramped around the grounds and shone their torches into the bushes that formed part of the fence. Hiero directed them to the back rooms, the housekeeper's lodgings.

'The forensics boys say the pool was poisoned,' Hiero said, confirm-ing Abioseh's suspicions. Taking out his notebook, Hiero paged through. 'Someone wanted to kill you,' he said. 'The pool is full of hydrofluoric acid, which is very corrosive. They say here that it causes no painful burns on contact and this allows it to seep deeply into your tissue without you noticing. The acid can separate the calcium from the bones, causing them to liquefy. Then, skin, muscle and fat necrosis follows soon after.'

'Showa didn't have a chance,' Abioseh said.

'Someone,' Jacqui told Abioseh, 'must have wanted you not just dead but *disappeared* as well.'

'Shouldn't we go and see what had happened to Abdullah?' Abioseh asked.

'Let's give the police a chance to do their work,' Hiero said, his eyes on Jacqui. 'Did you hear anything since coming in here?'

'I heard nothing,' Jacqui replied, 'except music.'

Just then the police team returned from their search. Even though Abi-oseh was the most senior person around, an MP, the man they treated with overwhelming deference was Hiero, whom they referred to as Lieutenant. They even addressed him as 'The Lieutenant' in third person singular.

A slightly embarrassed Hiero was aware that, in contrast, when the policemen deigned to speak to Abioseh, they simply called him Mr Gondo. *Yes, Sir, Mr Gondo. No, Sir, Mr Gondo*, their blank eyes damning him, perhaps for not being the man his father was. Even though this was Abioseh's house, and the violation that had been committed by persons as yet unknown affected him, Hiero was sure that they saw Abioseh as one of the spoiled brats of the Reform, cashing in on his valuable name, knowing bugger-all about struggle. And this one was even fucking his late father's bitch. This class could have its dogs – and cats for that matter, take your pick – boiled in a cauldron, it didn't matter to the cops. Hell, they didn't have the luxury of owning pets; in their dwellings they didn't have room to swing a cat, let alone pamper one.

As for Jacqui, they couldn't lift their eyes to look at her above her neck, there being a rule that officers were authorised by tradition to probe the region around a woman's chest where there might be a concealed weapon. Hiero watched the minions of the law with an equal measure of amusement and annoyance. *They give us all a bad name*, he thought.

More urgently, the police had found Abdullah. Or to be more precise, the police dog had sniffed him out as he lay gagged, bound and blindfolded with a hood favoured by executioners over his head. His assailants, he was able to recount now that he had been rescued and given a stiff shot of brandy, although he wasn't a drinking man, had been loose with their tongues, as they went about the back room, waiting for Abioseh to arrive.

'One of them,' Abdullah recounted, 'was a tall man in a tracksuit. He had led the poisoning of the pool, since he had it from a reliable source that the Bossman . . .' he gulped guiltily, 'Master Gondo, liked to take a swim before going to bed. He said that he wanted to hear Boss—, Master Gondo, scream as he thrashed in the water and started being chewed by his pool. They laughed, promising to lie in the deckchairs and watch the action up close.'

'Maybe,' Jacqui put in evilly, 'they might even have sent out for popcorn?'

'How many were there?' asked Hiero. He detested frivolity.

'Four, Sir.' Abdullah was definite.

'How did you count them if you were blindfolded?'

'Before someone hit me on the head,' said Abdullah, who was lanky and as dark as night, with tired, unsurprised eyes, 'I'd seen what looked like three shadows. At first I thought it was the people from Armed Response, but as I was about to shout out, someone grabbed me from behind.' He gingerly felt the bump at the back of his head before looking at the speckling of blood.

'This was the tall man?' Hiero prompted.

'Yes,' Abdullah said. 'He had a long forearm covered in tracksuit fabric. He pushed me and hit me with something hard. I saw stars and I thought I was going to die. Then as the others came to where I lay, I heard Tall Man ordering someone who smelled of liquor, *Give me the fucking jerry can*. The others laughed and the tipsy man grumbled that Tall Man wasn't his boss; they were all equal in the eyes of the law. *The law?* queried Tall Man. *Don't make me laugh!*'

Not liking his vocation being ridiculed, one of the cops asked, 'Should we take Mr Abdullah to the station to continue with the investigation?'

'No,' Abioseh intervened. 'He's been through a lot. In fact, he should see a doctor. His light-headedness might be the result of taking a knock on the head.'

Bristling visibly, one of the officers started to pull himself up to his full height before Hiero snapped him a warning look. Jacqui went into the bathroom. Hiero helped Abioseh support his somewhat groggy helper to the back room to change and prepare for a ride to the clinic.

'I hope to God they're open,' Abioseh prayed. Hiero sympathised with him. The service levels of the public sector did not inspire confidence.

Inside Abdullah's lodgings, the look on Abioseh's face told Hiero that the 'Bossman' knew very little of the life of the man who was at his beck and call. Abioseh looked stunned, as if it were he who had taken a knock on the head. The cottage consisted of a single room dominated by an austere iron bedstead supporting a sagging and lumpy mattress that was covered with a patchwork quilt duvet. Abdullah had used curtains and Masonite room dividers to demarcate a bathroom, kitchen and closet. The only ornamentation on the walls were small, framed daguerreotype pictures of pastoral scenes and portraits that must have been taken almost two centuries ago. On the bed was a neatly arranged pile made up of a hymnal, an Old Testament, a folded Zion Christian Church tunic and a silver-grey iron star set into a green velour ribbon, a medal of his sanctity.

The men turned their backs to give Abdullah the privacy to change and then splash his face with water. He groaned, presumably when he touched the sore spot on his head. Then there was a rustle of clothes being hastily donned. 'We all set, Boss,' Abdullah said.

In the 4.00 AM gloom, Abioseh and Hiero watched Abdullah locking his rickety door. 'I'll need to get a stronger door,' Abioseh murmured, but it was clear that he was a little distracted. 'He seems a lot better, doesn't he?'

'Let's hear what the doctor says,' Hiero responded.

Jacqui joined them. She took Abdullah's hands in hers. 'How do you feel?'

'He'll survive,' Abioseh said, more out of nervousness and wishful thinking than out of authority and conviction.

Jacqui gave him a look. 'There you go,' she said, 'taking away his voice. He's the one who got roughed up, so how would you know how he feels?'

Sensing that he might be the cause of disagreement among his benefactors, Abdullah was quick to smile. 'I'm fine, Boss,' he said. To demonstrate this, he took a couple of steps up and down the edge of the garden, swinging his arms — and then folded, slowly, as if about to inspect a particularly niggling clump of weeds among the marigolds, and sank into a flower bush with a sigh.

2

IT WAS WITH a certain bitterness that two weeks later Abioseh the Anointed One, as the newspapers had taken to calling him, buried his trusted housekeeper whom he had never really got to know. He felt removed, estranged from the rest of the people, even though he had paid for all funeral arrangements and had been present in all developments, as well as establishing contact with the Zion Christian Church officials. Abdullah's relatives came and camped in Abioseh's house. They ate his food and drank his liquor; one cousin even made a pass at Jacqui, who had become a regular visitor to the house. Abioseh organised for a tent to be erected to accommodate the increasing population of Abdullah's friends and relatives. Abdullah, they said, was so blessed to have had such a great man as his patron.

Abioseh participated in some of the night-time activities, but mostly he went to bed, listening to the same syncopated beat to the hymns, hands clapping, feet stomping and tent shuddering as if in celebration, until the vigil of the last night and, mercifully, the funeral on the following day. Later, he arranged transport back to the hinterland for Abdullah's people.

The funeral over, Abioseh was overwhelmed by fatigue and was confined to bed for nearly a week. He blamed his father for having cultivated an environment in which his leadership position had been so coveted that people were willing to commit murder in its pursuit. This was a situation where the whole of government had revolved around the president to the extent that Cabinet ministers and the ministries and departments they piloted through the administrative maze tried to second-guess the president's wishes and aspirations.

The handful of mavericks, the ministers or other high officials, who had dared to challenge the Colonel's policies, had not lasted. Media commentators, seeing the turnover, remarked that the real kiss of death for officials was for them to be publicly commended and referred to as presidential material.

The same media started sniffing around soon after Abdullah's burial. In finely managed pieces, someone (and Abioseh couldn't rule out one of the disgruntled policemen) had leaked the story of Abdullah's dog and its owner's subsequent death. Abioseh's residence was now kept under surveillance by both police guards and photographers looking for a scoop; perhaps the next time a horse might stumble into the drink.

In private, however, journalists asked questions, probing, until they cornered Jacqui. They got the story of the attempt on the life of the heir apparent and the actual killing of his housekeeper. Somehow, Hiero's name was kept out of the controversy. In no time, Carlos Nobrega was fingered as the one responsible for the assassination attempt. This was whispered in the long queues as people waited for taxis; it was spoken in slightly louder tones in taverns and at sports grounds where spectators watched soccer while they savoured their brews.

A rumour that had started as a small seed grew into a tall and sturdy plant that could withstand the buffeting winds. It was a plant whose seeds would harden inside the pod and would scatter at the season's end, spreading everywhere.

One by one, those implicated in the plan to cut Abioseh off from the presidency became casualties of investigations that were kept alive in the newspapers. Suddenly, confidential psychiatric records were broadcast in the public media, in this country where any form of mental illness could banish a patient from the human race. Others found their private financial dealings the subject of headlines that were framed with the sniffy suggestion of graft.

When Carlos Nobrega was implicated in a multi-million-dollar property development project that would situate primary schools next to strip clubs, there was an uproar from parents and a call for an inquiry, which was invariably a call for someone's head.

At around the same time, Dr Caramel Sebone-Prah left the select committee on communications and Abioseh was promoted to chairman in her place. His star rose in inverse proportion to the reverses suffered by Nobrega and his faction.

The sleaze that attached itself to government was so widespread that strikes and huge unrest broke out. The junta chugged along for two more years to complete its five-year mandate. An electoral commission was set up to pave the way for national elections and most of the incumbents were relieved of their duties. The junta was dissolved.

On the 13th of January, Abioseh Gondo became the president of the republic.

His inauguration happened on the afternoon of a day of remarkable ordinariness. The sun shifted at noon to create shadows under people's eyes. It caused those who could not have been accused of having a sinister bone in their body to seem more like Hiero's henchmen. Their distinguishing marks were shaded glasses even in the gloomiest of hours.

For some reason, even as he stood taking the oath before the Chief Justice, hearing as if from a great distance the weighty words relating the range of his future responsibilities, Abioseh recalled another gathering where people had sat unflinching under the sun, their collective brow tinted by a light that deepened the shadows under their eyes, at his father's funeral. His mother had occupied a seat among the honoured guests at the top table, overcome by grief she could not express. Here she was now, proud in her new dress of navy-blue crushed cotton set off by orange organza piping, a stylish modern hat that must have challenged the milliner, because it was fronted by a veil that was itself patterned with intricate designs that must have been inspired by a bridal exhibition. She appeared, even to him, to have been overwhelmed by a quiet pride, like deceptive embers that are capable of generating great heat.

Abioseh felt a surge of guilty delight, as if he was indulging in something delectable but which should be consumed in moderation. That his ascension to power had been written on his birth certificate did little to assuage the feeling of entitlement. If his father had paved the way for him to accept this sceptre of power, then, so be it. Not normally a believer in fate, he nevertheless accepted the notion of some form of ineffable cosmic design, which set in motion a series of interconnected events. He was the son of the Colonel, a man who had sweated blood to bring about the Reform, and *he* had deserved to be president, no matter how much he, Abioseh, might have had difficulties with the deployment of power. With his mother beaming somewhere off to his left, Abioseh, right hand raised, swore in the name of the Father, the Son and the Holy Ghost.

3

EVEN TEN YEARS after the Colonel's death, Hiero still got occasional reminders that he needed to go over his lineage. When he rifled through his father's old things and scrutinised old photographs, he saw nothing that connected him with his dada except for a fondness for alcohol. Even physically they were like chalk and cheese. His dada had been small and very dark whereas he was tall, big-boned and light-skinned, sometimes being mistaken for a Creole in the half-light of a bar's interior.

In his dreams he encountered shadows that urged him to go deeper into his past and peel the various layers of memory to discover his life's purpose. In one dream, he was a newborn baby as Emma-May listened to a seer telling her that Hiero had been brought into this world bearing gifts needed by the community. *What gifts? What community?*

When he asked his mother, she glared at him, her eyes narrowed. 'What are you trying to say?' she asked. 'Are you aware of the implications of your question? Are you saying I cheated on your father? Why don't you get a wife and give her a child and be satisfied that that's *your* purpose in life, instead of stinking up my house with your vomit?' End of enquiry.

But it didn't end in his mind. Time and again he visited the shamans who spoke to him in the obscure language of the spirits. There were rituals and sacred methods of divining a person's purpose. Hiero should know, however, that the price could be high if he engaged with that world but didn't see the course to its logical end. Was he ready for that? Did he have time and the spiritual resources to enter those sacred spaces where consciousness could be moved backward through time? Dabbling with spirits in a half-baked manner could lead to madness ... was he ready for that?

He wasn't ready for anything that could lead to madness. He decided to visit Baluba Jambo. Baluba's proximity to the dead could perhaps provide a short-cut to spiritual insights without offending ancestors and incurring their wrath. Hiero believed that he had a much bigger role to play in Bangula other than providing security for Abioseh Gondo, the president of the country. Reviewing his dada's photographs, he noted a passing resemblance between Abioseh and his dada. Shrugging off that possibility, Hiero started suspecting that perhaps the madness had already taken root a long time ago.

Baluba Jambo's secretary, a bewigged middle-aged woman in dark glasses ushered Hiero into a cold chamber darkened by maroon drapes. Baluba Jambo's hugeness, as well as his deep ebony complexion, seemed to absorb any light in the room. A family of five, consisting of a reedy middle-aged man, his distracted wife and two disinterested teenage boys and a girl, stood before a casket containing the body of an elderly man, definitely someone's grandfather, his nose and ears stuffed with cotton wool. Baluba Jambo was reciting the virtues of his funeral service, making it sound like a package tour to the mainland. 'We're now offering an aftercare programme,' he added, 'which has been known to help the survivors work through their individual grief.' As he handed them glossy leaflets, which he called 'informative literature on the many different situations, such as the loss of a spouse, loss of a child, suicide, etc.', a nervous look passed between the couple. Then they glanced at their children as if monitoring someone's reaction to the promotion of a dodgy cult.

Hiero wanted to laugh. Baluba hadn't changed one bit.

A few minutes later, Baluba escorted the family members out, his arms managing simultaneously to hug and guide them up the stairs into the sunshine outside. After waving the family goodbye, Baluba drew Hiero into the workshop section of the mortuary. The large, brightly lit hall the size of a small warehouse buzzed with activity, three men attending to cadavers on trolleys. Hiero almost gagged at the sight of one of the young attendants plugging a hole in a skull with cosmetic cement, rearranging the scalp and smoothing the hair of a respectable-looking corpse. 'Gunshot wounds,' Baluba explained. 'Pure murder.'

'Can we talk somewhere else?' Hiero asked.

Re-emerging into the sunlight Baluba asked, 'What brings you here? I like business but I hate to be of service to people I know.' He frowned. 'Emma-May?'

'I'm not here officially,' Hiero replied. 'And my mother is fine, thank you for asking.' He paused, thinking. 'I've a peculiar bone to pick with you.'

'In this business,' Baluba said, 'I've come to expect people to throw at least one or two curveballs at me. Death brings out latent creativity in all of us.'

'Mine is really strange.' Hiero was suddenly at a loss for words.

'Try me.'

'I wish to find out,' Hiero said, 'if the Colonel was in any way related to me.'

'You mean,' Baluba Jambo asked, 'if he was your real dada?'

'Yes.' Hiero started to squirm. 'I feel like an idiot.'

'You *are* an idiot,' Baluba said simply. 'Everyone knows the Colonel's *your* dada.' He gazed down at him. 'Matter of fact I was going to call you.

You and Zebulon.'

'Really?'

'Really.' Baluba Jambo released a small smile. 'What does your ma say?'

'She'll hear none of it.'

'Well, what did you expect?' Baluba Jambo said. 'Mothers have to tell lies to reassure the world that there's no such thing as infidelity.'

'What about Abioseh?'

'I don't know about Abioseh,' Baluba Jambo said. 'There's no telling how many children really came out of the Colonel's testicles. Some look like him, others look like other men who're supposed to be their fathers. Who's to tell?'

'Is there a way we can verify things … that I'm his son?'

'Like how?'

'Through the shamans. You must be close to them. The traditionalists … in your line of work …'

'The shamans have other pressing matters to deal with right now.' Baluba sounded a little irritated. 'And the traditionalists want to introduce a few changes in Bangula. They don't like the way things are going.'

'I need to verify things,' Hiero said, ignoring the line that the conversation was taking, 'so that I can claim what's mine.'

'Ten years *after* the man is dead and you want to stake a claim?' Baluba's tone betrayed real wonderment. 'Look. Forget that. There are better routes to power. Trust me. There's a lot we can accomplish together.'

'What?'

'Let me tell you what the people have in mind.' There was a finality to the offer Baluba was about to make. 'And *you* judge if you want to be a part of that.'

'Tell me.'

TWO WEEKS LATER, Hiero broached the idea with the president that the masses wanted to commemorate the first decade of the Colonel's death.

Wary of perceptions that he was promoting a personality cult, Abioseh asked Hiero to give him evidence that the proposal had support. Inside a week, the conservatives were loud in the land, pinning the increase of blood plague infections on Abioseh's administration. Even though some of the more discerning editorials pointed out that the epidemic had actually soared during the Colonel's time and reached its peak during the junta, there was already a groundswell of opinion against any of Abioseh's initiatives. There was resistance to quarantine; when the government indicated the virulence of the contagion, the relatives simply accused it of a cynical form of genocide by not finding effective remedies. It was a no-win situation. The crunch came when the burial grounds were full to capacity and the mortuaries were bursting at the seams. Hamilton Sodoku, the minister of health, proposed to Cabinet that a mass grave under controlled conditions was the only way to obviate a catastrophe. There was an uproar when he suggested that the dead bodies could be impregnated with chemicals to ensure that the disease spread no further.

Sitting in on the Cabinet meeting, Hiero knew that the proposal was stillborn. Later he had a private chat with Abioseh.

'With all due respect,' he said, 'using bulldozers to shovel bodies into a big hole can't be acceptable. People will rise up against you.'

'Is that a view informed by intelligence?' Abioseh asked. 'Or is it informed by the ambitions of the conservatives?'

'It could be both,' Hiero said truthfully. 'But you'd do yourself a favour by taking a softer line on one of their wishes.'

'What's that?'

'To commemorate the Colonel.'

'Well,' Abioseh said, considering. 'If it really means so much to the people ...'

ZEBULON HEARD OF the planned commemoration while en route to Napa, a village on the valley of the Gomano. Napa had been in the news on account of thirteen-year-old Timi Seramen. He was in such a state of shock that he had lost his speech and was known as the saddest person in Bangula. Once a sleepy hamlet, Napa now resembled a holiday resort.

Timi's legendary sadness had drawn a succession of religious men from various denominations to the Seramen home. Those from charismatic sects that were familiar with exorcism and hand-to-hand combat with the Evil One, lit candles, sprinkled mysterious spring water and called upon God's miracles. When the boy's sadness intensified, they asked the Almighty to send not only His only begotten Son, but a host of angels as well, as this enterprise called for divine reinforcements. Timi continued to fix his absent eyes on these ineffective attempts with stubborn silence. Chastened, the men left, promising they would return. The villagers knew they were seeing the last of them.

Zebulon discussed the boy's case with Zoya. She wasn't convinced that it was worth the journey, suspecting that the boy was a spoilt brat. She also couldn't accompany Zebulon for that was her week on call at the meteorological centre. 'You can go,' she said, 'and save the boy. *I've* to make sure the rest of humankind won't get caught napping if a cyclone hits us.' Although they'd both laughed at her feigned self-importance, Zebulon knew that she took her work seriously.

He eventually met with Timi's family; although the parents weren't interested in politics, they easily linked Zebulon to the trouble brewing in the mountains. But since they wanted their son restored to health, anyone would do.

He spent a week in Napa, visiting the boy every morning, taking him on walks, listening to him even though he couldn't talk. Zebulon had already established that Timi's condition was mute hysteria. On the sixth day, Zebulon learnt that the boy's greatest wish was to meet the president. Using his hands, Timi conveyed that he would 'tell' the president what had traumatised him. Zebulon promised that he would do all in his power to arrange a meeting. With his mission partly accomplished, Zebulon went back to Jambora.

'Are you really going to do it?' Zoya asked him in the evening.

'I've no option,' Zebulon said. 'I gave my word.'

'Good luck,' Zoya said. 'If you ever crack the meeting, please tell the president we need help at the Centre.'

Zebulon merely nodded. He didn't relish the prospect of an encounter with Abioseh.

'Promise you'll tell him.' She looked at him, something beginning to dawn on her. 'Oh,' Zoya said. 'Before I forget, Baluba Jambo came looking for you.'

'What does he want?'

'He refused to tell me,' Zoya said. 'I suppose it's men's business.'

'I don't want Baluba coming here when I'm not around,' Zebulon growled.

'You know what I think?' Zoya asked. 'I think Baluba Jambo is up to something. And we'd better be on our guard.'

'I'm always on my guard.'

'And the people applauded,' Zoya said.

HIERO SOON SAW evidence of how much commemorating the Colonel meant to the people. Hundreds packed the city hall, the crowds overflowing onto the street outside, blocking traffic and causing it to detour. They came from all regions, using all forms of transport. Hiero saw reports of hordes on foot, donkey-drawn carriages, minibus taxis, buses, long-distance trucks and the most modern sedans. They came singly or in groups, as families or neighbourhoods, all impelled to pay homage to a man credited with starting a movement that resonated with their hearts.

Seeing the multitude, hungry, tired, some weary, others bright, the young and the old, the lame and the crippled, Hiero remembered that the Colonel had been more of a symbol than a hands-on leader, believing in delegation and the distribution of power. That way, he had as many friends with power as he had enemies, the two camps cancelling each other out and leaving him free to plan. The Colonel had held that a leader's strength lay more in maintaining a polity without drama than in increasing the number of vocal supporters. According to the Colonel, countries whose leaders always featured in newspapers, where they commented on this or that issue or laid out measures to combat this or that problem, were in trouble. The effective ones were quietly running their affairs without drama. As far as he was concerned, bodies such as the UN were merely amphitheatres for political performances. In that regard, you hardly ever came across a public initiative by Switzerland, yet it was one of the most successful economies on the globe. Africans, he maintained, were so full of drama that they couldn't do anything without fanfare. 'Africans,' he would say, 'confuse effectiveness with noise. That's why some even get buried with their drums, to continue the racket as ancestors.'

There was a rustle of plastic bags containing fried chicken, roast potatoes and cabbage. This fare would be washed down with tepid, over-sweetened tea as the eaters' greasy hands ceaselessly waved off swarms of flies. Some would break out with the bawdy corruption of a hymn, the lyrics of sanctity substituted with indelicate references to what Abioseh and Jacqui were assumed to be doing in private.

Hiero marvelled at the inventive use of technology, something that he couldn't immediately link to traditionalists. The Colonel's colour photograph had been blown up into a giant presence across the wall, presiding in death much more intensely than when alive. *I'm supposed to be the spymaster here*, he thought, *the spook, but I know precious little about what's going on.*

Baluba Jambo seemed to be in charge of the programme. Chairing a panel with three speakers on either side of him, he facilitated the afternoon's agenda with great skill. He introduced the speakers and their topics while ensuring that people bore in mind that the Colonel was the man of the hour. Speakers, mostly men in big coats even though it was thirty degrees Celsius in the shade and ridiculously humid, flayed Abioseh's regime, lamenting the extent to which it had strayed from the path. Watching the goings-on, with her face resting on her hands, was the sixth panellist, Zoya Badawi, in a lemon two-piece calico suit and a matching headscarf. Now and then she straightened up to whisper something to Baluba, who nodded and then scribbled on his notepad.

An elderly man, who had been sitting quietly fanning himself with a bunch of newsprint, raised his hand. Baluba Jambo noticed him. 'Yes, Damaseku?'

'Yes, You-Who-Sits-On-The-Chair,' Damaseku said. 'What is *this* path?'

There was a brief confusion at the table, as the speakers conferred, like sappers drawing straws as to who will go out first to defuse an anti-personnel landmine. Baluba then turned to his neighbour on the panel. 'Zoya?' he called. 'Want to take the question?'

'Nope,' said Zoya, her face impassive. 'I just sing. I don't do paths.'

There was a general titter. An unamused Baluba Jambo stood up and waddled to the edge of the stage. Sweating in his black undertaker's suit, he constantly wiped his brow with a white handkerchief as broad as a pillowslip.

'The path that Damaseku's asking about,' he started, 'and which Ms Badawi — our esteemed weathergirl — doesn't *do*, whatever *that* means, consists of all the things that held us together as a people. In the days when Ramala was the president, a lot of trouble stalked us. The Colonel arrived like benevolent rains and introduced measures that benefited the native people of Bangula. Certainly, there was illness and death ...'

'And of course the undertaker made a killing!' someone shouted, his raucous voice eliciting a ripple of merriment.

Baluba Jambo raised his hand, smiling thinly and staring with mock sternness at the bright spark. 'I look forward,' he said, 'to being of service to you soon, Sonny.' He laughed at his own witticism before getting down to the serious matter at hand.

'The brother's right,' he continued. 'Death happened, but it was in the acceptable context of nature, the journeying of man into the land of the spirits. But now, there is something unacceptable about the frequency of the burials, and I should know something about that. The gravesite is protesting and saying: *No more; enough is enough*, at the sight of so many of our dead.'

To Hiero, Baluba's fluent recital bore the hallmark of a rehearsed piece. As the heat rose in the packed hall where no one was laughing, Baluba dismantled Abioseh's government as he elevated the Colonel's legacy, destroying any possibility of a meeting of minds between the two. 'They might have been related by blood,' Baluba said, 'but, without casting aspersions on the miraculous mechanism of birth – and without sullying the integrity of the Mother of our Nation, MaZembe – we cannot help but ask: *Is this really the Colonel's flesh and blood?* And if so: *Why is there this dissimilarity?*'

Hiero experienced a moment of immediate identification with Abioseh, who had declined an invitation to the memorial. Aware that his father was revered even though he had been a knave, Abioseh couldn't help but hold in contempt his praise singers. But, and there was the nub, Abioseh must have felt a twinge of envy: the Colonel had lived life to the full. Hiero drew a parallel between the Colonel and his own dada; both men had feasted on fresh female flesh and had lived their lives on their own terms. Panicked, Hiero realised that he and Abioseh had no offspring. He recalled a chilling line in the Book of Job: *His remembrance shall perish from the earth and he shall have no name in the street*. His mother's earlier rebuke that he should get himself a wife echoed in his ears, as did Baluba's lecture, which had become a harangue.

'It is also easier,' he was saying, 'to glorify one who's no longer alive, who cannot embarrass us. But we know that the Colonel wouldn't have embarrassed us. Or put up with police inaction. The other day, thieves crated off an entire surgical operating room's equipment. The only items lacking were surgeons and scrub nurses. In the time of the Colonel, you'd never see bank robberies in broad daylight, with the robbers no longer bothering with disguises ...'

Hiero stopped listening. He had heard the litany of woes, many of them unverifiable as there was no record in the police files. Of course, as with any country, things were bad and poverty was undermining the gains made under the Colonel's administration. Hiero headed law enforcement. He knew. But then, the earlier dream and the issue around his life's purpose returned – and he imagined something unstoppable that he'd have to embrace.

'The present government has failed us,' Baluba Jambo thundered, 'and we need a new race of men and women to rise and take control.'

The same joker of the rough voice shouted again, his voice now devoid of levity, 'I propose that we get Zebulon Gondo to lead us.'

The hall exploded. Chants resounded and filled the corners of the building, rousing exhausted travellers from afar who had seized a brief moment to nod off. A quivering alto started another song, no longer lambasting Abioseh's government but welcoming a future guaranteed by the continued good health of one Zebulon Gondo. Listening to the song Hiero wondered vaguely if Zebulon really knew what lay in store for him.

'WHAT DO YOU think?' Josephine asked her two life companions. Jumaima and Jutaita, not used to hearing their opinionated crony voicing uncertainty, looked at each other, hoping to find answers in their eyes. However, having witnessed so much through the years, their eyes had learnt to reveal nothing.

Josephine knew that the pressure of silence, the weight of the things that lay unspoken in their hearts would finally loosen their tongues. So she turned her back on her friends and looked at the crowds streaming out of the hall. Some people were resolutely trekking to the taxi rank; others looked warily about as if wondering where they would get shelter before embarking on the long hike back to the hinterland. The three women were more fortunate as they had temporarily vacated their house in Cinnamon Hill to enjoy Zoya's hospitality. They waited for their hostess to drive them to her place to freshen up and have a cup of tea.

'They should stay put in the hall,' Josephine said to herself. Having long lost the sense to keep her thoughts private, she was overheard by both Jutaita and Jumaima, who naturally concluded that she was speaking to them.

'Who should stay put, homegirl?' Jumaima asked.

'Yes, who?' Jutaita also wanted to know.

'Those country yokels,' Josephine replied, 'should stay put in that hall.'

'Maybe,' Jumaima suggested, 'they got revved up, got to shake the bones.'

'Yep,' Jutaita agreed. 'Baluba Jambo sure knows how to set a crowd afire.'

'He does that,' Josephine agreed. She returned to her opening question. 'What do you think, homegirls?'

'You're not really asking us anything,' Jumaima lamented. 'You're actually telling us that something doesn't sit right with you, *homza*, is that it?'

'Which aspect makes you unhappy?' Jutaita asked. 'The Baluba Jambo part or the Zebulon part?'

'I figure both,' Josephine answered in a small voice. 'This thing is huge. Maybe people like Baluba Jambo are built for it, being an undertaker and all that, but Zebulon …'

'Zebulon *is* a big boy,' Jumaima said, 'if one goes by the smile on Zoya's face.'

'*Homza*,' Josephine insisted patiently, 'this thing is serious. We're talking about someone taking on the *president*, here.'

'*Another* big boy,' Jumaima put in. They shut her up with dark looks.

'The thing we've got to ask ourselves is: *Is this the correct thing?*' Jutaita pondered. 'We've got to weigh things up. What kind of changes do we want to see? Has Abioseh really failed? Is Zebulon the correct candidate for president?' She paused. 'Sometimes he strikes me as a little crazy.'

'Wouldn't you go crazy, too,' Jumaima asked, 'if you spent your waking hours staring at dead people?'

'Don't *we* do that every day, girls?' Josephine asked. 'Watch them walking up and down the streets, some even occupying the seats of the mighty?'

'Yep. Only someone needs to tell them they're dead,' Jutaita said. Her face lightened up as Zoya wove her way through the crowd, which was thinning but still considerable. Her progress was slowed down by well-wishers who shook her hand or embraced her, looking up at her face, which was flushed from the combined effects of late afternoon heat and excitement. 'Here comes the princess!'

THAT NIGHT, GLOWING from having accomplished something, Zoya played host to her grandmothers, demonstrating that their cooking lessons had not been wasted on her. She boasted about the alterations to their recipes, showing her ingenious capacity to scavenge in the remotest parts of the island to get the ingredients for mango chutney.

'You can't find fresh garlic or ginger in the stores or the market,' she said, 'so I used dried ground ginger and garlic.' She also had no pepper sauce to make her grandmothers' chicken recipe, which they'd filched from some academic dreamer from the Caribbean. 'I rustled up some red pepper and paprika spices, oregano and coriander. I don't care what you say,' she added, eyes bright as if she'd just taken a hit from a reefer, 'but *I* believe this tastes great!'

'We agree with you,' Jumaima said, smacking her lips in an exaggerated show of appreciation. 'Your cooking has improved considerably.'

'And so has her modesty,' Josephine observed slyly.

Zebulon arrived accompanied by Baluba Jambo, who looked merry and smelled a little of alcohol. The presence of the two men brought a chill into the evening, as if the four women were suddenly constrained. Zoya was irritated with the way Baluba Jambo showed off the property, which he had rented for Zoya and Zebulon, until, he had said, they found their feet. It was a beautiful villa on prime real estate near the sea, the kind of place where tourists spent plenty of time barbequing or swimming and taking in the local sights. She and Zebulon sometimes explored the surrounding areas, the rocky and sandy beaches, mountain-top look-out vistas and the quaint fishing village of Amutiya. It had a small bay lined with white sand and an unpaved road for leisurely walking and, depending on the availability of merchandise, shopping.

Zoya escorted the old women to their sleeping quarters, past the private swimming pool that was surrounded by a patio, a lawn and several large palm trees. They finally ensconced themselves in the guest bedroom, which had a king-size bed, a sofa and a small kitchen. 'This,' Zoya said, 'is only ten minutes' walk from the beach and very close to public transportation points.'

'Answer me this one,' Jumaima said. 'With a place like this, where you get to heaven without first dying, why would you want to fight the government?'

'That's a very good question.' Zoya used the old women's own ruse to deflect the enquiry. 'But it's been a long day and we're starting early tomorrow.'

'That,' said Josephine, already under the sheets, 'is my little girl.'

SHE LEFT THEM, three little wizened dolls who were too worn out to engage in further banter. Zoya wondered whether it had been a good idea to give them wine, which they had drunk with great enjoyment. But their light-headedness, she knew, came more from the joy of reconnecting with their favourite granddaughter than from intoxication. She accepted, also, that they were no spring chickens and the excitement of the day would tax the healthiest of people.

The warning light that flashed in her head when she got a whiff of alcohol on Baluba's breath was set off by a distant memory of her own father, a man she had once worshipped and lost. In momentary confusion, she almost launched an attack on Zebulon, suspecting that he'd also had a drink. Firmly he assured her of his sobriety. 'I will not disappoint you,' he said. 'Trust me.'

Zoya sensed his anger, however, and it created complications for their evening. She could tell that he was dissatisfied with something, perhaps a matter relating to Baluba Jambo. Whatever it was, she knew it would seep into the room like water from a sewer. Looking at him and seeing him as if for the first time, she noticed a forehead that was broad and high and eyes that were set wide apart under almost-girlish lashes. 'Is something the matter?'

'I hear you were rude to Baluba Jambo today,' Zebulon said.

For a moment, Zoya thought she might have misheard him, but then the jumble of words rearranged themselves into an accusation. Standing at the sink, looking down at the pile of dishes and wondering where to start, her own anger brewed in some small spot in her gut and rose up to her mouth, tasting of bile. She wanted to tell Zebulon that organising today's commemoration service had taken its toll on her. She had been part of the committee ensuring that people were transported, sheltered and fed; Baluba Jambo had been nowhere near the arrangements that needed his muscle. She wanted to say that he embodied the kind of leadership that arrived only when all the work had been done to claim the credit. Moreover, the man got on her nerves; he was creepy. Instead she said, 'Baluba Jambo is an idiot.'

'Well,' Zebulon answered, 'it's perhaps best to bear in mind that the idiot subsidises this villa, where you can entertain the Three Wise Hags.'

'They're my friends,' she snapped back, 'and you'll have to live with that. They might be hags, but doesn't it bother you that their combined body mass is less than that of One Fat Politician?'

'What's Baluba Jambo's size got to do with it?'

'Everything. Unless a politician has glandular problems,' Zoya went on, 'that person has no business putting on weight. It's a visible symptom of self-indulgence.'

'Well,' Zebulon said heatedly, 'that's just childish prejudice. And I'm ashamed of the *self-indulgence* in your thinking.'

'Fine,' Zoya said, squirting dishwashing liquid into the sink, turning on the taps and lowering her face into the swirling steam.

She watched the foam, the globules eating into the grease, the evidence of the meal she had cooked with love and care disintegrating into nothingness. An observation her father had once made returned to her. 'Humankind,' he said, 'from the cradle to the grave, is in the industry of making refuse. Half of what you cook ends up as trash; you buy a car and its final destination is a scrapyard, metal trash. We go to the toilet and flush away our trash. Even death is a form of manufacture of garbage, which is either burnt in a crematorium or stored six feet under a layer of dirt and rock.' Dr Badawi's lesson to his daughter was that she should minimise making garbage. A human being should conduct his or her affairs with care, ensuring that nothing of their own personal baggage (or garbage) spilled over into the next person's domain.

Why am I thinking about garbage?

'I'd thought,' she said sadly, averting a face now moistened by steam and tears, 'that you were different, a democrat. But I can see that you're just another despot.'

'Perhaps,' Zebulon countered, 'that's exactly what this country needs. A strong hand that will put to rights some of the ancestral wrongs.'

'And you believe that *you* have that strong hand?'

'Indubitably.'

Like someone learning a new language, Zebulon practised the latest words he'd acquired from night school on her. It seemed to her that he was also getting lessons in attitude. She supposed it was all part of his preparation to govern with a strong hand. She wondered bleakly whether she wanted to have anything to do with it. He looked at her, his shirt unbuttoned. 'I've got a heavy day tomorrow. I'm taking the boy to see the president.'

'Is that right?' Zoya feigned interest. She couldn't give two hoots, really. 'I suppose you'll be scoping out Mariposa, your new residence if everything goes according to plan?'

'There's no room for anything to go awry,' Zebulon said, making the last word rhyme with *cowry*. 'Plans never go wrong; people do.'

Zoya let that one pass. 'As I've asked you before, could you do me a favour, when you talk to the president? Please bring to his attention the state of the equipment at the weather station. It's scandalous.' She stared at him for a minute. 'Think you can do that?'

'If there's an opening,' Zebulon said. 'You know how these things are.'

'I'm sorry,' Zoya said, 'I don't *know* how these things are. I thought you just spoke to the president and gave him a list of your needs … am I right?'

'You make it sound like going to a supermarket.'

'It *is* a fucking supermarket of the country's inventory of needs.' Zoya was fast losing it. 'A president is just a supermarket manager, ensuring that we get all our groceries. The cashier's the national treasurer working with the taxman. They give us the goodies and then slap us about if we buy too much on tick.'

Zebulon stood stock-still. He started to say something but thought better of it. 'I'm pleased to know you regard me as future flunkey-in-chief of retail,' he said with a self-deprecating shrug, a peace offering. 'Well, I'm hitting the sack. Coming?'

'It's dubitable.'

4

FOR DAYS, MARIPOSA buzzed with activity once the visit was arranged. Child psychologists were called in to supervise the decor of the lounge where the president received visitors. *Shouldn't we place a stuffed panda here?* the organisers asked one another, *near the chaise longue, which the boy will occupy? And what kind of chow must be supplied, so that the kid could have a nibble while chatting to the Big Man? But won't that be a sign of excess? The boy, after all, is known to be a fussy eater.* 'Jesus,' one official said, 'what a palaver!'

Believing that parks were a source of joy, landscape gardeners revamped the grounds of Mariposa and ensured the safety of guests. A month earlier, the president had been embarrassed when a section of trellises festooned with creepers peeled off the wall and narrowly missed the French deputy minister of culture on a walkabout in the garden. Simulating laughter, the politician had said that Mariposa reminded him of the magnificent Chateau de Villandry in his native country.

Although Zebulon had already heard so much about Mariposa, he wasn't prepared for the expanse of floor space, the pine flooring and panelling, and the polished floors covered in sections by miles of strip carpeting. Tables of various sizes sported vases with exquisite flowers that looked artificial until Zebulon touched them, sneakily, so as not to spoil the order of things.

The splash of colour contrasted with the simplicity of the president's appearance in a cream calico shirt, a simply cut pair of black trousers and sandals. It was Friday, an opportunity to dress down. Feeling slightly out of place in the plush surroundings, Zebulon wore a khaki suit and Hush Puppies, his light-blue denim shirt open at the neck.

The men shook hands; their mutual awkwardness was cut short by the Chief of Protocol announcing that the other guests were already in the lounge. The sprightly man, charged with anticipating his principal's needs, choreographed the seating of the president and his main guest. Then he wheeled the drinks table towards Ministers Bhele, Stone, Sodoku, Baraka and Sebone-Prah as the young Timi Seramen entered, escorted by two leggy usherettes.

'So,' Mr President said, breaking the ice, 'how goes it at the salt mines?'

'Things are looking up, Mr President,' Zebulon answered. 'But I'm not here for union work.'

'I know. I know,' Abioseh said hastily. 'You've brought us our little visitor; we have to thank you profusely for that.' Cleaning ladies and some of the staff started ululating, presumably at the sight of the boy, who had reached near-movie-star status. A look of irritation crept across the president's face. He hadn't bargained for a carnival, not here in his bailiwick. The look went away quickly, like a distant thunderbolt not sure of its target.

'Are you comfortable, young man?' He looked around for help. He wasn't used to dealing with children … *Where's the damned child psychologist?*

Marcia Baraka had been sitting quietly and looking around with an obliging smile. Seeing her president struggling to converse with the young man, her expression changed and something, perhaps from her own days as a social worker, drove her to act. Flouting procedure, she rose and wedged herself between Caramel and Wonderman, forcing them to give her room. Leaning forward, she looked straight at Timi, who sat across from her next to Zebulon.

'When you were ill,' Marcia said, 'you talked to your parents, didn't you?'

Timi nodded. He turned and glanced at Zebulon, like a trial witness mutely seeking counsel's guidance on tricky questions. Zebulon merely shrugged and spread his hands. *Go ahead, answer the question.*

'I'm asking,' Marcia continued, 'because here's a man, the leader of this country ...' turning briefly to indicate Abioseh to her right, she glared at Zebulon, '... who's opened up his house for you and we're all here to welcome you. And you? You can't even answer a simple question. Do you think that's right?'

'Marcia?' Caramel started to speak but caught her breath as Wonderman's elbow dug into her ribs. She gave him a look that promised he hadn't heard the last of it.

Timi mumbled again, something caught in his throat.

'Speak up,' Marcia prompted. 'The president can't hear you.'

'*I'm very well, Mr President,*' Timi said. It came out as a guttural whisper accompanied by exaggerated lip movements.

'You'll have to practise speaking up a lot more,' Marcia said, softening. 'Go into the bathroom or an empty field – and shout.'

'I want all of you to listen to what Timi has to say,' Abioseh said, 'because a government that works is a government that listens to the people. All the people. This is one thing my father taught me. He believed that we learn so much from those we treat with contempt. Which means that on occasion *he* listened to *me*.' He spread his hands at the memory of his late father's imprudence.

As the president talked, his ministers stole a look out of the giant windows to admire the lawn that formed a broad spread of viridian on which stood a white wicker gazebo. Beyond that was an enclosed pool, its gleaming water inviting. Five bathers, whose near-brazen display of female flesh marked them as foreigners, soaked up the sun on the deck-chairs. Cocktails in tall glasses topped by miniature umbrellas completed the effect of holidays.

Zebulon turned to Timi. 'I remember the clash between the workers and the police in Pengezi,' he said, 'when two stevedores were injured and one of the fellows remarked from the stretcher: *We're busting our balls here, so that some people can enjoy paradise on earth without first dying.* He was bleeding, but felt he had to tell us that. He died in hospital.'

'And you feel,' Marcia Baraka spoke again, more calmly this time, 'that those women outside are freeloaders, enjoying the taxpayers' money?'

'I'm not accusing anyone of anything,' Zebulon said, 'except that many people are suffering out there.'

'While others are lazily enjoying the fruit of their sweat?'

'I haven't said that. *You* said it.'

As if to add insult to proletarian injury, one of the women rose in a fluid motion from her lounger and started shimmying slowly. Picking up a small transistor radio and carrying it around the garden, she continued dancing, to the amusement of her colleagues.

'Those women,' Marcia said, 'are part of a delegation of world trade unionists. They have come to us to support a whole series of initiatives of solidarity with countries like Venezuela, which are threatened with in-vasion or subversion by powerful countries like the United States. They have launched a Hands Off Venezuela campaign, which coincides with the celebration of International Workers' Day, and they have come to us for support.' She studied him for a moment as she mentally plotted a course through a forest of words. 'But I suppose you wouldn't know that, would you?'

'I didn't know,' Zebulon admitted. 'But *we've* always encouraged our workers to form alliances with the working people of the world.'

'Maybe that could be the case,' Wonderman chipped in, 'if the labour movement got off its butt and did some real work instead.'

Abioseh had been silent, staring at the goings-on outside, now and then turning to give Timi a reassuring smile. He cleared his throat. 'That's not a very correct characterisation of the workers of this country, Bhele,' he said. 'We must thank our lucky stars that the trade union movement is in responsible hands; otherwise we'd be dealing with wildcat strikes and chaos.' He paused as if visualising the crack of batons on skulls and Molotov cocktails flying.

'There have been failures in certain crucial areas,' he continued. 'We took over from Ramala and promised people a veritable utopia. The Colonel's Reform amounted to elegant promises whose fulfilment would have emptied our treasury. Homes for the poor; work for the unem-ployed ...'

'Not to mention free medical care for pregnant women, children and senior citizens ...' Wonderman put in, repairing the damage of his earlier inapt remark.

'Yes,' Mr President concurred. 'We overpromised and underdelivered. People held us to the things that we'd dangled in front of them and got angry.'

Turning his attention to Zebulon, he balanced his elbows on his knees and cupped his chin. 'What has been your experience?'

'With respect,' Zebulon started, 'my feeling is that this government has treated people with astonishing callousness. It has lurched from one disaster to another, as it can't listen. It's not a case of overpromising and underdelivering as the president says, but an unwillingness to deliver on even the small things that you have the power to deliver on. For instance, there was a hue and cry in Panza when the blood plague started affect-ing young people – and there was the question to which the government never responded: *Where is the future of Bangula if its young die like flies?* No one answered. The question, like many others before it, fell into a bottomless pit of official indifference.'

Eyes smouldering and face tightened in annoyance and disbelief,

Marcia Baraka prepared to wade in, but Abioseh blocked her with his
hand. Outside, the Chief of Protocol stepped briskly up to the foreign
women and, bending from the waist, he said something to them. The
volume was immediately softened but the performer continued with her
dance; from inside the lounge the tableau was as surreal as a film sequence with the soundtrack off.

'Maybe,' Zebulon said, 'you should let Ms Baraka say her piece.'

'Mr Gondo,' said Mr President, 'the two of us might come from different sides of the tracks, but I'm sure of one thing, and that is, both
of us *must* have benefited from proper upbringing.' He paused. 'This is
my official residence, the closest thing to my house. If we go along with
one of the sayings of the wise that a man's home is his castle, then it
shouldn't be too difficult for *you* to do me the courtesy of letting *me* decide who does *what*, here.'

'The people of this country,' Abioseh went on conversationally, 'put
me in this position where I can expect that courtesy from you. You might
not think much of me, Abioseh, but you *should* respect the office or we
open the gates into chaos. Try to see me as the foreman of this sugarcane
plantation we call Bangula. If something goes wrong with any aspect of
production, *I'll* be blamed. So, when it's Minister Baraka's turn, *I'll* give
her the chance to talk.'

'Thank you for the correction, Mr President,' Zebulon said. 'Or should
I dare say, Mr Manager of the Supermarket?' He seemed about to laugh.
'But we came here on your invitation to present Timi.'

'Of course,' Abioseh said, slapping his forehead. 'The floor is yours,
young man.' Then he added, 'Before the media come in, we must all remember that so much has been done to rectify past injustices, but it's not
in the nature of the population to be thankful.' He pondered his own
remark. 'Call them in.'

The Chief of Protocol dashed outside and called the journalists. Led
by an older, heavier and seemingly sadder, Sarsaparilla in a two-piece suit
the colour of a neglected garden, the media contingent trooped inside

and took their places. In a minute, the lounge was transformed into a studio, complete with cameras, photo-flood lamps and aluminium reflectors, microphones on boom poles, wireless intercoms, production monitors, digital audio recorders, even teleprompters and an autocue. Sarsaparilla pouted playfully when the Chief of Protocol turned down her request to apply make-up to the presidential party. For Bangula men, cosmetics were used to give the dead the appearance of being alive.

Sarsaparilla thanked the Chief of Protocol for having allowed the media into the reception lounge of Mariposa. Curtsying towards the president, she said that this was a rare occasion when the media were allowed into the 'holy of holies' of the government of Bangula. She then checked the mikes before the interview with the president, his half-brother and the boy. These three would be actors in a drama, which, Sarsaparilla maintained, would have the country talking long after 'all of us have gone to that great studio in the sky'. Holding the microphone up in front of Timi's face, she urged him to tell his story.

The president, Zebulon and the ministers visibly primed their ears for Timi's words. Although too young to appreciate the significance of the occasion or the power of broadcasting, Timi was grateful for Abioseh's presence. Clearing his throat, he started to speak, his voice still shaky from lack of use.

There was a slight disturbance at the lobby as Hiero came in, clearing the obstacle course of cables, boxes, cameras and lights. He mouthed an apology to the president and perched himself on the armrest of the settee, his eyes on Sarsaparilla. She suddenly seemed slightly flustered.

'I was a close friend of a boy called Gaza,' Timi said, 'and we attended school together. There are many other boys my age, but everyone liked Gaza because he was the smallest boy in the class. He was smart and could do things that put other boys to shame because he had the spirit of a lion. Sometimes when we wouldn't play with him, he would stand there with his eyes brimming with tears but he wouldn't let them fall. He wouldn't let them fall.'

'And then, one day, he didn't come to school. We didn't know why he wasn't at school and we thought it was because of the flood, *so much water*, and we feared that perhaps he had drowned because he liked school so much he would walk for miles to attend classes. It was the only place where he could get two square meals a day and had friends, even if we sometimes treated him like shit.'

'So when he didn't come for the second day and the third day we started asking questions, like you're asking questions now. At first, the people merely looked at us and looked away as if the question shouldn't be asked. We asked again.' He paused to take a sip of water.

'Then we heard that Gaza and his mother – his father had died years ago – had been killed and their house set on fire because they carried the blood plague and the village feared it would spread and kill everyone. Twelve minivans came with men armed with homemade knives and they chopped them into fine little pieces and they put the house on fire and said that the blood plague would end there, in the fire. So,' Timi said, ending his tale, 'he hadn't drowned after all.'

Sarsaparilla expelled a gush of air as if she'd been punched in the stomach. 'There it is, to you listening or watching at home,' she said, 'the sad, sad story of the consequences of neglect. Mr President,' she asked, raising the mike to the level of Abioseh's lips, 'what do you make of little Timi's grim account, in the light of government policy towards the blood plague?'

'Government policy?' Abioseh asked. 'What government policy?'

'Oh,' Sarsaparilla said, eyes widened in a parody of surprise – or horror. 'Mr President, you mean to tell the people of Bangula there's no policy with regard to a pandemic that's decimated so many of our people?'

'You're twisting the facts, Ms Sarsaparilla,' Mr President said, levelly. 'The government has always prioritised the pandemic and has spent millions of Bangdos to stem the tide of new infections . . .'

'But the message is not getting to the people, Sir,' Sarsaparilla insisted. 'Is this due to the fact that you were quiet when the disease first broke out?'

'Mr President?' Breaching all protocol, Hiero was bypassing the ministers in his quest to catch Abioseh's attention. 'Mr President?'

Turning his eyes to Hiero, Abioseh asked, '*What?*'

'Please ask Seraphim—' Hiero began before he was interrupted.

'*Sarsaparilla!*' snarled the fearsome journalist. 'My name is Sarsaparilla.'

'Whatever,' Hiero said. 'Just direct her, Mr President, to ask the boy where *he* was at the time of the murder of Gaza and his mother.'

'What's that got to do with this interview?' asked Zebulon, who'd been listening intently. 'We're just wasting time here with this flimflam.'

'Ask him, *please*,' Hiero pleaded, 'what *really* struck him dumb?'

Sarsaparilla shrugged her shoulders. 'What did you see?'

'In truth,' Timi said slowly, 'we didn't *hear* about Gaza and his mother because we were *there* when he died.'

He glanced at Zebulon and quickly looked away. 'You see, the men grabbed me on my way home from school. They got hold of me and covered my head with a sack that smelled of stale urine and bundled me into a minivan and took me on this long drive.'

Timi must have passed out for there were gaps in his recollection of the drive that was taken in malodorous darkness. They slowed down along the busy taxi rank, for he could hear the hubbub of vendors and customers and touts exhorting people to various taxis for diverse destinations. Timi could hear the gentle bullying by the area boys and car guards advertising parking spaces and the virtues of the island's most accomplished car wash. The absence of familiar smells lent weirdness to the journey. About an hour later, the minivan stopped.

'They took off the hood,' Timi said, 'just as the men ... there were many of them, their cars forming a half-circle around the house, which was a distance from a cluster of other shacks in the neighbourhood. I was scared. They dragged, first, Gaza's mother, who was screaming, and someone stabbed her in the neck and blood poured out. Then she fell and the men continued. Then Gaza came out running; he was still in school uniform, his white shirt flapping over his grey shorts, but his feet were bare. He saw me and waved as if we were just meeting near the soc-cer field – a greeting. Gaza.'

'What happened to Gaza?' Mr President wanted to know.

Sarsaparilla gave him a baleful look. *This is my show.* 'What happened next?'

'There was blood and shouting everywhere,' Timi said. 'Then the first man, who was now a scarlet scarecrow, signalled that they bring Gaza to him. With a mighty heave, he beheaded him. The head rolled to the side while the body quivered and then became still. What happened stunned us. Gaza's eyes were open and he blinked once while he was looking at me. I noticed that his eyelids and lips were working as if he wanted to say something. Then as his face relaxed and his lids closed on his eyeballs, he was able to whisper a few words.'

'What did he say?'

'He whispered: *There will be no songs this year.*'

PART FIVE

PLOTS

I

'SOMEONE HAS TO do something about these children,' said Zoya as she wove her way through the busy Jambora traffic, slamming on the brakes to avoid hitting a boy who'd jumped from the pavement into the road. She and Zebulon watched as the boy sauntered between cars, tapping on the windows and alerting drivers to his hunger while sniffing glue from a plastic bottle. Above the shouts of vendors and beggars and the restless early evening traffic, they could hear the *foo-poo, foo-poo* sound of the boy gulping in and exhaling the intoxicating fumes of the solvent.

The traffic circle was clogged with cars that inched forward more out of habit than a need to take the occupants anywhere. In the centre of the circle was a graffiti-covered plinth that that had once supported a statue glorifying some ancient conqueror. Watching from the plinth and smiling beatifically at the chaos below was a naked man whom everyone knew was mad.

'No one,' Zebulon said, 'will lift a finger to help. This is perhaps the boy's last summer.' Even to himself, he sounded listless, preoccupied.

'What a depressing thought,' said Zoya. She cursed under her breath as another ragged figure holding a bottle and a miniature squeegee slid between the cars and banged on the roof of her Peugeot, gesturing that he wanted to clean the windscreen. Before she could react he had squirted the window with a viscid liquid.

'Hey,' Zoya shouted, 'leave my car alone or I'll kill you, I swear to God!'

Convinced he was dealing with someone more unhinged than the naked madman on the pedestal, the guerrilla-cleaner sauntered off, shouting an obscenity.

'Did you have to yell at him like that?' Zebulon asked, his bad mood finding an outlet. 'I mean, the kid's only trying to make a living.'

'He'd better go make it elsewhere,' Zoya said. She pointed at the substance that dribbled slowly down the windscreen. 'Take a look at that stuff. You call that enterprise? A man just splashes his shit on your window ...'

'Perhaps,' Zebulon interrupted, 'he saw your face and thought: *Ah, a kind lady ...*'

'Zebulon,' Zoya said hotly, 'don't try to guilt-trip me with *your* sanctimonious shit. I'm not a kind person, or a lady for that matter — and I have no intention of trying to be something I'm not cut out to be.'

'So,' Zebulon asked, 'what are you cut out to be?'

'Just li'l old me,' Zoya said. 'A weathergirl by day and a blues singer by night.' She paused for a while and then asked, 'Did you speak to your brother?'

'I don't have a brother,' Zebulon snapped. 'I've told you that a hundred times already. I don't have a brother.'

'All right,' Zoya said. 'Did you speak to the *president?*' She looked at him. 'Who is *not* your brother.'

'About what?'

'Don't tell me you've forgotten,' Zoya said. 'The meteorological centre is operating at zero capacity, and no one can get through to the minister to tell her that this is a serious problem. We need new equipment, for God's sake. Bangula could get hit by a cyclone tomorrow without any warning.'

'What makes you think *I'm* the one to tell the president that?'

'You had access,' Zoya said. 'Not many people have that opportunity.'

'Yes,' Zebulon conceded, 'but I'd gone on a different mission. You don't just bundle issues when you deal with officialdom.' He paused. 'And relaying your request would have meant asking him for a favour.'

'You mean,' Zoya said testily, 'you'd rather thousands of people were swept away by floods than swallow your pride just this once?'

'I think,' Zebulon said, 'we should get off the subject before we say things we might regret tomorrow.'

'*Je ne regrette rien*,' Zoya said under her breath. 'You'll have to come to terms with the fact that Abioseh Gondo is the president of the republic and he's your flesh and blood. Also that he's a mightily flawed man who's hung up on the fact that he's not revered the way the Colonel was, who also happens to be your old man. Even if you hate Abioseh Gondo's guts, if you have the slightest chance to warn him off the precipice, you are duty bound to do just that, not so much for him as for the millions of people who get damaged when he stumbles. He's got to be told that he's being kept in the dark by his advisers and close lieutenants. When they speak to him, they feed him a barrelful of lies.'

'I don't believe that leaders are *kept* in ignorance,' Zebulon countered. 'I think they *like* creating the impression that they might have been misinformed about this or that, so that they don't take responsibility. How many times have you heard them saying: *I was quoted out of context*, or: *The media have an axe to grind*? They're no different from a character I heard about ... I think it was in one of Kofi Awoonor's stories, who, found copulating with an underage girl in a toilet, offered the excuse that it was a slip of the penis. They play the victim and find a scapegoat.' He didn't tell her that it was Melinda who'd read him the story.

'And you feel Abioseh Gondo is like that?'

'I don't know what he is like,' Zebulon said. 'I only know that I definitely wouldn't like to be in his shoes.'

'I think,' Zoya said levelly, 'you men are all the same. You don't know what the other guy's got but you suspect it's much better than yours – and then on the strength of that, you construct an enemy.'

'You're so smart,' Zebulon said, 'you'll end up outwitting yourself.'

'At least the victim of my delusion will be just one person,' Zoya said, stepping on the accelerator as the traffic congestion eased. 'Your paranoia is as widespread as the blood plague, and it will claim as many victims.'

As the evening approached and the road to the township cleared, Zoya and Zebulon drove in uncompanionable silence. Individually they looked ahead into the ill-lit street, the words they had exchanged returning to them at intervals and fuelling the anger that had sprung from nowhere, like an assassin, to ambush them. They both accepted – although they would never verbalise this – that their anger originated from another plane and made itself felt exactly at the moment when they were together and vulnerable to each other. Their tussling was like pain, which started off elsewhere and referred itself to a different part of the body. But their anger could fuel and fulfil itself and block the mind from seeking a way out that would return them to a moment of original tenderness. And so they fed their anger with silence and imaginings of silent and unimaginable things.

AT BALUBA'S JOINT, Zebulon watched Zoya singing and the band playing. Stefan's absence was evident in the repertoire. They'd added a violinist, the vibrato complementing Zoya's voice, but the overall effect was quaint but unimpressive. It was a stew that lacked vital ingredients. Zebulon gnashed his teeth when he caught Baluba slinging a proprietary arm around Zoya's shoulders. Fearing that jealousy would give him a heart attack, Zebulon wondered whether to confront his benefactor or just let it ride. In other circumstances, he'd have been up like a shot. Was he getting soft?

The question of whether any of Zoya's previous lovers were in this lounge came unbidden. What about that pointy-headed clown in the front who was clapping and whistling like a steam engine – was he one of them? Had he tasted the nectar of her kiss or been enclosed in the soft warmth of her firm thighs? Are pointy-headed clowns good in bed? *Zebulon*, he told himself, *get a grip or you're heading for the madhouse.* In a strange way, he missed Stefan. Without familiar enemies, he concluded, life was a torment.

'DID YOU ENJOY the show?' Zoya asked as they got into the car two hours later. Before he could answer, Cameron Jele's voice rang out; he came running across the lawn and, panting, asked for a lift. Zebulon had hoped for some private time with Zoya but they could not refuse his trade union colleague a ride; it would be the height of bourgeois churlishness.

Zebulon never got to answer her question because Cameron hogged the conversation from the very start, praising Zoya to the heavens. In the course of the drive, she and Cameron chatted about every subject from favourite musicians to macramé, finding mutual areas of agreement, the discovery of this treasure trove expressed via high fives and loud declamations. When Zebulon cautioned Zoya against theatrics behind the wheel, she called him a party pooper, at which point he lapsed into sullen silence. The more Zebulon gritted his teeth as a sign of disapproval, the more blatantly Zoya ignored him. He couldn't quite figure out how he had so swiftly become so unimportant, and not just in the present context.

Even though he had climbed upwards in the trade union movement, he was not part of the top executive. Instead, he was a voice among many that, admittedly, was taken seriously. But he felt that this respect derived from the surname he shared with the president of the republic; it had nothing to do with his own intrinsic value as a man. It rankled that he would always be the Other Son while the *other* son of a bitch lived off the fat of the land. He was not given to using profanity, especially since he had great regard for MaZembe, but there was something about Abioseh Gondo that just riled him. That lecture in front of all those people … But there was more, only Zebulon couldn't quite figure out what it was. Was it that air of detachment, perhaps, as if all that was happening – even that which happened in Abioseh's own name – had nothing to do with him?

'A penny for your thoughts,' Zoya said. It was time to cease hostilities.

'A million Bangdos would be the correct figure,' Cameron Jele said from the back, exploding with laughter. Zebulon couldn't see him in the dark interior, but he imagined the folds of his stomach rippling and threatening to pop the buttons off his shirt. Another joker on the way to early heart failure.

'You'd be wasting your Bangdos,' said Zebulon, 'since I'm not thinking about anything of substance. That is the sole preserve of the good and the great.'

'And since you're in *that* illustrious company,' Jele said, 'we reserve the right to benefit from your sagacity.'

Zebulon let it go; he watched the lights that seemed to shine brighter as they approached the city. The air was crackly with electricity, a condition that preceded a storm. He mulled over Zoya's earlier concern that the coastal region might be hit by a cyclone. The old obstinacy returned. *If she is so concerned*, he thought, *let her tell Abioseh herself*. He was done with running errands.

As they approached the hotel to drop Cameron Jele, who was now quietly snoring in the back, they came upon a squad car, dome light flashing, which had pulled up behind a minibus. Two policemen stood on either side of the vehicle. An Asian driver, probably Korean, sat behind the wheel. He was in the company of five or six young black women, one in the passenger seat and the rest in the back. As Zebulon alighted from the car to open the door for Cameron Jele, he saw that a third policeman was struggling to open the side door. The women were cowering inside the minibus, waving their hands as if signalling that they hadn't deliberately locked the doors. All the doors seemed locked.

'Open the door!' yelled the first policeman, a big man with a beer belly that bulged out of his shirt, his hand on his holstered firearm.

'Yes,' agreed the second policeman, a leaner version of his colleague.

'Let's go see what's up,' Zebulon told Cameron Jele. Zoya got out of the car and laid a restraining hand on his shoulder.

'Be careful,' she said.

'No,' Jele said, 'don't go. You want to keep away from that ...'

'I'm going, anyway,' Zebulon said, heading towards the commotion ahead. For Zoya, everything became like a series of freeze-frames, an action film sequence. Here, the first policeman's antennae picking up the arrival of the newcomer, and there, the third policeman releasing the fastener on his holster and gripping the butt of his gun as if for reassurance. Zoya prayed that this was merely a display of strength, the primeval preening of a male sensing either danger or the presence of a female of the species – and not a trigger to set off some homicidal maniacs. She had seen enough bodies punctured by heavy-calibre weapons to last her a lifetime.

'Is there a problem, Officer?' Zebulon asked.

'Is there a problem?' the first cop asked in a high falsetto. 'We're the ones who're supposed to ask that question.' Grinning, he regarded Zebulon as if opening up his file in his mind. 'What's the matter with you – can't sleep?'

'Why don't you follow your friend's example?' added the lean policeman, jerking his head to the side, pointing to a terrified Cameron at the hotel's entrance. 'Keep your nose out of things that don't concern you; let the cops do their work.'

There was more vigorous tugging on the doors by the two cops. The Korean and his party of desperate women continued hammering on the windows, their laboured breath misting on the glass, the minibus beginning to look like a mobile bordello. The handle on the passenger-side door snapped off in the policeman's hand and he looked at it in surprise, as if his hand had grown an extra thumb. With the women becoming more agitated, the policemen got even more furious.

'If you don't open this fucking door,' threatened the third policeman who'd been standing nearby, surveying the tussle, 'I'm going to shoot the lock …'

'I don't think that would be a good idea, Officer,' Zebulon said.

'… and then give you a beating you'll remember for the rest of your life …'

'… 'cause you're obstructing the police in their work …'

'… you Chinese bastards smuggle all the time …'

'Maybe we should see your badges,' Zebulon suggested mildly. This time all three policemen momentarily forgot the man they'd dubbed Chinese and his black women and focused on Zebulon.

'What?' the three officers shouted in stereo. '*What?*'

'I said,' Zebulon said, not budging, 'maybe we should see your badges …'

'What do you think we should do with this fucker, Cecil?' the first policeman asked, already drawing his gun.

'Don't fucking call me Cecil, here, Basil,' said the thin man. Snarling, he stepped towards Zebulon, grabbed him by his shirt-front and pushed him up against the minibus, his aggression eliciting a series of audible whimpers from the women. Their Asian companion gripped the steering wheel as if his life depended on it, his lips working.

'You … are … going … to … die!' Cecil said, slamming Zebulon's head against the roof to punctuate each word. Zebulon scrunched his shoulders and let them absorb the impact, at the same time studying every pore and wart on Cecil's sweating face, noting the stained teeth and getting a blast of whiskey-laden breath.

Fearing that Zebulon was most likely going to be killed, Zoya stepped into the street and flagged down a busload of celebrants who were chanting gospel songs. She directed them towards the scene of mayhem. 'Please help.'

The passengers, who were still in the grip of the Holy Spirit, peered through the windows down at the woman – a sister, no less, whose apparel denoted how far she had strayed from the path of sanctity – who was gesticulating wildly and pointing at the fracas in front of the hotel. But if the singers had chosen a life of singing praises to their Maker, they were still of this earth and its tribulations. Their attention was drawn to the scene where Basil was now lashing out with his truncheon, its *thwack-thwack* sound reverberating into the night.

'*No!*' This scream came from the lungs of a huge black woman in a voluminous evening dress. She must have been the lead singer because her cry was taken up by the rest of the choir as they stepped out of the thirty-six-seater, all in formal gear – the women in frilly evening dresses, even high-heeled shoes, and the men in tuxedos, dress-shirts, bowties and shiny black shoes.

Even though driven by a common purpose, they all differed in size, age, race and possibly class, since some wore their festive apparel with aplomb while others seemed awkward, as if wearing rented clothes.

The initial second soprano scream, issuing from lungs that had been exercised in choirs, christenings, birthdays, weddings and burials, was amplified and broadcast by other voices, driving dogs in suburban kennels in the distance to howl in solidarity with the gospel choir.

'Isn't that Holy Boy getting a right royal pasting over there?' asked someone young, taking time off from screaming.

Even as pain shot up his spine, Zebulon had to admire his fellow citizens' inventiveness. So, now, *he* was the Holy Boy. He would have laughed under different circumstances. The hands that held him pinned against the side of the vehicle relaxed their hold when it finally dawned on his attacker who his victim was. 'Hey, Basil,' Cecil said over his shoulder, his voice laced with guilty wonderment, like a child who'd just realised that the clock he'd taken apart was a prized family heirloom, 'know *who* we've got here?'

'I *hear* say it's the Colonel's kid,' Basil said, suddenly less interested in the terrified Asian man and the women than in making a getaway. 'Let's bounce.'

But the crowd, swelled by the arrival on the scene of hotel guests in various stages of undress and the general public, who collectively possessed internal antennae for trouble, wouldn't let them bounce, not just then. The spring air was suddenly filled with tension. The traffic, which had roared indifferently on, appeared to have slowed down, eventually coming to a standstill as if guided by the hand of a magician.

Zebulon felt rather than saw the rage that had taken hold of the crowd gathered outside the hotel. It prickled and gathered momentum, becoming an electric impulse that transformed the gait of young men with serious eyes into a frenzied dance routine that was always a prelude to mayhem.

Desperate to stop a course of action for which he felt somewhat responsible, Zebulon raised one hand to speak, but was pulled off balance and pressed into the jaws of the throng. He heard, as if from the depths of a well, Cameron Jele, now emboldened by mass action, urging people to fight the power structure.

Power structure? What was he on about? These were just ordinary thugs posing as policemen, Zebulon thought. He had figured out that Basil, or whatever his name was, could *not* have been a policeman, not with that ill-fitting tunic with a nametag that certainly couldn't have belonged to him, and not with those high-top sneakers.

Another fresh batch of young but hard-eyed faces joined the crowd. Leading the charge, they pressed forward, grabbing the three men, pummelling them with a rat-a-tat of blows, carrying them aloft like they had scored the winning goal in a soccer cup final, then dropping them onto the ground and kicking them as if they were sacks of cement.

Finally on firm ground, Zebulon shouted for the youngsters to stop the violence, having a fair idea of where this would end. Scenting blood, the crowd roared for the men to be stripped naked.

'No!' Zebulon shouted. 'No!' Two or three of the attackers turned their eyes to him. 'That's *not* the way to do it.'

'How would *you* do it?' One of the young men with ageless eyes asked, an odd smile on his lips. 'Tell us.'

'That's just *not* the way to do it,' Zebulon repeated, impelled by something he couldn't quite explain. 'That way we'd be playing into *their* hands.'

'What the fuck are you talking about?' A second young man yanked Cecil by his shirt-tail and spun him around with a staccato of slaps. 'They're in *our* hands, now ...'

'And *we'll* do one thing with them.' The first man drew a forefinger along his throat. 'That way they won't be bothering anyone for a long time.'

'No!'

'Young man,' shouted the woman who'd earlier raised the alarm. 'You'd best listen to Holy Boy if you know what's good for you.'

'Holy Boy, my ass,' said the youngster defiantly. 'This is our prisoner.'

'*Prisoner?*' the woman scoffed. 'Get out of here ...'

Still intent on making his speech, Zebulon was distracted by a well-dressed, middle-aged man hefting a brick which seemed, initially, destined for the would-be robbers, but which landed with a wet crunch against the window of the police van, the sound hanging in the air before dissolving into the tinkling of glass.

Taking their cue from this respectable vandal, the adolescents, no longer bereft of a role model, found more missiles with which to pelt the car, the impact like automatic gunfire. Except for the women who stood jeering as the rioters vented their frustration on the police van, the crowd largely ignored the now naked trio who had started the trouble. Zebulon sidled towards them. 'Get out of here!' he hissed.

'What?' This was Basil, his hands cupped to protect his genitals. '*What?*'

'I said, get out of here!' Zebulon repeated above the clamour, shoving the men to the edge of the crowd, past angry young people and defeated old people.

The night air was suddenly thick with the blue-black smoke of charred rubber. Astonishingly, while flames engulfed the police van, its radio crackled messages and the siren wailed the vehicle's agony. Jubilant people danced in the street. Above the bobbing heads across the square – and there were suddenly six or seven clusters – Zoya waved her arms to catch Zebulon's attention, the car doors ajar. A tear-gas canister shot up into the air and landed a few metres away from Zebulon, an acrid cloud of gas dispersing and enveloping everything within range.

His eyes burning, Zebulon was suddenly the leader of a four-man delegation, three of them naked and he as blind as a bat. But the desperate men tagging along now held tightly onto his belt. Unseeing, Zebulon ran forward, shoving anonymous bodies, hearing a grunt, a yelp of pain or a suppressed oath as a fist or elbow connected with a midriff. In that period of blindness, there were even briefer episodes when sound was suspended, like the infinitesimal moment of the jagged streak of lightning preceding a thunderclap.

Opening his eyes, he heard a deafening crash as a shadow threw a garbage can into the plate glass fronting the hotel. A loud explosion followed, igniting the square in a light as brilliant as a tropical sunburst. As if conjured up by the luminescence, three men staggered purposefully along; his vision restored, Zebulon saw it was actually two men supporting an automatic teller machine between them. Rigged atop a skateboard, the ATM seemed to lurch like someone's thickset kid brother who'd had a bit too much to drink.

The night was split by a series of loud blasts from sirens that were pitched at different registers, a cacophony much like a battle royal involving tipsy trombonists. The emergency services rolled in, the ambulance first, followed by the police truck, a fire engine and a sedan bringing up the rear. 'The police are here,' someone shouted, his excited voice trailing behind the flaming arc of a Molotov cocktail that smashed and fizzled out against the wire mesh window protection. But if the incendiary bomb had failed to inflict damage, its very potential fanned flames of defiance against the representatives of law and order.

As the paramedics stepped out and tended to the fallen, mainly injured in the stampedes, the riot squad, looking alien in dark protective gear replete with helmets and shields, formed a phalanx and advanced slowly into the entrails of the crowd. The ringleaders were isolated and subdued, their wrists tied behind their backs with strips of plastic flex. Then they were forced prone on the fetid tarmac, examples of the futility of resistance. Zebulon thought he'd caught sight of Hiero in an unmarked car but he couldn't be sure.

Still running, Zebulon heard a bottle zing past his head, a trace of flammable liquid in its wake. The naked and the reprieved were still tethered to him by unspeakable terror. Zebulon briefly thought of surrendering his wards to the police, but the sight of two uniformed cops clubbing a man down and kicking him in the ribs decided him otherwise. He could have sworn that one of the assailants was Cameron. But that was impossible. Eventually he neared a clearing where, as if in a vision, Zoya waited in the car, the engine running.

'Where's Cameron?' Zoya asked as she gunned the accelerator and the car sped away from the scene of destruction. 'What happened to him?'

'No idea,' Zebulon said, truthfully. 'Probably still in the mix, swinging.'

'You mean the fat geezer who was with you?' Basil was a little bolder now. 'I saw him sliding fast into the hotel with the fat sister.' He giggled.

'Shut up, Basil,' Cecil said. They might have escaped a lynching, but as they were still naked, they were technically not out of danger. 'Just shut the fuck up.'

'You boys,' Zoya said, 'keep it down there in the back – and *don't* swear so fucking much in my car.'

'Yes, Ma'am,' someone said. It was Basil. He still couldn't keep quiet.

AS ZOYA DROVE off, Hiero stepped out of his car. He scanned the scene of battle and started taking notes, his tongue working, following each word.

2

THE MIDNIGHT RAID on the president's private office in Mariposa came as
Abioseh Gondo was having fun, dreaming of a campaign for the citizens
of Bangula to reclaim the beaches for themselves. He'd seen a few seaside amusement parks, especially the exercise courses, seesaws and picnic
areas. It was a pity that thugs invariably took these over and terrorised
couples who were out to have a good time. But he had something different in mind, a train, perhaps, or one of those monorails featured in Dis-
neyland. The Bangula version would be without the showiness associated
with the American way of life.

He lamented that the term 'American' had become shorthand for almost anything sought-after and capable of elevating the seeker into a
world of endless possibilities. In his heart of hearts, he'd have wanted
his country to be like America, but without the attendant hostility. Unfortunately, everything militated against that. The economic reality of
Bangula, with its long wish list, meant that there was no way to meet all
the needs. The poor would continue being poor.

This depressing situation didn't dampen his upbeat mood. The day had been a breathtaking wonder. An earlier shower had cooled the land, signifying a break with the heat wave that had broiled the island for weeks on end. As the city lay still beneath the filmy sprinkle of mist, the children dragged their parents out from under umbrellas and forced them to horse around. The sun shone while the rain fell, leading some people to say that this was a monkey's wedding; others crossed themselves and spat three times to drive out the Devil.

But the good fortune dogging the day prevailed; the rain had now become a breeze that started out cold but had grown milder. Without the faintest hint of a storm, the wind blew landwards all that was associated with the healing power of the sea. Abioseh took advantage of the day. He went to a mid-morning session at the gym and worked up a good sweat.

Later, he held his fortnightly lunch-hour meeting with Wonderman Bhele, who briefed him on the security situation in the country. It was a glib and upbeat report that flew against what the president knew, arousing some unease. When anxious, Mr President called his bodyguards and went jogging, the exertion taking his mind off potential mishaps. Fighting the need to stop and give relief to his lungs, his heart kicking against his ribcage, he pressed on. His anxiety was forgotten with the sight of puddles on the ground, a sign that nature existed to rebuild even if human beings were hell-bent on destruction.

The run took him up onto the wooded dirt road that skirted the vast graveyard. The headstones shimmered, the crosses and various symbols adding to the knowledge that underneath the stone slabs lay the remains of people who had once believed in some canon with such passion that, if needed, they would have gone to war. Tended by clergy and laity from the Order of St Augustine, the graves and the disused church represented the most distilled version of Catholicism on the island.

Sometimes, on Sundays, Abioseh would fight the urge to enter the ancient oak doors of Father Mitchum's downtown church, if only to be imbued, however briefly, with the power and the glory of ancient spirits that had authored the liturgy in Latin. Although not a believer himself, he loved the drama and bravura of the rites and rituals. But he had been advised that gracing any order of worship could send the wrong signal and give grist to the mill of cynics who doubted that there was any separation of powers between church and state.

Hearing the bodyguards panting behind him, picking up the pace just for the heck of it, Mr President reflected on his own conflicts. He had no bad conscience for he trusted the integrity of his decisions. He had never taken a decision lightly, however minor. He always applied his mind.

It was this sense of integrity that had led him to probe the treasury on the financing of the Reform. Since taking over, the Colonel had seemingly performed miracles. Through the departments of public works and transport, he had undertaken massive projects, improving roads and bridges and physically narrowing the developmental divide between city and village. Wide swathes of unutilised public land – either choked by weeds or sporting derelict buildings – were reclaimed to make each acre tillable and fit for human growth. Even dusty plains were parcelled out to farmers. Factories sprouted up in areas where despair and laziness, regular bedfellows, had once been the order of the day. This was the Reform. It saw young women take their places as heads of companies and become captains of industry. The clinics and hospitals catered to the needs of patients without demanding payment; one of the rallying cries of the Reform was that health care and primary school education would be free and accessible to all. But all of these 'achievements' were a drain on the treasury.

As he jogged back to Mariposa, Mr President had made his decision; he felt worn out, the fatigue internal, spiritual. It was late, around 5.00 PM, when he sent for Wonderman Bhele again. Dressed in a blue tracksuit and trainers, the minister was in ill humour, as if he'd been interrupted in a pleasurable pastime.

As always, Mr President was struck by Wonderman's imposing appearance, standing at close to two metres and probably weighing about one hundred and twenty kilograms, a giant whose favourite party trick was impersonating Idi Amin Dada. Wonderman complemented his physical endowment with mental acuity. He could hold his own in any situation. His vast knowledge of history and the classics put paid to the stereotype of the big galoot, even though Abioseh jocularly referred to him as a little dictator gone to seed. Mr President had been careful to adopt an attitude that left no room for doubt as to who the boss was.

As with all people who started out as friends and then had to negotiate a hierarchical relationship, Wonderman and the president conducted the second meeting of the day massaging those aspects of their lives that had drawn them together and skirting around the prickly bits that snarled silently in the room. Knowing that he was sometimes dismissed as soft, Mr President quickly dispensed with pleasantries and got down to the heart of the matter.

'I've got concerns, Wonderman,' Abioseh said, 'about the budget. Things don't seem to stack up.'

'Would the president please clarify,' Wonderman answered, 'what he means by concerns with the budget, as I'm not the minister of finance.'

'I'm aware of that, Wonderman,' Abioseh said patiently, 'but we have a covenant, an agreement. You're the pointsman I have to raise these concerns with since they have implications for state security.'

'Well,' Wonderman said, his tone ironic, 'that's a first for me, Mr President.' He looked at the floor. 'State security indeed,' he mumbled. 'I thought I *was* the one who had first claim on information relating to state security, but I see Mr President has other sources ...'

'Don't insult my intelligence, Wonderman,' Abioseh snapped. 'I don't know what games you have been playing, but I do know that a lot of money is unaccounted for. It seems to have been buried under phantom projects related to ...' he studied some notes scribbled on a piece of paper, '... pushing frontiers for the advancement of the Reform.' He looked up. 'What the hell is that?'

'With respect, Mr President,' said Wonderman, the epitome of patience, 'there's no such a thing as a phantom project; these are projects that had to be subsumed under other ongoing capital initiatives, for any number of reasons. Some of the government departments had under-spent and some had used up their budgets, but, at the end of the day, both the Colonel and the then minister of finance had stressed the need for the Reform to be prioritised. I have memos in my office to that effect. I have, moreover, communications signed by you, Mr President, which authorise the expenditure.'

'I don't remember signing any item authorising spending to finance the Reform.' *I'll be damned if I'll cave in to my own Cabinet minister's sophisticated bullying.* 'Maybe you should bring those documents.'

'I'll bring the documents, Mr President,' Wonderman promised; it sounded like a threat. 'But you'll do well to remember that the Reform is the political and socio-economic philosophy of this country. Your own father promoted it. He impressed on us that the Reform wasn't any one thing that you could label and say: *This is the Reform. It is round in shape and blue in colour.* No, the Reform is what makes us who we are, from the cradle to the grave.'

'Thanks for the lecture, Wonderman,' Abioseh said dryly. 'That was also drummed in to me from day one.' When he was eight or nine years old, he had found the Colonel no different from the preachers who promised a better dispensation in the future.

Wonderman seemed to have trouble getting off his seat. Finally on his feet, he went to the drinks table and poured himself a shot of brandy topped with Coke. He turned to the president, raising his glass, enquir-ing if Abioseh also wanted a drink. Abioseh hesitated and then shrugged his shoulders. Wonderman handed him a large whiskey and water.

Even though there was tension in the air, the men were at ease, like ex-lovers who could still entertain the enduring memory of tenderness. 'Problem is,' Wonderman went on as he settled back into the cushions, 'you're again approaching this as if we're in an ideal world, which doesn't exist in the cut and thrust of political realities. Your old man was a master at making everyone feel good. He reminded the public of the benefits of the Reform as opposed to life before the Reform. People need to feel good all the time. The moment you fail to provide that, you allow them to remember the past – which might have been horrific indeed – but from which they might start isolating certain elements of what was good. Give them time and they build that mosaic into a reality that repudiates the one you've provided them with – and then you're up shit creek.'

'However hideous the past was,' Wonderman went on, warming to his subject, 'it contains a kernel of goodness, or a benefit – or we wouldn't even be talking about that past. The Second World War was a hideous period, but it threw up heroism and an understanding of patriotism. The evil of oppression broadens our knowledge of the resilience of the human spirit.'

'Next I can hear you singing anthems to colonialism … the Palestinians won't thank you for your treatise, my friend.' Abioseh looked at his watch; it was nearly 6.30 PM. 'In time you'll be talking about the empowerment that comes out of forgiveness, because, in understanding the nuts and bolts of what led people into all these different brands of madness, something shifts in our hearts and we make room for forgiveness.'

He looked out at the gazebo, which seemed even more isolated as the evening gathered. A thought took hold of and released him at the same time – and he shivered.

'The word out there is that you want to dismantle what your father built,' said Wonderman after a silence, like someone who'd finally decided to confess.

Abioseh Gondo looked at his one-time friend with hurt puzzlement. Then he sighed. 'They might have a point,' he said. 'My father thatched his roof with borrowed straw. The Reform was an illusion. It took attention away from what really needed to be done here. All the failed agricultural schemes; the ambitious promises of one family one house, which floundered when most of the dwellers of shanty towns refused to move;

the airport expansion initiative, when no one really flies into Bangula; the waste when the Port Authority constructed what was going to be a dry dock that would accommodate the most modern ships, which now looks like a scar on the waterfront. All of these things cost huge money, but the money wasn't there. Nevertheless, they had to be built – and broadcast with fanfare – because they were manifestations of the spirit of Reform.' He laughed bitterly.

'The people wanted all those projects,' Wonderman persisted. 'Even if the monument's foundation is shaky and the stone crumbles long before the damn thing's erected; even if the bridge wobbles and threatens to send vehicles tumbling into the Rugamo; even if the dry dock doesn't service a single vessel and the airport runway is pockmarked, potholed and overgrown with elephant grass; so long as it's all to the glory of the Reform, people will support that.'

'Yes,' Abioseh agreed. 'But I can't be party to that level of deception.'

'What are you going to do, Mr President?'

'I'm going on national television,' Abioseh said, 'to tell the people that the Reform was a farce. We need to reform the Reform.'

HIS WORDS HUNG in the air, joining all the weighty conversations that had been held in the lounge since Mariposa had become the official residence of an incumbent president. The drapes, which had now been drawn by the resident wraith, and which had not been changed since the inception of the chamber of secrets, were weighed down by the confidentialities that leaders had exchanged in their time in power. They had not been replaced because that reputedly brought about bad luck for the office bearer. Instead, they were freshened and sprayed and dusted with a broomstick, beaten until their fabric frayed and screamed for relief, but they were not removed from the curtaining rod. Countless dignitaries from home and abroad who had been entertained there remarked on the texture of the brocade material and the majesty of the deep purple. That evening, the drapes conspired with the dark to muffle the last moments of the secretive conspiracies being hatched. Abioseh Gondo and Wonderman Bhele heard the wind rising and then, after a lull, their nostrils were teased by the fecund smell of the sea, followed by spatters of rain; they could imagine the drops slanting, becoming in a few minutes a curtain of water.

Abioseh refilled his glass. As he heard the driving rain he suddenly remembered the Monster, the cyclone that was synonymous with his boyhood. How it had lashed the island and left a trail of destruction. The wraith reappeared, tiptoed in and headed for the light switch. 'Leave it as it is,' Abioseh said. 'Thank you.'

'Yes, Sir,' intoned the ghost in a voice softer than a whisper.

'If you do that,' Wonderman said, 'you'll open the floodgates and allow in something we won't be able to control.'

'Maybe,' Abioseh answered quickly, 'we lost control a long time ago. Only we've been too coy to admit it.'

'Be that as it may, Mr President,' Wonderman conceded, 'but as the government we can't afford alarm bells and theatrics. That will sow panic among a populace that's already quite skittish. Just a couple of days ago, I got an anonymous tip-off from someone, a woman, at the Bureau of Meteorology.'

'There's no such thing as an anonymous tip-off, Wonderman,' Abioseh said. 'You know who it was.'

'I forget the kind of man I'm dealing with,' Wonderman said half to himself, smiling in defeat. 'It was Zoya Badawi.'

'Zebulon's woman,' Abioseh mused, his face thoughtful. 'How strange.'

'Yes,' Wonderman said, 'but she paints a grim picture. They've got outdated equipment, which could spell disaster if we're suddenly hit by a cyclone, no early warning and all that. In any event, we've been sent urgent data by the Météo-France research base in Réunion. It seems like Bangula is potentially in the path of a category-five cyclone.'

'And that's pretty severe?'

'The most severe.'

'It makes it all the more imperative to go on air tomorrow,' Abioseh said. 'People have to be warned.'

'Well,' Wonderman got to his feet. 'You have a few trump cards. The Americans have been messing up the world climate settings. Global warming, Africa in the dilemma of droughts and floods … but …' his voice trailed away.

'Yes, Wonderman?'

'If you issued a warning,' Wonderman said, 'there would have to be a massive evacuation. And that costs money.' He let this sink in. 'Which we don't have.'

'We would have to do it.'

Lost in thought, Abioseh didn't even see Wonderman out, weighted down as he was by a great tiredness. He sat back into the settee, debating whether to call Jacqui over, needing – and at the same time blanching from – companionship, feeling at once alone and crowded. Outside the breakers crashed against themselves, a collision as timeless as creation.

He heard a car start up, the engine igniting effortlessly, purring above the loneliness of the sea's endless journeying. He got up and poured himself another drink, then sat down to a solitary supper of lamb chops, lentils and sweet potatoes. Cracking open a chilled bottle of white wine and taking a sip from his glass, he gazed absently at the television monitor, an indifferent face announcing the 8.00 PM news. A voracious consumer of news, Abioseh knew that something was wrong with him when he found himself distracted, the images dancing across the screen, the words of the newscaster tremulous like waves, at once absolutely clear and garbled. The picture oscillated between a blurry snowstorm and highly defined lines, the colours bleeding into one another and then separating into prints so vivid they assailed his eyes.

Abioseh tried to reach for the remote control. It suddenly seemed miles away. Finally he grabbed it and pressed it to increase the volume. He saw and heard the clean-shaven newscaster detailing the news of the day. In Panza, the army had mutinied, following the soldiers' complaint over poor pay. The report cut back to visuals. Mouth hanging open, Abioseh watched as a general dashed across a sugarcane field and shut himself in an armoured personnel carrier. As the vehicle drove off, men took aim with their rifles and the tyres caught fire. Someone in the foreground took aim with a rocket launcher and fired, the recoil setting a clump of grass ablaze. The grenade whooshed and missed the APC, landing slapbang in a cluster of flats. The general's vehicle disappeared into a thicket; soldiers and civilians dashed towards it in the company of the camera crew. As the general was brought back, now stripped to his underpants, women ululated and children screamed and jumped excitedly. A knife flashed and suddenly the general, who had earlier tried to maintain some dignity, dropped to his knees, like a bull that had finally accepted its role in a sacrifice. The camera whipped away from the slaughter, but the sound of hacking was all the more haunting off-screen.

Horrified, Abioseh couldn't take his eyes from the screen. The camera returned to the man lying alone in a pool of blood. Mr President heard voices, close by, followed by the chatter of small arms fire. He knew, then, that Mariposa was under attack. Meaning to run towards the lever on the wall that sprung open the trapdoor to the underground room, he slipped, cursing the whiskey and wine. Face down on the carpet, he crawled under the desk. Without thinking about it, he braced himself. He didn't know about and couldn't hear the explosion; he felt it as a faint rumbling, a shock that came up from the floor. Then everything was sucked up in the most complete silence he had ever experienced. *Where in hell is Hiero?*

3

IN THE TEN days before the raid on Mariposa, Hiero had been having a series of nightmares. In the dream he was always driving in his car and it was late at night. Somehow he knew that he was going to lose the car. He didn't know how he knew this, but he was never surprised to find himself walking along a narrow tree-lined street whose ominous gloom was simultaneously leavened and heightened by an irregular sheen from an earlier drizzle on the tarmac. As he approached a large shadow that could be a hut standing in the middle of the road, his hair stood on end. He knew that the silhouette would change into a group of men dressed in cloaks topped by hoods under which the watcher could only see the eyes that burned with the intensity of live coals. Hiero wanted to detour or even turn back, but was drawn nearer by the smouldering eyes and by his own need to make sense of the materiality of those numinous figures. Running the gauntlet between the shadowy ghosts that now numbered hundreds, he could feel their heat through their strange robes and make sense of their words as they spoke in tongues. The figures represented Vezi and the rest of the men who were executed. There was a rustle of blankets as the corpses-come-to-life divested themselves of their grey robes. Seeing them raise their arms that ended in stumps, Hiero ran and ran, eventually waking up drenched in sweat.

Finally he decided to go and see Father Mitchum, for in the few years he had been heading Security Affairs, he'd found inside himself a great darkness, which saw the logic of death in clear lines. Like almost all Africans, Hiero believed that ancestors had a role overseeing the lives of the living. That some people acted like animals didn't place them outside the realm of the ancestors' influence. The offenders would in time be transformed into spirits that would hover restlessly above, looking for human bodies that could render them corporeal.

'You don't really believe all that mumbo-jumbo, do you?' Father Mitchum asked Hiero as they sat in the priest's office. It was separated from the main part of the church by a thin brick wall bedecked with notice boards. There were posters, yellowed newspaper clippings and ancient photographs that formed a visual history of the parish and Father Mitchum's role in the story of Bangula.

The small room was stuffy with old newspapers and magazines piled haphazardly in every available inch of space. Father Mitchum's chain-smoking didn't help matters much; the blue acrid wisps from the pana-tella vied for dominance with dust motes. The lived-in quality of the room, which complemented the lines of experience on the Irishman's face, gave Hiero a sense of comfort. It seemed to him that the more priests heard confessions, the more their faces became reassuring to the sinners. Although using different methods, he and Father Mitchum were in the same trade of ridding people of the onerous weight of transgression. Even though there might have been little doubt as to what constituted the final destination, there would always be some healthy disagreement on the best route to the core of the human soul.

'I'm surprised you regard it as mumbo-jumbo,' Hiero said, 'since I've been hearing that the Vatican promotes the tolerance of other faiths ...'

'If cannibalism were elevated to state religion in this country,' Father Mitchum said, 'which it is in many lands, the Vatican would find some obscure historical text to support it. There've been so many violations on the basis of religion that we've become schizophrenic on what constitutes sin.' His blue eyes seemed to have turned grey in the swirling curtain of smoke. 'We have to forgive so much. Mainly the wrongs that we're still fated to commit.'

'If you're so depressed,' Hiero asked, 'where will you find the energy to hear confessions? And will your Ave Maria have any validity?'

'Ah,' Father Mitchum said airily, 'in this electronic age, you don't need me to hear your confession. You can get absolution from the Internet. Or via sms.'

'In that case,' Hiero joked, 'why don't you slip me God's mobile number?'

'*You're* in the business of extracting information,' Father Mitchum argued. 'I'm sure you already have the number at headquarters.'

'That's what I wanted to talk about. Finding out what everyone thinks we have.'

'And what's that?'

'Peace.'

Father Mitchum clucked his tongue, telling Hiero that peace was a very difficult thing to find. 'Especially now,' he said, 'now that we have a new country with so many needs. Men in your trade have to balance the attainment of their own personal serenity against breaking bones to ensure the protection of peace.'

'And that means some people must bleed,' Hiero said. After a brief silence, he went on. 'I oversaw the torture of a man I knew was innocent the other day. When he screamed, I felt an excitement that was like a sexual charge. I knew even as he admitted to various plots against the state that he was lying, and something in his eyes told me that he knew that I knew.'

'What did you do? I hope you released him.'

'Yes. But he committed suicide.'

This death and many injuries in the name of preserving law and order were no longer reported to Abioseh Gondo. Hiero explained that the president had a role to play to ensure that there was a government in place. The job of security officers was to ensure that nothing whatsoever was allowed to disturb the peace. Recently people had been captured at the marina, three of them with crates that had been taken from a boat with a false bottom. The crates were full of small arms and ammunition, material, no doubt, to help foment unrest. The president, Hiero felt, was not to be exposed to unnecessary alarm over ineffectual rebels. He had a country to run.

Since his unwritten covenant with Baluba Jambo, Hiero had overseen that the president received only an acceptable ration of news. More than ever, Abioseh had been kept busy with ceremonial tasks: opening a multi-purpose community centre here, a bridge there, commissioning a housing project on its way to being a slum long before the cutting of the ribbon.

It was during one of these launches on a sweltering morning that Hiero understood the president's dilemmas. Abioseh was notoriously averse to the aggrandisement of leaders, living or dead. He'd cite examples of the pitfalls of the personality cult. But even he had had to succumb to pressure and preside over the naming of a little-used theatre after the Colonel.

Among the dignitaries was MaZembe, solemnly turned out in a black, forties-style formal dress, replete with sheer lace overlay, a sweetheart neckline and pleated cummerbund with a back bow. Her crowning glory was a hat of soft velour felt trimmed with satin face organza and delicate peacock feathers. Since this launch was in her late husband's name, it seemed as if MaZembe wished to invest the happy occasion with the qualities of a stylish wake.

The proceedings included a dance troupe, drum majorettes, musicians and speakers from various arts disciplines in addition to Mr President himself. About a kilometre from the waterfront, the voices and the drumming were occasionally trumped by the tootle of a horn, some boat warning off a stray craft. Beneath this were the general discordant calls of seagulls that dipped beneath the chatter of schoolchildren enjoying a rare treat of ice cream and cold cuts.

As Mr President strode to the microphone stand, behind which sat the dignitaries with their backs against the double doors leading into the theatre, Hiero overheard MaZembe. 'Let *me* also say a few words,' she whispered, earnest and forceful in the same breath. 'He was after all *my* husband.'

'Ma,' Abioseh hissed, 'you will sit down and behave yourself.' He smiled a presidential smile at the curious assembly.

'You've done *nothing* for your father,' MaZembe persisted. 'Even this theatre … this poky little excuse for a theatre … I know theatres … people had to beg you on bended knee to be here. Otherwise the Colonel's name would appear *nowhere* in the public life of this country – he who contributed so much.' She paused, out of breath. 'You couldn't even bring yourself to name the new airport after your own father.'

If the guests within earshot heard MaZembe's lament, they must have decided that this was private family business, because no one betrayed any anxiety. The ministers, members of the diplomatic corps and a choice selection of local celebrities and businesspeople, maintained their composure in their suits and formal dress under the hot sun. Some must have wished they were part of the watching masses who came out in loose floral dresses, dashikis, T-shirts and jeans. Sometimes, to be somebody came at too high a price. The notables shushed one another quiet when the president rose to speak.

'My mother,' Abioseh said, visibly shrugging off his mother to address the guests, 'always chivvies me about not paying sufficient homage to the Colonel. But I believe in formal arrangements in the exercise of power. I believe in our institutions, the courts, parliament and various agencies that push forward the agenda of governance in Bangula. In that regard, I believe that the correct route to the naming of structures and institutions – especially houses of culture, which is the crystallised form of people's experiences and aspirations – must take place via serious consultation. I believe that there should have been competitions for young people in schools to grapple with the most appropriate name for a bridge, or even this theatre itself. My father had no time for music or theatre or drama. The ongoing drama constituted by his life was engaging enough for him.'

'*Abi!*' MaZembe whispered from her seat. '*Abi!*'

Abioseh ignored her and went on. 'In that regard,' he said, 'I want to challenge the teachers and arts administrators to engage the youth, the students, and the community of artists in this country. They must find creative ways in which to memorialise the heroes and heroines of Bangula. They must give us names that will reflect the nature of society and engage entrepreneurs and big business to chip in. Let's have reality prevailing once and for all.' Turning to the master of ceremonies, he said, 'In the light of all that, I'll hand the scissors to my mother to open this theatre. This poky little theatre where young people will maybe have a chance to dream dreams and hope hopes. I do not have the authority to do it.'

People clapped. MaZembe took the scissors from her son and they suddenly looked like a dagger in her hands. In that moment, Hiero wondered what would happen to Bangula if Abioseh met with a fatal accident. It was not unique for the widow to succeed her late husband, although, in this instance, it would be her son. Hiero was somewhat saddened that he was already thinking of the incumbent in the past tense.

Holding herself with stubborn dignity, MaZembe sliced the ribbon with the expertness of a seamstress, smiling benignly at the throngs and guests who cheered her with heartfelt joyfulness. Looking at her, Hiero was struck by her physical resemblance to the late Colonel, down to the old man's modest expansiveness. The five ministers present, Bhele,

Sebone-Prah, Baraka, Sodoku and Stone, stood in line to take turns to hug her, possibly alive to the influence of powerful matriarchs in history.

Suddenly diminished by this exudation of power, Abioseh stood among the dignitaries. It dawned on Hiero that the people present had not come for lofty speeches about principles. The country was marching on and the masses needed less of a lecture on the finer points of accountability than simple reassurance. Right then, they would have embraced the cruellest despot if only that person guaranteed stability. Hiero regarded Abioseh as his friend. But he was a dreamer who imagined that people were guided by reason. He seldom polished his arguments, believing that since everything was clear, reasonable people would come around to seeing things his way. Assuming leadership at the ceremony, MaZembe had proven that the public longed for moments that recalled a secure past.

HIERO BROUGHT HIMSELF back to his present company. Father Mitchum was subdued, his gestures hinting at an anger at something he was unable to control. Presently he opened his heart to Hiero.

'I'm sixty-eight years old now,' he said. 'And I've been present in almost every arena of trouble. In my own country where we gave the world an understanding of white-on-white violence.' He laughed grimly at his macabre wit. 'In various parts of Latin America where I saw a succession of regimes that worshipped on the altar of Mammon and Uncle Sam. People disappeared and death squads thrived, even in preternaturally beautiful lands like Brazil. They unleashed terror on the vulnerable, the poor. I believed that people with nothing, those who find themselves on the lowest rung of the ladder, can only rally together and help one another up, up from slavery. I learnt that people at the bottom use others' bodies to climb to the top. It happens everywhere; it happens here. I have seen Bangula transform itself from an idyll into a little hell. I know that people are dissatisfied with your friend, Abioseh. But I know that an alternative to him, that Zebulon, will bring strife into this country. I don't know where you stand in all that, but I hope you'll be on the side of healing this country.'

'I don't know where I stand myself.'

'Well,' Father Mitchum said, 'if nothing changes soon, you'll have an explosion. The man you tortured … the man who committed suicide, will multiply like fungal spores into thousands. In no time the jails will burst at the seams. The torturers will get tired and the sea will throw up the bodies from its depths.'

'But,' Hiero asked, 'what the hell *do* people want?'

'It's human nature to seek change,' Mitch Mitchum answered. 'They want a chance to move away from poverty, which humiliates them. They look at the social stratifications of Bangula. The whites are still at the top, followed by a layer of Creoles, who are enjoying the benefits of whiteness without the burden of colour. Then you have the blacks at the base of the racial pyramid. When liberation came, sections of the white population, second- and third-generation Portuguese and French and English, fled, imagining the worst. Ramala preached reconciliation. They came back and, seeing there would be no retribution, became more emboldened in their chauvinism, because now they had the power of the state and the laws behind them. The Creoles played both ends against the middle, sometimes loudly proclaiming that they were in it for the money. Look at their family structures, how they keep to themselves; you'll never see a Creole marrying anybody except another Creole. That's also how they've kept the money among their families, how they've survived a hostile Africa. The blacks see all this, how everyone holds them in utter contempt, something that's made even more bizarre by the notion that they are in power, and all hell breaks loose. Those in power scramble and amass wealth to bring them closer to the former oppressor. Over and over, the old paradigm of power. I came across a lovely passage in Eduardo Galeano's *Days and Nights of Love and War*, where he recycles an Argentinean cynicism. *Power is held by the left hand and played by the right.*'

'If the confessional yields so much information,' suggested Hiero as a form of goodbye, 'shouldn't we install some listening devices into the booths?'

'You may do that if it pleases you,' said Father Mitchum. 'But you'll first have to bug the minds of the people to get results. That's where all the secrets lie.'

DUSK HAD SETTLED on Revolution Boulevard, the main thoroughfare that bisected Jambora. The diminished visibility was a signal for drivers of three lines of vehicles including motorbikes, minibus taxis and tankers, to let loose with their hooters. Hiero's ears were still attuned to the rumble of traffic and the cacophony of horns, idly watching street children dancing nimbly along the narrow lanes and dodging motorbikes that could still advance in intermittent spurts of speed, when he noticed a shadow that was blocking his view of the traffic from the side window.

Suddenly alert to what might be happening, he reached for the pistol in his waistband. As he struggled to get a grip on his gun, Hiero heard a muffled crash as his side window shattered, the glass popping onto his lap like a blister pack.

Looking up, he saw two hooded figures from his recurring nightmare. Instead of fear, he had an irrational urge to question them about their strange headgear since it was so hot. Strong hands simultaneously opened the door on the driver's side and pinned him against the seat; another hand that was softer, almost feminine, managed to imprison his gun hand against his crotch.

His training in various academies told him that he was in the hands of professionals. They would readily inflict maximum damage – kill him, even – if what they wanted was withheld. Hiero felt a sharp pain in the back of his hand and wondered if he had been stabbed. Drifting away, he realised that he'd been drugged. He cursed himself: *You stupid idiot, how could you be so . . .*

WHEN HIERO CAME to, he was lying on a mat on a stone floor in the middle of a bare room, the taste of chemicals in his mouth, a residue of something that he knew would wreak havoc with his system. Through a wooden door standing ajar, he could see an outside perimeter wall enclosing a compound; he could hear voices and, beneath them, the stammer of waves. Somewhere, a horn blared, trailing into the distance, a sound suddenly freighted with great longing.

When he tried to raise himself off the floor, he found his arms tied at his elbows behind his back. Trussed in this way, he could be tortured to someone's heart's content. A vulture that had hopped onto the compound wall, glimpsed from the floor, confirmed his fears. Two others joined the bird and they all sat in a line. Fascinated, Hiero watched the trio putting their heads together as if in consultation, the first vulture nodding sagely. Forgetting for a moment his own discomfort, Hiero half-expected the animals to shake on the clinching of a deal. *I never knew we had these scavengers in Bangula,* he thought, wondering whether this piece of information would die with him. *Will these creatures feed on my flesh?* He knew that vultures only roamed in areas where death or its promise thrived. *So, what's happening in Bangula?* he wondered.

The answer came soon enough, personified unsurprisingly by Baluba Jambo, who was preceded into the room by his belly. He was in the company of two men whom Hiero couldn't place, but who seemed vaguely familiar in the manner of people once encountered fleetingly in a crowded market. Baluba cut such an incongruous figure in army fatigues that Hiero had to struggle to stop the laughter that was bubbling up from inside him.

Perhaps sensing that Hiero was not about to take them seriously, the three men started assaulting him. As the blows rained down, Hiero was most worried about his teeth, and so he strove to minimise the surface area of his body that could be punished, curling himself into a foetal ball. Since he hadn't offered any resistance, he wondered at the point of the beating, concluding that it was a softening exercise. Law enforcement agencies loved this tactic. They sometimes enclosed a suspect in the back of a canopied pickup truck and then drove over uneven terrain, bouncing the man up and down, scrambling his insides. Carried to extremes, these procedures could result in fatalities.

It was at the moment of hoping that his captors knew what they were doing that he passed out.

When he regained consciousness, Hiero could smell his own bodily waste, caked vomit and urine. Although it was dark and his eyes were closed, he could tell that he'd been transferred to another room. For a long moment, he lay motionless before opening his eyes to gaze at the swirl of faces above him. He shook his head, tasting blood inside his mouth, feeling with the tip of his tongue if any of his precious teeth were loose. At least they'd untied him. Everything seemed intact except for a splitting headache.

Hiero was genuinely puzzled with the treatment meted out to him by Baluba. At Alfredo Romero, he had counted Baluba among his friends. That friendship had been cemented at David Kone's funeral. Their most recent encounter at the funeral home had been marked by friendliness and cooperation. Passing out twice in a row, and at such short intervals, could signify brain damage. That was scary. Hiero had seen people reduced to cabbages, and some as a result of the enthusiasm of his own subordinates.

As the darkness deepened and the sounds of life outside diminished, Hiero broke into a cold sweat. There was no way his captors would let him leave this place alive, unless there was a guarantee that there would be no prosecution over his seizure. Because, whatever their attitude – whether or not Baluba Jambo and his cronies had almost killed themselves laughing at Hiero's obsession with his bloodline – Hiero was a high-ranking member of government, responsible for law and order and state security at the highest level. *You can't smack me around and only expect to give an apology*, he thought. *There is no 'oops' in these matters.* Suddenly very angry, he vowed: *Someone's going to pay for this.*

They came and defused his anger at midnight, introducing him to a level of anxiety he hadn't expected as he was marched out of the compound. On the side of the road was a military-type jeep with Zoya Badawi at the wheel and Baluba Jambo in the passenger seat. One of the two camouflaged men held the back door open and ushered him in. As Hiero sat sandwiched between the two men, he offered no resistance when they blindfolded him and then snapped handcuffs on his wrists. 'Sorry about the rough stuff,' Baluba said, his regret sounding genuine, 'but you know how it is.'

Hiero remembered Timi Seramen in the blind dark of a bone-jarring journey through the night. *How does Zoya Badawi fit into the picture?* he asked himself. *Is it out of allegiance to Zebulon? And where is Zebulon? His presence in this whole operation has been marked by his absence.* Zebulon hadn't shown up at the hall, which had been less of a tribute to the Colonel than a coronation of an unclaimed son. Somewhat frightened, Hiero reasoned that Zoya Badawi was an educated woman. She'd be loath to engage in escapades that could land her in jail, unless all the conspirators operated on the principle that dead men told no tales. Obliquely, Hiero was mortified at the knowledge that he might just make history; never before had a murder been associated with a woman from the meteorological station – weather forecasting was meant to be about saving lives. It was like being smothered by a paramedic.

'You okay there, Hiero?' Zoya addressed him for the first time.

'I'm okay,' he said. 'Where are we going?'

'Patience, Hiero,' said Baluba. 'We'll be there soon.'

SOMEWHERE ALONG THE way, in a stretch that smelled of cut sugarcane and rotting pineapples, the jeep stopped. Hiero was bundled into the back of the vehicle where he lay coiled around the bulge of the spare-tyre magazine, in a space that smelled of diesel and rags. He was covered with grey blankets and ordered to be still, otherwise the men in the back had the authority to shoot him.

'Don't even fart,' he heard one of the men saying; then the sound of a silencer being screwed to a pistol. The thought that the roads were corrugated gave him the jitters; accidents did happen. *Well*, Hiero thought resignedly, *if shit happens, at least my body will be in the hands of a professional undertaker.*

He soon understood the logic behind his concealment when the jeep stopped at two roadblocks, each incident as surreal as it was scary. Hiero knew that a roadblock was normally manned by a squad with an assortment of arms including an RPG-7V anti-tank grenade launcher for adventurous drivers. Twice Hiero heard the police allow the party to pass in response to Baluba Jambo's oleaginous tones. 'Take care, Boss,' the men said, laughing. Faintly, from his stinking hidey-hole, Hiero heard Zoya's coquettish undertaking that the next television weathergirl would don a wet T-shirt to match a rainy day forecast. Then, as the jeep was gunned into gear, her long-drawn-out sigh, *'Fuck!'*

'*FUCK!*' CURSED HIERO.

He couldn't remember the last time he had sworn in public. Sometimes when Emma-May bugged him, especially when he was a little hung over, he would mutter a mild profanity, but nothing this coarse. Around him, seemingly having decided to release him to make his own discoveries, were Zoya and Baluba. By the time Zoya had helped him out of the back of the vehicle, the two gun-toting assistants had vanished. Hiero now had use of both his hands and his eyes.

What his eyes were seeing, which had elicited the expletive, made him wish for blindness. First there was the village that had been sentenced to death. As it was dawn, Hiero had initially thought that the rows upon rows of tents were an optical illusion, a condition that could be blamed on the earlier wholesale assault on his cranium. But, probing deeper into the clearing mist, he saw that the village of canvas had been built in the middle of a forest of ragged, dome-like thatched huts that seemed unhealthy even from a distance.

It was not difficult to enter the camp, for that is what it was, for refugees and for relatives of people condemned to death by the blood plague. Thousands had escaped from the quarantine centre, which had been christened the Camp of Bones. Skeletal people who had seen other skeletal people had walked, in groups or singly, across the plain and set up in this valley. In time, some benefactors had arrived and provided the refugees, who were sleeping on hessian matting under the open sky, with tents and other forms of support. The donors had to bribe a lot of officials, from the health ministry to the military, to turn a blind eye.

The early pioneers, who were certainly mostly dead, had scrounged for materials until they were able to build a fence, which stood ten feet high. There was now a rickety gate and a guardhouse that was manned by some of Baluba Jambo's militia. The fence secured just one end of the camp; the beach and the savage breakers of the ocean formed the border on the other end. The fence couldn't, of course, stop anyone from leaving the camp. It stopped those crazy enough to want to enter. There were a few of these, volunteers and outcasts who had found so-called normal society hugely unbalanced.

Hiero walked in step with Zoya and Baluba, following their guide, a young man with an accent from the mountain region. Leading the way to a multi-purpose tent, he warned them before opening the flap. 'It smells in here,' he said, and ushered them inside.

Hiero was struck by the smell of human waste and despair. It took him back to the final days of his dada's struggle to hang on to life. In the dim light of reluctant daybreak, he realised that he knew nothing about suffering, for there, on pallets, like offerings on an altar of neglectful deities, lay what remained of human beings for whom everything had lost meaning. Twisted limbs the size of broomsticks pulled at blankets to hide nakedness that was expressed most profoundly in the staring eyes. It was difficult to tell the living from the dying, the hopeful from the utterly hopeless. The camp was clearly more of a hospice than a hospital, the survivors merely there to do their duty as part of the human race, before they, too, were rendered helpless.

'We brought you here,' Zoya Badawi said, 'to this place, to see for yourself what you've been shielding your eyes – and the eyes of your leader – from seeing. These bags of bones are people; once upon a time they loved and laughed and gave birth and had orgasms and cried. Now the smell alone tells you where they are going. We're not saying that the government must save them or stop the blood plague. You cannot stop something whose inner workings you do not know. We do not know where this disease comes from. We do not know when it will end. But we do know that there must be a way for things to be done differently.'

'First, this disease must be brought out into the open. Then the government must sponsor a series of discussions coupled with an end to the denial of its existence. Otherwise we end up with situations like these. And, lastly, people must go to the grave with a lot more dignity. This is where *you* and Abioseh Gondo have failed.'

I knew there was a place for isolating victims of infection, Hiero thought. *If the walking – no, sleeping – corpses had escaped from quarantine, what does the quarantine centre look like and what is the condition of the inmates? There's a lot I don't know about my own country.* He realised that he had been deliberately kept in the dark. The briefs from Wonderman Bhele, assigning him to the interrogation of suspects accused of various crimes and misdemeanours against the state were all a sham, a camouflage for the real crime against the people of Bangula. The games that were being played were suddenly clear. He had thought he was keeping so much from his president. But who had had the last laugh? His president had actually foxed him and played him. *Ye are liars,* the biblical ruling came unsummoned, *and the truth is not in you.*

Then Baluba Jambo interrupted his chain of thought. He said, 'Some of the ministers, not all, know what's going on. It's tolerated because it removes the onus of setting up hospices and mass graves from them. Furthermore, they don't even have to field the police or the army to control the refugees' movements. They leave that to the villagers around, who patrol the roads and make short shrift of any of the refugees unwise enough to stray outside the perimeter fence.'

'But why?' Hiero asked.

'Why?' Baluba Jambo sounded tired. 'We think that if we expose our weakness, people will take advantage of us. People will think less of us. We plaster the cracks and everyone thinks we're okay when we're rotting inside. I see this daily. I make corpses resemble the living; some of them so convincing that you'd expect them to get up from the trays and demand breakfast.' He paused. 'Death will always be with us. But it's how we arrange the transaction with death that provides a judgement on our suitability to hold public office.'

'So,' Hiero asked, 'in your opinion, do undertakers make the best leaders?'

'No,' Baluba said. 'But they've got a more realistic grasp on what constitutes being human. They see it often in the expression of loss. People know how to behave after bereavement. Before that, it's all abstract.'

'Is that why you tried to kill me?'

'No,' Baluba answered. 'That was to bring you closer to valuing life. People who've had a near-death experience become philanthropists.' His teeth gleamed in the gloom. 'We've actually done you a favour.'

'It almost killed me.' Then, after a pause, Hiero asked, 'Where's Zebulon?'

'You mean in all of this?' Zoya responded. She and Baluba exchanged a look. Hiero suspected that, for all their bravado, accoutrements of the military and revolutionary platitudes, they were uneasy. At that exact minute, their eyes were no different from those of the people paralysed by dread in the camp. No government had the right to instil such fear among its citizens.

Hiero nodded. 'Zebulon, yes. He's pretty scarce in all this.'

'Zebulon has been chosen to lead,' Baluba said. 'Although the people have nominated him as their leader, they are confused. On the one hand, they remember the Colonel. But they know that their troubles actually began with the Reform. On the other hand, they are attracted to the radical anarchy of Vezi – and Zebulon is the direct heir of both men. He comes from two branches of a strong tree. Since our people believe that power derives from the sovereignty of the dead, Zebulon will have to be initiated in death first, before he can be allowed to lead.'

'How is that possible?'

'Everything is possible.' Baluba looked at his watch. 'Let's get moving.'

'What about the president?' Hiero asked.

'Everything is ready,' Baluba said with real sadness. 'I wouldn't want to be in Abioseh's shoes right now.'

4

'MR PRESIDENT? MR PRESIDENT?' The voice that accompanied the hands shaking him was as insistent as it was courteous. 'Mr President?'

Abioseh Gondo became aware of his surroundings slowly, like a man coming round from a blackout induced by vicious concoctions. Although he had been unconscious, he was sitting on a rigid chair and not laid out on a bed. The room was familiar in the way hotel rooms look the same, but it was rigged with glass, chrome, and aluminium fittings constituting general medical equipment.

Wonderman Bhele and a man in a white coat came into focus. The man prodded the president's skull with cold fingers, now and then peering through thick glasses at his face. *Someone ambushed me*, Abioseh remembered, *and now it's open season on my flesh*. Feeling a surge of resentment over his self-pity, he started to ask for his personal physician, but then felt the need to be sparing with his quota of questions. He was the president but, somehow, the hotel-room-turned-hospital-ward instilled in him the need to take his cue from others.

The doctor barked an order that the room be vacated, save for his assistant, a young nurse with expressionless eyes. Her conduct disturbed Abioseh. She seized every opportunity to rub herself up against him, as if testing whether or not his sexual wiring was still functional. The doctor asked questions and seemed interested in the dream, the blurred line between dream and reality. Now and then the doctor, whose face Abioseh couldn't place, and the nurse, also a stranger, exchanged meaningful glances. Abioseh was very uncomfortable with the session. They left and sent Wonderman and his companions back in.

One of the men with Wonderman drew back the curtains and let in a splash of harsh sunlight, the beams sending needles straight into the president's brain. Abioseh blinked and Wonderman, who was still wearing the same tracksuit, made a cutting gesture with his one hand. The room returned to bearable blandness.

Wonderman sat on the bed and leant forward, his elbows resting on his thighs. Making a tent with his fingers, he told the story as he knew it. 'On the evening in question ...' he began. The president raised a hand.

'Hold it right there,' he said. 'What do you mean *on the evening in question?* Didn't this ... this confusion ... didn't it happen last night or something?'

'No, Mr President,' Wonderman replied; he looked about him as if soliciting help from the security men. The men seemed awkward, like youngsters discomfited by an elder's incontinence. 'You've been in a coma for nine days.'

Nine days! Abioseh was aghast. *Surely not ...*

'What's going on?' Mr President asked. He looked down, memory returning in disjointed snatches, like a film sequence delivered through a faulty projector. Someone had divested Abioseh of his jogging gear as he was now in hospital greens and cotton slippers. 'What's going on, Wonderman?'

'It seems you had a little accident at Mariposa,' Wonderman explained. At around 8.10 PM on the evening of the meeting with the president, he had met an ambush at the gates. Men in army fatigues opened fire, riddling his car with bullets. Wonderman managed to escape unscathed, but two of his bodyguards in the lead car sustained fatal injuries. Praising the power of German-made engines, Wonderman gunned the car into reverse and sped back to Mariposa to warn the president that they were under attack. Two other men were with him. By then someone had raised the alarm and the rag-tag army was put to flight after a furious firefight with the presidential guard. It seemed that one of the rockets had smashed through the southern wall of the lounge and exploded, flinging the president into the air. When Wonderman and his men entered, they feared it was all over, but they took the president for emergency treatment.

As Wonderman spoke, Abioseh felt his head gingerly with his fingertips. He still couldn't believe he'd been in a coma. He'd been asleep for nine days.

'Who were the attackers?' asked Mr President. 'And how could you not have known of such a threat, Wonderman?'

'It came like a bolt out of the blue, Mr President,' Wonderman explained. 'We'd been getting reports about bandit activity and we thought that the security measures we'd taken were enough. But we hadn't bargained on malcontents within the armed forces. I think the dissatisfaction emanated from the pay dispute and went full blown.'

In a nutshell, thought Abioseh, *you're selling me a lot of hot air*. 'There *must* be a ringleader,' he persisted. 'Soldiers don't just rise like that.'

'I'm expecting a consolidated report,' Wonderman replied. 'Hiero should be here. But the man in our sights is Baluba Jambo.'

'Where is he? The suspect?'

'Mr President,' Wonderman went on, 'Bangula is under martial law now. We invoked the special powers when the head of state got incapacitated. A five-person junta, which I head, is now in control of the state machinery. It's the Provisional Authority for Progress.'

'PAP?'

'Yes, Mr President, PAP.'

IT WAS STILL too early to report the number of casualties to the president, especially the fact that a school on an outing had been caught in the crossfire. Wonderman wanted to tell Abioseh about small bodies lying in various unflattering poses of death. Wonderman told himself that it was this outrage, more than anything else, which propelled him to take power. He recalled the wreckage, people running helter-skelter, the sirens and car alarms, a bedlam that gave voice to the fire, smoke and crumbling masonry. He would tell the president once he'd built up a comprehensive picture, and he wanted to take his four colleagues from PAP along with him. Then there was the little issue of the Commission of Inquiry.

'We are setting up a Commission of Inquiry, Mr President,' Wonderman said.

'On the disturbance?' Abioseh asked.

'Yes.' Wonderman paused, thinking. 'That was partly the reason why we moved you from Mariposa to the hotel.'

'Am I the subject of the inquiry?'

'I'm afraid so, Mr President.'

'So,' Abioseh said, jerking himself up and regretting the sudden movement as it sent a sharp pain coursing down his back from his neck to his coccyx, 'what exactly is my status? Am I under arrest?'

'The country was plunged into confusion during your stewardship,' Wonderman said, reciting a rehearsed speech. 'There was the mutiny of the men under arms, given the crisis over salaries. What is it that a soldier gets here? A few hundred Bangdos a month. A pittance. Do you know that a fisherman earns more than the man or woman whose life is dedicated to the defence of this island? The deaths from the blood plague: you're not God, but you didn't pay attention to the deaths – and these were mainly young people, especially women. The soldiers were sickened by the journeys to the north, where we had to incinerate the bodies because we were running out of burial space. The mortuaries are a disaster. In your absence, we did a comprehensive inspection. While we had a full measure of the mess we were in, we had to remember what the Colonel once said: *We must always discourage indecision. The people must know that their leadership …*'

'… *is the best leadership in the land.*' Abioseh finished the sentence for him.

'In fact,' Wonderman continued, 'it should be a leadership that people trust implicitly, if not instinctively.'

'And you feel that I did not inspire that … instinct … implicitly?' Abioseh felt the onset of a massive headache.

'Do you choose to forget how I catapulted this itty-bitty island into the international arena?' He asked the question more as a soliloquy than as an attempt at conversation. 'How we, a small atoll with a small population, punched way above our weight? A peasant, a fucking populist philanderer, who must have engineered from his loins a tribe that will rise up and smite all of you sanctimonious bleeders, drafted your manifesto. You're transported on the musings of a man whose sole fixation was making uncomfortable things about governance go away.'

He stopped, suddenly drained. 'I tried to even the playing fields. What will your regime do?' Raising his hand, Abioseh motioned for one of the security men to pass him a glass of water. Taking a sip, he seemed to relax and ease himself into his hospital greens, like an adolescent making a choice that the birthday present, whatever its limitations, was something he could live with. 'You know what?' he asked. 'Go right ahead and set up a commission. Do whatever. I believe that things happened because some of you – and this includes you, Wonderman – some of you were white-anting my leadership.'

'Mr President?' Wonderman said; irretrievable sadness had crept into his tone. 'The men here will ensure that you are kept safe. It's my responsibility as head of PAP to make certain that you're provided with all the amenities – including a radio, television and a telephone. I'm sorry that all your calls will be monitored, so don't go overboard with little Jacqui.

Be kind to your mother; you said some nasty things when you were blacked out.' He shook his head as a thought seized him. '*White-anting?* What a curious word.'

PART SIX

FLAMES

I

THE DAY PROMISED to be uneventful. It was slightly overcast with cumulus clouds scudding across the sky, looking like floating candyfloss. Thanks to Zoya, he paid more than passing attention to the weather and its whims. Zebulon could say with certainty that a thunderstorm was on its way. Suddenly remembering Zoya's appeal for the equipment for her weather centre, he cursed his hesitancy with Abioseh Gondo.

The city looked dazzling, especially the new, whitewashed structures standing uneasily next to the old face-brick buildings long abandoned by the Portuguese. Zebulon entered the shops in the mall, which stayed open and crowded even past midnight. Not an economist, but rather an astute listener, he had come to know that even as unemployment rose to alarming heights and poverty stalked the majority of households, the economy was in good health, in fact, booming.

This success, which reflected on world stock exchanges but was an enigma to the man and woman on the street, was credited to Abioseh

Gondo's monetary policies. Bangula was an investors' paradise and a living hell for the poor. Zebulon knew even as this thought entered his head that the state of affairs in Bangula was replicated elsewhere in Africa, Asia and Latin America. The taxi driver honking his horn and trying to scare up an indifferent trade had cousins far and wide, as did the man in a threadbare suit and shoes with thin soles – *soul-less shoes*, he called them. These were some of the worker bees who, even though imbued with meekness, would inherit nothing.

He thought of his mother and the trouble she had seen, which, with the benefit of hindsight, he could now appreciate. Immediately he started comparing her with Zoya, she who made his pulse quicken. And then wondered what Madu would have made of what people expected of him.

Zebulon was still sifting through a tangle of memories and thoughts when, on a patch of lawn close to the street corner ahead, he saw a man playing marimbas, his back turned to the street. Coins and two or three crumpled Bangula dollars of different denominations were scattered on a garish carpet. An amplifier stood on one corner of the carpet. From the intensity of the volume, Zebulon guessed that the speakers and the power supply had been rigged somewhere on the lawn. Something about the player triggered instant recognition, the spare frame in a black suit and a panama hat – *that hat*! Meaning to avoid the man with whom he had once argued, Zebulon was about to make a detour when Stefan called out to him.

'Hey, Playboy!' Stefan was in a jovial mood, even though it was clear that he was down on his luck. 'Playboy? Don't you run away from *me* now.'

Zebulon turned and approached the group that had gathered around the musician. They looked at him with undisguised curiosity, this man with such an interesting name. A few recognised him. Zebulon noticed that Stefan's eyes were red from alcohol or a lack of sleep.

'What is it?' He was irritated; Stefan had no right to talk to him like that.

'What I want to know,' he asked, 'is have you now found the power?'

'Power? What power?'

'Don't act like you don't know what I'm talking about in front of these people,' Stefan said, punctuating each word with a tap on the keys with a mallet. 'I'm asking about the *power* you went to get with the bitch, Zoya.'

'Now, look here ...'

'Listen to him, folks,' Stefan said, his voice hoarse with indignation, doing what comes naturally to musicians, weaving a spell to attract an audience. 'He's all coy now that he's not swanking around with the weathergirl on his arm. Look at him, this dogshit-eating, cunt-lapping, cock-sucking, liver-lipped, fucked-up ...'

The noontime crowd had at first consisted of workers taking an early lunch, shoppers to and from the sleepless mall or young schoolchildren having break, for whom such a distraction was a godsend. Now the crowd had changed subtly into a mass of bodies – men, women and children of all shapes and sizes – who detected in the drama on the lawn a promise for the slaking of their undying thirst to know what was happening in the lives of others.

The assembled people, united by a single purpose, witnessed Stefan's bitter hysteria. They marvelled at Zebulon's seemingly stoical acceptance of the profanities that oozed as though with rehearsed eloquence from the younger man's lips, like mango juice dripping into a glass.

As the words rained down and scattered like the coins on the carpet and settled in the minds of the crowd, the people took a closer look at Zebulon as if trying to make sense of the kind of man who could stand unmoving while his insides were opened out for the world to smell. They hardly glanced at Stefan, for to hear the words was enough. There was no need to look at him and see the way his eyes burnt with rage and hatred and how his lips were twisted. No, they concentrated their gaze on Zebulon, remembering him now from some earlier moment when death had been on the agenda. Some of the members of the audience, who heard the rush of obscenities underscored by a series of gongs from the gourds and timber that formed the keys of the marimbas, suspected that death was perhaps not far, especially when they looked into Zebulon's eyes.

'... misbegotten-bastard-son-of-a-no-good-whore ...'

At which point Zebulon struck Stefan flush on the mouth with his fist. The soft crunch of knuckles against flesh and bone momentarily shut off the stream of profanities. The blasphemer tottered and then landed spread-eagled on his carpet. Its extravagant patterns changed with the introduction of fresh crimson. Some of the children saw vomit and bloodstained teeth and mistook the fetid mixture for kernels of maize in beetroot juice.

Somehow Stefan drew himself up into a sitting position, his gaping hole of a mouth still working, the swearing all the coarser because it was wordless and allowed the fascinated watchers to exercise their imaginations.

There were many versions of the moment that followed. Some people remembered the punch, delivered with lightning speed and Stefan falling, falling like a pebble into a well, his plunge seeming to take a very long time, much longer than the string of curses he was delivering. Still others would swear that Zebulon never touched the man. What happened to that foul-mouthed busker was an intervention from above, the Almighty having lost patience with the use of language so corrosive it could have scoured industrial coating off a ship's hull.

The shooting, then, was all the more confusing, because some of the people would swear, when they made depositions at the police station, that it was Stefan who drew a pistol and fired at point-blank range at Zebulon. Others said that the shooter came from within the body of the crowd that had surged forward to witness Stefan's collapse. These recalled that the assassin, for that was how he came to be known, was a slightly built, middle-aged man in a grey suit whose facial features were so unremarkable he could have been anyone there. When asked to try to remember what the man had looked like, a woman witness from the crime scene, who was giving evidence at the Jambora Central Police Station, looked

around and described the killer by pointing a gnarled finger at the homicide detectives. 'He looked like you and you and you,' she said. Then she
burst into tears, perhaps beginning to suspect that she herself could have
been mistaken for the killer. 'Holy Boy was killed by a chameleon.'

The detectives were livid. Who the hell did this old crone think she
was? They were already feeling the heat, expecting Hiero and other top
brass to make an appearance soon. They felt it in their bones that there
would be hell to pay. 'Does she expect us to send out an identikit featuring a fucking chameleon?' someone exclaimed.

The ubiquitous Sarsaparilla and her team were first on the scene,
which the police were busy cordoning off with sawhorses and tape.
Other officers were busy taking down statements from the witnesses,
the majority of whom, like the old Mrs Chameleon, didn't add much
to what the police didn't already know. In addition, many of the people
were wary of talking to the police, what with the security situation on
a knife-edge. There could be no telling which faction, in a country that
was grappling with the question of taking sides, would gain the upper hand with this public slaying. But Sarsaparilla's microphone and the
promise of instant fame achieved results where the police investigation
had stalled. A schoolgirl of about fourteen, her hair straightened in defiance of the grooming regime stipulated by her school principal, stepped
forward and looked unblinkingly at the camera. 'The gunman,' she said,
'looked like Mr President.'

The gunman looked like Mr President. The words had hardly escaped her
teenaged lips when the microphones broadcast them to the rest of the
country. The paramedics zipped the body up in a bag, placed it on a
gurney and wheeled it towards an ambulance. Emerging out of the swirling crowd, Zoya wailed, slapping her own head and face in intense grief,
driving several watchers to tears. Sarsaparilla focused on Zoya. To the
many witnesses of the fatal row, the day was filled with wonder. A man
who had shown the skill of a boxer had been reduced, in the wink of an
eye, to a corpse.

Zoya's grief was like a whirlwind. It stopped the paramedics in their tracks. They recoiled as she, helped by a group that included Baluba Jambo and Zoya's three grandmothers, Jumaima, Jutaita and Josephine, seized the body in its bloodstained cover and carried it above their heads as they forded the crowd. Suddenly the mass of people who had appeared stunned in solemn disorder began gyrating to a song that had sprung up from the entrails of the multitude:

The lizards chew the meat
And think they've got us beat . . .

And then the chorus:

They're starving, starving, starving . . .

The singing gave rise to dancing and chanting and ululation that inflamed the blood of the men and women and even children, and brought back memories of times when people had gone out with weapons in hand to bring back wild boars or the heads of the enemy. In the fading light, the women danced, their limbs softened. In the night, which had lost its own shadows, the people started their own Festival of Lights, an ancient carnival marking a declaration of war, which would continue for nine days. Everything and anything burnable was brought onto the lawn in the square, now transformed into a shrine, where Zebulon had fallen.

The people danced well into the morning. At first light, at the traffic circle at the centre of the city, near the plinth of the absent statue commemorating the Portuguese conqueror, Zebulon's body lay in a glass-topped coffin. On either side were another four coffined dead, making up nine, the magical number for Bangula believers in the resurrection of the dead. Reciting age-old praise songs from memory, the poet Ezekiel Manolo predicted the end of the regime.

TO A SLEEPLESS Abioseh, hardly a kilometre away, the excitement on the square came as part of the city stirring awake. But the buzz had infiltrated the dream he'd been having since the attack.

In it, wearing a smile of sad triumph, Carlos Nobrega stood tall with thin electrode wires attached to his head and partly obscuring his face, like false dreadlocks. 'See how heavy the crown is,' he recited. 'You sit there watching power. The oppressed becoming oppressors in the name of the common good.' He shook his head; the beaded ends of his wild tresses clashed like castanets.

'All of us in leadership,' Nobrega continued, 'started out as patriots, but we have no power to heal what has been dishonoured by time. We explained our impotence by enacting more laws to cover up yesterday's mistakes. We all tried to be like the Colonel. We even talked like him. But we couldn't approximate the ways of his spirit. Much later, we learnt – and by then it was too late to get back to our original selves – that the Colonel was also acting a role.'

Nobrega said that the Colonel had been imitating Vezi, the man whose death he had caused. The Colonel had died wishing he could punish the beneficiaries of plunder and rapine of the past. But he couldn't. The laws he had sworn to uphold had outlawed retaliative tendencies. 'Our modes of expression,' Nobrega went on, 'and our thinking were shaped posthumously by a man whose memory was akin to treason. Your father was Vezi's greatest victory.'

As Nobrega disappeared, MaZembe entered the frame, like someone emerging out of a mist, and regarded her son. Bowed at the waist like a dancer introducing a complex routine, she stretched her arms, her quivering fingers directing Abioseh's gaze to her extraordinarily long crimson nails. A bearer of hard memories, MaZembe recounted in a sing-song voice how difficult it was to love Abioseh as a child because he strove to create distances between himself and others. She'd stopped breastfeeding him at a tender age, instead giving him a mixture of mashed maize and milk through a straw.

Abioseh asked: *What was wrong with me, Ma?* With the shamefaced smile of someone not entirely certain of her suitableness in the world, Ma-Zembe answered, 'You looked too much like your father. At some point, I wanted to poison you, too, so that you'd stop reminding me of him.' Abioseh asked: *Is that how he died, then?* MaZembe laughed. 'Once you've made up your mind to turn your back on unhappiness, it's better not to confide in anyone, not even the closest friend.'

Suddenly, coming from behind, he heard the rustle of clothes as people stripped naked and he remembered Abdullah dying. Turning with difficulty, his neck stiff, Abioseh saw Wonderman and his bodyguards disrobing, at first slowly and then with urgency, as if their garments were full of red ants. Motionless in the half-light of the dream, Abioseh felt powerful hands grabbing him and bending him almost in half, the men positioning themselves behind him. Suddenly and unaccountably naked, he despaired as a cold breeze caressed his genitals: *They're going to take turns ... I've never been so vulnerable.* He screamed, '*No, no!*'

On the morning after Zebulon's shooting on the square, Abioseh Gondo phoned for his personal physician. It was time to confess.

2

THERE IS NO *such thing as innocence*, Wonderman Bhele thought. It was an original thought, although somewhat sparked off by an essay on Palestinian Judaism in the Greco-Roman period, which also analysed religious notions of the apocalypse. He longed to formulate a theory on his own relationship with Abioseh and the function of power in Bangula. He was in top form, delighted by his status as the junta chairman with a casting vote. He liked being called 'chairman'; politically correct jargon alone hadn't brought in any gender equity.

Formed soon after a comatose Abioseh was whisked to the makeshift hospital room in the hotel, the junta was formally called the Provisional Authority for Progress. Knowing that people preferred 'junta', with its hint of despotic rule in banana republics, he favoured the short form of PAP. He had almost lost his temper when told that the country's comedians would sometimes append an 'a' to PAP in their skits lampooning ministers' expensive lifestyles. This added a spicy flavour to the hilarity when the country's radio stations regularly acceded to requests for James Brown's timeless hit, 'Papa's Got a Brand New Bag'.

Long before Abioseh had faced his current challenges, political pundits had touted Bhele as a likely successor. That the two men shared a commitment to transformation had displeased traditionalists who, ironically, were the main sponsors of the major changes. Now that these changes had come to haunt them they had become hard to accept.

Both men were uncomfortable with the whispers and innuendo about deals and kickbacks among some of the ministers and senior government officials. Abioseh and Wonderman were roughly the same age, give or take, and both prided themselves on having graduated with flying colours from the same leadership academy – the street. They had also both avoided using family connections to go forward, preferring to climb to power on their own merits.

Bhele came from a successful line of sugarcane tycoons. He had joined the unions and, having made his mark there, amassed support in the various federations that rattled the cages of both big business and government. Fearless to a fault, it was inevitable that Wonderman would be given a high position in the Colonel's government following his recruitment from the unions. He started out as a deputy minister before promotion to his current portfolio of safety, security and national intelligence.

Before relocating to the offices set aside for the operations of PAP, Bhele's was a huge ministry with numerous directorates whose main focus was ensuring that the citizens enjoyed a good night's sleep in the safety of their homes. Although Hiero reported directly to the president, in administrative terms Wonderman Bhele was his real boss.

Bhele's star rose when he canvassed for the return of the death penalty, not because he believed in it, but because the people still held that it was a deterrent. He had long decided that the war against crime wasn't going to be won while the law enforcement agencies of the state wore kid gloves.

He then dedicated a large part of his term to win Cabinet backing to effect an undeclared shoot-to-kill policy against armed robbers. Bhele enlisted sections of the media to run campaigns advocating the need to be tough on crime while the government simultaneously sought to eradicate the immediately identifiable causes of crime such as poverty, disease, unemployment and inequity.

The slogan that preceded the nightly news bulletin on all television and radio stations was: 'To make the omelette of national safety, the government has to break some eggs; you, the loyal citizens, are the griddle.' This refrain, accompanying a catchy tune, found resonance in the public mind in a country where cooking – especially barbecuing – was very popular. Children in their school uniforms sang the jingle with zeal. Such was the fervour against transgression that it didn't occur to anyone to question who had composed the motto – probably some pony-tailed consultant fresh out of some fly-by-night arts college – about a planet where eggs were prepared on a griddle.

During this period, which lasted thirty-six months, the police were given extra powers to search, seize and detain suspects without trial for ninety days. A dusk-to-dawn curfew operated, during which time citizens were encouraged, under the rubric of Operation Cipher, to expose felons in their midst. Although there were abuses of the system, such as people accusing their enemies falsely, there was a dramatic reduction in violent crime. Some of the accused who had got off on technicalities in earlier court appearances were discovered in unbecoming poses of death, usually with bullet holes at the back of their heads.

Although a rumour did the rounds that this was the work of Bhele's death squads, no one seemed anxious to lay a charge with the Civic Complaints Directorate that was responsible for investigating alleged excesses by the security forces. One complaint was, however, pursued, when a conscientious citizen reported her neighbour's eight-year-old daughter to the authorities for impugning the dignity of the anti-crime campaign by chanting, during a game of jacks, 'The government has to break some legs.'

CONTROVERSY HAD ALWAYS followed Dr Caramel Sebone-Prah, Bhele's de facto deputy in the junta. She had fought with Abioseh from the day of her appointment to the presidential commission on infrastructure price regulation. Having been her successor at the select committee on communications, Abioseh couldn't help but raise concerns about the mess she had made of her job.

Dr Sebone-Prah always insisted on being addressed formally, although few could remember when, where or if she had actually graduated, some saying she got her Master's degree in biblical studies through a correspondence course. Her detractors said she was equipped for nothing but invoking holy writ. Since she made it known that she was on first-name basis with Carlos Nobrega, it was not uncommon for her to suspend proceedings while, she'd announce proudly, she consulted the vice-president on a debatable issue. Whatever answer she came back with would be accepted as the course to be taken, for it came from the VP.

The likelihood that this might have been a charade and that the feedback or official *line* – ostensibly from the exalted lips that were a heartbeat away from the highest office in the land – had been made up by the good doctor herself, was never subjected to scrutiny. It was generally accepted that querying the bona fides of someone this close to the oracle was not such a wise career move.

The Colonel – many said on the basis of Nobrega's prompting – appointed her as the deputy minister responsible for infrastructure coordination. Although she was later blamed for the torpor that affected most of the infrastructure cluster of ministries, which largely came from indecisiveness in a competitive world, commentators laid the blame squarely on the president's doorstep, saying his blind reward of loyalty resulted in the sacrifice of delivery.

It was with a certain amount of amusement that analysts observed how the tide turned when Abioseh succeeded Carlos Nobrega and confirmed Dr Sebone-Prah to full minister. A believer in not fixing what ain't broke, Abioseh had built on what his predecessors had put in place.

Few knew when the relationship between them had soured, but perhaps it went back to Abioseh's success in the position that she had been forced to vacate. What was clear was that Dr Sebone-Prah strove with cunning to undermine every decision that Abioseh sponsored. Of all the ministers, she was the one who more than diligently read her document pack and arrived formidably prepared to every meeting, with choice passages of the president's proposals already highlighted with a purple marker.

Wonderman Bhele knew that he would have to carry a big stick when dealing with Dr Caramel Sebone-Prah.

If someone was likely to throw a spanner into the works, however, it was Marcia Baraka, because it was difficult to know what she was thinking. Her political allegiance and commitment to the Reform Party were unquestionable. But she had on numerous occasions stymied proposals sponsored by the Party, which she felt were either unconstitutional or would in time expose them to charges of human rights' violations.

Hers was a strange portfolio of tourism, culture and energy. The first two tasks were unproblematic. Culture and tourism had always coexisted in most situations, with many countries setting up booming tourism industries on the back of their cultural vibrancy. Examples were found in varying degrees all over the globe, with more marketing aggressiveness seen in the UK, France, Italy, the USA, some choice islands of the Caribbean, parts of South and Latin America and Hungary, to name just a few.

By contrast, Africa, perhaps with the exception of Egypt and the Maghreb, had very little of a strategic approach to arts and crafts, culture and tourism. Bangula was particularly bad. Marcia Baraka had travelled, sometimes with Caramel Sebone-Prah, through the length and breadth of the country. She had found that policy-makers were totally out of touch with steps to break the cycle with an imprisoning past.

The violence marking the end of Ramala's period had seen some theatres, libraries, museums and various treasuries of society's refinement and achievement put to the torch. Aware of the challenge, Marcia Baraka committed herself to rebuilding. Sometimes, tired and weary, she would wonder if it was worth the trouble. The youth still seemed hell-bent on aping anything American, from fashion design through to the visual arts and musical comedy. The adults appeared to take their cue from fantasists, never showing any leadership. The middle and upper classes also participated in the self-hating mimicry that was inspired by the never-never images on television and glossy magazines; they splashed out on unaffordable cars, clothes and palatial homes.

Notwithstanding the feeling of forever shovelling manure against the tide, Baraka took pride in her portfolio, which also aroused her passions and curiosity. She fervently believed in the importance of ethics, reason and justice. She also believed in, and sometimes conjured up in her magic moments, the unappreciated griots and village oracles – and was consequently the sum total of their intellectual energy.

Even in her most despairing moments Marcia Baraka accepted that the young did not uniformly display a sheep-like adoration of all things Western. There *were* young musicians who went into the remotest corners of the land and captured for the coming generations the sounds of music, the forgotten songs and chants of grace and valour. Other young people painted and carved and constructed astonishing installations that would never be exhibited or mounted in establishment galleries that were usually branded with the logos of banks or various financial institutions.

Energy was another matter, it being understood that the more natural a resource, the more people in influential positions guaranteed that it be held in as few hands as possible, preferably theirs. The offenders included one or two of her Cabinet colleagues. She was therefore inundated with irritating hints that she stood to be as rich as Croesus if only she'd overlook some irksome regulation or provision in the statute.

Marcia was known to be angry with the president, to whom she had dutifully reported the whiff and reality of graft to no avail. In Wonderman's reckoning, she would readily throw him to the wolves, just to teach him a lesson. But then it was also no secret that she was one of Abioseh's steadiest supporters. She held him in high esteem for his demonstrable commitment to the women's cause and for his pragmatic management of the economy.

And what about the Zebulon factor? Wonderman Bhele couldn't tell: he had seen her chatting to Zebulon, her intelligent brow furrowed as she listened to him, head tilted to the side.

But nothing on her face would betray what she was really thinking. 'I fear snakes, scorpions and all sorts of creepy crawlies,' Marcia would say with a visible shudder, 'but being taken for granted frightens me the most.'

Someone who seemed almost incapable of fear was Hamilton Sodoku, minister of land, agriculture and defence. Whenever the Party needed a troubleshooter, Sodoku was almost always the candidate fielded. This derived from his popularity with the grassroots. 'I am,' he was wont to say, finger raised like someone about to invoke the wisdom of a holy book, 'of the grassroots, although I'll never get choked by the grass.'

Very few people, including journalists, academics and respected commentators, knew that the last phrase had been slightly reworded from a poem by the Last Poets, and led many to conclude, incorrectly, that Sodoku was a secret weed head.

But a weed head Sodoku was not; in truth, he hated all forms of weakness and had never drunk or smoked in his entire life.

When his younger brother, Khalifa, who had been a musician (and who had actually made him listen to the Last Poets) died of a heroin overdose in a fleabag hotel, Sodoku became a favoured spokesman against substance abuse. He would appear on Sunday television and on radio talk shows. His ubiquity presented itself as funny to some of the users. 'Boy,' remarked one crack cocaine addict, lighting a pipe, 'you know you've got it bad when, after Sodoku's spiel, you get such an instant craving you *want* to phone up your dealer.'

This was his problem, Bhele thought. Sodoku was too damn earnest and this cast doubt on anything he did or said, and therefore had the opposite effect from the intended one. In shebeens, there was 'Sodoku' lager in direct contrast with his vaunted crusades; and pharmacists nearly ruptured themselves laughing when they learnt that their shelves stocked a brand of ribbed condoms known as 'Sodokus', following a scandal that involved him and a pop diva.

Dogged as he was by an undeserved attention that sought to label him as mediocre, Sodoku was good at his job, especially in his stewardship of the combined land and agriculture ministries, which had left many of his predecessors bruised and disfavoured. He had cleaned up the top layer of officialdom and promised to widen the purge in the middle echelons, although there was inevitably still rot that dated back to the first decade of liberation.

And there *were* proportionately more native Bangula farmers now. The land-tenure legislation ensured that the land-buyers, mainly from Europe and Asia (enviously dismissed as Euro- and Yellow-trash respectively), would not willy-nilly gobble up swathes of land that belonged to the people.

This was where Sodoku had seemingly found agreement with Zebulon's union, whose slogan was simply: *Land for Africans!* Although Wonderman would never publicly admit this, he suspected that Sodoku shared many more of Zebulon's sentiments, especially those questioning if humankind's fate had actually improved as a result of the last century's momentous developments.

Sodoku was passionate about his other portfolio of defence. For him, this was the cornerstone of a state's ability to define itself. It was also known that Sodoku modelled himself on the Colonel, whom he missed. 'He was a real soldier,' he'd tell anyone willing to indulge him. 'A military man to boot.' Sodoku would smile at this witty pun, his moustache twitching slightly, giving his square face a look he believed people associated with the military, the way the Brits supposedly had stiff upper lips.

He hadn't minded Caramel's cutting comment. 'Why does he do that with his moustache?' she had once asked as the ministers filed out of the boardroom after a meeting. 'Doesn't he know it makes him look like he's trying to forestall an overdue bowel movement?' Someone – Marcia, perhaps – had shushed her while asking why she seemed to have proctological fixations, whatever that meant.

It was this lack of respect, these constant put-downs, which could have turned Sodoku, in his quiet but stubborn manner, into an opponent of anything that Dr Caramel Sebone-Prah supported and a supporter of anything she opposed.

This friction among some of the ministers was just another problem that could give rise to internal collapse if left unattended. This was caused in no small part by the president's reluctance to discipline his ministers. Wonderman knew that a shrewd chairman, namely himself, could put this to good use.

The best way to run the inquiry would be to present himself as a sympathiser with the president while at the same time ensuring that he would respect – and uphold – the rule of law. History was full of people who had been sacrificed on the altar of fairness. Wonderman was familiar with the implications of the phrase: *We'll give him a fair trial and then hang him*. He could only imagine the media feeding frenzy that would follow Abioseh's downfall.

Someone else who appeared destined to raise the ire of the media – who'd been quoted as having said that journalists were fit for the hangman's noose – was the minister of health, education and welfare. Whether Caswell Stone had actually said this – or had been misquoted, as seemingly happened with troubling regularity to government officials – was beside the point. What was clear was that Stone's seeming intolerance of his former colleagues had won him a certain measure of popularity among some members of the public that held the media responsible for the troubles besetting the world. A former journalist himself, Stone had seized the moment when media vultures had descended on lower-ranking department of health officials. This was due to rumours that Minister

Stone favoured traditional methods of healing for the blood plague.

Knowing that a rumour becomes a fact once it's been officially denied, he called in favours with some of the editors to explain his side of the story – and this, he assured them, wasn't spin. He told them that the people of Bangula were sick and tired of being exploited by international cartels – and the use of the word 'cartel' was not an accident. The pharmaceutical plunder was the obverse side of the cocaine coin and the customers at pharmacies were the willing junkies being serviced by legalised pushers. The promotion of traditional methods and the subsequent sitting of the healers on councils that decided the strategies for health provision, found resonance with the majority who had relied on the service from childhood.

From the mightiest to the lowliest there was a common experience with healers. While some made use of herbs and animal fats and mysterious bits and pieces dug up in faraway lands, others used holy water and faith in the human body's capacity to heal. Both schools regularly called upon the extra muscle of the ancestors, who were expected to lend their timeless weight to tackling certain complications, especially where evil spirits were involved.

However, the blood plague's mutability made it hard for the real nature of the disease to be detected in time. Many countries – even poor ones – had depleted their meagre research resources in trying to tackle it. Stone had been among those who had sensed that this was a huge and enduring pestilence, but had been dissuaded from immediate action by Abioseh, who cautioned against precipitate action and advocated a wait-and-see attitude. 'See the way the cat jumps,' he said. The media cat, of course, jumped at Stone's throat with claws bared.

Those familiar with the matter, who knew it was actually Abioseh Gondo who had stalled progress towards dealing with the blood plague, could still criticise Caswell Stone as having been derelict. He was, after all, the minister of health. There were howls of protest about the quarantine, especially when families of the sufferers were prohibited from entering the isolation facility. In people's minds, the bleak place of high walls topped by coils of razor wire, which was patrolled by men armed with high-calibre rifles and guard dogs, had become a prison in which the inmates had been sentenced to death. The hospice section of the two-storey, L-shaped building was known as Stone's little charnel house.

Wonderman had tried to help his Cabinet colleague redeem himself. As he mulled over the events of the past two or so weeks – the establishment of the junta, the assassination of Zebulon Gondo, something with which the country still had to grapple – he supposed that there must be a way in which Caswell Stone and his beleaguered ministry could be given teeth. The final benefactor of that proverbial dental health would, of course, be Wonderman Bhele himself. His legacy would address all that had been ruined by Abioseh's indecision.

Abioseh was neither corrupt nor self-serving. *Take Jacqui's case*, Wonderman thought. *Any powerful man would have installed her in a plum position that would also have benefited him indirectly. But not Abioseh. He had watched her wiggle on the fishhook of the beauty industry, a place that was infinitely cold and unattractive. Through her own efforts, she had set up a few boutiques, understanding that modelling was an industry with as limited a shelf-life as gold mining – and as precarious.*

Abioseh's general conduct gave an impression of the weakness of government. Baluba Jambo's ill-conceived attacks and the display of dead bodies at the traffic circle's plinth had shocked everyone to the core, leaving the president wounded, physically and symbolically, and damaging the trust of the electorate in the leadership.

What had driven Baluba Jambo to such destructive anger? There were the elections, oh, so long ago, in which Jambo's father had lost by such a margin it would have curbed the enthusiasm of a saner candidate. Bhele looked forward to the day Baluba Jambo would sweat as he danced to the crackle of electrodes attached to his testicles. Then he would tell everyone what had brought about the crazy stunt he had pulled with the band of hoodlums dubbed the Vezi Brigade. *Why were outlaws so lacking in imagination, so unoriginal?*

However, Wonderman acknowledged that the Vezi Brigade had given the security forces a run for their money. They had exposed the soft underbelly of the nation's intelligence networks, which had failed to anticipate a campaign of such proportions. Were Abioseh still in control, he, Wonderman would be on the carpet. In these situations, people didn't just accept any excuse.

The only way for the people's anger, bubbling under the surface, to be appeased was through a public act of sacrifice that would echo throughout the land. It would vindicate the security men who fell at the grounds of Mariposa, when the grenades arced high into the air and their low detonation rumbled like thunder. It would douse the fire, repair the gutted school bus whose paint had peeled off and silence the screams and the hiss and burst of flesh. The inquiry would achieve that.

By assuming leadership, Abioseh had taken responsibility for the journey of his people from the darkness of the past to a future characterised by safety and security. Most leaders retained that crucial portfolio. Gondo had mortgaged it to the nebulous principle of friendship. He had trusted Wonderman. Rubbing his hands together, Wonderman smiled as his palate tingled in anticipation.

This sense of being on top of his game recalled the moment when his Master's thesis on the implications of ceremonial scars among the Buzaki was not only praised by his university supervisor as the acme of scholarship but was also accepted for publication by the prestigious Pershing Bros Press. Their books were usually optioned for film production. What had thrilled Wonderman the most was the endorsement of his postulates by academia. He had been on edge, fearing that only Western social anthropologists would embrace his thesis, which would have led to a feeding frenzy by the black nationalists. Although his dissertation was gathering dust in the archives of the University of Bangula, Wonderman was determined to insinuate some of its findings into his summing up of the Commission of Inquiry. He could hardly wait.

3

'YOU HAVE TO give it back, Ma,' Abioseh Gondo said.

Although it was only mid-morning, he was already tired. It was some two weeks since the 'fall of Mariposa', as the rebel attack had come to be known. The papers and the radio had been alive with breathless reports about the 'fall of Mariposa'; sometimes, changing tack, a speaker would mention the 'raid on Mariposa' in gentler tones. As it was one of the hottest days in August, where the needle danced in the upper thirties, Abioseh was sure that the announcers' tongues would be sunburnt.

He'd had a good sleep that was full of dreams about everyday things. The absence of a quest for power in the dreams, the fact that he woke up without his chest heaving with anxiety, meant that he was beginning to relax and accept as inevitable that unexpected things could happen to him. He was starting to recognise that he was no longer in control of time; he couldn't bend it and shape it to his will – or even squeeze it into a capsule so that certain urgent tasks could be completed. The

five-hour clock was losing its time; it was fast getting erratic. Abioseh
had decided to throw in his lot with time, rather than race against it. He
would henceforth allow it to determine the pace of things.

For instance, MaZembe had arrived unannounced a little more than
three hours ago, before his nap. It dawned on Abioseh that a whole range
of people were dropping by without first checking with Presidential Protocol.

YESTERDAY HAD BEEN the busiest day so far. At noon, five priests had
visited him; each was determined to coax out of the president an undertaking that, whatever happened, their respective church denominations
would continue enjoying constitutional protection. The phrase 'whatever
happens' had sounded like an elegant expression of the leaders' anxiety about the real possibility of Abioseh's dying. It was also an indirect
claim that the clerics had first dibs on administering the last rites. That
assumption could be made because the president's religious affiliation
was still a closely kept secret and the Almighty had been reticent about
the final destination of his particular soul. The clerics, then, reserved the
right to take their chances. Before getting them out of the suite, Abioseh
had pointed out that the priests were asking for guarantees from the
wrong man. Constitutional protection was the domain of the judiciary;
he was merely the head of the executive branch of government. He could
not interfere. The looks exchanged among the priests told Abioseh that
they were not swallowing that particular story. They'd heard it all too
often and all too often it had proven to be a monumental lie. So they
left, their faith tested somewhat, with a promise that they'd come and see
him again. But the way they glanced at him from the door told him that
they didn't expect him to see the end of the month. On his side, Abioseh
prayed that he hadn't antagonised the holy ones.

He had, however, succeeded in annoying the two women in his life.
Jacqui arrived at about 4.00 PM, her wet Mackintosh telling him it was
raining outside. The knowledge that life was going on increased his iso-

lation and fed his touchiness. 'I'm cooking for you tonight,' Jacqui said, proceeding into the bedroom where she removed her overcoat and draped it over the radiator. She was in a pink, low-cut blouse, stonewashed blue jeans and black high-heeled pumps. She kicked off her shoes and sat on the edge of the bed, massaging her feet. Looking up, she signalled for him to come closer; he kissed her, realising that her face and hair were still wet. 'I wish,' Jacqui said, still stroking her feet, 'I wish we had one of those foot spas.'

'Want me to call the front desk and have them bring one up?' he asked. ' I wouldn't mind my feet also getting some TLC.'

'No,' Jacqui said. 'Let's just stay as we are. I don't want anyone coming up here tonight.'

'But your feet?'

'The feet shall benefit from benign neglect,' Jacqui said. 'That way they'll walk the path of the righteous.'

Abioseh considered himself a modern, liberated man, someone who was fairly sophisticated, but he would never understand women's capacity for self-imprisonment in the clothes they wore, especially their shoes.

'Your toes must have been screaming for relief,' he said with heartfelt sympathy. 'Why can't you just put on comfortable shoes?'

'Do you want a lesson on shoes?' Jacqui asked. 'You have time for that?'

'Enlighten me.' He was genuinely interested. Maybe this would give him an insight into his mother and her quirks.

'One. Shoes with heels will make your legs appear thinner,' Jacqui said. 'This is known and respected by women worldwide. The heels don't have to be terribly high, but a bit of a heel will help dramatically. Two. Shoes with pointy toes will help make your legs appear longer. So, even if you think your legs are long enough, if it's a thinner appearance you're after, try shoes with pointed toes. Three,' she said, putting up her small left hand with three fingers extended. 'Shoes with open toes or high-heeled sandals will give your thighs and calves a slimmer appearance than a closed-toe shoe will. Four. Please avoid shoes with ankle straps as they will give the appearance of shorter legs and, lastly, if you wear sling-back shoes instead of pumps, your legs will look thinner and longer.'

'I like ankle straps,' Abioseh said. 'They make women look sexy.'

'Well,' Jacqui said carelessly. 'That's for the full-bodied, voluptuous look. I'm not for that.'

'What *are* you *for*, Jacqui?' Abioseh asked, realising that he knew relatively little about the woman with him in the room.

'The real question you're asking me, Mr President,' Jacqui said, 'is who am I?' She laughed. There was a hiss as the rain came down with renewed vigour. Jacqui seemed attentive to the rainfall, bracing herself as if against a thunderclap she knew to be coming. 'Don't you find it strange,' she asked, 'that we've spent so much time together, doing all the things we've been doing, but I still remain a dirty secret that's known to all and sundry, the president's little floozy?'

'Oh,' Abioseh said, a touch nastily, 'so, it's payback time now, is that it? I thought both of us knew what the deal was?'

'No one,' Jacqui said, '*knows* what the deal is, Mr President. Not in these matters. Just before your accident I was intending to leave the country.'

'So why didn't you?' Abioseh asked, a little surprised at how harsh he sounded. *This is not me*, he thought. Inwardly he tried to resist the impulse to hurt, to lash out. 'Hope it wasn't on my account.'

'No, Mr President,' Jacqui said. 'I stayed, mainly because I needed to do something that would tell me if I still wanted to be a part of this society. I wanted to discover things for me and me alone. No altruism; no Jacqui Morgan Benevolent League for Flaccid Organs.'

Abioseh laughed bitterly. 'Is that how you see me?' All his organs were intact, the doctors had assured him; except for his pride, the other injuries were surface burns and contusions. He suspected, whenever he felt weak, some mental damage; his brain might not have been affected but his mind was.

'You cannot imagine what I have to go through,' Jacqui said, 'the egos I have to stroke just to make it through the day.' She gazed into the air, lost in some unflattering memory. 'But I had to get back to all the things I feared. I've had nightmares reconciling me, the real me, with what I think *you* want me to be. In a sense I've been invisible for most of the time; the person you've seen, shared meals with, sometimes laughed with – and fucked – that person has been a construct to mediate between our disparate realities. You've been dealing with an envoy who has accreditation for social contact with you. In a sense, then, I wanted to escape my avatar, the lingerie model, and find other means to define me.'

It never fails, Abioseh told himself. It starts as a romance, a flirtation flowing from a chance meeting at the marina, the smell of marijuana, the sea, someone else mellowed by wine, which also calms you down. Then the feverish and infectious days, the nights of laughter and wine and the love-making that transcends imagination, everything possible, nothing untried, no taboos. I love you, I love you, I love you ... And then reality sets in, that this is actually some other mother's child; those legs are connected to a live human being with the faculty to think and negotiate her way in the world independent of my penis.

'I went back to Panza, to search for the women who'd helped me grow up,' Jacqui said, 'and they were all gone. But I found an old healer, who said that unless I took part in a ritual, my blood, which had gone bad, would drive me insane.' She jiggled her foot, still perched on the edge of the bed.

Abioseh's eyes were suddenly drawn to her high instep, the curvature of her calf outlined against the fabric of her jeans, visualising the legs that went up into a part of her body that left him weak with imaginings. Unaware of her effect on him, Jacqui went on in a sing-song tone. 'The ritual involved spending three days in the river that everyone says houses the snake, the first ancestor of Bangula,' she said. 'Men came in droves to dive with me and we all watched one another's nakedness, but it was completely natural. I came out of there and drank a potion made of ingredients I couldn't name and I vomited out all the fire – and desire.'

Abioseh was unsure if he wanted to hear the rest of her tale. Yet he was desperate to hear everything. The room had gone very quiet, the rain all but a memory, the dark having descended stealthily, giving the suite a near-domestic atmosphere.

'In the three days in the water, I saw you.'

'Me?'

'Yes, you. I understood the trouble you're in,' Jacqui said. 'Trouble you can't avoid even if you wanted to. Your birth. The struggle to be who you want to be when all of us, the country, all the people around you – some of whom speak with forked tongues – all of us wanting you to see things with our eyes. Not understanding that we're driving you to blindness.'

Jacqui stood up to switch on the lights and, swiftly, Abioseh got up to block her hand. *No lights*, he heard himself saying, although that could have been a mere thought. The abrupt move sent needles shooting up his spine, upsetting some equilibrium that the doctors had tried to inject into his injured body. Seeking an anchor, suddenly adrift, Abioseh put his face into her neck and stroked her shoulder, his nostrils taking in her odour. It was raw and heated like the breath of a freshly planted sugar-cane field following a spell of rain.

As he looked down, he noticed the pink fabric that clung to her hips and the curvature of the jeans over her bottom. He let his arms fall and encircle her waist, the fingers fumbling uselessly with buttons and zips and encountering flesh that singed his fingertips. She was telling him, as his hands struggled against her own struggle against him, that he'd better take off his pants, couldn't he see that he was with a lady? And Abioseh said: 'Yes, the pants.' He felt her tugging at his belt and wished for the hospital greens: *Trousers with belts are a fucking nuisance.* And then he was free from the encumbrance of cloth.

He felt the air on his genitals, cool like a summer breeze. Then her fingers curled around him, hotter than the fires of hell, handling him with something akin to viciousness, a reprisal for all the humiliation she had endured. And then she dragged him back towards the bed and pushed him so that she was actually above him, straddling him. Borrowing a manoeuvre from a lizard, with its power to dispose of a part of its tail to elude a predator, he twisted his body under her, lifting her and positioning her thighs above his face. Then, he stuck his tongue into the wet thatch, the tongue guiding and lips tweaking. Taking hold of the globes of her bottom, his fingertips lingered over the already moist, puckered spot before slipping a finger inside her, feeling her body tensing, before she arched her back and sighed. As the heady smells of their thrashing bodies wafted all over the room, Jacqui took him in her mouth, releasing him, licking him once and then retreating to assess her handiwork. Squeezing the base of his shaft and running a fingernail from behind his scrotum up to the head of his penis, Jacqui bathed him with her tongue. 'I love you,' she said once. As the clock chimed 6.00 PM, Abioseh felt everything in his body pouring out like a geyser and cried out. Her whole body juddering above him, Jacqui showered him with juices tasting of jungles and rivers. After resting awhile, they resumed a less frenzied exploration of the maze forming the human body.

They fell asleep, inhabiting each other's worlds, entwined and dreaming each other's dreams, until urgent banging on the door woke them up. Somewhat annoyed and disoriented, unwilling to readapt himself to the unhappy world, Abioseh let out a mild oath.

A towel wrapped around his waist, he exited the bedroom, closing the door behind him. He surveyed the lounge, debating whether to tidy up, then shrugged off the urge to decency and peered through the peephole. His uncle Malachi stood in the hall, his smile indicating that he was aware of the surveillance. Abioseh was put out that Malachi had chosen a most inopportune moment to drop in. He'd get rid of him quickly and then give the Chief of Protocol and hotel management a real tongue-lashing. He imagined using strong language: *This is completely unacceptable.*

The bedroom door opened and Abioseh turned to glimpse a naked Jacqui dashing to the bathroom, her clothes tucked under her arm and her face showing impish panic. The bathroom door clicked shut as she latched it from the inside. Abioseh opened the door for Malachi, meaning to use his state of undress as a compelling reason to be left alone, someone on the way to a shower before dinner, but Malachi had MaZembe, his sister and Abioseh's mother, in tow. The two entered the suite, Malachi with an apologetic look and MaZembe calmly triumphant now that she had finally entered the room from which she had been barred. Ushering his visitors to the lounge, Abioseh excused himself while he retreated into the bedroom to change into something suitable, at least for his mother.

He returned to the lounge in a loose grey tracksuit and hotel sandals. Abioseh watched MaZembe crossing to the window and standing still, as if contemplating the curtains. Even to Abioseh, now that he'd had his fill of the pinkness of the decor, they appeared hideous, patterned to motivate guests but managing to dispirit. Nose in the air, MaZembe sniffed like an eager hunting dog. Abioseh was aware of the whiff of recent sexual activity permeating the suite, something that couldn't be masked by all the perfumes of Jambora. His mother couldn't have missed the smell; the confirmation was in the conspiratorial smile on Malachi's face.

Like a little boy about to be scolded, Malachi sat hunched on the edge of the settee, his hands folded on his knees. Sensing the tension, Abioseh wondered what had happened. 'Can I offer you something to drink? Malachi? Ma?'

'I'm fine,' MaZembe said, turning away from the window. She found her own corner on the settee. 'Unless you've got a soda?'

'I'm fresh out of soft drinks,' Abioseh said after checking the small fridge. 'Do you want me to call room service downstairs? There's some beer – and scotch.'

'No. *We're* fine, then.' She glared at Malachi, daring him to propose an alternative choice of beverage.

'I'm okay, too,' Malachi demurred. MaZembe gave him a withering look before turning her attention to her son.

'What's this I hear about you and the doctor?' It was a question that had been bothering her for a long time.

'What doctor?' Abioseh asked. 'And what did you hear?'

'The head doctor. The psychiatrist.' She wasn't at all happy. 'I hear you told him I poisoned your father.'

'Whoa, Ma, wait a minute.' Abioseh was genuinely surprised. The session with the doctor should have been confidential. 'I told him about a dream I had.'

'A dream in which I poisoned your father.'

'In which you *said* you'd poisoned the Colonel.'

'But really,' MaZembe said, her eyes registering extreme pain, 'really, how do you dream something like that?'

'That's not a very nice dream about your own mother.' Malachi was actively trying to curry favour with his powerful and wrathful sister.

MaZembe wouldn't let him worm his way out of the dog box. 'Keep out of this, you bloody drunkard!' Turning, she asked, 'Abi, just for once, couldn't you have chosen a more pleasant dream about the memory of your father? Instead of shaming *me* all over Bangula.'

'Bangula might be seventy-five per cent peasant, Ma,' Abioseh put in, 'but people are still smart enough to tell a dream from reality. People dream dreams every day, Ma. They might dream that you and I are dead – and here we are, alive. We cannot haul them all over the coals for that.'

Abioseh could see that even though an issue had been aired, Ma-Zembe reserved her right to be dissatisfied. The altercation had left him tired and unreasonably angry. His mother and his uncle had no right to barge into his room, especially since they must have known of his condition. His mother's first words to him had no bearing on his injuries, especially the burns, which were still visible along his arms. His movements, slow and stiff, should have elicited some form of maternal concern, an enquiry, even, on the state of his health. There was none of that. She was merely concerned about how people regarded her. As for her brother, Malachi, he'd discredited himself with his dependence on the bottle, which had made him untrustworthy and pitiable.

Abioseh became determined, there and then, to take control of his life. Acting accordingly, he left the two in the lounge and went to knock on the bathroom door. 'Jacqui?' he called softly. 'Open up.'

'Have they gone?' The voice from the other side was tentative.

'Yes,' Abioseh lied. 'I've just seen them out. Come on, open the door.'

Just as the door opened, MaZembe shouted from the lounge, 'What's going on, Abi? Do you have someone in there?'

Jacqui stepped out, already dressed, her blouse a little rumpled. She looked at Abioseh with a puzzled and panicked expression. 'You said to me ...' And then her face took on a determined cast. 'Are you sure?'

'Yes,' Abioseh said. 'Ma,' he called, 'I've got Jacqui here with me.' He led her into the lounge, holding her hand.

'Who?' MaZembe shouted. But it was obvious, when Abioseh and Jacqui appeared, that she'd heard him loud and clear, the question a refusal to accept the reality of the woman who now stood in front of her. Malachi started to get to his feet, but plopped back into the settee in response to a look from his sister. MaZembe continued sitting down, seeming to sink deeper into the folds of the sofa, something changed about her face.

MaZembe's face had caved in and she looked like a defeated old woman. As she opened her mouth to speak, Abioseh noticed she had taken out her plate of false teeth, allowing him a glimpse of dried-up gums. 'Are you trying to send me to an early grave?' she lisped. 'First you soil my name and then this ...' She fumbled with her handkerchief and stuck her dentures back into the cavity of her mouth, restoring her face to its original appearance.

'*This*, Ma,' Abioseh said, 'is Jacqui Morgan.'

'I know who she is,' MaZembe hissed. 'Everybody knows *what* she is.'

'I don't think you really know who or what I am, Madam,' Jacqui said conversationally. 'You only know what you *think* you know — or *want* to know.'

Standing up abruptly, MaZembe snapped her fingers at Malachi as she picked up her handbag, preparing to depart. 'We're obviously not wanted here,' she said, 'where children dream obscene dreams and flaunt their strumpets.'

'I don't think what you're doing is correct, Madam,' Jacqui said. 'Your son is the president of this country, elected on a popular mandate. He's a grown man, no longer a child, whatever you think. As for calling me a strumpet, I suppose you think you have the right to insult people you regard as not your equals. You carry the mantle of being the Colonel's widow, the official curator of his legacy.'

'You stupid bitch!' MaZembe hissed. 'Don't you *ever* mention his name!'

'Ma!' Abioseh started to intervene. 'This is going too far.'

'Keep out of this, Mr President,' Jacqui said, her chest heaving. 'I'd sworn that I was going to take this with me to the grave.' She took in great gulps of air; the lounge was still, everything quivering in malevolent silence. 'I thought I'd keep the promise I made to the Colonel, but now I feel that I would be piling sin upon sin if I kept quiet.'

She turned to Abioseh. 'You've always wondered what took place between the Colonel and me. And I never contradicted you, even when I knew that it was eating you up, whenever there was the suggestion that we'd had a sexual relationship. But,' she added, now turning her eyes to MaZembe, 'there was nothing of the sort. And she knows it!'

'Now,' MaZembe said, but the fire had gone out of her, 'you wait a minute . . .'

'Let her speak, Ma,' Abioseh cautioned, simultaneously scared of the implications of Jacqui's disclosures.

'She's telling a bunch of lies!'

'No,' Jacqui continued, putting up her hand like a pointsman. 'In the past I have chosen to keep quiet rather than tell lies. The Colonel was impotent,' she went on. 'He had been incapable of an erection since shortly after Zebulon was born. He was injured during an operation against the warlords.'

'Lies, lies, lies!'

Jacqui told her story in unemotional words. The Colonel had come across Jacqui, homeless and scared, living on the streets. Through him, she had attended school and started a new life. Then she went to Panza and was cared for in a nursery run by old women, before getting a job in the hotel. She had kept in touch with the Colonel and later with Carlos Nobrega, who both had an interest in Zebulon. She'd known Zebulon from the streets, but had never really been friends with him. He was too scary, too intense.

Listening to Jacqui's story, which had become entangled with his own destiny, Abioseh realised that he knew nothing about his own mother. He concluded that if she'd kept anything from him, she had kept everything from him. He realised that it was eminently possible for people to travel from childhood through to adulthood and thence to the grave oblivious of the forces that had conspired to give them the names that they carried with pride. Mothers, he started to understand, were the ones with a monopoly on the truth about the lives, loves, triumphs and despairs of society. Fathers were possibly the most swindled sector of the world community, alert only to the fact that they could sow their seed into fertile regions, but could never be entirely certain of the nature of the harvest. *Every day*, he thought, *after every nine months in the year, somewhere in the world, a man beams as he is presented with a bundle that will soon bear his name.*

But in this realisation, in this moment of admitting that his parentage would be forever shrouded in mystery, for there was no way he was going to interrogate his mother, Abioseh recognised that MaZembe had also been shaped by the fear that had stalked her throughout her adult life. It must have produced moments of pure horror to be the spouse of the most powerful man in a country where power needed might to be effectively sustained. And then, as a mother, in a place festering with intrigue and infections – especially the unpredictable seasons of the blood plague – she must have been eternally vigilant, a state that brings about mental fatigue. And lastly, living with the threat that she could be replaced, the world being so full of nubile young women attracted to power. Abioseh knew that the insecurity that women experienced had a lot to do with the way men saw the world and themselves – and how their own insecurities could be assuaged.

'Uncle Malachi,' he said, 'please take your sister home. We'll find time to discuss these issues. If we ever we do.'

'I think,' Malachi put in, 'MaZembe had another matter to raise.'

'Ah, you,' MaZembe said to her brother, a soft reproach. 'You're useful sometimes.' She turned to Abioseh. 'You might not like this, what I've to say ...'

'Well,' Abioseh asked, 'what can beat today's eye-opener? Tell me.'

'I've bought Carlos Nobrega's boat,' MaZembe stated.

'Have you lost *your* mind? Can you imagine the stink when this gets out?'

'I paid for the boat with my own money,' MaZembe said stubbornly. 'Far as I know, there's no law against fair trade.' Malachi, on the side, nodded.

'It's called corruption, Ma,' Abioseh said. 'You don't even need to be actually corrupt; there must just be the teeniest whiff of impropriety – and you're sunk. You're the mother of the president ... what do you think people will say?'

'But you're no longer even a *practising* president.'

'Ah, and that alone means the store's open for looting? A looter continua?' He sighed. 'You have to give it back, Ma. The Colonel would have raised Cain.'

'Then you don't know your father,' MaZembe said, the earlier revelations seemingly forgotten. 'Here you are, broken, an ex-president even before you've been officially voted out of office. How's that for making history?' She gave a short, unpleasant laugh. 'Most people are killed or driven out of power ... you ... you had to be unique. You went into a coma that took you out of power.' She gave him a sidelong glance. 'Your father would *never* have gone into a coma.'

'Yep,' Abioseh agreed. 'He took the short-cut, straight to the Pearly Gates.'

'You joke,' MaZembe said, unamused. 'Truth is, no one would even have *thought* of attacking Mariposa during your father's time. Or even in Carlos Nobrega's. People attack you when they think you're weak. Do you know what they're saying out there? If Baluba Jambo had got hold of you, he'd have made you his woman.'

'That's fine, Ma,' Abioseh said. 'Fact is, here I am, not dead. I'd have thought that's all that matters. That and the understanding that the men we call our fathers are exactly that on account of the way they've helped us grow and face the world. Fatherhood has nothing to do with the ownership of sperm. The Colonel was *my* father because he cared for me.'

'I want to talk more about this,' MaZembe said, but she was clearly terribly upset. Out of her handbag came a wad of tissues and she dabbed at her face. She looked at Jacqui. 'I will want to talk to you, too, young lady.'

'With pleasure,' Jacqui said. She didn't move; the two women didn't embrace.

PART SEVEN

THE WEIGHT
OF RAIN

I

AT 4.00 AM on the day of the Commission of Inquiry, which coincided with the climax of the Festival of Lights, Zoya Badawi woke up with the feeling that something was wrong. She half suspected that a premonition was behind her wakefulness at this pre-dawn hour; the other reason, which she wanted to keep from acknowledging to herself, was the absence of Zebulon. Ever since he had been gone, she had been sleeping at the weather station, distracting herself with work. She sometimes guiltily found that she actually enjoyed the mindless routine of her profession. She'd be quick to chide herself, though, as distraction and being on emergency watch didn't go hand in hand, the same way inebriety and air traffic control were mutually exclusive.

Well, girl, she mused, *you've made your bed, so you might as well get used to its lumps.* She couldn't say, though, which bed she had in mind: the futon in the other room was quite comfortable; the only problem was the struggle to roll it up and then shove it under the table, making space for her colleagues. Not that the two men and a woman, who were the permanent staff, bestirred themselves to come to work. The absenteeism had started slowly until it became a simple stay-away. She could live with that, the principle; it just meant that she had to mind the store on her own – and, she knew, if shit happened, it would be on her head. Or she made do with volunteers, university students, who were mostly in it to be the first to experience the deluge that they expected to be coming.

The other proverbial bed, her life, was a different thing altogether. Contrary to what she knew people believed, her activism hadn't started with her relationship with Zebulon. It had a deeper and bloodier genesis in the years of her ignorance as a small girl when, one evening during supper, her father had politely asked to be excused from the table. This was itself a departure from custom that should have set alarm bells ringing. Dr Ahmod Badawi wasn't given to airs and graces, *excuse me*. He then locked himself in the bathroom where he shot himself in the head with the pistol he had been given as a present by the Colonel.

When Zoya, her mother and three elder brothers and her sister heard the shot, Mrs Badawi initially sat slumped and stunned beyond movement in such a manner that Zoya thought a stray bullet had hit her. After a minute, she also got to her feet and rushed to the bathroom. She called softly, but with an urgency that Zoya had never imagined she could muster: '*Ahmod, Ahmod,*' as if she feared disturbing him in the middle of his toilet. '*Ahmod? Open up!*'

The brothers, renowned for their toughness in rugby and wrestling matches, mobilised their muscular shoulders and hardy boots and sent the door crashing open. Their momentum dislodged the corpse from its original position and slid it away so that blood and brains painted a crimson arc on the tiled floor, something that later earned the young men a severe tongue-lashing from the homicide detectives. Zoya had wondered what difference it would have made in terms of garnering clues for forensic purposes. It was clear that the man had taken his own life; where was the fucking mystery? Could they work out from the position of the body or the blood-spatter pattern if the cause of suicide had been money troubles or love or despair or simply fatigue?

Some of these wonderings happened much later with the benefit of hindsight and the comfort of selective amnesia. As a girl, Zoya had seen her father lying in a pool of his own blood, half his head in sections on the floor; she had looked at her mother and seen that she still had a knife and fork gripped in her left hand, the tines of the fork still retaining the burnt umber tinge of chicken tikka masala and saffron rice. It was this sight, rather than her broken and bloodied father, that sent Zoya scampering to the toilet bowl, where, mercifully, the seat was up, and she heaved until she felt empty, like an upended vessel.

That was the first time she saw Zebulon, who arrived and commiserated with the family while her brothers poked fun at him, making faces, for he was a sight in his threadbare black suit, scuffed shoes, a yellowing white shirt and a hank of tangled hair. Soon after the funeral, which had to be quick in accordance with her father's religion, her mother suffered a massive breakdown and had to be institutionalised. Zoya's sister, Fawzia, who had stood unblinking throughout the drama, got a scholarship to the USA and proceeded to cut off all ties with her family. The last Zoya heard of her, she had married a Canadian dentist and was living in a small town in Saskatchewan, where she raised her children and ran a small store selling honey, exotic breads and sweetmeats. Two of her brothers were still around in the national army; the youngest had emigrated to Morocco, where he was briefly held for suspected racketeering. On release, he had fled to Spain.

ZOYA SWITCHED THE radio on but left the room in darkness. She proceeded to the small kitchen, a corner really, which supported cracked cups, sugar and powdered milk in Nespray containers, and made herself a cup of instant coffee. Someone had tacked a sign to the wall: *Keep the kitchen area clean.* She thought wistfully of filter coffee and cream, or even a double espresso, and immediately banished the tempting images, which, she knew, would trip her up in her resolve.

Looking out the window, she caught her breath at the sight of the sea, a majestic body that stretched silently to a horizon that fought to emerge from the gloom. The pinpoints of lights and the scything flame of the lighthouse caused the water to dance and seem at once peaceful and ominous. The craft bobbing on the water cast their own shadows and contributed to the solidity of the dark.

Feeling the stirrings of an even deeper darkness inside her, Zoya turned away from the window. The lights flashing on the monitor of her personal computer were almost a mirror image of the lights operating outside. She imagined the two realities clashing, the sea becoming a weather station, exploding with a rich array of dynamic and colourful gauges, dials, graphs and charts – and the desktop hosting fish and seal and whale, supporting boats and barges carting dreamers and merchandise to distant locations.

Knowing that her flights of fancy and craving for coffee confirmed one thing, she sat down in the straight-backed chair and rested her chin on her fist, wondering what Ahmod Badawi would have made of the knowledge that he was to become a grandparent.

She remembered one of his repeated monologues, a warning to his children. 'I'm like a fallen angel,' he would say, 'no longer capable of achieving all that I sought to mould with my hands. If we do not teach ourselves how to cook, we will always eat the saliva of others. In a land where the eyes of the confined people are eternally calculating the distances, we shall have a population obsessed with flight. In the situations where we imprison ourselves with the fear of betrayals, it is time to learn that pain is inevitable and we have to strengthen ourselves for its advent. The strongest of the people is not the one who has slain the greatest number of enemies, lifted the heaviest burden or stashed the largest sum of money in the vaults of a bank. It is the man or woman who has eventually discovered the secret of conquering loneliness, not by running away from it but by looking it in the eye. When the time comes, we must be strong enough to cheer the one who has left us to make a new house with someone else, because that spirit has moved on and negotiated its destiny elsewhere.'

Zoya had never been able to make sense of her father's words, although she had known they were important and that they came from a deep and wounded place for him to recite them each time he came home drunk.

That habit had been a mystery, which he had taken with him to the grave. He had been as abstemious as a mullah, saying his prayers five times a day and scornful of fleshly weaknesses. And then one day he had come home dishevelled and smelling of liquor. It was as if the family's world had come to a standstill. Although he flatly refused to tell anyone what had brought him down, Zoya came to believe that his alcoholism and loss of faith – contained in his words of disillusionment – were just a few of the elements that had finally led to his suicide.

It was a few years later, when she was already settled with her three grandmothers that Zoya learnt that her father had been conducting sensitive research for the government. There was pressure to find a vaccine for the epidemic that was killing people in the most horrific manner. Badawi had been on television and made national headlines vowing that a breakthrough was imminent. His despair must have been crushing when the bodies piled up as people dropped like flies, necessitating the first flush of quarantines.

Soon his status had changed from national hero to national scapegoat. What was galling for Zoya was that her father's funeral had been the epitome of desertion, attended only by family and close relatives. There was a terse message from the president: *Dr Ahmed Badawi applied himself selflessly to the struggle of our country to rid her of the scourge of disease. He will be sorely missed.*

Zoya seethed: 'Dr Ahmed.' They couldn't even get his name right! And the dreaded pandemic remained framed in unemotional generalities: a disease. To look it in the eye and call it the blood plague was to conjure up horrific images of viral infections represented by the lead Horseman of the Apocalypse, medieval pestilence or the slaughter of the first-born.

She remembered her own fright when she thought she had contracted the blood plague; it was a fright that wasn't sudden as suggested by the word 'fright', with its connotations of immediacy, but a gradual listlessness and night sweats that at first made her think she was experiencing a rather unpleasant menstrual period. But then as the week passed – and as more and more people took the returnless journey to quarantine – she asked Zebulon if in his travels and ministrations to the bereaved he had strayed and slept with another woman.

She didn't know where this came from, except that, from the day he had murmured Melinda's name in the throes of passion, she had been determined to treat all men as potential betrayers and to take anything they said – no matter how compelling – with a liberal pinch of salt.

Her question had been unexpected and he was hurt by it. It confused her, also, that the illness, for that was what it was, that had gripped her, coincided with a moment when she was re-examining her life with Zebulon. At first, theirs had been a relationship made in heaven, full of joy and expectation. Then she had started feeling the onset of a restlessness that left her silent and uncommunicative, for, as a singer, she believed that no introspection is possible while a person has his or her mouth open. In time, she had been returned to health. This was corroborated by a three-letter legend against the blood tests, NAD, nothing abnormal detected. Still, she maintained her silences.

In these silences, Zebulon suffered. Although puzzled by the changes, he took comfort from the reassurances of other men, people like Baluba Jambo, who boasted an encyclopaedic knowledge of women and their ways. Zoya was certain that Baluba Jambo knew fuck all about women. In her experience she found that men who flaunted their masculinity were usually hiding something.

She had heard stories about Baluba but had embarked on a single-minded track to pursue her vocation in music, seeing that her stint at the weather station looked to be an unrewarding task, and Baluba had promised to help launch her career. In time, however, he had effectively convinced her that there was a bigger goal to be pursued. He spoke of the necessity for the people to fix their eyes on the prize, a statement whose lyrical cadence told her that Baluba had most likely filched it from somewhere. He'd found her when she'd started probing her father's suicide, mainly because the chosen method of death ensured that the survivor carried the injury of the deceased to the grave.

She had been somewhat uneasy around the dead bodies; Baluba Jambo had used his prodigious knowledge of death and the restoration of bodies to treat the cadavers with mysterious unguents and decorative crèmes and dyes with such skill that some of the dead men – there were only two corpses of women, no gender equity here – seemed more handsome dead than when compared with the photographs the families had provided.

'There are people who'll disagree with what we're doing,' Baluba said on the morning that Zoya found him working on the corpses. 'They feel that we should either bury or cremate the dead and that anything else is disrespectful. But,' he said, wiping his latex gloves on the plastic-coated apron, 'that would be a deeper insult, for the deaths will have been totally useless. You see,' he went on, meticulously wedging a measure of flesh-coloured cement into the corpse's cracked cranium, 'this man snuffed it a while back, so he's useless; his body has no value except as compost – and that after a long time. To make him part of a living protest, a means of rallying people to a cause, is to resurrect his spirit.'

She remembered him laughing, the sound at odds with the solemnity of the task and the sterile ambience of the workshop with its porcelain tables and outsize sinks. 'We cannot waste the power of the dead.'

'The dead will rise, you mean,' Zoya asked, averting her eyes from the sight of the unclothed cadavers of women on the trays, their breasts suspiciously firm and nipples erect. She shivered as a thought seized her and she wanted to bolt out of the mortuary.

'Yes,' Baluba said absently, his head bent as he concentrated on the task at hand. 'In more ways than one, the dead have *already* risen. They've catalysed the ferment in the blood of our people.'

IN THE STATION, Zoya looked at her wristwatch, wishing that the three crones or even, impossibly, Zebulon, were with her. She knew that if she wanted to have a healthy baby, she'd have to leave the island – leave behind its small-mindedness, its indecisive leaders and its even more pusillanimous public. She glanced at the dials, studying the lines dancing across the screen. Some movement here, like the anticipated flutter in her belly, only more capable of havoc. A crackle of the lines, a communiqué from Météo-France. Time seemed to crawl before the ceremony of committal as a centrepiece of the Festival of Lights. Then, she thought bleakly, we'll see to the burial of the dead.

2

AT 5.00 AM, on the day when believers and unbelievers would assemble
and commune with their different gods in the Festival of Lights, which
would start at sunset, Abioseh readies himself for a date with his own
destiny. *Today,* he thinks, *is one of the most fitting days for an execution.* He
doesn't know why the thought comes to him unsummoned and unasked
for. In the wakefulness at dawn where the sky looks reddened as if with
fever, he knows that he should be thinking about survival. Abioseh has
slept his five hours; he wonders whether he'll ever be the same again after
all those countless hours of sleep when he was in a coma. Ah, but the
dreams of that time. He'd forgotten to ask the doctor whether he'd been
dreaming or hallucinating. Is there a difference? He'll ask Malachi, who
never dreams but is exceedingly knowledgeable about nightmares.

He is aware of dreams and their nuances as one becomes conscious
of the heaviness of a downpour, which one might have earlier dismissed
as a mere drizzle. *Baby, the rain must fall,* he remembers, a song and a black-

and-white movie that portrayed accurately how Steve McQueen and Lee Remick had failed to acquire the American Dream.

The memory of the film brings back memories of long nights of rain in his childhood, the people who got lost in the storms and the ones who forged ahead in spite of the hand that life dealt them. These people form the bulk of those who seek him out of the way. *Where did it all go wrong? The fishermen and their wives and the vendors at the market; the women at the hotels and lodges and places frequented by tourists and the moneyed of the land – what would they think of him? What really goes on in Jacqui's mind when they are together? Does she think that maybe, somewhere, sometime, he, Abioseh, soon-to-be-ex-president of Bangula will marry her? Is she the marrying type? Where is she right now? Possibly hopping from shop to shop in the mall, trying to find the most exquisite outfit for the Festival.*

When he and Jacqui started out, possibly in her attempt to bring him back to earth, she'd asked him to accompany her to the once highly desired suburb of Vipima, which had deteriorated into a stone slum with boarded high-rise flats and stairways choked up by garbage and human waste. It was here that refugees from all points of conflict, not only in this country but also in other parts of Africa, converged.

The wretched of the earth, he'd realised, were the true embodiment of the adage that misery loved company. People lived cheek by jowl in unimaginable squalor. The stink of rot and despair wafted like a pall over the square mile of fetid and decrepit buildings. The buildings towered over a mingle-mangle of meat and vegetable market stalls where disembowelled fruit littered the ground and rose, together with offal and the stained feathers of plucked poultry, to a mountain of garbage that was topped by a carpet of green flies that buzzed with fulfilment. A teeming riot of humanity in colourful prints existed here.

Men, women and children strained to be heard above the cacophony of speakers rigged outside shops that blared a medley of hip-hop, house, salsa, soul or jazz. Cyclists or pedestrians jostled for space with minibus taxis, smoke-belching lorries, luxury sedans and gimcrack jalopies. Some of these unsafe vehicles were steered by jumpy young drivers on the look-out for the merchant who'd help them reach narcotised ecstasy, some laughing, others crying, all seeming to give an individual rendition of the blues. In the heat, vendors shouted their wares in almost all sub-Saharan languages, the bolts of cloth decked out on zinc tables spoke of the journeys these stateless men and women – and their wide-eyed and uncomplaining progeny – had taken to reach the latest version of the Promised Land.

Abioseh now hears the slow rhythmic thump of tablas and the rattle of tambourines, the drummers revving themselves up as they rehearse somewhere in the bowels of the hotel for the festivities to come. A woman sings softly in a voice that gets swallowed up in the sounds of the morning. Barefooted, he pads to the window, the city revealing itself to his sleepy eyes, casting off the robe of the night, the amber lights flickering palely against the stronger rays of the sun, the sky red like judgement. He hears the breeze whooshing through the pipes of the hotel, the incoherent snarl of the air-conditioning, which continues to be as capricious as a fallen monarch.

Looking out the window, he sees the city shaking itself from slumber. *We have created so many sleepwalkers*, he thinks. *And today is the day for the repayment of old debts. Everyone will get his or her pound of flesh.* With this sufficiently despairing idea taking root in his mind, Abioseh retreats into the bathroom, where he does his daily toilet and prepares himself for the morning cup of coffee and his paper. In a few minutes, the orderly knocks and hands the president his paper. The man's face is bland, his eyes refusing to make contact. The headline reads: 'WHAT WILL HAPPEN TODAY?'

THIS QUESTION ECHOES in the ballroom of the Commodore Hotel, the same ballroom in which people have danced in celebration during weddings and banquets in honour of sons and daughters of the notable of the land. But this time, the ballroom is the venue for the inquiry into the conduct of the president. It is thus dressed, intentionally or accidentally, in dark colours matching the grave nature of the occasion.

But it is outside that the true character of the inquiry expresses itself. Standing at the entrance are the doorman and, in observance of the equality of the sexes, the doorwoman. Their uniforms have been changed from the frivolous costumes aimed at titillating tourists into the seriously elegant and simply-cut maroon Nehru suits with epaulettes striped with the colours of Bangula's flag.

Although the hotel lobby is the most democratic space in the establishment, the two affable though serious sentinels guard the entry judiciously. They have the final say on who can or cannot enter; they cull the riff-raff from serious citizens whose credentials have the power to open doors.

However, as happens even on the most exclusive of occasions, the unwashed somehow find a way inside the exalted venue. They marvel at the design of this space, which, while accommodating so many people, somehow manages to avoid creating bottlenecks. It is an area which flatters even the most unappealing figure. Illuminated by crystal chandeliers that bounce off the breathtaking opulence of gilded furniture upholstered in imported silk, the bank of tinted mirrors renders each face, each figure, in the most complimentary light.

Behind the long and highly polished reception counter well-dressed staff hover; these are men and women whose ages simultaneously insist on style and the stability of old money. It is here in the lobby that some of the people, intimidated by the magnificence contained in the glass atrium and the central apse that rises to the sky to remind them of cathedrals, decide to sidle out of the hotel and watch the events in more familiar surroundings on their televisions. The braver ones duck into the bathrooms and cluck their tongues at the extravagant fixtures. They test the taps and the toilets from which water hisses as if delivering a sibilant rebuke to undesirables who should be elsewhere.

IN HIS ROOM, President Abioseh Gondo sits waiting for the agents of PAP to come and escort him to the venue of the inquiry. Although his mind is crowded, he appreciates the pulse of life in the corridor where people converse in anxious and raised tones; it is in the sun streaming into the lounge, scattering itself through glass decanters. These lighten a dominant thought: *The end is coming.*

Increasingly, he acquires a sense of peace that borders on the irresponsible. A great weight eases itself off his shoulders. It is a rare feeling, no different from a runner expecting a gruelling marathon to be much longer, only to find that he or she has already crossed the finishing line.

What is it about the days and nights of his leadership that have drained him to the extent that the prospect of surrendering power, this divestiture, leaves him weak with a sense of illicit freedom? But, then, this relief is short-lived. A grimmer scenario presents itself unbidden. In his mind's eye, he sees himself stripped of all trappings of power and reduced to a beggar.

This image of future calamity causes him to smile because it brings him to a great debate with himself, which he has always deferred. *If reduced to that state,* he asks himself, *will I have the guts to commit suicide? Killing oneself —* he remembers some joker remarking — *is the highest form of self-criticism.*

Am I so critical of myself? To what extent will my final self-destructive act — among an illustrious array of enormous cock-ups — give lifelong joy to my enemies? Which is better, for them to rejoice at my downfall while I'm alive, or for them to falsify history and demonise me endlessly with impunity when I'm dead and incapable of answering? But which beggar has a voice loud enough to be heard in the higher councils of power? Which of the wretched of the earth has recourse to agencies that could amplify his or her voice and make a case that could reach the ears of the powerful? Who, of the powerful, would want to hear when deafness could be so convenient? But, then, he concludes, *if I take the easy way out, I'll be beyond reach — and nothing will matter.*

Instead of leaving Abioseh somewhat elated, this thought brings back the morning's headache. *Will have to rustle up an aspirin,* he thinks. He wonders about Hiero, whether the security chief will be able to bear being in the midst of people baying for the president's prestigious blood. *Well,* Abioseh shrugs on hearing footfalls preceding a knock on the door, *whatever will be, will be.*

WHATEVER WILL BE, will be. These were Jacqui's exact words yesterday morning, when, still stunned by the exchange with MaZembe, she had told him that he had turned out a much better leader than she had expected. He had thanked her. 'Thank yourself,' she'd said. 'Pity the people who will be left in the mess. Leaders hatch up all these conspiracies against each other. At the end, the people are left betrayed and bewildered.'

'That sounds like a valediction,' Abioseh had said.

'True,' she answered. 'I might not see you again after this.'

Looking at her as she showered and prepared for the day, transforming herself with the aid of the contents of her compact, Abioseh could only marvel at the ease with which women turned their backs on yesterday's world and embraced the unfolding moment. As she applied eyeliner and buffed her cheeks with an assortment of brushes and cotton wool, Jacqui delivered a rapid-fire commentary on what the day had in store for her. Not once did she allude to their love-making that had carried on until dawn; the passionate words of endearment were cancelled out by the exigency of the strategies for her meetings later that morning. It occurred to Abioseh, who felt the stirrings of desertion, that there was no bleaker sight than a condom being flushed down the toilet.

It was his Uncle Malachi, however, who deepened his sense of abandonment. 'You live in such isolation,' Malachi said, arriving unannounced again, this time to apologise for being used as a cat's paw by his sister. 'Seems to me your father robbed you of your real calling. You should have been a monk.'

'What would that have solved?' Abioseh asked. 'Monks set themselves on fire protesting against war.'

'You could start by protesting against our own war against ourselves,' Malachi said. Tall and gangly, he looked unwell today. He coughed a lot, sipping water from a glass with the hotel insignia. 'Too much whiskey.'

'Why are there nine coffins on the square?' Abioseh asked. This had bothered him from the very start but there hadn't been a single soul he could have asked. He couldn't ask Wonderman or anyone from PAP; all of them, he felt, were part of the conspiracy to erode the presidential office.

'Isn't it a little late to be wondering about such things?' Malachi asked.

'Why late?' Abioseh asked. 'Think I'll be the tenth corpse soon?'

'It's not outside the realm of possibility,' Malachi said dryly. 'Not with the way things stand.'

'Well,' Abioseh said, 'it's refreshing to hear the unvarnished truth, even if it's about one's own demise.'

'Relative to someone like me, you're still a kid,' Malachi said, extracting a pinch of tobacco out of a leather pouch tied with a drawstring. Arranging the strands of tobacco into a line on Rizla paper, he managed a slim, even roll-up with deft fingers. After lighting up and expelling twin blue streams of smoke, he spat out the bits of tobacco stuck to his lips. 'I'm seventy-eight years old,' he went on, 'but I still see myself as a young man within the framework of this republic. Modern Bangula is ninety years old. That's when the second flush of modern liberation movements waged war against the colonialists. The weapons were rudimentary and ineffectual against the superior forces armed with twin symbols of contemporary civilisation, the Gatling gun and the Holy Ghost.'

'So,' Abioseh asked, 'a coffin for each decade?'

'Well,' Malachi said, 'it has got the whole town agog with excitement. Death does wonders for the tourism industry, with folks crawling out from all sorts of holes to come and gape.' He shook his head. 'It's funny how all of us might know that death exists, but we go gaga at the sight of a dead body.'

'Perhaps,' Abioseh said, 'others are mere models that pose for our benefit, so that we'll know what we'll look like when our turn comes.'

'You must do me a favour when it's my turn,' Malachi said. 'A quick interment please.'

'And so when is the big burial?' Abioseh asked. 'The bodies can't stay out in the open forever.' He ignored Malachi's lapse into morbidity.

'They'll be given up for burial on the Festival of Lights,' Malachi said. 'I thought you knew.'

'But that is tomorrow,' Abioseh said. Then, almost to himself, 'No one tells me anything.'

'The announcements have been made,' Malachi said, 'that there'll be the Commission of Inquiry during the day and in the evening – the Festival of Lights.'

'A fitting closure to a wonderful era,' Abioseh said, his tone containing a resigned shrug. 'Strangely,' he went on, 'all of this leaves me ... numb.'

'Be careful,' Malachi said, getting to his feet. 'Numbness sets in as a preparation for death.'

'Death doesn't bother me,' Abioseh said. 'It's the thought of claustro-phobia in a coffin that kills me.'

'Imagine then,' Malachi said with a hint of malice, 'how the nine bod-ies must be feeling.' Apropos of nothing, he said, 'By their smell, ye shall know the size of their buttocks.'

'Well put,' said Abioseh. This was what Uncle Malachi always said when he took leave of people. No one knew what it meant. 'See you, hopefully, at the Festival.'

'See you at the inquiry first,' Malachi said. 'I wouldn't miss that for the world.'

Alone, Abioseh sat at his writing desk that had been salvaged from Mariposa, but which had a different feel in the hotel, much like a religious icon used for ceremonies in a strange land. The sunlight filtered through the curtains, creating shadows that danced like wisps of smoke.

Burdened by something he couldn't quite articulate, an emotion close to the remorse associated with people who had neglected to save a life, he fiddled with his papers, searching absently among the notes for a thread that would connect him with life. There was nothing important except for a collection of nasty little truths about his existence and his steward-ship of a reluctant polity, a people wedded to tradition. These would be buried under the weight of love for fallen idols. A few jumbled words scribbled on the margin of a notepad jolted his memory. *An African is a stranger in his own land*, he read. Ezekiel Manolo.

NOW, HE WALKS at the head of the men and women who will adjudicate his case, more a leader than someone on a journey to judgement. As he proceeds, he ensures that the presidential gait people must have seen on television doesn't falter, not now. Walking on the wooden floors, through back passages that are darkened by design, he hears the hum of electricity and the thrum of air-conditioning through the thin walls. They pass the huge kitchen in which giant cookers issue flames that shoot up hungrily like ferocious tongues. The chefs in high hats and white uniforms mop perspiration off their brows with their aprons. Some of them stare incuriously at the passing parade, one suddenly concentrating on her pot as if the bottom of the vessel holds the answers to all of life's unasked questions.

Abioseh feels a great need, which he promptly suppresses, to wave at them in expansive gestures of reassurance, for he knows – it has to be like that – there are some here who root for him.

Eventually he, Abioseh, son of the Colonel, the most revered or reviled man in Bangula, emerges into the mote-laden light of the ballroom, now converted into a solemn arena. His Cabinet colleagues guide him decorously past a long table to his own enclosure, the dock, the furniture smelling of varnish, the table bare as if waiting for him to inscribe history on its smooth surface.

When seated he has a view of both the members of the Commission of Inquiry at the slightly elevated table and the public, which feels like a breathing weight on his shoulders. Then someone shuffles up deferentially and sits beside him, his elbow tentatively claiming a section of the table – and then manicured fingers place a pile of papers and files on the table.

Abioseh turns and sees the bespectacled face of Gwandon Kone, the retired judge and whimsical investor in women's lingerie, who now defends the same people he helped send to prison. 'I recycle justice,' he is famously quoted as saying in a moment of immodesty. The jowly face attempts a smile; the smooth-shaven stack of chins moves up and down like a physical stammering of flesh.

All along, Abioseh has surrendered himself to the fate of the inquiry, but one look at his counsel and it suddenly dawns on him that the road to a lengthy prison sentence is paved with the good intentions of inept defenders. Even before Kone opens his mouth to present his credentials and commitment to fight the good fight, Abioseh raises his hand and requests an opportunity to speak.

While Kone harrumphs that this is most extraordinary, Wonderman hastily confers with his Cabinet colleagues, putting up his hand, as if signalling traffic to halt, to ask both the defendant (for Abioseh is here to defend his name if not his life) and his counsel to wait.

From where he sits, Abioseh can sense the attentive stiffening among the spectators. People are enthralled and yet embarrassed at the negotiation of power between Abioseh (who is still the president) and Wonderman (who'd love nothing more than to be enthroned as one) in this charged space. The brief consultation over, Bhele tells the assembly that as presiding officer, he first needs to outline the terms of reference of this inquiry – and to remind all present that this is not a court of law although it will be guided by legal precept.

Standing there, gazing directly at the many camera lenses aimed at him, Wonderman reads out the terms of reference, how the commission has been constituted, and what has brought about the need to impeach ... no, he corrects himself, *not impeach*, but set up a Commission of Inquiry to investigate the events that have put the country in jeopardy.

He thunders on, citing occasions when there had been a systemic breakdown of law and order and the attendant crumbling of organisational discipline among the armed forces, which could have easily precipitated widespread and uncontrollable civil unrest if the Provisional

Authority for Progress hadn't stepped in. In the morning, with the heat rising and promising rain, Wonderman recites instances of 'leadership responsibility', 'manifold errors', 'criminal neglect and compromise of people's health stemming from the president's cavalier handling of the blood plague crisis' – and *murder*. 'These circumstances,' Wonderman declares, 'were exacerbated by inaction and flawed leadership …'

'Why,' someone, an elderly woman by the sound of it, shouts, 'don't you also charge him with adultery, so that we can stone him with his whores outside?'

'Madam,' Wonderman says, without missing a beat, 'you wouldn't be able to stone a brick wall if it were erected outside your window.'

Some of the people in the ballroom-cum-courtroom titter nervously, which Wonderman cuts short with a bang of the gavel on the table. Having called the house to order, he continues itemising the terms of reference.

Abioseh listens as the voice drones on, hearing the rolling syllables that are now and then submerged beneath the murmur of traffic outside and the hum of the air-conditioning and, above all, the distant buzz of the wind rising, rising, and carrying within itself the beginnings of rain.

The far-off sounds of drummers and the choral groups rehearsing for the Festival of Lights float in waves into the hall and weave out like tangible images of revelry. The light, which has blazed and allowed the eyes to locate every object, goes dim like a softening storm.

As the hotel's lights flicker on and off and create their own confusion of shadows, Abioseh swivels his chair some sixty degrees and thus partially gives his back to the inquisitors, for that is how he sees them now, their little game of power, and turns his eyes on the curious onlookers. Temporarily deaf to the declamations of his one-time compatriots, he studies each face, starting at the back row, where the shy sit like reluctant congregants at a sorcerers' mass.

He looks at his people who are here for excitement or something more profound with which to leaven their lives. Unintentionally, as his eyes cover the middle rows, his action attracts the attention of the cameras, which, slightly dissatisfied with Wonderman Bhele's play to the gallery, now focus on the face of the accused. It's as if Abioseh can hear their thoughts whirring.

Since most dramas are about the picaresque adventures of the rich and famous, here, the producers decide, is a human tragedy that eclipses your daily soap opera. And so, cameras whirr and mobile phones crackle with messages to headquarters of television newsrooms and production houses. In real time, depending on the political or aesthetic impulses of the producers, images that convey innocence or guilt find their way into people's lounges, in living colour.

But above all that, most dramas are successful not so much by what they reveal as because of what they allow to linger unsaid but alive and vivid in the public mind. For here are men and women, elected representatives, who clasp each other fondly in public gestures of shared affirmation, but now employ legal artifice to cut one another to pieces. At which point of their relationship was the seed of this enmity, at once polished and primeval, planted?

Abioseh realises the futility of power, the fact that it actually doesn't exist except as an ideal in people's minds. *What is it? What is power?* As a president, he knows that there could never be a decision that he takes as an individual, which comes from some dream or original thought: the Cabinet has mulled over policies and determined everything he says, especially on foreign platforms. Certain doctrines are ascribed to certain leaders, but they actually belong to the collective of the hour. There might, here and there, be strong-willed men and women – leaders who wish to put their individual stamp on particular policies or decisions. They, too, are mere showmen and -women, actors in the theatre of state, who are best able to articulate the lines scripted by the ensemble. The leaders are also energised by the applause, the frills, the five-star hotels and presidential suites. At the end, he knows that there are so many conventions, signing ceremonies, heads-of-government meetings, reviewing troops, honour guards, gala dinners in tails, even on the hot African soil, shaking hands and embracing some truly despicable people with whom he's forced to agree, merely because they are leaders like him ... Many of these are unnecessary. They don't change the living standards of the men and women of Cinnamon Hill, Vipima, Panza or the Jambora market. Many of them could be delegated to functionaries in government departments, who, in any event, are at the coalface of all that is happening in the country. He shakes himself from the reverie.

Wonderman still holds the floor. '... events that transpired in Bangula when Zebulon Gondo was murdered,' he roars on. 'These impugned the reputations of individuals, the Bangula military and, indeed, the nation itself. Here, we cannot blame the Security Forces, for they work on orders of the leadership, represented by the President of the Republic of Bangula, His Honourable Excellency, Mr Abioseh Gondo, who expects subordinates to be held to standards of accountability by which he and whoever aided and abetted him in these heinous crimes were not prepared to abide.'

Listening to Wonderman's voice, which oozes a mix of venom and scorn, Abioseh experiences great tiredness and wishes to take a nap, just a lie-down to let nature take over. For perhaps the first time, he realises the full impact of leadership. Whatever people make of it, it does finally take its toll on a person, much like the fabled bolo punch, which Muhammad Ali made famous, whose effect could be felt for days and sometimes weeks after a fight.

His five hours of sleep a day, Abioseh senses, have accumulated into decades of denied rest owed to his body, like an engine ruined by years of operating to defective calibration.

Realising the probable source of his fatigue takes him back to the day he took the oath to protect and defend the republic; he accepts that translating those noble principles into reality calls for inner resourcefulness and luck and a gallery of supportive ancestors. Any leader of any country in Africa needs this. For what is one to make of an African country that is defined not as a place known for its history or culture, unless all that coincides with the prejudices existing in the minds of those who have benefited from colonialism, racism or slavery?

For instance, for an African country to be defined and make sense to the world, if such a place exists, Western registers have to be used: *Madagascar is slightly less than twice the size of Arizona* and *the Democratic Republic of the Congo is slightly less than one-quarter the size of the USA.* The space that the county occupies is described in lingering detail not so much for what it supports or represents as for what it lacks. Bangula lacks important arterial rivers or lakes (an anomaly for an island) thus necessitating extensive water-conservation and -control measures.

The experts will always include pollution of the few rivers that exist and blame agricultural run-off and urban discharge. In the minds of the West and its handmaidens, native Bangulans who had made their money in blood, this country is not a country, but an assemblage of confusion. It is hot, humid and it rains daily; in the interior it has a temperate climate; it is mostly mountainous with narrow, discontinuous coastal plains and is subject to wild winds that sometimes get upgraded to hurricanes. Bangula has a population of close to a million people, with high life expectancy and low infant mortality rates. These shot up during the period of the blood plague, but have now stabilised to acceptable levels, whatever that is.

The people are therefore not live, pulsating beings but ciphers representing the number of births or deaths in every one thousand. These people are only known as statistics of blood plague sufferers, ethnic groups, languages, prevalence of major infectious diseases and religions and here, the quainter – that is, charismatic churches, syncretic sects and indigenous beliefs – the better.

Why the hell, Abioseh asks himself, *did my father, of all people, become party to the persecution of the movement of people that sought to reclaim the blood of the ancestors?* But what about the governments, those administrative machines that purport to embody and execute the will of the people? What about the presidents, prime ministers, potentates, monarchs, emperors, kings, rulers, some of whom, like himself, were not really elected but erupted onto the epidermis of the country's surface, like a boil or a growth that suddenly announces the importance of its presence?

And democracy, in whose name everyone speaks: what is its value when it can be bent into shape and made malleable for the moneyed of the land? Abioseh realises – and this shakes him – that he has been at the helm of the country, drawing his monthly salary like everyone, giving a hefty percentage of it to the taxman and using what's left to take care of his mother, MaZembe, who in turn saved some of it towards buying Carlos Nobrega's boat. But he has nothing in the form of reserves in the bank – and, strangely (for he knows that many of his compatriots are a lot more enterprising) he has no savings in any foreign bank.

Most of the people he knows, and the thought brings about a rueful smile, *have got serious cash invested in financial institutions offshore. I'm one of the few presidents who is overdrawn at the bank! Would he have been a better man, then, had he stashed something away and made his escape rather than sitting here swallowing insults from half-men like Wonderman?* Almost involuntarily, Abioseh gets to his feet. 'I'm really tired,' he says. 'If you people want me, you'll find me in my suite.'

'You will do *no* such thing!' Wonderman roars. 'You're on trial here!'

Caramel and Marcia look at each other, their gestures indicating disquiet not so much with Abioseh's conduct as with the tone taken by Wonderman. This was not in the script. Moreover, a Commission of Inquiry is a medium for investigation. Even if, at the end, serious blame is ascribed to Abioseh, the commission can only recommend – and not exact – sanction.

The women's eyes say that Wonderman has perhaps overplayed his hand. They don't seem to want to be associated with this.

Suddenly there is the loud crash of a thunderbolt striking something, a tree perhaps, in the middle distance. This sound is followed by a series of muted rumblings that shake the hotel to its foundations. The lights flicker again and then go out momentarily, showing everyone how gloomy it actually is outside.

'The eclipse,' someone shouts excitedly. 'The eclipse.'

The television crews rush to and fro, checking that their lighting apparatuses are still functional after the brief surge of power. Some of the spectators stay glued to their seats as they watch the performance unfolding before them, now given a piquant flavouring by the difference of opinion between Wonderman and the president. Others crowd the window while a few rush outside to watch nature's wonder, the sun darkening and the shadow of the moon creeping in like a black coin, investing the land with menace.

'There's no need,' argues Gwandon Kone, determined to earn his fee at all costs, 'for the honourable chairman to lose his temper.'

'Under the present circumstances, Judge,' snarls Wonderman, 'the honourable chairman has *every* right to lose his temper. So,' he goes on, the stridency slowly leaving his tone, 'I suggest you get your client to sit down, otherwise there'll be consequences.'

'*Abi,*' a voice calls from the gloom. '*Abi.* Do what the man says.'

It's MaZembe. '*Ma?*' Abioseh is exasperated and yet somewhat pleased that she's made it to this inquiry, which he increasingly regards as a circus. 'I thought I'd made it clear that you shouldn't come here.'

'Don't talk to your mother like that!' It's the shrill elderly woman who earlier suggested that Abioseh be charged with adultery. Turning to a young photographer busily snapping away at the main players in the scene of agitation, she suggests, 'They ought to drag him outside!'

'And stone him to death – right?' interjects the photographer, smiling, humouring her. *Click! Click!*

'*You're damn right!*' Her indignation, it seems, is so profound as to bring about a renewed onslaught of thunder. The rumbling goes on for what seems like a long time. The windows are suddenly stained by a drizzle, which builds up to a howling torrent. Leaning forward with her one hand on Abioseh's jacket sleeve and the other gripping the timber backrest of the long pew, MaZembe turns to gaze at the elderly woman and shakes her head.

'MaD'junne,' she says softly, 'please comport yourself. This is a serious matter being discussed here.'

Visibly stung by MaZembe's unemotional tongue-lashing, MaD'junne shrinks into her seat and suddenly seems irretrievably old in sullen silence, her protruding lower lip quivering like a leaf in a storm.

'Ma,' Abioseh repeats, 'I agreed to cooperate, as long as the inquiry was going to follow acceptable standards.' He points at Wonderman who's still objecting to Abioseh's departure, his hands flapping ineffectually. 'The inquiry has overstepped its terms of reference and busies itself with irrelevancies.'

He feels a great sadness as he sees the anxious faces of Marcia and Caramel, their hands also working vigorously as if in lieu of conciliatory language that would improve the situation. In their expressions, he reads frustrated resignation, people who've stumbled upon a fatal flaw in the character of someone they might once have loved and held in high esteem. 'Perhaps,' Marcia Baraka suggests in an urgent whisper, 'we should go into recess and discuss this in the breakaway room?' Abioseh thinks he can see Wonderman scowling and mouthing an obscenity: *Fuck him.*

Where, Abioseh asks himself, *is the source of all this venom, my brother?* Reaching into the remotest recesses of his memory, he does a mental exercise, to triangulate the exact moment that could have turned Wonderman so bitterly against him. Could it have been an insult or some throwaway remark uttered within the hearing of others that must have cut to the quick?

Feeling the weight of his mother's sad eyes still on him, Abioseh wonders what his father would have made of this situation. The Colonel didn't give a hoot what others thought; he just did what had to be done.

So, Abioseh asks himself, *where did I go wrong with people like Wonderman, whose antipathy must be shared by most of the people here, in this room, awaiting my downfall?*

'Do you know,' MaZembe asks, possibly reading his mind, 'what your father would have done under these circumstances?'

'No, Ma,' Abioseh answers, taking a deep breath to control the annoyance he feels welling up inside him. 'I don't know.'

'He'd have done *nothing*,' MaZembe says, nodding in agreement with her own inner truth. 'He'd have sat here and let them hit him with everything they have — only to turn the tables on them.'

'How,' he asks, 'do you turn the tables on idiots who don't even understand what they're doing?'

'Trust me,' MaZembe puts in with grave determination, 'these people know what they're doing.' She pauses, gives him a sidelong glance. 'Maybe it's you who should start knowing what's going on.'

'What's going on, Ma?'

'See how he talks to his own mother?' MaD'junne pipes in, addressing the island and the world at large, letting them take responsibility for filial disobedience. 'And you tell *me* to shut up.'

Abioseh realises that he has raised his voice. 'I'm sorry,' he says.

'And so you *should* be!'

'Never mind her,' MaZembe murmurs, circling a forefinger alongside her temple. 'She's not all there. But,' she goes on, straining to be heard above the roar of the storm outside, 'it's you who's required to give leadership here.'

She looks past him, almost through him, at the table behind, where the members of PAP continue with their heated though low-toned argument. The rain intensifies its fury, audibly crashing against the awnings, bending and shearing branches and leaves off the trees outside, creating puddles that will soon build up into rivulets. Even though no one inside can see this, they can well imagine it. This storm, Abioseh knows, will deepen the darkness that has always posed a problem for fishermen out at sea.

And the fishermen are my people, Abioseh thinks. *I've not been able to build a paradise for them, but they have thrived. The people eat. There have been setbacks, mainly with the activity in the mountains by rebel devotees of the creed of the Blood of the Ancestors, but the country is relatively at peace. In comparison to other lands where widespread conflict triumphs daily — notwithstanding the recent upheavals provoked by Baluba's supporters — Bangula is still envied as an example of stability.*

Although a strikingly beautiful country with choice areas that are pic-ture-postcard quality and mountainous regions that abound with flora and marvellous beaches, Bangula still battles unpredictable storms that periodically lay areas of the island to waste, leaving scores dead in their wake. There are capricious hurricanes and cyclones that befuddle the most talented of meteorologists. So, in the main, tourists favour other countries, where the only calamities are insane traffic accidents and ran-dom crime.

In short, since Bangula has something for everyone, from the investor to the voyeur frequenting beaches for nudists, where did I go wrong?

'The real problem,' his mother says, 'is that you've never understood power.'

At that moment of truth, he hates her; it is a hatred borne of all the years of her having been a helpmate to his father, a man, he always suspected, who never really loved him. And now he knows the reason for this. Abioseh is somewhat rocked by his mother's pronouncement. He knows that she must have raised it with the Colonel. Like Zebulon, the Colonel doesn't allow death to stand in the way of creating controversy.

He wants to tell her, his mother, something that will hurt her; turning towards her and closing his ears to the murmurings and declamations by his former colleagues, from whom he feels so remote, he sees her eyes and remembers them when he was helpless.

The affectionate watchfulness is still there and will be there, he knows, until hell freezes over. MaZembe has been the power behind the throne. He wonders, bleakly, if things would have turned out differently if she had been in his corner. She had punished him through the simple ex-pedient of withdrawing affection. In his mother's face, which, paradox-ically, looks at him with unconditional love, he encounters the faces of the women and men he has wronged. It hits him like a fist below the heart that there are legions of anonymous people, mainly women, who mourned their loved ones – and many of these deaths had been in defence of follies.

Inside the ballroom, the first of the giant screens projecting television images flickers to life, reflecting at first what seems like a snowstorm before the image stabilises to show that the action is actually taking place at the Revolution square. Here, the gloom is relieved by thousands of lights, flares and torches and an occasional incandescent explosion from a firecracker from someone, possibly kids, for whom the Festival of Lights is recreation. Although it is raining, the downpour does little to dampen the spirits – and the fires – of the revellers, many of whom are ready to struggle, in rough jeans and T-shirts and loose dresses with capacious pockets.

Under the tent that shelters the dignitaries, mainly religious leaders who will officiate the committal of the unburied bodies, nine coffins are arranged atop a long table fashioned out of rough timber, the side with the head being farthest from the crowds. There is an artificial passage between the high table and chairs of the clerics, which allows the throngs to pass and gaze at the bodies under the glass covers. The spectators and wielders of lights must number in their thousands, their vigil made all the more eerie by the absence of sound.

And then Sarsaparilla appears and talks to the microphone, her luminous eyes seeming brighter than some of the pinpoints of light. The ballroom, where the Commission of Inquiry seems briefly suspended, is suddenly filled with her excited voice. She points at the crowds, estimating them to be close to two thousand and rising, people who have come from far and wide for the committal of the deceased and the climax of the Festival of Lights.

Abioseh catches sight of Baluba Jambo, who seems to have gained an incredible amount of weight. He jostles people and ensures that the camera crew sees him. Distantly Abioseh wonders why this man hasn't been arrested yet, since it's common knowledge that he was behind the plot to kill the president. And where is Hiero? It is quite dark now with the total eclipse of the sun; the combination of the unexpected darkness and the violent rain brings about a strangeness to the day, darkness at noon.

In artificial night back at the square, the camera suddenly picks up and stays on a running Zoya, who has a sheaf of papers in her hand. She tries to push to the front, shouting inaudibly, the crush of bodies forming a wall. The camera closes in on her and zooms in on the papers she clutches with desperation. Abioseh recognises the logo of the weather station. The camera pulls away from Zoya.

Inside the ballroom, someone — a man with a voice that must have enlivened countless political rallies — shouts and punches the air. 'Viva Zebulon Gondo, *viva?*' And the congregation, for that is exactly what it has become, responds, '*Viva!*' These slogans, some praising Abioseh, others damning him, ring out and fill the ballroom. The giant screens show people rushing to gaze at the progress of the committal ceremony on the square.

And then the rain seems to let up a bit and cameras centre on activity around the dead Zebulon, on his face, which seems remarkably alive in death. And then everyone gasps as Zebulon's eyes flicker open; he raises himself from the encumbrance of the box. Slowly but steadily he rises to a great clamour and stands arms akimbo, legs bent at the knees in a fighter's stance. Dressed in a frilly white shirt and black trousers, Zebulon seems to have grown bigger in death. His resurrection causes a stampede. People run helter-skelter. Some scrabble to touch Zebulon, the way pilgrims strive to make contact with icons possessing healing powers.

Then, as he starts walking, cars hoot and people shout as if they've just won the soccer world cup. The frenzied march swells as more and more people join in, oblivious to the rain that has now reduced to a drizzle.

Abioseh notices Hiero walking alone, almost hidden at the edge of the ecstatic crowds. He wishes he could direct the camera to concentrate on Hiero's face: *Could you give us a close-up on the head of Security Affairs, please?* But he knows that it's just wishful thinking, almost like knowing the exact thing that pulses in Hiero's heart.

He turns to regard Wonderman Bhele with something close to pity. Wonderman seems no longer at ease, as if something momentous has introduced a huge change into his world. The inquiry dissipates into nothingness, like a football match where the referee refuses to blow the final whistle.

'They're coming this way,' the man with the booming voice shouts, his excitement reaching fever pitch.

'*Zebulon Gondo!*' people scream. '*Zebulon Gondo!*'

And then another bolt of lightning strikes somewhere in the hotel complex. The whole area is plunged into inky darkness. People yell and scrabble for matches and flares. At that moment, Abioseh Gondo takes his mother's hand and tells her, 'I think it's time to leave.'

'Yes,' MaZembe agrees. 'Let's go.'